Twenty years before the Great Trek of the Boers, resentment of the English is smouldering in the wild country above the Great Fish River. Here the pious free burghers, who seek to live according to their lights, are whipped into resistance by the

(Continued on the back flap)

shooting down of old Frederik on his own farm as another link is welded in the three-generation struggle between the Boers and the English. How young Kaspar van der Berg finds himself trapped in the conflict and how his desire for the appealing Aletta comes to rich fulfillment is told by the author of 'The Turning Wheels' in this powerful novel of love and border warfare projected against a backdrop of the vast African bush.

BOOKS BY STUART CLOETE

The Turning Wheels

Watch for the Dawn

WATCH

FOR THE DAWN

BY STUART CLOETE

HOUGHTON MIFFLIN COMPANY — BOSTON

The Riverside Press Cambridge

1939

·CG214w

The Riverside Press
CAMBRIDGE · MASSACHUSETTS
PRINTED IN THE U.S.A.

DEDICATED
TO
M. V.

To everything *there is a season,*

And a time to every purpose under the heaven:

A time to be born, and a time to die;

A time to plant, and a time to pluck up that which is planted;

A time to kill, and a time to heal;

A time to break down, and a time to build up;

A time to weep, and a time to laugh;

A time to mourn, and a time to dance;

A time to cast away stones, and a time to gather stones together;

A time to embrace, and a time to refrain from embracing;

A time to get, and a time to lose;

A time to keep, and a time to cast away;

A time to rend, and a time to sew;

A time to keep silence, and a time to speak;

A time to love, and a time to hate;

A time of war, and a time of peace.

Ecclesiastes

CONTENTS

WATCH FOR THE DAWN

CHAPTER I

TWO MEN CAME

NOTHING moved in the Great Fish River Bush. Not a bird. Not a beast. Even the small leaves of the trees were closed or hung sideways. Over everything was the intolerable weight of midday, a silence in which not a cicada sang. Out of an empty, washed-out sky the sun struck at old Frederik's house; at the bare earth round it; at the solitary tree in front of the house; at the two bay horses tethered beneath it.

With his back against the tree, squatting on his bare heels, a Hottentot rested, looking from the dogs that watched him to the house.

Andries liked neither the place, the mission on which his master had come, nor the dogs. They were great, rough-haired hounds, of the kind that all Boers kept in numbers to guard their homes. Two of them lay on their sides in the shade of the wagon. That they were asleep he doubted, knowing from experience that such dogs never slept, not heavily like a Christian man. Another, broken lemon-and-white in colour, bit the thorns from between its toes, stopping every now and then to gaze at him; while a fourth, an old, scarred brindle bitch with torn ears, stared at him out of

savage golden eyes. Her dugs were distended and somewhere — in the house, perhaps, or in the rough thatched
shed near it — she had young pups.

He would have liked to walk round to investigate the
farm, or, failing this, to lie sleeping till his master called,
but the dogs made him uneasy. There was no feeling of
safety here, no peace.

This was a land ill-spoken of, peopled by renegades,
rebels, and those rough farmers who, by accident, by enter-
prise, or from sheer dislike of all authority, had gone
forth to lie, like a spiked fringe, along the edges of the
Cape Colony, a prickly buffer between Kaffirland and the
sleek Burgers of the south. Here, scattered among the
kloofs, the highland plains, and the small vleis, were their
farms — mean, desolate holdings set at the ends of the
valleys or backing onto the rocky krantzes that fissured the
mountain-sides.

These folk asked for nothing save to be left alone. It
was for this they had come so far. It was for this they
stayed, valuing their liberty above their lives, life on the
Border being held of small account so easily was it lost —
a slow, solemn people who feared nothing but the Lord
their God, the jealous God of Israel.

In front of the house, a few yards from it, was a heap of
buck skulls, the skulls of buffalo (koodoo), bush-buck
(duiker), and steenbok, some of them whitened and rid-
dled with worm-holes, some with fragments of meat still
clinging to them, the piled accumulation of the years.
Along the orchard walls two rows of dark-leaved citrus trees
bloomed and fruited, bearing their golden harvest while they
still flowered; and mingling with the sickly scent of the
orange blossom and putrefying flesh, embodied in it, was
the humming of the bees that sucked the honey from the
flowers and the flies that blackened the fresher bones.

Caught up in waves of shimmering heat, sight and sound
and scent were merged into one prolonged vibration from

which the senses could distinguish nothing, so inextricably were they blended.

Near Andries, almost hidden by the dry, untrodden grass under a thornbush, a red hen sat brooding her eggs. Here was a subtle problem, in which the hen, the eggs under her, the dogs, and the closed door of the house, were all inter-dependent, the success of the plan hanging, as it were, in the correct gauging of the balance between them.

Without moving his head Andries' eyes flickered be-tween them. He swallowed. The hen was out of the ques-tion; she would make a noise, and even if he killed her quietly she would be difficult to secrete. The door of the house seemed likely to remain closed. It was always like this when his master presented a summons. They were busy in the house — his master and Groot Frederik Bezuidenhout, a savage man called to court for the ill-treatment of his serv-ant. But the dogs...He concentrated on them now. The resting dogs could be ignored, but the old bitch was another thing; whenever he looked at her, her eyes met his. Yet his mouth watered for the eggs. That they might contain half-formed chicks was little to Andries. He was hungry.

Unmindful of the heat, a chained baboon sat on the top of his pole, hunting his belly for scurf and vermin, picking his hide over with neat black fingers; and a large, blue-throated lizard, running forward, halted and ran on again. Suddenly the baboon looked up, gave a bark of alarm, and the dogs, rising, walked with raised hackles towards the house.

Here was his opportunity. Smiling maliciously and giving a quick glance towards the door, Andries detached himself from the shadow of the tree. So swift and gentle were his movements that the red hen hardly pecked him and the horses never raised their heads. But with the prospect of food his expression changed from one of angry cunning to a leer. Ai, he was a slim thief. One would have to go very far to find a more cunning man, and if no one else appreciated him it was a small matter, for he knew his own value and his stomach was a lucky one; rarely did it go empty. Not for long were the rumblings of his spirit unattended.

Again he looked at the house, nodding his head wisely. So there was trouble. Well, all the way along, as they rode here, he had been telling the Baas that there would be trouble. This was a verdomde country and it was all very well to say that he was a servant of the State, that nothing could happen to him. Yes, he was a servant of the State — he looked at the brands on the horses' quarters — but the State was far off, and how would the State help him if those great dogs were set upon him? Would the State buy him new trousers? Of course it would not. Instead, there was little doubt that he would be beaten for getting them torn. Truly there was little justice in the world, and since this was a white man's quarrel, let his master see to it.

Getting up he began to saddle the horses. It was in his heart that soon they would be going. As he pulled the stirrups down on their leathers, the door of the house was dragged open and he heard old Frederik shout:

'I am an honest man. What does the Landdros think? What does Stockenstroom think? I tell you, I do not care for my life. Nee, I care for it just as much as for nothing.'

'But, Father Bezuidenhout,' his master said, 'I come not to quarrel; only to summon you. Tell me,' he went on, 'if you will appear or not?'

'I cannot appear. It is impossible, I say, because my bodily constitution does not permit it.'

The brindle bitch stood apart, watching his face, waiting for his word. The other dogs were grouped round the old man, growling, their lips drawn back from their teeth.

With his head hidden under the saddle-flap, Andries watched the scene.

What a great devil of a man. Bent, half-crippled, leaning on two sticks, he still towered over his master. Drunk with rage, his small blue eyes flamed and his stained white beard rose and fell as he shouted. He was like an old tree, twisted but thick and strong. He was like a great boar held by dogs. And there was the Baas pricking at him with words, and angering him still further.

Standing away from the horse, Andries pulled the tight girth up another hole. It was like his master to argue with a madman, but white people were without sense, and, surely, if there was a time for talk there was also one for silence. He himself liked talking; no one liked it more than he, or was more skilled in argument; but alle-wereld, unless it were a serious matter, one in which drink or women were concerned, he never prolonged it dangerously.

'Then you will not come? That is your last word?'

'I will not come. I cannot.'

'You will not come because you are sick — because you cannot ride?'

'Ja, that is why, and if I could...' The old man paused. 'I wonder which way I should ride — to the south, or to the north. What are these questions that you torment me with, meneer? What do I know of the courts? And have you no eyes to see that I stand alone in an isolated place? Have you lived so long among women and attorneys that the ways of men are strange to you? Go now, I say, and tell them what you will. Say that I cannot come. That I will not come. Say that it is, in all circumstances, impossible for me to come. But in God's name, go!'

With his thumbs in his heavy belt, his palms spread over his buckskin trousers, old Frederik watched the court messenger and his servant ride away. Only thus had he succeeded in controlling himself. With the sticks in his hands, or with his hands loose, the Almighty God alone knew what he might have done. Before they had turned the corner, while less than two hundred paces from the house, he saw the Hottentot drop his reins, feel in his pockets, and throw back his head.

So it was not enough that they must come with their summonses, but must also bring their servants to steal his eggs. For a moment he thought of calling his dogs. A word and they would have pulled him from the saddle.

Picking up his sticks, he went to the nest of the red hen; only one egg remained beneath her.

His rage now boiled like water in a pot. Would this business ever end? Ever be done? With a final look down the valley he turned and went into the house.

Thirty years ago he had built it and twice in that time had been driven from it by the Kaffirs, returning to find the walls still standing but blackened by the burning of the thatch.

For a moment he saw nothing in the half-light, and then slowly he perceived the room, seeing it in its entirety as a part of his life. He had made it, and now it, in its turn, held him fast. He looked from the big Bible on the table to the guns hanging by their slings to the wall. It was by these, the Bible and the guns, that he had lived his life, and the sight of them gave him comfort against his mounting anger.

Below the long glinting barrels were his powderhorns: two of curved ox-horns that he had made himself, and one, with silver mountings, of buffalo. This last had come to him from Barend Prinsloo. 'Before God,' he thought, 'if Barend was alive he would stand by me now.' But Barend was dead. And his own wife and children were dead, too; they had been killed in this room. He stared at the floor of hard earth. Dagga-smeared, dressed with cow-dung and ox-blood, and polished with wild beeswax, it shone dimly. She had died here, fighting to the last; wondering, perhaps, if he would come in time. He had found her like that — dead, with her children dead at her feet, and her dogs dead too, and many dead Kaffirs, all under the ashes of his roof. And on that day his heart had died. On that day he had become an old man, uncaring, very much alone. From the past, his thoughts swung to the present, to the court messenger, to his servant who had stolen the eggs. They had been nearly ready to hatch and soon he would have had the pleasure of seeing the chicks running with their mother while she scratched for them. At night he would have brought them into the house and set them in a box, taking them out in the mornings. Such things as this gave him pleasure; a hen with her chicks was a glory to God and a mystery which gave one much to ponder on ... and all this wrecked by a thieving skelm of a Hottentot. Tears filled his eyes. Before God, what had he done that he should be teased like this, like a lion surrounded by Kaffir dogs?

As if it were a living thing, his fury gripped him. His great hands sought the muscles of his neck to ease them. He could feel his eyes burning. Blotting out everything, his anger spread over him. His blood thickening in his veins threatened to burst them; and trembling, he held onto the table for support.

It was thus he had been as a young man when he had hunted and fought. It was so God had made him — a peaceful man, slow to anger.

Nee, he would not go to court. Nothing would make him go. He was sick of the gout. He could not leave his farm. He could not leave Selina and the child. There were a thousand reasons for not obeying, the best of them that he was a free Burger, not one to be told to come here or to go there, a Border Boer mounted and armed, driven beyond his strength by the sharpened goosequills of petty clerks.

For a moment he thought of crossing the river into Kaffirland and joining with Coenraad Buys and the outlaws and rebels who had gathered round him. Had he been younger he would have done this. But he was tied by his age — his memories. Here lay his wife and his children, and here was his sworn word that in death he would lie beside Paulina as he had done in life. The old bull did not run. He stood his ground, and if they wanted him they must come and take him from the home that he had made. He had made everything here. Ja, even the food on the table he had made: the meat was of his killing, the earth-apples he had planted, the bread was from his wheat, and the milk he drank was from his cows. Only the sugar and the coffee were bought things. Here he had plenty and it was all his; little by little had things come to his hand, forming a fullness that was renewed with the seasons. It was his vineyard that had been hardly planted; a solitary corner wrested from the wildness of the veld, and today, even his right to his land was questioned. He was expected to pay rent for it. He was asked for his title. If he had gone to court about his Hottentot Booy, this matter would have come up also. He looked again at his guns. Those were his title; those and the years he had spent here; those and the blood of his children. Was it nothing to the lawyers and judges that a man should take a place and make it live? That he should take rough land and tame it so that it was cut with water-furrows and the low hills smooth with the grazing of his beasts? He had planted fruit trees here and white poplars by the spruit. There were flowers, too, that he had brought from afar. He had built kraals and a house of stone. He had done all the things that a man can do who serves a piece of soil faithfully and well, loving it as a woman loves her child; for truly the farm had come out of him; not from between his thighs in a few hours, but out of his hands, out of the sweat of his breast, out of the thoughts of his head, spread over many years. Magtig, it was his. For two hundred miles round this valley was known as Oom Frederik's Plek.

For a time he sat at the table, his head bowed over the dark leather binding of his Bible. Then he got up and took his greatest gun down from the wall. The door opened and a young coloured woman came into the room carrying a child on her hip. Frederik did not look up. He knew who it was. He knew how she would be standing with her weight on her right foot, her left foot slightly forward and raised to throw out the hip on which the child rested. From her slim, honey-coloured body that was covered only by a single garment of pale pink cotton; from her sleek oiled hair under its magenta dook, her heart-shaped face, her full lips, to her oblique almond eyes, he knew her; knew how she looked, how she felt — soft and supple, with skin that was like silk to touch. As she hesitated in the doorway, he could feel her looking at him, feel her eyes searching him; but he would not meet them. Often they saw more than he meant them to see. Not white, not black; neither of the east nor of the west, this girl saw too much and knew too many things by instinct. Long ago she had told him to get rid of Booy and he had not done so. Often her advice had been good, but he had always been too proud to take it.

'What are you doing, Frederik?' she asked, coming in and closing the door.

'I am thinking of past times, Selina.'

The child that she had put down, letting it slide along her thigh, crawled towards him.

'You think with your roer on your knee and the Book in your hands.' The girl's eyes widened, their whites suddenly very clear in the gloom. 'Something has happened,' she said, coming closer to him.

'Ja, much has happened, woman, and it is not ended. This time they have piped a tune that I will not dance. Make coffee, Selina, for I would think.'

'I have made it,' she said. 'I saw them go. Had all been well, they would not have ridden off like that with their heels driven into their horses' flanks, forcing them to gallop with high heads. Nee, this is no small thing that you have done, setting yourself up against authority. Now,' she went on, 'either you must submit or you must run.' Drawing herself up, she stood beside him, her breasts rising and falling as she cried passionately: 'Let us go, Frederik!

Let us go over the Border to Gaika, to Coenraad, and the others who are our friends. Let me send word that we come. Let me send a boy at once.'

Through his shirt Frederik felt the warmth of her trembling body as she pressed it against him. With his hands he sought the comfort of her, but his mouth was tightly closed and his eyes were still fixed on the lock of his gun.

'Nee, little one, I am too old to run; besides, this is my place. I have made it,' he said slowly. 'And surely they must see that I have done no wrong. To run would convict me of fear; and to go to them, after this, of weakness. And what is all this but lawyers' nonsense? Consider the letters I have written, Selina. All is explained in my letters, and things will come right. Ja, alles sal reg kom, of this I am certain.'

But, despite his words, Frederik was troubled. What did he know of the law and the ways of those who administered it? And, for that matter, what did they know of him?

He drank his coffee in silence. Wiping his mouth on his wrist, he put up his gun, and taking his sticks climbed the kopje behind his house. He climbed laboriously, his feet as heavy as his heart.

It was from here that he had surveyed his ruined homestead and had replanned it, more beautiful, so that it might be at once a monument and a sepulchre; a small ornament in a waste country which would show those who passed by that he was faithful to his trust. Always, when troubled, he came here to seek peace — in the silence, in the immense outlook, in the panoply that was spread below him from horizon to horizon. Here in this vast land was escape, a place where none would lay hold upon him; but he was too old to flee like a shadow; too old never to continue in one stay. Too old, and too well-rooted to be moved.

In the void above him a vulture circled, its shadow falling upon him as in one of its ever-narrowing circles it came between him and the sun. More came spiralling down, and one sailed past him on strong, level pinions, the air hissing past its cutting wings. So near was it that he could see its eyes and the skinny folds of its ruffled neck that was pushed out as straight as a ramrod, while its head moved from side to side.

Something was dead down there, under the blanket of the bush. Something that the aasvoel saw and which was not apparent to him. A dead beast? A dead man? Much died there and much lived, but all was hidden, secret. It was said that aasvoels lived forever. This he could well believe, for in his life he had never seen one dead.

His eyes swept over the farm below him. There was his house. There were his kraals, his orchard, his little water-land, the small cemetery with its headstones cut and carted by his own hands; and there, outside the house, was Selina, the coloured girl who had replaced his wife ... Selina, the Bastard woman he had taken, walking with their child upon her hip.

Women were scarce on the Border — that was why he had taken her — and it was neither good nor possible for a man to live alone, untended; and now, after his fashion, he loved her. She had been good to him. Selina's words came back to him: 'Run, Frederik ... let me send word that we come.'

But it was also from a high place that the Lord Jesus Christ had been tempted, and it seemed to him that the place where this was done must resemble the one where he now sat: the exceeding high mountain from which all the kingdoms of the world were visible. And this, too, was the hour of his own temptation, and he wrestled with it, for, despite what he had said to Selina, he knew himself well able to flee; but did it not say: Blessed are those who are persecuted for righteousness' sake; blessed are ye when men revile you and persecute you and shall say all manner of evil against you, for so they persecuted the prophets before you?

And still the Devil whispered in his ear: Run, Frederik Bezuidenhout, run. What is your promise to a dead woman compared to the joy you have in a live one? What is this little thing you call honour to set it up against your life? Ride and be free; take your woman, the child of your loins, your servants and your beasts, your oxen and cattle, your sheep, your horses, and your dogs, and get you gone.

'Baas! Baas!'

A naked picannin stood beside him. In one hand he held a letter, with the other he fingered a scratch in his leg where a thorn had torn him. He must indeed be getting old when a child could come upon him, over rough ground, unperceived. To the old nothing but their cunning remained — the vast store of things experienced to be set against their waning faculties. This was God's balance, to set the cunning of age against the strength of youth. But he had decided against cunning, for it was by appealing to it, by appealing to his knowledge of the forest, that the Devil had sought to snare him.

'Give me the letter,' he said.

It was from his brother-in-law, Rudolf. Maria had given birth to a daughter and many were coming to see the child. It would be good to go. It would make him forget his situation. He would see many that he had not seen for a great space and there would be news. From all round farmers would come to the little festival in carts, in wagons, or on horseback, and all would have gifts. For it was the custom when a child was born to give cattle, horses, sheep, and goats — these were the birth-gifts of relations, friends, and neighbours. Even at this moment people would be on the road and, with good luck and good years, their gifts would give increase, becoming the portion Rudolf's daughter would one day take to her husband.

So eighteen hundred years ago had the wise men gone across the deserts of Judea, seeking diligently for the young Child that had been born. They, too, had brought gifts, but of gold, of frankincense, and myrrh. What was myrrh? he wondered. And to what use was it put? He smiled gently, for his heart was tender to the child he had never seen. Was she fair like his race, or dark like her father's people? Had she hair on her head, or was she bald? Still smiling, he went slowly down the mountain-side. Tomorrow at dawn he would set off. He would ride Witbooi, who was very tame, and he would take the child a cow: a cow with her calf at foot. There was one that he had bought from Rudolf which did not take kindly to his place, but always returned to the farm where she had been bred. How Rudolf would laugh when he saw her! He would say, 'Oom Frederik, you give my child a cow that you cannot keep.' And he would say: 'Ja, Rudolf, that is the truth. I give the cow because it is too much work to keep sending Kaffirs to fetch her back.'

A small stone dislodged by his feet rolled down the mountain-side. Picking up others, some larger than itself, it went on; and as he stood to watch them leap and thunder down, it came to him that this was not the only stone he had set rolling since the sun rose. The first, too, would go on, gaining impetus and volume as it went, becoming a landslide that was like to overwhelm him. But he had acted in good faith, acted as it was in him to act. And did it not say, That the thing which hath been is that which shall be, and that which is done is that which shall be done?

Once again, with tired eyes, he sought the vultures, but they had gone; they were sunk beneath the canopy of trees. In hope, still believing against hope, he went on down, but, magtig, he was tired. There were too many dead in his life and his strength was forsaking him. Now at last was the reckoning, and the fevers and hungerings of his life were extorting payment from the body that he always neglected, counting himself above sickness or disease. He was a man who had always rejoiced in his great muscles, but today his back was bowed and his legs hardly supported him. Once they had been so strong that when wrapped round a wild horse he could make it grunt in agony as he pressed its ribs between them. Today, the full weight of his years was upon him. Today the mountain had failed him.

CHAPTER II

THE LITTLE FESTIVAL

I

WHEN old Frederik had gone, driving the cow and her calf in front of him, Selina went to the fountain behind the house.

Where yesterday the man had gone up the mountain to think — staring out at the void beneath him; turning his eyes upwards to the emptiness of heaven; or striven as he gazed at the hills to recapture his strength in the memories of the days he had spent among them; repeating the names of the mountains over and over to himself as if their names mattered — the woman went down, descending into the depths of the kloof, crouching on the flat rock where she washed the clothes, to seek the truth in the dark waters: to watch the living waters of the mountain die, absorbed into the blackness of the pool.

Ever since she had belonged to Frederik, Selina had loved this place, coming here to think; to allow sensation to flow over her to the accompaniment of the falling water and the slow humming of the bees that nested in the krantz; to dream with her dark eyes fixed now on the slowly overflowing cup beneath the spring, now on the tree-trunks which shot up like spears towards the upper light or lay, writhing and twisted by the creepers that held them strangled. Out of the crevices, between rocks too shadowed for grass, maidenhair fern grew, unmatted, separate as feathers. Like a small flower this little kloof was hidden from the sight of men, but the beasts knew it and came here to drink. On the sand beside her was the small heart-shaped spoor of a steenbok; and once, almost the first time she had come here, she had surprised a koodoo bull at water. For a moment the woman and the buck had stared at each other. Selina had looked into his great liquid eyes; seen the symmetrical white mark on his forehead, the fringe of long dark hair that hung from his dewlap; and then he had gone up the hillside, his nose high, his long spiral horns laid flat against his back, his hooves clattering the stones.

On the ledge beside her the brindle bitch lay extended, watching; and between her knees, dappled by the sun, her child sat, restlessly struggling for her breasts with his small hands. Half impatient, half in play, she kept him from them, covering his hands with her own, holding his tiny nails between her fingers, rubbing them backwards; and, then, giving way, she let him drink, wriggling and pushing, his lips avid against her, his mouth bubbling with the milk he drank: the milk which, hot as spilt blood, ran down her flanks. He drank till he was full and she was empty; then he slept, and she sat on, lulled by his pulling into a hushed unquiet, a frightened content, a feeling that she was trapped by events too great for her understanding, and a confusion of mind in which, unable to weigh out true values, she sought relief in an overpowering solicitude for her man and the child she had had by him.... In the cleft above her the buzzing of the bees went on; the buzzing they made as they flew out empty in long lines strung into the sky or came back laden. And all the time from inside came a deep murmur, the vibration of a thousand beating wings. The bees were labouring to make honey. The thought of the bees and of the work they did pleased her. That they went on made her feel more secure. Frederik said the cave had once been the home of a leopard. Looking up, she could see the dark crack in the rocks. There was a small track running up to it from the pool. It was this that Frederik used when he stupefied the bees with smoke to take the honeycombs.

Frederik had been kind to her, and in her life she had known little kindness! Behind his rough words there was always a gentleness of look or touch; behind his anger a smile; and if he struck her, afterwards he was tender. But why in God's name would he not run? Bred of slaves, Selina was conscious only of expediency.

2

That Frederik Bezuidenhout's farm was deserted meant nothing to Kaspar van der Berg; the hospitality of the Boers went beyond their presence. Those who had gone would return, and everything pointed to a short absence: the chained baboon, the poultry, and the wagon with its yokes stacked against the wheels. Dismounting, he off-saddled, knee-haltered his horse, and prepared to wait.

The horse moved forward with his head low, sniffing the ground till, finding a depression, he lowered himself carefully, and swinging over from side to side he kicked his free legs in the air, grunting with pleasure as he drove his back into the sandy soil. Pausing, he lay still, and then, scrambling to his feet, shook himself, snorted, and, standing on three legs, stared about with his head high and his ears cocked.

Satisfied that all was well with the horse — he had watered him on the road, and a sick horse did not roll like that — Kaspar stood his wet saddle on its flaps in the shade, and sat down beside it. Still watching the horse as he moved awkwardly off to graze, his eyes took in the homestead, the orchard, and the kraals. He examined the details, for a man's place spoke of the man who had made it. And this place was better than most he had seen; more carefully, more lovingly constructed. Old Frederik Bezuidenhout must know something of beauty or, unknowing, had achieved it.

The eaves of the thatched roof were wider than usual, giving an impression of covered comfort. There were potato creepers growing up the rough posts of the stoep and some plants — geraniums and lilies — in broken butter-barrels by the door. Except for the heap of skulls it might have been a farm in Stellenbosch or Paarl. It was a dwelling place, neat with its outbuildings and kraals, its cultivated land and grazing. It had known joy and sorrow. Children had been conceived and born here. Here also had men died. It was lovely, but with its loveliness went a brooding sadness. It was like a woman who led a blind child by the hand: no matter what she did, the child was blind, and her lavished care was lost.

At the side of the house were the sheep and cattle kraals, stone-fronted, and cut back into the living rock of the hill; and between the kraals, from the hillside, the bush crept, straggling down towards the flat. Thrown flesh-side upwards on acacia and kareebos, the crinkled skins of sheep lay drying.

Kaspar ran his hand over the dog that sat beside him, and, pulling a tick from under its elbow, crushed it between the nails of his thumb and finger. His other dog had trotted off to the house as soon as they had reached it. Kaspar smiled as he thought of old Wolf: a very careful dog, as faithful as Witvoet, but of a different nature; a dog that was more curious. In any new place, before he settled down, circling round and round to lie curled watchfully, he would make a tour as if to know what he might expect. Truly the ways and temperaments of beasts were as variable as those of men, and each was different from the next. This was well known and universally applicable to all animals, both wild and tame: equally to the lion or the ox, the quagga or the horse. Kaspar loved beasts. First his

horses and dogs and after them his cattle. But all beasts
he loved, understanding them and knowing their ways, for
he was a farmer, a man concerned with beasts, and that he
was up here trading did not change his feelings. Stretching
himself out, he pulled his hat over his eyes. His gun stood
ready to his hand, and, with his dogs on watch, he could doze
in peace.

From here it was but two days on to Leendert Labuschagne's farm. Leendert had married his mother's sister,
and that was where he would make his home in these parts.
He wondered what Leendert was like. He had been a child
at the time of the marriage.

This north into which he had ridden was an adventure,
the realisation of a dream. Since childhood he had thought
of the Border, listened to talk of it, and sought out those who
knew its secrets and had penetrated into its fastnesses.
This was the land of mystery whence ivory, gold, and rhinoceros horns came. The place where lost men drifted never
to return: a country all but unknown, all but uncharted;
where blank spaces were marked on the maps as the country
of Zulus, the country of the Swazis; where great rivers faded
into a line of dots that indicated their probable courses.

It was no chance word that had sent him here, but a
series of circumstances, the one following upon the other:
the stories he had heard in his youth, the piles of ivory he
had seen on the docks of Table Bay, the wish of his father
who thought him in need of experience, and finally the scene
in the market place of some six months ago where, by accident, he had come upon a slave girl being publicly whipped.
Stripped naked, tied to the stocks, two Hottentots had
whipped her, striking alternate blows, with rods of split
bamboo, till the blood ran down her back; and then, taking
salt from a little bucket at their feet, they had rubbed it into
her wounds. Mounted, he had seen all, from the beginning
where they tied her to the end when, loosened, she sank at
the feet of the grinning men.

His feeling of anger had been a new thing to him, for he had always thought of himself as quick and hot-tempered. Yet his anger then had not been hot, but was, on the contrary, cold. It was as if he had suddenly ceased to be a boy; and he had hardly recognised his own voice, so soft and gentle had it been, when he enquired of a man near him what this girl had done.

The man was a small trader dressed in broadcloth. In his hand he held a gold-headed stick and behind him stood a slave holding an umbrella to shade him from the sun. The man had blue eyes that were flat and cold, and a thin-lipped, smiling mouth.

'What has she done, meneer? Very willingly will I tell you, for her owner, Karel Fourie, is my friend. Two years ago he hired her out to a man, a discharged soldier who farms near Simons Bay; and when he could no longer pay for her, my friend fetched her back for his own use. And so little did she understand of God's law that three times has she run back from her lawful master to the man that hired her. Magtig,' the man repeated, 'three times!'

'It seems to me possible that she loved this man,' Kaspar had said.

'Love!' the merchant gasped. 'A coloured bitch does not love. She belongs. And now she will learn, and so will the others who hear of it.'

'I also have learnt much today,' Kaspar had said, and, turning his horse, he had ridden slowly home.

He thought of the government slave-lodges where every day one could see strings of soldiers and sailors entering the quarters of the female slaves. They remained there till nine when they were required to leave, and this practice was not discouraged by the authorities, since by it the slave population was increased and the slaves bred at home were more tractable and docile than the ones imported from the East.

He could not talk to his father of this; for his father,

brought up in the old way, would say it was an isolated case and speak of their own slaves who were treated almost as members of the family. And this was true. At home the farm was filled with slaves who were happy: young ones who worked in the fields, in the vineyards, and in the house, or among the beasts; old ones who, past work, sat brooding in the sunshine, doing such little things as they were able — braiding whips, fashioning walking-sticks, stitching harness; and as they worked, talking interminably.

Much of what he knew, not only of birds and beasts but of men also, came from the hours he had spent with these old slaves: crinkled crones who, squatting in the great kitchen while they watched their grand-daughters at work, had carried his mother as a child in their strong arms; old wrinkled men who had ridden behind his father and his father's father. These old slaves had much simple wisdom. To them they were not his slaves; to them he was their possession, the young Baas to whom they came asking for this and that. Was a child sick? Did they need new clothes? It was to him they turned.

And about the cottages at home the slave children played, swarming, naked, like brown and golden-coloured mice that ran, unafraid, to anyone, expecting a sweetmeat or a pat.

At home there was nothing but mutual good-will and trust. The halt and the lame were succoured, the sick helped. At Weltefreden none cried in vain, and never, that he could remember, had he seen a man or woman punished. It was a good farm and there was plenty for all. Aye, plenty; and much over. And both men and beasts were sleek and well liking.

But that this was so was because his father was rich and kindly. It did not alter the fact that elsewhere things were otherwise. What he had seen proved it once and for all time.

For some years a new idea had been coming in from over the sea; an idea that was Christlike in its simplicity: the idea that all men had rights and that perhaps they need not wait till the final reckoning to stand equal in the eyes of God, but might yet do so whilst they lived. A heresy very widely condemned. But nevertheless an idea — and the one on which Napoleon's army had striven so successfully, carrying his eagles all over the world; each soldier knowing that he might be carrying a marshal's baton in his knap-sack; that he need not stay in the situation in which the Almighty God had seen fit to place him.

Came also the word of Voltaire the cynic, whom God did not strike down, and of Rousseau. For the Cape of Good Hope had much traffic with the world. News swept in from the East on the spreading sails of tall East Indiamen laden with spices and treasures. It came in from the West, outward-bound, with troops, with merchandise, and with convicts on their way to Botany Bay.

The population of Cape Town was multicoloured. The East flared here, meeting the West. Here were the red coats of the soldiers, the blue of the sailors, the broadcloth of the Burgers, the dressed-skin clothes of the farmers. Here were Dutch and English, Scottish and Irish. Here were Flemings and French, Germans high and low, Austrians, Poles, Italians, and Portuguese. Here were human skins of every colour, bastards of every nation, language of every kind, and to the breeds and the cross-breeds of the slaves there was no end. Hottentots, tame Bushmen, slaves from the Guinea Coast, from Madagascar, from Batavia, from Bengal, Amboyna, Java, Candia, Surat, Malabar; from the Rio del Goa and bush Chinese from Malaya; all bred to-gether according to their opportunity, desire, or the caprice of their masters. Some clothed, some naked, some in chains, they moved about their business among the soldiers, the traders, the advocates, and the publicans. Here were the heavy wives of solid Burgers, with their slim maidens; and here were the fashionable ladies of the garrison. For to each kind of man was there a female counterpart in this place — a wife, a mistress, or a prostitute.

Flanked by other continents, a halfway house between them, the Cape was the clearing-house of races, of merchandise, and of ideas: the place where the flotsam of the world was washed up. And always there was change; men came and went with the ships or disappeared into the interior. It was the end of the known world. South of the Cape there was nothing, only a waste of sea. To the north also was nothing — a vast black continent that the wise ignored.

3

Behind Kaspar, an hour away, rocking and rolling on their wooden axles, his three wagons crashed over the rough bush roads. Many times in the last months they had been overturned; many times had he had to halt for days while he effected repairs or rested his exhausted beasts or waited for flooded rivers to run down; but still the convoy had gone on. The pace of his small Zuurveld oxen was slow, but it was sure; long trek, short trek, but always on; seeing mountains ahead, they came to them, passed them, and left them behind.

His wagons were loaded with lead and powder, with bolts of material, with beads, copper and brass rings, with muskets, tobacco, with brandywine and tiger's milk in casks. He had also spare draft oxen and a troop of horses, young stallions and colts to trade. It was these horses that were his pride. All were by the Blue Spaniard, a horse taken from the French ship captured in 1807, and they were out of his father's best mares. In them ran the blood of Sébastien's Loyalist, Cricketer, Mambrino, Selim, Zarlot, Hercules, and Paul Jones. Such horses as he brought had never been seen in the north before, and even at the Cape there were few to equal them. It was a bold venture for so young a man, but from what he heard it should pay him well.

4

It was the brindle bitch that first saw the stranger. She had gone on ahead, anxious to get back to her pups. And Selina trembled with fear. The Border was changing when visitors came daily. Had this one anything to do with those who had come yesterday? Whence was he? Where did he go? What did he want? Surely nothing could have happened yet: it was still too soon. Unable to collect her thoughts, but fearful, conscious that the peace of her life was threatened, she stopped, standing very still in the shadow of a tree, waiting, watching her dog and the man. His own dog had come forward, and another which had been near the house joined it; but ignoring them the bitch went up to the stranger. Without moving from his seat, he reached out his hand, palm upwards. The bitch smelt it and looked round. The man turned his head and saw Selina.

Could she have gone back, she would have; but to go might arouse suspicion. Also she wished to know who this man was. He might have news. He was alone; from his clothes he looked a farmer. Holding her child very close, Selina went diffidently towards him.

When he got up, she saw he was tall — taller than she had thought at first, and younger. She looked at his face, seeking to read it, and ready to fly; but there was nothing there to make a woman run.

His face was smooth, unlined, and his grey eyes gentle. His mouth was not hard set. By instinct she knew that she need not fear him; by observation — by the quick look that had taken in his arms, his dogs, and his horse — that he was not poor. He was a free young man; a man in the making, and as yet there was nothing written on his countenance. By a man's eyes you knew him, and by his mouth. His eyes God gave him, but his mouth he made himself, loose, generous, mean, or sensual: the character of a man was in

his mouth, written there for all to see. Selina knew much
of men. She had belonged to many.

'I am Kaspar van der Berg,' he said. 'And I am come to
visit my uncle Leendert Labuschagne.'

'I am Selina, and this is Frederik Bezuidenhout's place.
Come in, and I will make coffee, meneer. Afterwards I will
tell you how to find your uncle's farm. From here you must
go to Rudolf's place, and from there it is but a day on.
There is a gathering at Rudolf's. The Baas is there, and it
may be that Meneer Labuschagne is there too, for he is
cousin to Rudolf, and Rudolf's wife is my master's sister.
The festival is for her child,' she added. And leading the
way into the house she said, 'Sit, meneer, while I make
ready.'

So this coloured girl belonged to Bezuidenhout — and no
doubt the child was his. It was almost white, with fair
hair.

Kaspar looked round the room. How alike all these
Boer houses were. Each had the same rough, home-made
riempie-seated rus-banks, the same beds, the same tables,
the same mud-plastered walls that retained the marks of
smearing fingers. In each house there was a Bible on the
table; in each there were guns on the wall. On some shelves,
recessed into what had once been a window, tin plates and
beakers shone brightly; and on the table, near the Bible,
was a bullet mould. From the rafters hung bundles of
riems, strips of biltong, and some specially big mealie cobs
tied together by their husks which he supposed had been
saved for seed. There was one big chair in the room, of
stinkwood; over its back a large leopard skin hung in loose
folds. The light from the half-open door caught the skin,
painting it brightly; almost gold in the gloom, pierced with
black spots, it stood out — the hide of the savage beast the
only thing of beauty in the room, its only comfort.

Kaspar had hardly finished drinking when he heard his
wagons coming.

First faintly, borne on the little wind which had sprung up, came the clap of whips, growing clearer and clearer as they approached, and then the cries of his drivers and the claps much louder, like pistol shots, one after the other. Now he could distinguish the names of the oxen as his boys called to them ... Witkop ... Bles ... Bokveld ... Blauberg. Loop ... Loo-oop, you duiwels! Loop, Geelbek, Donker, Stompie, and there, mounting the drift, was the first wagon, the oxen almost lying in the yokes as they strained against them with bent knees; pair after pair appeared, and then as the wagon topped the rise they trotted down with slack trek-tous behind the running voorloper, gaily, as though they knew that the morning's work was done.

Behind the first wagon came the second; and the third, all lumbering and rocking down the slope with shoes on their wheels. The drivers no longer sat on their boxes, but ran beside their spans, their long whipsticks bent like bows under the weight of the clapping thongs. Clap and echo sounded into the mountains; birds rose from the trees; and the peace of the valley was broken by the coming of a multitude. Kaspar's people had come with his goods and his driven herds.

Standing outside the house, Kaspar forgot everything in his pride and joy. Here was a fine thing to see on a summer's day; a sight that filled your heart, bringing it up into your throat. He loved his oxen; they were the best procurable. All were matched in spans; two spans of red and one of black; all were in their prime, rising six; brave, willing beasts with full mouths. And despite all the noise he knew that not one would bear the mark of a whip on its hide. The clap of the whips and the shouts of the men were for encouragement. No Boer used his whip until he must, and then he used it to effect, drawing blood at every stroke; but this was only in emergency, in heavy drifts, or on the mountain passes.

One after another, in response to the long-drawn whistles

of the drivers and the stones thrown into the faces of the
oxen by the leaders, the wagons pulled up. Painted light
blue, their wheels red and very bright from the water that
ran down the spokes streaking the dusty hubs with scarlet,
they lay side by side — red wheel to red wheel — their torn
tents and bucksails a testimony of the difficulties through
which they had passed.

Pair by pair the riems were undone and withdrawn from
the horns of the beasts; first the middle oxen were spanned
out, then the leaders, and lastly the wheelers; and each as
he was released sprang away from the yoke and drifted off
to graze, the matched spans broken, the oxen spread over
the veld, followed by the herders.

Sending a boy to catch his horse and telling two others to
come with him, Kaspar prepared to ride on. He wished to
see this festival that Selina spoke of; the wagons could
follow on more slowly.

That he took two armed and mounted men with him was
because he knew his countrymen. Before he could sell he
must impress, and Boers would not care to see his coloured
servants better mounted than themselves.

Opening a case, he gave Selina some needles and cotton
in return for her hospitality and questioned her as to the
route he should take.

'You will find it easily, meneer,' she said, pointing up the
road. 'Go on till you have crossed the second drift — the
one where on the far bank the rocks lie piled like watermelons in a field — and there turn right, up the small path
that runs along the randjie. It ends in a hill shaped like a
sugar loaf. From there you can see the house. It lies near
a great tree.'

She moved uneasily, as if she had more to say, and Kaspar
took his foot out of the stirrup.

'It is a fig tree,' she went on, paused, and then said, her
words coming out quickly: 'What was the talk in Graaf-
Reinet, meneer? Did you hear anything?'

'Hear anything?' Kaspar repeated. 'Hear anything of what?'

'Of the old Baas. Yesterday they sent to summon him and he refused to go. I thought you might have heard something. You must have passed the messenger on the road, meneer,' she added. 'He had a Hottentot with him and they were mounted on government horses — bays with fine black tails.'

'I saw them,' Kaspar said. 'They passed me, but beyond a greeting nothing was said, nor did I hear anything in the dorp.'

'I do not know what to do,' the girl said. 'He must do as they say, or he must run, and he will do neither. What can I do, meneer?' she asked. 'What can I do with my master? He is old and obstinate. He still thinks of the days when we were safe here, but it is in my heart that we are no longer safe; that they may send soldiers to take him.'

Her eyes looked past Kaspar, staring at the mountains in the north.

'Up there they would not catch him, meneer,' she said, 'for he is a slim man, one who holds the byeways of this country like a bird in his hand. But I delay you, meneer,' she said, recovering herself. 'From the sugar-loaf hill you will see the house. It is nearly hidden by the wild fig tree beside it.'

CHAPTER III

THE LION OF THE NORTH

I

FREDERIK'S arrival was greeted with shouts of laughter; all the louder since, unable to restrain her, once on the familiar road, his gift had begun to run and, preceding him, was standing near the kraal, lowing to be let in when he came.

'Have you come to fetch your cow, Oom Frederik?' they asked, all pretending she was no gift, but that, having escaped again, he had followed his cow, and was now, by the circumstance of the festival, saying that he had brought her as a present for his niece. 'Nee, nee,' they said, 'it is not you who gives. It is the cow who, hearing that her old Baas has a new child, has come to give it milk. Ja, a rhenoster bird looking for ticks has whispered the news into her ears and she has come. This is what we believe,' they cried, 'for look, was she not here before we even saw the dust of your horse?'

'Ja, that may be so,' Frederik said, very seriously. 'But who sends rhenoster birds to seduce my cows? At least,' he went on, 'she is here now and can remain. She is a good little cow, but obstinate. Never before,' he said, 'have I known such an obstinate little cow, so put your small daughter's mark upon her, Rudolf, and let her be the mother of a herd. But of this I warn you: if her progeny resemble her, your son-in-law will have to live in your house, for he will never get his herd away.' Laughing loudly he got down from his horse. 'I must see the child, Rudolf,' he said. 'Ja, before I take anything I must see the kleinkie. And how is Maria?' he added. 'Did she have an easy time?'

He picked up Klein Kattie. Till last week she had been Rudolf's youngest child. 'You have a sister now,' he said, 'and I have brought her a cow.'

'Did you bring me a cow?'

'Nee, I did not bring you a cow.'

'What did you bring me, Oom Frederik?'

'I brought you nothing, Kattie; but I will bring you a puppy next time I come.'

'A puppy?'

'Ja, a puppy.'

She broke from him and ran into the house shouting, 'Uncle Frederik is bringing me a puppy!'

2

By such gatherings as this was the Border life cemented. They were the ferment of an otherwise static existence, the loose net drawn about the very separate lives of the Boers, and important, since Boers only met for great causes: to worship God; to assemble mounted and armed for war; for a birth that they might welcome a new soul into the community, or for a death that they might mourn the passing of one from it. At such meetings were old quarrels made up and from such meetings did new ones arise. Here age argued with age and youth made calf's eyes at youth; and here, concentrated into the few hours of their occasional association, was the whole social structure these people epitomised: perfect, in the simplicity of its devotion to God, in its lust for life, in its striving where each individual, while realising his responsibility to the others, went his own particular way. No Boer was servant and none acknowledged a master or superior. Here boys of twelve were men, and men of forty grandfathers.

And each hour more people came, their carts and wagons filling up the space in front of the house. All were eager, men and women to whom a birth was a great thing, an event, an occasion: a boy was another gun, a daughter would become the mother of men. To them a birth meant a simple feast, a thanksgiving; meant some prayer, some drunkenness, and among the young people some love-making. But above all it was the chance to meet friends, to talk, giving and gathering news. And for this they came from all round: from Daggaboor's Nek, from Zwaager's Hoek, the Bush Berg, the Groen Berg, and the Zuure Bergen. Brothers who farmed far apart met and talked, slapping each other's back; sisters compared children, putting their babies into one another's arms so that their great weight could be felt.

Newcomers were greeted with cries of delight, guns were fired, young men showing off to the maidens made their horses dance, and the maidens looking down watched them out of the corners of their eyes, for from these men must they choose the fathers of their children. The older men spoke heavily, laying down the law, of hunting, of cattle, of Kaffirs, of wars that were past and possible wars to come, of the English and the new administration to which they were still unused. While the married women discussed children born and unborn, confinements, remedies for sickness, and the laziness and incompetence of their servants, when they were not talking, directly and without undue modesty, of men.

And all the time the sun shone bitterly upon them so that even as they stood or sat talking they must rub the sweat from their eyes: except for the big wild fig tree, which had, by common consent, been left to women with young children, there was no shade in that place, no ease from the heat.

For every white person there were six coloured; for every adult many children — boys, girls, little ones that trying to walk fell on their faces, suckling children in the arms of their mothers or slung on the backs of slave-women; and dogs everywhere, dogs of all sizes that stole the food from the hands of the children, fought, walked from place to place by their masters, or slept under the wagons. A tortoise-shell cat very heavy with young sat imperturbably by the doorway of Rudolf's house. Laying back her ears, she hissed at the strange dogs that approached, but apart from this, unmoved by the noise or the crowd, she licked the pink soles of her feet and washed her face continuously.

Smaller than many of the white children, a few tame Bushmen, pale yellow, with peppercorns of hair widely distributed over their heads, wove in and out of the throng as watchfully as animals. These were men and women who had been taken as babies from parents that had been shot, and reared in the homes of the Boers who had killed them.

A group of tame Kaffirs, their assegais driven into the ground beside them, sat devouring the sheep they had been given, swaying as they ate to the rhythm of the small drum that one of them played. Holding it between his knees, he beat upon it, striking it with his fingers and his wrist. Naked but for their kilts of wildcat skin and their ornaments, they were apart and alien, visiting Kaffirs, able to come and go as they willed and conscious that where they ate today they might fight tomorrow, for there was never real peace between the white and the black — only truce and armed neutrality. There could never be a lasting peace where good grazing, hunting, and water were the issue.

The assembly at Rudolf's bore no resemblance to a Nagmaal of the south. It was less orderly, and even in the way these folk outspanned their wagons their independence was apparent; for all faced different ways, each having chosen the place that was best suited to his purpose, and many had swung their spans round so that the poles pointed homewards

— a wise precaution at a festival and one which enabled those who had done it to enjoy greater freedom, for if one thing only was certain in life it was that the horses and draft oxen would remain sober. There were no drunken beasts save only the pigs that ate the husks of the grapes after a pressing.

3

On Frederik's right was old van Ek, who said, 'Is it true what we hear?'

'Ja, it is true, Christiaan.'

'Then eat well, and when you have eaten talk. Tell us the truth, Frederik, for it is in my heart that many have come to hear of this, using the festival only as an excuse. Events ripen like fruits,' he said, speaking softly, 'but like fruits they must be plucked from the tree when they are ready.'

'It may take guns, Christiaan,' Frederik said.

'We have guns, Frederik.'

For a moment van Ek rested his hand on Frederik's knee and then turned away.

Christiaan was still the same. As the years passed he seemed to get no older, only tougher, drier, and more wizened. His beard, cut after the French fashion into a point, still jutted out when he talked. His black eyes still sparkled. And he remained what he had always been, a man without family, without land; a man of bitter humour; one whose questioning spirit was only countenanced because of his tried courage and the known goodness of his heart. Of his past none knew anything for certain, save that he had been to Europe as a young man — taken there by his mother who was French and, it was believed, of great family; that he spoke English and hated the English; and that he was educated, knowing many things — history, philosophy, and natural science, so that he could for hours tell tales of ancient wars or of travels in strange places that he had seen or had read about. Of his life, few knew much. Of his words, most, fortunately for him, were misunderstood and believed, where he meant them, to be a perversion; for who could take seriously the words of a man without a wife or a child? Uncle to all and father to none, was what they said of Christiaan van Ek. Loving him much, they understood him little and had come finally to accept him for what he was: an old, wise man, a great hunter who came and went like a shadow on the Border, disappearing sometimes for months into the deep north that no man knew; but all were agreed on one point: that among good shots he was the best, and to him they came when they wanted the sights of their guns adjusted. This he would do for them, taking infinite pains and charging nothing.

On Frederik's left sat Joachim Prinsloo, an ox of a man, as silent as van Ek was garrulous. Buttoned tightly, despite the heat, into a bright blue cloth coat with big silver buttons, Joachim concentrated on his food, stopping only to take off his hat so that he might scratch his head when the curry made it tickle. His movements were clumsy, since it was less than a year that he had been mauled by a wounded lion. It had got him by the shoulder and dragged him into the bushes, and there Joachim had killed it, feeling for the beating of its heart with one hand while he drove his knife into it with the other. He seldom spoke of this exploit, for, as he said, 'If I had not killed the lion, it would have killed me. Was I to lie there and let it eat me, kerels?' Then he would laugh till the tears sprang to his eyes. 'Nee, nee! Joachim Prinsloo was not made for that. He was not made to be a lion's breakfast. That would be a fine thing for his children to say when they were asked where their father was. For his children to say, "Our father is in the belly of a lion." Nee, I am not one to make my children to be ashamed.' And more than this no one could get from him.

'Did it hurt?' they asked.

'Ja, it hurt,' he would say. 'A lion's teeth are not nothing. And, ach God, how he smelt! He carried me so that I could hardly breathe, with my head turned under him and my face in his mane. And when I got home my wife pulled many hairs of that lion out of my beard, and to this day she says I must have bitten him. It may be so, but if it is, then I am the first man to bite a lion.' And once more he would be off into laughter, and recovering would go on to talk of his wife.

'Katrina is a fine woman, as all can see,' he would say, looking fondly at her as she sat simpering modestly with her hands folded in her lap. 'She weighs three hundred pounds and is so comfortable to live with that it is like being dead.'

'To live with me is like being dead, Joachim!'

'Ja, because it is like being in heaven. No man has a more comfortable wife, and not even in a great town is there a better woman to be found. It is as if the good God made her for me. She fits. Ja, she fits me like a yoke fits on an ox.'

'Ag sis, Joachim, me a yoke,' she would say, blushing happily as her husband pointed out her manifold perfections in company. Not that she didn't know them. She knew that she was good and beautiful; perhaps not quite so good as Joachim thought she was, but with her looks what could be expected? Men desired her — they could not help it — and she was kind to them. And though she agreed that God had made her, fashioning her very exactly to be the wife of Joachim, she felt that he should restrain his talk about such matters, but on this subject her Joachim refused to be silent, and though she protested it made her glad. It warmed her to know that she made him happy; and that wherever he was and in any company it remained the only subject on which he became voluble.

4

Rudolf had given of his best. Nothing had been spared, for thinking his wife likely to die, so long had been her labour, he had spilt out his firstlings. To make this feast there had been a great killing: of oxen, of sheep, of goats; of chickens, ducks, geese, and turkeys; of wildfowl, guineas, pauws, and pheasants; and of bucks fresh-killed also. There was wine and brandywine and peach brandy. For this eating was to the glory of God, given in the thankfulness of a father's heart for the pleasure of those friends who had come to rejoice with him.

Frederik ate all that was offered: curry, rice, chicken, potatoes, pumpkin, peas, cabbage, and three slices of a roasted buck, whose haunches were served up like a child to be whipped. He had pieces of hard-boiled ostrich egg with vinegar dressing. These eggs had been preserved by being rubbed with oil and packed in bran. He had konfyt of melon and little oranges; he had mebos and raisins and sun-dried peaches. And as he ate, he drank, his heart warming as his belly filled.

Time after time Aletta, Rudolf's adopted daughter, pressed him to eat more, saying, 'You have eaten nothing, Oom Frederik' — which pleased him, for, though there was no blood between them, he loved her, recognising a spirit that was kindred to his own, and tied to her, too, by the fact that where he had lost his children by Kaffirs she had lost her parents, and that it was he who had found her among them and had brought her back. Seemingly fragile, she was a maid who was unbreakable, whose mind, under its small golden head, would trek its own way and find its own path through life. Who her parents were no one knew. Why the Kaffirs had spared her no one knew. And with his own wife dead, he had given her to Maria, his sister.

And as much as he liked Aletta did he dislike Stephanie, Rudolf's daughter by his first wife. That one was too quiet. He mistrusted her, thinking her like a river thick with hidden weeds in which men drown. For all her downcast eyes, Stephanie had plucked the fruit of knowledge and was already skilful in using it, but subtly, and for all her reputation for piety, very certain on whose hills her cattle pastured; and though, like Aletta, she also served men with food, it was the young ones to whom she took it, and among the young ones those with the widest farms and the greatest herds.

The eating was silent and the men and women ate apart, grouped according to their taste, spread out into little parties that merged into each other as some went for more food or broke up when, full-fed, they prepared to doze.

Frederik was well content. He loosened his belt and looked from bearded face to bearded face. Once again he was a man among his folk. Christiaan's words had comforted him and Aletta's ministrations had soothed him. He only wished that his brother Johannes was here. He shouted across the table to Gerrit, another brother who sat with his four sons. He did not get on with Gerrit, though he lived near him: perhaps that was why — nearness led to disputes — or perhaps he was jealous of Gerrit's sons. In his opinion Gerrit, though large in size, was small in heart.

Gerrit shouted back to him. Today they were friends. Frederik tried to forget his last argument with his brother. It had been about some sheep, which Gerrit had claimed wrongfully.

They said Johannes was looking for cattle he had lost — two heifers and an ox, but he could send him a message by Jan Bothma who would pass his house. When he heard of his trouble, Johannes would come to see him. He was a certain man, one who stood by his family and friends, but hot-headed and lacking his own restraint. Frederik began to think of the past few years. Ever since he had taken that accursed Hottentot into his service, he had known nothing but trouble, and he hated trouble. To this all men could bear witness. If asked, they could do nothing but say that he, Frederik Cornelis Bezuidenhout, was a most peaceful and law-abiding man. Ja, from the Snewberg to Graham's Town he was known as one who lived at peace with his neighbours and treated his servants well. But Booy was a bad Hottentot. He should have got rid of him before, and would have if it had not been for the oxen that he owed him.

And then he began to talk. Before God, these were his people; they should hear his words. It was in his heart to testify, to tell them what was passing in his mind.

'Put him up!' Rudolf shouted. 'Set him up so that all can hear!'

'I will get up,' Frederik said, and swaying a little he made his way to a wagon.

It was fitting that he should speak to them from a wagon; fitting that they should stand and sit round one. For a moment he said nothing, but holding on to the wagon-box he searched them with his eyes, searched them as though he would see into their very hearts as they clustered round him. They were very large, most of the men being six feet or more in height and wide in proportion, and many of the mature women mountainous. Wearing their best and brightest apparel — green, pink, and scarlet dresses; blue dresses; mauve dresses; prints, ginghams, taffetas, silks, and chintzes — the girls and women flashed as brightly as birds in the hot sunshine. These were his people. Many were related to him distantly, or closely, but all he knew. There was no stranger here. Their fathers had hunted and fought with him, and many of them he had led on commando. He knew them: the Prinsloos, the Bothas, the Krugers, the Bothmas, the Nels . . .

And they knew him. They were ready to listen to him, for he was their uncle. He was Oom Frederik, their friend. Nowhere in the world were there people like this, so strong, so bold, so free. Looking from those nearest to him to those farther back, he raised his eyes to the distant mountains, and began.

'I want no more than justice, kerels. I want no more than that. No more than a true reckoning. Let what is Booy's be rendered unto Booy, and what is due to me, to me; and let me rest in my place. I am too old to ride far, this all men know — this all who see me here can tell. And what are the charges against me? That I broke a stick over Booy's head. It was a rotten stick, vrot, or it would not have broken. That I killed

one of his sheep. Ja, I killed it. Magtig, and what could I do
with a mad sheep but kill it? I killed it, and I wrote to
Philippus Opperman to tell him so, saying: "I have killed
none of Booy's sheep but one, and that a mad hammel"; and
this is the truth, that I do not know what otherwise to do
with a mad sheep.'

The crowd laughed. 'Ja, Oom Frederik,' they shouted,
'what else could you have done?'

'And what of my side of the story?' he went on. 'Are the
times so changed now that the word of a Hottentot is taken
against that of a Burger? And did not Booy make away with
twenty-one of my sheep, break my kitchen iron against a tree-
trunk to obtain wild honey for himself, and steal a new spade?
All this I wrote to the Veld Kornet, but, like all those in
authority today, Opperman sides with the black against the
white. Beyond this I am owed two fat oxen by Booy, a debt
already four years old. And now they summon me. Now
they say I must ride two hundred miles to Graaf-Reinet to
answer the charges against me at the Drosdy. That is a thing
I cannot do — will not do — for I am without blame in this
matter.'

Frederik felt the virtue leave him. He was giving all that
it was in him to give and it was having no effect. His words
were a thin stream poured onto the aridity of their hearts;
yet he was giving them his blood, wringing his soul dry, like
a wet cloth, squeezing it out drop by drop. Surely there must
be some way he could stir them; some appeal that he could
make, or was his effort wasted? Was he crying in the wilderness?

Talking more slowly, he began to search for words. He
was an old man, a little drunk, talking of his wrongs.

His eyes met those of a stranger, a tall young man who
stood near the back of the crowd with the reins of his horse
looped over his arm. He had two servants dismounted behind him. Was it the coming of this boy that had disturbed
him? And what was he doing here?

Frederik concentrated his attention on the stranger. Words, more words, kept pouring from his lips. His throat was dry, his voice hoarse. Once he had been able to hold people, to sway a crowd as he willed by the power of his oratory; once, like a loving woman to the body of her lover, they had clung to his words, following his thoughts unhesitatingly. But now, when he needed them most, his power was gone; the woman no longer loved him, her eyes instead of meeting his were seeking. He could see by the movements of their hands, by the shufflings of their feet, that, ill-at-ease, they wished he would end, wished he would mount his horse and ride away. They were tired of him. No longer with him, they were against him, resenting the appeal he made. He could no longer hold them. But he must hold them. All that he held dear was at stake: the Border life for which they had all paid so much. He halted, and, covering his eyes with his hands, cried silently upon his God. Seeing him pray, many took off their hats and stood bareheaded. Father Bezuidenhout was a good man. Old, yes; but entitled to respect on that account. Moving awkwardly, they waited.

Pulling himself up to his full height, Frederik began again. His voice was now firm, and louder than it had been. He was without doubt or hesitation.

'Listen again,' he said. 'Listen, I say, for I would go beyond what I said when I spoke only of myself, for those things are but straws in the wind. They are stones cast into a pool and their ripples move slowly outward. Today it is I. Tomorrow it will be you. And what do you, who are children, know of the history of this land? Can you remember old Adriaan van Jaarsveld, who led us against the Kaffirs in eighty-one, and the battle at Naudes Hoek when we killed three hundred and took five thousand head of cattle? Or the war in eighty-nine, when we were forbidden to attack, although assembled, and sat on our horses watching our cattle being driven away? Or that of ninety-three, when we took seven thousand beasts and they all died in the drought? Or

the little republic we made in ninety-five with old Carel
David Gerotz as Landdros and Adriaan captain general?
Or how in ninety-five they took Ons Adriaan and we took
him back? Or how, later, he was betrayed and taken finally?
... Nee, I say you do not know of these things, or have forgotten them. Only such men as Coenraad Buys, Jan Botha,
Martinus Prinsloo, and some others can remember. But it is
always the same: men forget. Ja, even their promises they
forget, and think that things will pass. But what has passed?'
he shouted. 'Has the paper money passed, have the monop-
olies, or the tax on our beasts? Ja, they have passed with the
English. Ja, things are changed, and yet they are still the
same. Nothing has changed, I say, but the Boer heart. You
are mak now, you are tame. Before God, you are tamer than
women; and when you have the world in your hand like a
sweet lemon, behold you will not take it. Ground under the
heel of the English, you whimper like hungry children and lie
waiting, as meal, to be ground yet more finely. By the English on one side, the Bushmen on another, and the Kaffirs on
a third. Where will you go, then, when they have finished
with you? Where will your children farm? There is but one
place left. There is the sea. Our children becoming a nation
of strand-loopers, eaters of shellfish. Ja, your children can
have the sea-wide farms of fine salt water.'

Frederik felt the tide of feeling turn from ebb to flow.
Imperceptibly this change had come over the people. Where
there had been no enthusiasm, it rose; slack mouths tightened; and the women and girls who had hung on the out-
skirts of the crowd came closer, pressing in and clinging,
bright-eyed, to their men.

Anger was succeeding apathy, and Kaspar felt himself
caught up in it. Their cause was his cause. He was among
them and, though none had spoken to him, of them. Now
he saw that his dream had been true; that these people were
different, less grasping, less cynical, less wise, perhaps, but
cleaner in their minds, more urgent in their natures than

those of the south. A folk that some might call simple; but their simplicity was that of innocence. They were children, but with the passions and feelings of men and a great faith in God. Knowing that all men were not created equal, they were true to themselves: the great, great without pretence; the small, small without shame. What chord in him the old man had touched, Kaspar did not know, nor did he think of it, but was, with the others, caught up and with the others he pressed closer, sweating, shouting, waving, and throwing his hat in the air when they threw theirs, as they seethed nearer and nearer. Slow like all their race to be roused, they were now up, and a thousand smouldering grievances flared into open fire. Each man shouted his wrongs; and where before each man had had a mind of his own, where each had been listening with one ear thinking of his own affairs, they now had only one mind, and their women were with them. This struck Kaspar forcibly — the courage of these women who stood foursquare with their men, equal to any eventuality. Gripped by the old man's words, Kaspar listened. Old Frederik was like a prophet, he thought, as with his white mane of hair flowing about his head, his eyes brilliant with passionate anger, he went on.

'I would go beyond this and warn you. What they do to me is but the beginning, for they question our titles and would have us back under their hands, away from the Border. But this I say they cannot do. One generation goeth, another generation cometh, and only the earth abideth forever. All the rivers run into the sea, yet the sea is not full. All but the earth is vanity. All but our land is a striving after the wind. I say that there is time for all things, that to everything there is a season. That there is a time to plant and a time to pluck up that which is planted, a time for peace and a time for war. Nee, this land is ours, and the land is everlasting. God made it, dividing it from the firmament; and it is beyond the strength of man to undo what God has done. Before man there was the land, the field and the forest, the little streams and the great rivers, and with the passing of man they will remain. The land is God's trust to man, and it is in my heart that first God created the land and then put man upon it to serve it. And we are indebted to no man. We made these places, felling the trees and moving the piled rocks with spans of hauling oxen, turning the soil with our ploughs. And now it is tame land and many have died to achieve it: by savage spears, in contest with wild beasts, in childbed and in sickness. And despite adversity we have endured, increasing our people, our flocks and herds; and because it was the Lord's will that we should do this thing did He prosper us.' He paused for breath. 'And if they take me ...'

'We will see that you are not taken!' someone shouted.

'Nee, he shall not be taken! He is our Oom Frederik who led us on commando before our sons were born.'

All were shouting now. The stranger was shouting. Their faces were blurring in front of him. The bright colours of the women's clothes would not keep still, they ran into each other. Frederik put his hands up to his face — it was wet with tears. He felt his knees give under him. He was going to fall, as an elephant fell sometimes, going onto its knees and then rolling over. He heard Coenraad shout: 'Help him down, you fools! He is stricken.'

But Coenraad's voice seemed to come from very far away, as if he were calling from a mountain. He felt a strong arm round him and looked up. The stranger had caught him. He must have come very near without his noticing it. He thought of the picannin who brought the message to him. He did not see things now as quickly as he used to.

'Give him to me.'

A man, bigger than all the rest with a great black beard, bent over Kaspar and took Frederik from him; picking him up as easily as if he were a child, he laid the old man on the ground by the high back wheels of the wagon.

'I am Coenraad Buys,' the big man said, holding out his hand.

This was the famous Coenraad Buys. The man who went with a price on his head. The man of whom all had heard and few had seen.

'I am Kaspar van der Berg.'

Buys' eyes flickered over Kaspar like the tongue of a snake.

'You may have heard of me,' he said, and withdrawing his hand he began to laugh. 'Ja,' he spluttered, 'I am the renegade, the rebel, the man who has married a queen. And one day I will sweep the English into the sea. Ja, one day I will do this, and you will help me.'

While Kaspar was thinking of an answer — he did not dislike the English nor did he think they would be easy to drive out of Africa — Buys left him. Moving quickly for so big a man, he went up to Kaspar's horse. Kaspar had handed him over when he jumped to catch Frederik. First Buys ran his hands down his legs, then taking a pace or two backwards he stood staring at him. Many men had looked at his horse, but Kaspar had never seen one look like this: as if he would fix him forever in his memory.

'That is a horse,' Buys said.

'Ja, he is a horse.'

'How is he named?'

'Tigernek, because when he was a foal a leopard got him down and scratched him,' Kaspar said, and going up to the horse he raised his mane. Under it, on the black and white hairs of the roan, were four clear white claw marks.

'And what happened?' Coenraad asked.

'His mother killed the leopard,' Kaspar said. 'She broke his back as he lay over the foal, and then we came.'

'Will you sell him?'

'I will not sell him. Nee, meneer, he is not for sale.'

'You are right,' Coenraad laughed. 'If the price of a good woman is above rubies, then the price of a good horse is yet higher. Ja, magtig, there are so many women that some among them must be good, though the good ones are generally ugly — so ugly that their virtue does them little credit.

Now, if Letta' — he turned to a girl who was passing —
'stays good, it will be something. Before God, if I was younger
I would take you myself,' he said. 'Ja, in front of them all,
I would set you on the pommel of my saddle and ride off
with you. Once I was a man, but I become timorous, and,
besides, what would my wife say? Ja, what would she say?'
and he laughed again till the tears ran down his face.
'Would you come with me, Letta?' he asked.

'Ja, meneer, I would come, and you would repent of it,' the
girl said, facing him angrily. 'I would come because you are
as strong as an elephant and would take me. But I would not
stay. And this I tell you, when I want a man I will have one
and I will choose him for myself. And how is it, meneer, that
you who are Oom Rudolf's guest come to mock me in front
of strangers? Is it because you are so big that you think you
can do what you like and override all men? Or is it because
women are such fools, confusing bulk with quality, that you
think them all yours for the asking, or without? If you think
it funny,' she went on, going nearer to him, 'to make a maid
blush and feel awkward in front of many, I can assure you
that you have done it. Ja, meneer, you can make me very
ashamed, but you cannot make me afraid. Nee, neither you
nor any man, for I hate them!'

For an instant she stood facing them all. In her anger she
had pulled her kappie from her head and stood twisting it
between her hands. Her fair hair was dishevelled, her eyes
dark with anger. Her lip trembled and, suddenly bursting
into tears, she turned and ran.

Kaspar was astonished at the wildness of Coenraad; at the
courage of the girl, who was so small that in talking to him
she had to throw back her head and stare upwards; at the
behaviour of the people about him: they seemed untamed,
uncurbed by restraint, or what he had learnt to consider as
good manners.

Ignoring the girl, Coenraad turned back to him and said:
'I also have a horse and I will match him with yours. Ja,'

he said, 'tomorrow we will ride a race. Will you match your horse against mine?' he asked.

'Ja, I will match him against any horse in the land,' Kaspar said. 'But I would tell you, meneer, that he has won many races at Sea Point, even running against the Governor's English horses. You asked if I would sell him, and I said that I would not. But I have others that are nearly as good that you can buy.'

'Where are they?'

'They come. They are following me with my wagons.'

'If they are even half as good, I will buy, for I need many horses.'

There were currents and undercurrents here that Kaspar did not understand. Not only was it all new and strange to him, but he had a feeling that it was dangerous. He looked about him at the people: they were very large, very quiet, and very determined. The enthusiasm of a few moments ago had gone. Or had it not gone? The talk was now of the race; it appeared that Coenraad's horse was well known both for its speed and its endurance. But Tigernek was also fast, and as for staying — well, tomorrow they would see how the Blue Spaniard's stock could stay. It was for this rather than speed that they were famous. It was a pity Leendert was not here. They said he was sick. He looked round as someone touched him and found old van Ek smiling at him.

'She is like a small bird, don't you think?' he said.

Pretending not to have heard, Kaspar went towards the open veld. It was here that they would race. Yes, Aletta was like a small bird, like a quail calling from the high corn, but how had the old man known what was in his thoughts when he had scarcely known himself?

CHAPTER IV

ALETTA

I

STEPHANIE followed Aletta when she left. Poor Aletta, who could not take a joke, who understood neither life nor men, who failed to see in Coenraad's words the compliment of his desire, who, preferring dreams to actuality, wasted her time listening to old van Ek's stories or ministering to Frederik's greed. And it was not as if she had never spoken to her of such things; she had, continually. But Aletta seemed unable — or it might be unwilling — to discuss them, and would listen, looking past her with vague, troubled eyes when she spoke of them. And yet what else was there to think about? For girls there were only men and, later, children. For men, there were only women and cattle. These surely were the reasons for existence: a husband, a home, and children. Of course men loved their children, but they, the children, belonged to the woman who bore them, who carried them in her womb, and the man was only incidental, little more than the instrument by which they were obtained. A woman might want a child by a certain man; might, achingly, desire to carry his child; but this was only because loving him she still knew that she could never possess him in his entirety, whereas the child of his loins was

helpless. It was the man, but the man reduced and manage-
able. The man small, and as weak in her hands as he had
been in the first flush of his possession of her.

She knew very well that the tale of men choosing their
wives was false. It was the woman who chose, and acting on
her choice so arranged matters that the man should think he
acted freely when he took her. But her arguments failed to
convince Aletta. She did not deny them. She merely ignored
them as though she were immune to life; to the strong, subtle
forces that clutched at you and made you do things, sometimes against your will, often against your principles; things
that, taken by themselves, were unreasonable, but which,
considered in the light of what had passed before and what
occurred after, were no more than single links in the chain
of events which together made up the life of a man or a
woman.

Men excited Stephanie and she acknowledged it: by their
presence, by the smell and the sight and the touch of them,
by the thousand ways in which they differed from women.
Their shapes were so much like her own. Their bones and
structure were not dissimilar, but they held something that
was hard, something unattainable, that challenged her fem-
ininity. Without men a woman's life could not be fulfilled.
It was an emptiness, and she liked to feel them want her —
to know what was passing in their minds when they saw her.
She liked the stolen kisses and the rest. And what harm was
there in it, since people were made that way? What harm
could there be in being young and well and strong? What
harm that your blood happened to run warmly? No, she
was right and Aletta was a fool. Look at the way she wasted
her time with old Frederik just because he had brought her
back as a child from the Kaffirs. Had he not picked her up,
another would have done so. It was just a chance that he
had seen her first, and how, having seen her, could he have
avoided doing what he did? Nor was it the first time such
a thing had happened: that a commando destroying a Kaffir

kraal had found a white child there and brought it in. True, he had looked after her for nearly a month, carrying her in front of his saddle and feeding her with biltong that he had chewed up to soften before he stuffed it into her mouth, and had risked his life milking one of the mares that ran with a foal among the spare horses till some cows had been captured. Stephanie laughed out loud as the picture came to her of old Frederik — not so old then — pulling at the teats of a wild mare. Did they have to cast her, she wondered, or did they just throw a riem, a spantou, round her legs above the hocks? And all about him, while he did it, the other Boers must have stood watching, smiling, trying to help and offering advice, not only on how best to milk a mare, but also on how to rear little girls. She saw them pulling at their beards and scratching their heads as they tried to remember what their wives did with their children. And for this Aletta was grateful. Grateful! Why, if it had been me, she thought, I should be ashamed to meet a man who ... But that was what was so curious about Aletta: she had no real modesty, and yet, if asked about this stranger, this Kaspar van der Berg, she would have no ideas about him. She would pretend she had not noticed that he was tall and slight with grey eyes; that he had on a brown coat of English cloth and an embroidered waistcoat. And it was more than likely that she would not even have noticed which way he had gone. In some matters Aletta was singularly unobservant, while in others — those of no importance — she missed nothing, and was as well-informed as a man. No doubt she would behave as if each time one went out, young men appeared mounted on blue-roan racehorses followed by three wagons full of trade goods.

Increasing her speed, Stephanie caught up her foster sister and flung her arms round her.

'Don't cry, Letta,' she said. 'It is nothing.'

'I know it is nothing, but why did he say those things? Why are men like that, Stephanie? What makes them so cruel, so ...' Breaking off, she dried her eyes and said: 'Come, let us get away from all these people. I hate them. Because I am small they think they can do anything, say anything. Ja, I am small, and I do not know who I am, and I have no place nor cattle, but I am not a child any more. I am a woman, and I am tired of it all — so tired of it!' she said passionately.

'Tired of it?' Stephanie echoed. Aletta was more than a fool — she was mad. Could it be the sun? she wondered.

'Did you keep your kappie off long?' she asked.

'Why should I keep it off?'

To show your pretty yellow hair, Stephanie thought. Why, if I had hair like that ... 'Then it is not the sun,' she said. 'I thought you must have sunstroke to speak as you do, for how often is there a feast like this, where we can wear our India muslins and see all the world? And then you say you are tired of it. I never get tired of it. What I get tired of is the veld, the emptiness of the mountains, the days and days when nothing happens and no one comes. And what did you think of Kaspar van der Berg?'

'I did not think of him.'

'Ja, I believe you,' Stephanie said. 'I believe that if the Archangel Michael came to the farm and tied up his horse to the stoep, you would not think of him.'

'You are blasphemous, Stephanie.'

'I do not mean to be, but I cannot understand you. A minute ago you said you were a woman, and then you say you never noticed Meneer van der Berg, and so I said if an archangel tied up his horse ——'

'But archangels come on wings,' Aletta said.

'On wings, then — though I would sooner a man came on a horse.' Stephanie laughed. 'But why did you do it?' she asked. 'Why did you argue with him? Everyone knows what Coenraad is.'

'Are you coming with me?' Aletta said, pulling away from her.

'Ja, I will come with you, but not for long.'

Linking her arm through Aletta's, Stephanie led her towards the vlei.

'If it had been you, I suppose you would have said nothing,' Aletta said. 'I suppose you would have let it go, and stood there looking modest, with your eyelids fluttering up and down, and then...' She paused.

'And then what should I have done?'

'Then you would have turned and walked away, but you would have looked back. Nee, Stephanie, it is good that we live in these days.'

'Ja, it is good; but why do you say so?'

'Because had we lived in other times, not once but often would you have been turned into a pillar of salt.'

'Me, Letta? How you wrong me! I should just have ignored him.'

'It would be a new thing for you to ignore a man, Stephanie.'

'New?' Stephanie said, pouting and raising her eyebrows. 'I never do anything.'

'You do nothing, and still men come.'

'I only sit as still as a flower on its stem.'

'You sit as still as a flower, but you show your honey. Do you think I am blind?' Aletta asked.

She had forgotten her own trouble in her indignation at Stephanie's behaviour. True, there was nothing specific; but some people could do nothing, and it was everything. Some women could, with every appearance of complete modesty, still be immodest, and by a look in their eyes, by a fold of their skirt, by a gesture, bring men to their sides and hold them there. She knew that Stephanie thought her stupid and without knowledge. But she knew that Stephanie was wrong. She knew that she had knowledge beyond the mere acknowledgement of the facts that seemed so important to Stephanie, and she had also a deep instinct to wait. One day, she felt, the waiting would end and she would become alive, not with the timid flutterings of Stephanie, but with a bold soaring of outstretched wings. But what was the good of talking? As little as she could convince Stephanie could Stephanie convince her. Especially now when all she needed was to get away for an hour that she might think. Beneath her calm acceptance of circumstances she knew that she was as taut as a bent bow and more sure than Stephanie, who often seemed like a child to her; for though she did so much, she knew not what she did, and was like a straw that was swirled upwards on every wind that blew.

2

Kaspar's hand ached. A hundred men had shaken it, but he could not remember their names or separate their faces. All were bearded, rather flat, with high cheek bones. They were the kind of men that he had seen in ones and twos in Cape Town, the kind that he had met on the road. But here, gathered together, they impressed him by their leanness and a latent savagery which he thought must come from their close contact with the soil, a hard soil, very different from the rich valleys of his country; from the lonely lives they led; from the fact that their hands were as accustomed to their guns as to their pipes. He realised that there had been women there — many women; but, with the exception of the girl who had faced Coenraad so boldly and the dark one who had stood near her, he had noticed none of them. Only Coenraad and the man who had made the speech — they said he was Frederik, the owner of the coloured girl — and old van Ek stood out. He tried to remember what he had heard of Coenraad; to recall the story of how he had been persuaded to return from over the Border when he had married Gaika's mother and abandon her; and of how, unable to settle down, he had, with the coming of the English, gone back again to become a thorn in their sides — a thorn that they were ready to pay two hundred pounds to have removed.

Already in a few hours Kaspar had come to think of the English as they did. This was a different world and very far removed from them. A place that seemed lawless because under such conditions the law, in its letter, could scarcely apply. This was the edge of the universe.

But what was the real Coenraad de Buys, he wondered. What was the man himself? Fact, fiction, and rumour all contradicted each other, and no two stories were the same; but even the most fantastic, now that he had seen him, seemed credible. There were stories of his fabulous physical strength, of his savagery — no doubt innate but developed by his wild life among the Kaffirs — of his golden tongue and capacity for leadership over both white and black, and of his quick temper which so often lost him the adherents he had made. All this seemed apparent when one met him — volatile, gigantic, a man flamboyant in the quality of his weapons and simple in his dress; a kind of land pirate who, from what he heard, lived beyond the Bushman country with a band of robbers, escaped criminals, deserters, and the like; fighting, hunting, and trading as and where his fancy took him; a mercurial force that stirred the already seething pot of dissension, not only on the Border itself, but beyond it into the very heart of the country, so that he was known and feared by the Amazulu, the Bushmen, the Griqua Bastards who lived by the Orange River, and even by other tribes as distant as the Swazis.

To Kaspar's eyes, accustomed to the more fertile south, the veld seemed very dry, and even the close-cropped grass of the vlei stubbly to his feet, crackling under them as he walked. With the rain he knew it would become luxuriant, waist-high in a few short weeks; but now it looked as if it had been scythed, and lay as smooth as the lawns about the Fort at Cape Town. Still, it would be good going, since there were no loose stones and few tussocks. To the west it opened out, becoming wider and the ground harder as the quality of the soil changed from the alluvial deposit along the river to clay, and here there was some low thorn scrub, scattered about like prickly cushions, which farther on thickened into a belt of bush. The mud of the river as he followed it was patterned by the feet of sandpipers criss-crossing each other in a design and pierced by their long beaks. A heron which stood in the water, waiting for a frog to come within reach of its beak, stretched out its neck, and spreading its wings, rose slowly in front of his dogs.

A wave of homesickness swept over Kaspar as he watched the heron. He thought of the time when, climbing a tree to obtain some of their eggs, the young birds had leant out of the nest and vomited over him, while all about him the grown birds had circled, crying harshly. But he had got an egg from another nest. As big as a goose's, but pale blue, it lay on a bed of white wool with the rest of his collection in a box at home. Old Frans, who was driving the first wagon, had cleaned his clothes, and a great fuss he made about it.

It was very hot; the earth palpitated with the heat, rising and falling like the belly of a man who has run fast, as if it sought to regain its breath. Waves of trembling passed over it. Seeing a bush on the slope of the hill, Kaspar went up to it and sat down. If there was one heron, there might be more. He wished old Frans was with him. They would have watched them and laughed about the incident of the heron's egg. It was very hot and he was very lonely.

3

Stephanie never knew what made her throw the stone. As she flung it, she thought, This is a silly thing to do.

It might have been anger. She had led Aletta this way hoping to meet Kaspar, and, failing, was not disposed to give way to the snake in her path; and having thrown one stone she threw another. And the snake, which had been about to slide away into the grass, turned and got up, standing a full three feet above the ground, its hood extended, its neck swaying, its little forked tongue darting in and out as it faced its enemies.

Here was something that could be destroyed. Coenraad had not noticed her, in spite of what had passed between them. It was Aletta he had joked with, and she had missed Kaspar. Picking up a third stone, Stephanie threw it with all her strength.

Aletta was unable to stop her. Stephanie was like that: flaring into sudden rages. This time the stone hit the snake and it struck. One minute Aletta was watching its small, cold, lidless eyes, the next she heard Stephanie cry, was knocked down, and heard a man behind her shouting.

4

Kaspar had seen the girls. He had seen Stephanie throw the stone and the snake get up. Jumping to his feet, he shouted to his dogs, 'Vang him, Witvoet! Vang him, Wolf!'

Like a flash the dogs left his side, and as the snake struck, the first dog reached it. When Witvoet sprang, he knocked down the smaller of the girls, the one that had faced Coenraad.

Livid with anger, Kaspar ran down the slope. Because of the stupidity of a girl, he was going to lose his dog, or perhaps both. Sometimes a dog could kill a snake; he had had one that did, but in the end they were always killed, and it was not possible to kill a snake in this fashion — not one that was aroused and ready.

When he got up to them, it was all but over. The snake had wrapped itself round Witvoet. Its fangs were buried in his foreleg and it held on, but its back was broken, showing the white flesh where it had been bitten. The older dog was still worrying it, while Wolf, growling savagely, pulled at its tail. Drawing his knife, Kaspar severed the snake's head, and, turning to Stephanie, said, 'Are you bitten, or was he in time?'

'It spat at me,' she said. 'I am blind.'

'Did it bite you?'

'Nee, it did not bite. It spat in my face.'

Going up to Stephanie, Kaspar snatched her hands from her face. Her eyes were bloodshot and inflamed. Before she could stop him, he had pulled down her dress and looked at her neck, shoulders, and breasts. The snake had struck high, but because of the dog had missed her.

'Sit down and wait,' he said. 'You will not die.'

With his knife still in his hand he bent over his dog.

'Can I hold him?' Aletta asked.

'He may bite. I am going to cut him. Give me your sash,' Kaspar said. Taking it from her, he tied it round the dog's muzzle, and straddling him said, 'Take his foot, and do not let go.' Pulling a thin leather thong from his pocket, he tied it tightly above the dog's knee. With his knife he forced open the snake's jaws, and then, with two swift cuts running at right angles to each other, he opened up the bite.

Aletta turned white, but never moved. Her hands were firm on the big dog as he struggled.

'Are you going to let him bleed?' she asked.

'Ja, he must bleed. If he is not bitten elsewhere, he may live. What did she do it for?' he demanded passionately. 'Why could she not let the snake alone?'

Aletta said nothing, but went over to Stephanie.

Kaspar undid the scarlet sash and threw it towards her.

'Thank you,' he said, 'and thank you for helping me. If I had been alone, it would have been difficult.'

Loosened, the dog could scarcely stand.

'Can she walk?' Kaspar said, pointing to Stephanie.

'I am blind,' Stephanie sobbed, 'and it hurts. Before God, I have never been so hurt before.'

'Stand up,' Kaspar said.

Obediently, Stephanie stood up while Aletta helped her. Speculatively, as if she were a foundered horse, Kaspar looked at her and nodded his head. 'Lead her,' he said. 'I will carry my dog.'

5

Above the pain Stephanie heard his words. He preferred to carry his dog and she could walk. Just when she needed his strong arms about her, he said she could walk; and it was all his fault. If, instead of hiding behind a bush, he had stayed in the open, if she had seen him — it was because she had not seen him, and because she was angry with Coenraad, that it had happened. And suddenly she knew that she wanted Kaspar, wanted this stranger with an ache that hurt more than her pain. She felt that this intolerable burning would have been worth while if he had carried her; still hardly able to think, she knew that she loved this man who had pulled down her dress so roughly that he tore it, who spoke to her so angrily, and who thought more of his dog than a girl. This was what she had always wanted. It was his lack of respect that had attracted her to Coenraad, that and the power of his hands — he had killed men with those hands. But who would have thought that a boy — and Kaspar was no more — could do this to her? And suddenly she hated Aletta for leading her home so coolly, who to comfort her said: 'We will bathe your eyes with milk and oil and soon you will be well. In a few days, in a week, you will see again.' It was true that the blindness from a spitting snake rarely lasted more than a week, but in a week Kaspar might be gone.

She began to sob again. Men were not like women. They did not stay in one place where you could find them. Men were as free as the wind and as unpredictable. She hated Kaspar; she hated Coenraad; she hated Aletta. And if she was well in a week, what did it matter even if he had not gone? It was like this he would remember her: crying with pain, with her face inflamed and her eyes blood-red. But he had seen more than her face. Stephanie thought of his hands on her shoulders. True, he had been looking for a bite, but could a man look for one thing and fail to see another?

'Take me in the back way,' she said. 'I do not want to be seen.'

'I will take you behind the kraals and we can get into the house that way,' Aletta said.

Stephanie could not be so sick if she still thought of her appearance, but there was no understanding Stephanie. She had missed what might easily have been death by a hair's-breadth and was wondering what people would think — not of having attacked a big ringhals so stupidly, but of how she looked. If the dog had been a little slower or had hesitated even for an instant, it would have been so different. And everyone knew about the way such snakes spat venom. Stephanie had known and still had come within its reach. It was all inexplicable and would doubtless remain so, for Stephanie rarely knew why she did anything, and when she was well again would refuse to speak of the matter, making little of it or distorting the incident till it was unrecognisable. It was not that Stephanie lied, for to lie one must know that one is lying, and Stephanie believed what she said.

Aletta felt tired. It had been a strange day. Old Frederik's impassioned speech had worried her; he had seemed so old, so tired; and the scene with Coenraad had left her exhausted. And in a little while, as soon as she had put Stephanie to bed and bathed her eyes, she must find Coenraad. She felt sick at the thought of facing him again, of having to speak to him and look into his hot, dark eyes — and yet, in a way, she was sorry for Coenraad. There was something about this man, with his recklessness, his bragging and his thick-lipped, laughing mouth, that made her sorry for him; behind it there was no gaiety. Underneath, Coenraad Buys was a hard, bitter man, cynically daring. It was as though he challenged the God who had made him. He was a man who did not care one way or the other. Whatever came, good or bad, he would take with the same scornful laughter — contemptuous of everyone, of everything. A man ready to kill, to make love; a man who by some twist of his nature had been set above other men; a great leader, a giant in strength, but bad because, not knowing good from evil, he played with lives — his own and others — as if they were dice to be rattled in a cup.

Aletta undressed Stephanie and, fetching milk, poured it into her eyes slowly, a drop at a time, holding back the lids so that it would run in around her eyeballs. She was in no hurry for this meeting. She was afraid of Coenraad.

CHAPTER V

THE RACE

I

COENRAAD was talking to van Ek when Aletta found him. Their faces were serious. But she did not hear what they were saying, for one of the tame Kaffirs, a man nearly as big as Buys himself, touched him on the shoulder as she came near. Having warned his master, the Kaffir stood like a shining brown statue, looking at her without insolence or curiosity. The sun was low, and in the light of early evening everything was very beautiful — the massed wagons, the livestock, the men and women about them, busy over their fires, stood out as clearly as if they were cut out of painted wood; each separate from its background, and yet each, adding itself to the others, formed a pattern that brought her heart into her mouth.

All these people belonged to each other. They came from somewhere; they would return again. Each had an appointed place, an appointed task. They had husbands, mothers, fathers, brothers, sisters, grandparents, cousins; they had ties — roots. It was not often that she thought of these things, but sometimes a great loneliness swept over her, a longing for a mother to whom she could talk, or a father —

for a home. And beyond this, that she knew nothing of her past or of her parents hurt her.

Van Ek scraped the tobacco out of his carved stone pipe, refilled it, and looked at her out of his pale blue eyes. Aletta was glad he was there. He was a very gentle man: gentle, with the wisdom and tolerance of age. She sometimes considered what held these two men, so opposite in character, together. Christiaan van Ek, even as a young man, had never been like Coenraad; nor would Coenraad, if he lived, ever resemble van Ek. Theirs was no bond of affection, but one of a common hatred and born of the respect they had for each other's capabilities. Van Ek, the old, cold man with his infinite resource, courage, and patience, and Coenraad with his wild, reckless spirit, his influence in the north, his immense strength and vitality, were a dangerous combination; and the Kaffir, leaning on his spear beside them, was a part of the pattern they sought to weave. It was men like this Kaffir who had killed her parents and who, for some inscrutable reason, had spared her and reared her till they themselves had been destroyed and old Frederik had found her. Yet she did not hate them as much as others who had less cause, for she had drunk the milk of their women and vaguely remembered the bare black breasts that she had sucked.

'Did you want me?' van Ek asked.

'No, Oom Christiaan. It was Meneer Buys that I sought.'

'So I am no longer Coenraad, but Meneer. Ja, you are right. I should not have said what I did, but I was a little drunk and my tongue was free, Letta. You are a mooi meisie,' he went on, 'though few but me seem to have seen it. But then I am very gifted. With men and women and horses I rarely am at fault.'

'It was nothing, Coenraad,' Aletta said, holding out her hand. 'It is already forgotten.'

'It is good to be able to forget,' van Ek said.

'What did you want of me?' Coenraad asked.

'Your stone,' Aletta said. 'Will you lend it to me?'

'My snake-stone? Nee, I will lend it to no one; but if someone has been bitten, I will come with you.'

'Who has been bitten?' van Ek asked, getting up.

'No one; but Stephanie was nearly bitten and Meneer van
der Berg's dog is struck. The dog saved her,' she added,
'and he is much upset. Something should be done, for he is
a good dog; one which his father gave him. He carried him
home in his arms,' she added.

'Where is he?' Coenraad asked.

'He will be at his wagons,' van Ek said. 'I saw them come
in. Those are his.' He pointed with his pipe to three wagons
drawn up apart from the others. 'The blue ones with red
wheels.'

2

As Kaspar had carried Witvoet he had felt his heart beating wildly and erratically. That he was not already dead
was a good sign. But with the bite of a mamba or a ringhals
the heart sometimes beat even after life had gone, for their
poison worked fast — much faster than that of an adder, and
without swelling or discolouration. He was thankful that
his wagons had arrived. Witvoet was more than a dog: he
was a link with his distant home. He was the friend and companion of many years. That he should be killed or die would
not have hurt Kaspar, for this was almost inevitably the fate
of a hunting dog; but that it should have happened out of
wantonness infuriated him. He would never have hesitated
to send his dogs to certain death where it was necessary: that
was what dogs were for; and as the dogs would risk themselves for their master, so would he risk himself for his dogs.
But why had Stephanie done what she did? A ringhals stood
up and would not move unless pressed. She could have
walked round it and it would have done nothing.

His servants, crowding round, tried to take the dog from

him. They said he would surely die; and as one of them touched him, Witvoet twisted in his master's arms and bit him. A shout of laughter went up from the others.

'He will live, Baas,' they said. 'Ja, he will live. He has the heart of a lion.'

'Get me water,' Kaspar said as he put the dog down.

Raising himself, Witvoet licked Kaspar's face and fell back panting. For a moment it looked as if his heart would burst out of his ribs. His breath came in great gasps; he fought for air as if he were suffocating; while Wolf stood over him, wagging his tail slowly. Except when they fought over a bitch, these two dogs were inseparable. As Kaspar waited for the water, he thought of the afternoon. Only an hour ago he had been sitting on the veld, watching for herons and thinking of the race he would ride tomorrow; and now Witvoet was dying; dying because of his courage. He had never hesitated, but had sprung straight at the snake, as he would have sprung at anything else, a man or beast, against which he had been set. Bending over the dog, Kaspar flexed his paw in the water, into which he had thrown a handful of salt, pressing the wound open with his fingers. Sometimes the dog winced and tried to push his hand away with his nose. Once he snapped angrily in Kaspar's face and then licked it again. And then suddenly both dogs growled thunderously.

Looking up, Kaspar saw three people standing behind him: Coenraad, looking enormous against the pale green evening sky; old van Ek, with his mild eyes fixed on the dog; and Aletta, very upright and small between the two.

'Coenraad has brought you his snake-stone,' Aletta said. 'It comes from the belly of a sheep and will pull the poison out. Give it him, Coenraad,' she said.

From a small pouch on his belt Coenraad took a little parcel of soft brayed skin and unwrapped a stone about as broad as a man's thumbnail and twice as long. It was a pale grey in colour and very light.

Another man came up. 'I do not believe in snake-stones,

'Coenraad,' he said. 'Nee, there is only one cure for a snake bite, and that is to take a chicken, either a cock or a hen, split it open alive, and put it upon the wound, holding it fast till it dies. In its struggles it draws out the poison.'

'A live chicken is good, too,' Coenraad said, 'but can a man carry a live chicken on his belt?' He gave the stone to Kaspar.

'If it was my dog, I would use a chicken,' the man said. 'I will give you a chicken if you want one.'

'No, thank you,' Kaspar said. 'I will use the stone.' He had already applied it to the wound, binding it tightly with a rag.

'Leave it half an hour,' Coenraad said, 'and then make loose the riempie on his leg.'

Van Ek, kneeling down, took the dog's head between his hands and stared into its eyes.

The dog, usually savage with strangers, made no protest.

'He will live, Kaspar,' van Ek said. 'I can see it. Always when you look into sick beasts' eyes, or men's,' he added, 'you can see if they are going to live or die. It is as if the spirit begins to fade from their eyes many hours before it leaves their bodies. I have seen much death,' he said. 'Ja, I have seen many hundreds of dead.'

'And have caused many to die yourself,' Coenraad said.

'I have killed men,' Christiaan said, 'but I do not kill lightly.'

What were these two men who talked like this of death; talked of it as of an everyday occurrence; something that one took as one took other simple things? Certainly Kaspar was sure van Ek would not kill lightly, but remorselessly, and with great precision. In a way the old man was more dangerous than Coenraad, more implacable, one whom nothing would move from his purpose. But they seemed to be his friends. Kaspar wondered what his father would think of his situation and of these people; but it might be that his father would not have been surprised. It might be because

he had known that he would meet men of this kind that his
father had encouraged him to come. It might be that his
father, knowing that to become a man life must be taken
between the hands fiercely, had sent him here to learn the
trick of it. And for the first time Kaspar wondered what he
knew of his father; wondered what he had been as a young
man. When he got home he would ask him.

3

Coenraad's horse was a chestnut, six years old and somewhat taller than Tigernek, a magnificent beast with a flowing,
pale golden mane and tail, and four white stockings; but
though an outstanding horse he seemed to Kaspar to be
lacking in quality. There was a certain coarseness about him,
and his hotness, Kaspar thought, as he watched him sweating
and pawing the ground, might only be superficial. Tigernek
looked very light beside him; but, whereas the chestnut was
showing the whites of his eyes and lashing out at anyone
who came near his heels, Tigernek stood quite still with his
head up and his ears cocked. Turning his head, he nuzzled
Kaspar's chest with mole-soft lips. Then he looked about
him again, less easily, shifting his feet and flicking his long
black tail. His wide nostrils were dilated and red, his eyes
wide and staring. Kaspar smoothed the horse's neck. It was
as hard as marble, but supple and warm, netted with a
hundred veins that stood out in relief, veins in which the
blood of the Blue Spaniard ran. Tigernek was still, but
strung like a bow that is bent. In the brilliant sunshine his
coat shone like satin, a cold, steely blue, shadowed with black.
Kaspar was far from calm. He loved racing, but the chestnut was an unknown quantity, and though he had ridden in
many matches, he always felt the same before them when,
stripped to his shirt and trousers, he stood beside his horse,
waiting for the start.
Spread out in a half-moon behind him, everyone waited

for the race to begin. In front of them the course lay open. They were to ride along the vlei, across the bush-covered flat beyond it and back again: some four miles in all. In the broken country Coenraad's horse would have the advantage, for his beast was used to this kind of going; but once on the vlei Kaspar felt he could pick up. He was clear as to the race he would ride. He would let the chestnut lead, follow him, clinging on his heels through the scrub; and then, when they turned and reached the open, would come the test. If he was right, the chestnut, hearing him behind, would extend himself, and then on the flat, when he passed him — if he did — his bad blood would come out and he would give in.

'Where is your whip, jong?' Coenraad asked.

'I do not ride with a whip, Coenraad.'

'Are you ready, then?'

'I am ready.'

They mounted, Coenraad's horse rearing and plunging as he swung up and fighting for his head when his rider was in the saddle. Most of the men were on horseback, and at the starting-point old van Ek sat on his dun pony with his gun across his knees.

'Are you ready?' he asked, taking his pipe from his mouth.

'Ja, we are ready,' they said.

'Then I will count three and fire,' the old man said, raising the muzzle of his gun.

The report rang out and the two horses shot forward. The chestnut was very fast, but Tigernek was galloping well, and Kaspar, feeling that he had plenty in hand, held his nose level with Coenraad's stirrup. He could hear nothing but the pounding of hoofs; feel nothing but the surge of muscles between his knees; could see nothing but the ground slipping away in waves beneath him. Tigernek had hold of his bit, but was not pulling. This had always been his advantage in racing, for Tigernek was not just a running-horse. He was his own beast, the one that he always rode in preference to any other. The bush was coming nearer and Kaspar dropped

back. Holding the reins with one hand, he reached forward
to pat his horse's neck and talk to him. The roan turned
back an ear to listen and slowed up.

In front of him the powerful quarters of the chestnut rose
and fell as he bent in and out of the bushes, and Coenraad's
great back and shoulders swayed as he swung with his horse.
An overhanging thornbush caught at Kaspar, tearing his
shirt and arm. Tigernek was bleeding where he had been
scratched on the shoulder. They were coming to the turn
where a Kaffir stood holding a whipstick like a lance between
his hands. It was more open here, and side by side they
wheeled their horses in a swirl of red dust with Coenraad on
the inside. Again Kaspar let him lead, clinging to the chestnut's heels and taking his dust as they galloped back through
the bush. If he could stay where he was, if he was not torn
from the saddle by a branch, there would be a great race
when they reached the open.

As they passed the last bush, Kaspar sat down to ride.
Now he was on his own ground with nothing but grass in
front of him. His horse knew it too; and as he raised his
hands the roan lay down to gallop. There was still a mile
and a half to go, and Kaspar wondered if he could keep up
this speed, for Tigernek was galloping as if it were the finish.
His feet seemed hardly to touch the ground as he extended
himself over it, and at his side the chestnut thundered.

'Magtig, this is a race!' Coenraad shouted.

He was using his sjambok now, and under it the chestnut
pulled ahead. Tigernek caught up with him. They were
riding neck and neck, stirrup to stirrup, and neither horse
showed any sign of faltering. Both were black with sweat
and powdered with red dust. On each side of them Boers
galloped, shouting and firing their guns. One of them on a
grey joined in the race, and though his horse — a good one
— was fresh, it could not keep with them and soon fell back.

The finish was near now. Kaspar could see the coloured
dresses of the women and distinguish old van Ek on his dun.

Already they were opening a path for them to gallop through. Now he must end the race; leaning forward, Kaspar called to his horse and slapped him with his open hand. As if a spring in him had been loosened, the roan increased his pace and pulled ahead.

'If only my father were here to see this!' Kaspar thought. 'If only...'

And then, in midair, Tigernek turned and fell. As he felt him go, Kaspar pulled his feet from the stirrups and went over his head. There was a shout from the people. He saw the big yellow hooves of the chestnut pass over his head as Coenraad jumped him, and as he got up with the reins in his hand saw Coenraad sweeping his mount through the passage in the crowd.

Tigernek stood trembling beside him. What had happened? Why had he fallen on open ground? As he looked about, dazed by his fall, he saw blood dripping from his horse onto the ground. Going round to the off-side he saw what had happened. As he had sprung away from the chestnut, Coenraad's horse had savaged him, taking a piece clean out of him just above the stiffle.

Dragging his horse round in an arc, scattering people to right and left, Coenraad came galloping back, and Kaspar had to hold Tigernek who, screaming with anger, reared and tried to chop him.

'Are you hurt?' Coenraad shouted. 'Magtig, I thought your neck would be broken. I am glad it is not,' he added, 'for one day we will race again.'

'I am not dead,' Kaspar said, having quieted his horse, 'and I do not think anything is broken' — he felt himself — 'but your horse is a skelm.'

'Nee, he is a good horse and very fast. Had the race been longer, he would have won it. But he does not like being beaten. Like me, he is not used to it.'

'Ja, meneer,' Kaspar said angrily, 'and when he is being beaten, he runs foul.'

'And when I am being beaten I also run foul,' Coenraad said. 'It is my nature, and we are very close, my horse and I. Nee,' he said, dropping his reins and throwing his leg over his horse's neck, 'I am sorry.' He held out his hand.

Kaspar took it, but his eyes were on the chestnut that stood quite still. 'How is it that your horse stands now when before he was so wild?' he asked.

Coenraad laughed. 'It is the way I have trained him. He is quiet like a child, but when I squeeze him he dances and plays. It is for the women and Kaffirs. They like to see it.' He went up to Kaspar's horse to look at the bite. 'It is a nice clean wound. Put some salt on it and then some tar to keep off the flies, and he will be well in a day or two. How is the dog?' he asked.

'The dog is better.'

'That is good, Kaspar. It is in my heart that you are a lucky man.'

'Yes, I am lucky to almost lose my best dog, to have my horse savaged, and nearly break my neck — all in two days.'

'That is what I said; for your neck is not broken, the dog is not dead, and the horse is not seriously hurt. One day you will see what I mean. Up here luck is different. Up here we thank God each day, not for His mercies, which are many, but for the simple fact that we are still alive. Yes,' he went on, 'everything is relative. Go and deal with your horse, and then we will talk. Don't leave it to your servants, for horses understand these things. Do it yourself,' he shouted at Kaspar's back. 'Your horses, your guns, and your women should remain under your hand, for they can all betray you.'

4

Still shaken by his fall, Kaspar led Tigernek away and attended to him. What did Coenraad mean by luck? What was it he felt and could not lay hold of? A whole new vision was opening up in front of him: one not based on worldly possessions, but on the possession of life itself. The fact of life was not accepted here as the basis on which prosperity was built. It was a thing apart, something from which one was easily separated. He wondered what Leendert would say when he told him of his adventures. He wondered if it would have been different if Leendert had been here instead of lying sick at home; and were things as simple as Coenraad and van Ek stated? Was there no more in life than the right to live it freely under the eyes of God among the solitary hills?

'Magtig,' old Frans said, as he felt his young master all over, 'we thought you were dead.'

The other servants crowded round him, agape. 'We all thought you were killed, Baas,' they said. 'And what would we have done up here so far from home?'

'You are sure the Baas is all right?' one of them asked old Frans again as he let go of Kaspar — 'that nothing is broken?'

Having washed out the wound and dressed it, Kaspar sponged out his horse's mouth and eyes; and then, giving him to Frans, told him to walk him up and down till he was cool before he watered him. Only now that it was over did Kaspar think of the race and of how well Tigernek had run.

'So it is as I said: the dog is better.' Christiaan van Ek stood beside him.

'Yes, he is better,' Kaspar said.

'That was a good race you rode,' van Ek said. 'You rode a good horse well, but when I saw him fall I thought — there is a good young man that is a dead young man. At that speed you should have broken your neck, and I was glad to see you get up.' He spoke reflectively, drawing at his pipe and staring at Witvoet, who lay on a blanket beneath the wagon.

'Perhaps I am lucky,' Kaspar said. 'Coenraad Buys says so.'

'Coenraad is likely to be right, for he is lucky and plays his luck. They say it is because he has a spot in his eye.'

'Has he a spot in his eye?' Kaspar asked. 'For I have one too.'

'Then that is why you are lucky. Have you ever thought about death?' van Ek asked. 'For you were near it today.'

'No,' Kaspar said, astonished.

'I have thought of it much,' van Ek said, lighting his pipe again and sitting down; 'partly because I have seen much of it and partly because I am old. But young or old, each day is one day nearer to the end; and let me tell you this, Kaspar, when a man dies his possessions are as nothing. He cannot take them with him. Nor do his children, relations, and friends count in the final issue, and it is in my heart that as a man dies he sees very clearly that all he laboured for all his life long is as nothing; that all is vanity and has been no more than a striving after wind. And, no matter how many be assembled about him when he dies, a man dies as he is born — alone. Ja, he dies alone, like a dog under a bush.'

Van Ek paused. He had spoken slowly with great detachment, staring into Kaspar's face, but looking past him.

'But let us talk of more serious things,' he said.

'More serious than death?' Kaspar asked.

'Ja, more serious; for death is nothing. It is an end. It is passive, not active, and therefore nothing. Perhaps it is like happiness — no more than peace, but a peace that is everlasting. Nee, horses are serious, and we have been to see them.'

'My horses?'

'Your horses; and we will buy them.'

'Who will?'

Van Ek hesitated. 'Coenraad and I will buy them.'

'How many?'

'The whole klompie.'

'All ten?'

'Yes, all ten; and you will be paid in ivory.'

'How do you know the price I ask?' Kaspar said. 'I want a hundred pounds for each of them.'

'It is not too much,' van Ek said. 'We pay well for the things we need. Now listen. Tomorrow you will go on to Leendert's place and we will send there for them.'

'And the ivory?' Kaspar asked.

'You must trust us. There will be a guide who will lead you over the river and through the Bushman country. Once there, you will sell your goods and load up with our ivory, and then . . .'

'And then?' Kaspar asked.

'And then you will go back to where you belong. You have a father and a mother. You have a home. Get back to it and leave us on the Border. I like you,' he said, 'and would not have you caught up in this. I am old and I do not matter. Besides, I am as slim as a rooikat and this is my country. The others,' he shrugged his shoulders, 'play for big stakes, but you have all to lose and nothing to gain. Therefore do as I say and keep your own counsel. Sometimes it is better to forget than to remember what you have heard. Better for everybody,' he added, turning away.

What did it all mean? Kaspar wondered as he watched him go. Something was brewing; and why did van Ek and Coenraad never move without their guns in their hands? He had only just noticed this, for they carried them so naturally, as easily as if they were sjamboks. Indeed, now that he came to think of it, in the race was the first time he had seen Coenraad unarmed, and always, wherever either of them went, some of the Kaffirs that he had seen sitting apart at the feast hovered about them, watching them with sharp, dark eyes.

But Coenraad liked him, and Coenraad held the key to the north, where there were ivory and gold. Coenraad, a strange, almost mythological figure. A man with two hundred pounds on his head. A giant who in one breath boasted that he would drive the English into the sea; challenged a stranger to a horse race, and taunted a girl till she cried; a man who had lived with a Kaffir queen and was by it adviser to Gaika, the greatest chief in the district. With Coenraad's friendship he would be able to take his wagons into the heart of the Kaffir country — a thing which was forbidden, but which could under such conditions still be done. And fortune was within his grasp.

Sitting by his wagon, Kaspar dreamed of wealth; of how he would return; of the presents he would buy for his mother, his father, for the house slaves, for everyone; dreamed of the hunts he would have, for from here on there was game in abundance. It was a strange world. Rather more than life-size, but one in which it seemed to him a man might make his way if he was fortunate in his beginnings.

CHAPTER VI

A COMPANY DISPERSED

I

AT THE hour of 'the cattle horns' — just before the dawn, when a man stooping can see the horns of his oxen against the paling skyline — Kaspar was awakened by the shouts of the herders bringing in the beasts.

All about him cooking-fires were alight; and slowly, out of the shoutings, the curses, the cracks of whips, came order, and some of the wagons, not waiting for daylight, rumbled off into the thick mist that lay like wool along the river.

The space in front of Rudolf's house was emptying itself; the wagons going, as they had come, separately.

Kaspar watched a young man standing by his horse as he talked to a maiden, saw him kiss her quickly, and then, jumping onto his horse, gallop away while she looked after him. The little festival was over.

By the time the sun was high, everything would be as it had been, except that the hard-baked ground would be more dusty, cut up by the spoor of the heavy wagons, blackened by the marks of many fires, and cluttered with those small things which remain when a company has dispersed — broken yoke skeys, bits of riem, the shards of a pot, some rags, and the bones of the beasts and the feathers of the birds that had been eaten.

Because it had been so full, the place now seemed very empty. Kaspar drank his coffee slowly. He was stiff and still tired. Both his horse and his dog were better, but he was sad and longed for his kin. The brilliant future seemed less brilliant today, and he wondered if he were big enough to seize the fortune that he saw. The words of his servants had upset him. 'What would happen to us, Baas, if you were hurt?' Suddenly he realised his responsibility to his people; realised that no matter where he led them they would follow; no matter what he commanded they would do. And he was planning to take them into the north where anything might happen. They had wives and children, and these trusted him to bring back their men safely. At twenty, what did he know of his capacities? What did he know of real danger, or how he would act under it? He was untried, and at once curious to know his qualities and afraid of what might happen if they failed him. Courage he thought he had, but would courage alone compensate for lack of experience?

His back ached, and when he raised the beaker to his lips a pain like the stab of a knife ran through him. Coenraad and van Ek had gone. With their Kaffirs they had faded away into the night, not even waiting for the dawn, his people said. Then there were those girls. How was Stephanie? He must see her before he left, and the other, the little one who had held his dog's foot while he cut it; who had faced Coenraad and who afterwards had gone to Coenraad to borrow his snake-stone. He had never seen girls like these, so reckless, or so outspoken in their ways.

Leendert's farm was not far away — a short day's trek would bring him to it. He wondered if he would be able to ride, or if he would have to travel like a woman on a kartel of his wagon.

2

Aletta was surprised to find old Frans at the door.

'What do you want?' she asked. 'Has the Baas sent you?'

'Nee, my meisie; the Baas has not sent me, and it is in my heart that he would be angry if he knew I was here.'

'Then why have you come?'

'I have come to see if the meisie has something to put on the young Baas's back?'

'Is he sick?'

'He is not sick and nothing in him is broken. I have been over him from the hair of his head to the toes of his feet, but he is very sore. Magtig, it was a fall that he had, and if he was not a foolish young man with a head as thick as a Kaffir's, he would no doubt be dead. Also he is unhappy.'

'How do you know he is unhappy?' Aletta asked absent-mindedly as she thought of the remedies she had at hand.

'How do I know?' Frans asked. 'I know all that is in my Baas's heart. Has he not been my Baas since he was born?'

'And he is good to you — good to his people?' Aletta asked.

'He is like a father to everyone. But he is foolish, as all young folk are foolish.' Frans sighed as he thought of Kaspar's foolishness, and went on. 'He is in my charge. But do not tell him this. It is not right that a young Baas should have an old slave set over him, but the old Baas said, "Watch over him, Frans, for he is my son." And before God, if he is the old Baas's son, he is also as much as my own sons to me — and more, for my sons are no good. They are so much no good that sometimes I think that they are not my sons. But you will send something?' he asked, 'for his back is very sore and he keeps touching it.'

'I will bring something,' Aletta said.

'And you will not say that I asked for it? The meisie will not say that I came to her?'

'No, I will not say.' Aletta laughed. No, she would not say. A young man whose servants loved him like this must be a good young man. She liked Kaspar van der Berg. She liked the slow way he smiled when he spoke. She liked the way he managed his horse. She thought of how she had seen him in the race, leaning over the neck of his roan, and of how, when he got up after his fall, his first thought had been for the horse.

In a cupboard, with the other simples and remedies that were kept against such an occasion, she had a pot of goose fat rendered down with turpentine and herbs. If this were rubbed into his back, it would ease his pain.

'What are you getting?' Stephanie asked from the bed. It was infuriating not to be able to see; to have to listen for sounds, and then from sound alone to have to reconstruct all that went on about her.

'I am getting something for Meneer van der Berg's back,' Aletta said. 'He is stiff from his fall.' Aletta was getting something for Kaspar's back, and no doubt she would rub it. She would think no more of rubbing his back than that of a sick Hottentot or a galled horse. Stephanie felt she could not bear the thought of Aletta rubbing Kaspar's back. She heard pots being moved, heard them clink against bottles as Aletta searched for what she wanted.

'How do you feel?' Aletta asked. 'Has the pain gone?'

'The worst is gone,' Stephanie said, 'but my face feels as big as a pumpkin.'

'It is as big as a pumpkin,' Aletta said. 'But it will go down. In a few days now it will be over.'

'Don't let him come in,' Stephanie said.

'Let who come in?'

'Kaspar van der Berg.'

'Why should he come in?'

'To see how I am. To say good-bye. He is going, I suppose?' she said. 'He is not too sick to go, is he?'

'He is going soon,' Aletta said. 'He wishes to get to Leendert's, and is taking April to guide him.'

But Stephanie was no longer listening. She had turned her

head to the wall and lay curled up with her legs drawn in to her belly.

3

The rubbing and the ointment did Kaspar good. With it the pain went and he was no more than stiff. Ordering his other horse — a brown that was almost black — to be saddled, he prepared to go, saying good-bye to Rudolf, to Maria, who sat outside the house with her swaddled baby in her arms, and to Aletta. Stephanie he did not see, but asked after.

'It is in my heart that you saved my daughter's life, meneer,' Rudolf said, 'and up here we have long memories. Let this be a second place to you.'

'Dankie, meneer,' Kaspar said. 'But what I did was nothing. It is only that I have good dogs; they are well trained and of high courage. What you owe — if you owe anything — is to my dogs and to the accident of my being near.'

'That was no accident, Kaspar,' Rudolf said, putting his hand on his arm. 'It was by the blessing of God that you were near.'

Mounting stiffly, Kaspar turned his horse, fired his gun, and, waving his hat in salutation, rode off with his mounted servants behind him and the guide at his side. Like ships getting under way the wagons wheeled and followed him, the rested oxen moving easily in their yokes.

'That is a fine young man,' Rudolf said as he watched them disappear, 'and I wish him well.'

Aletta said nothing, but stood at his side staring down the road. Something had ended. People had come, had paused, and had gone. The tangled skein of the festival was unravelled. A thread at a time it had been drawn out. That which had been was not, and never, no matter what happened, would things ever be the same.

Meneer van der Berg was going from Leendert's into the
land she feared, the north that was always with them, pressing onto them. She hated it. It was too full of Kaffirs; bursting with wild black warriors whose only outlet was over the
Border on which she lived.

Maria, still holding her baby, threw food fragments to the
chickens. She loved her chickens. They were entirely her
own, all descended from the few that she brought with her at
her marriage: the same strain that she had had at home,
except for the blood of the cocks that she had exchanged with
friends and neighbours. Chickens were like other animals:
they must have new blood. They were of all colours — red,
yellow, black, brown, speckled, white, and spotted. Some
had feathers on their legs right down to their toes. She liked
them the best. It was as if they wore trousers, and one hen
had feathers on her head like a big round hat. Oom Christiaan said there was a breed like that in France. It would be
fine to have a whole flock like that, she thought, each with
a bundle of feathers on its head.

Aletta watched the poultry for a moment. Then she
glanced at the sun. It was time to dress Stephanie's eyes
again.

4

Kaspar rode slowly, lost in thought. He listened with little
attention to the talk of the guide Rudolf had given him. He
did not know the men of whom he spoke; he did not know
their farms or how they lived.

How in the last few months his life had altered! How
in the last few hours it had completely changed in form!
If he were going to go back, he must go back now. Here was
a parting of the ways — a time when, alone, without advice
or help, he must choose between the right and the left; a time
when he could no longer hesitate with his mind divided.
Either he could wait for Coenraad's men and go with them

over the river, or he could sell his horses and goods here, using Leendert's farm as a base and hawking them round from farm to farm. If he did this, it would be because he was afraid, and because he was afraid, he would not do it. No; because he was afraid to go on, he would go on. He was strong; he had good servants with him; he was well-mounted, well-equipped, and above all he was curious. He knew that his mind had been made up from the beginning, and that he would only lie at Leendert's till Coenraad's men came in to fetch him.

Every hour the country got wilder and the road rougher, till at one point he pulled up and asked Rudolf's Hottentot if he had not lost the road.

'Nee, Baas, I have not lost it,' April said. 'This is the best road.'

'If there is another road, why did we not come by it?' Kaspar asked.

'The Baas told me to come this way. He said go the long way, for the road is better.'

Kaspar looked at the track winding in front of him. It curved along the side of the mountain; part of it was washed out by the last year's rains, and over the whole great boulders stood erect.

'So the other road is worse,' Kaspar said.

'Ja, Baas, the other road is bad.'

'Yet I do not see how we can get the wagons through this one,' Kaspar said, looking at the rock outcrops.

'There is plenty of room, Baas.' April rode on, and turning his horse said, 'Look, Baas, at the wagon spoor. This is the way we always come,' he went on. 'But of course if your boys cannot drive, I will take your wagons through, one at a time.'

'Who says we cannot drive?' Old Frans had left the leading wagon and stood beside him.

'I did not say you could not drive, old one. I said that if you could not, I would take your wagons through.'

'Magtig, do you think I would let you drive my Baas's

wagons? Kom, Hendrik, Lazarus,' he shouted to the other drivers. 'Baas,' he said, 'we will look this road over. Magtig,' he said to the guide, 'I was born on a wagon-box, I have driven horses and oxen since I was a child, and where wagons can go, I can take them. Because we are not half wild, you think that we know nothing; but soon you will see. Ja, soon you will see.'

Together they all went forward. The stretch was not more than a mile long, but Kaspar had never seen anything like it. With well-trained oxen it was just possible, but no more than that; for in many places, having come between two rocks, it would be necessary to halt the span and swing it at a new angle in order to pass the next, and owing to the heavy sand between all the rocks, the oxen must be in draft the whole time.

When they had been over it, Frans said, 'We can do it, Baas.' And picking up his whip, he went back to the wagon.

Pulling off his shirt and tightening his sandals, he shouted to his span: 'Loop! Loop! Trek! nou!' His whip cracked once, and then he sent the long lash hissing over the backs of the oxen to drop lightly on the quarters of the third ox on the off side, which flung itself into the yoke.

Running beside them, slipping over the disselboom, driving first from one side and then from the other, Frans drove his span, forcing them till the trek gear threatened to break, and then halting them with a long whistle while the voorloper swung them. Sometimes the wheels scraped rocks as large as the wagon itself; sometimes they rode up smaller stones, hesitated, quivered, and fell with a crash onto the other side. Now the front wheels, now the rear, rose, so that Kaspar feared the wagons would break their backs; but they were well built, the oxen strong; and everything held as, rocking like ships in a heavy sea, they rolled on, swaying over the boulders, their hubs screeching as they scraped past them; while the baboons on the mountain-side barked defiance and the hills echoed the claps of the whips and the shouts of the drivers.

Although it was still early, the kloof down which they went was dark and menacing, for the sun was hidden behind the hills and their bush-fringed crests were sharply black against the sky.

Accustomed as he had become to rough, mountainous country, this road frightened Kaspar. It seemed to him actively malignant. It seemed as if the rocks deliberately sought to breach the bellies of his wagons, to smash their wheels; as if the loose ground tried to slip away from under the feet of his beasts and precipitate them into the river-bed two hundred feet below. But once through the kloof he found himself in a pleasant valley. One in which trees grew sparsely on good sweet grass.

'We are here,' the guide said. 'The house lies over there hidden behind the randjie.'

5

'I do not like it, Kaspar,' Leendert said.

'You think he will not pay?'

'No, Coenraad will pay; he always pays. But I do not like your becoming mixed up with him. There are things' — he paused — 'things that are not good about that man. Did you like him?' he asked.

'I liked him,' Kaspar said. He also liked this new uncle of his who sat talking so quietly. He was about his father's age, very big, heavily built, with massive shoulders and a slow, deliberate way of speaking.

'They told you I was sick at Rudolf's,' he said.

'Yes, they said you were sick, Oom Leendert.'

'I was not sick. But I lay on my bed for two days because I did not wish to be in this: I had heard that Coenraad and Christiaan would be there. Is that answer enough for you?' he asked.

'Christiaan van Ek seemed a good man,' Kaspar said. 'He was kind to me.'

'He is good. But a good man spoilt. It may be by the English or by a woman. He hates them both, saying both are bad. And a man who hates, Kaspar, is an ill counsellor. Hate is stronger than love, for, feeding continually on itself, it grows stronger. Those who live by the sword perish by the sword, and it is not that I have not thought of this matter,' he went on. 'I have thought deeply; but the English are too strong for us, and it is our people's nature to fight only when they may win. Also Coenraad would raise the Kaffirs. He is not like us who hate them. He thinks with them and knows their minds. You have not seen a Kaffir war. You have not seen what they can do; or how they kill, sparing nothing.'

'I have given my word,' Kaspar said.

'Then you must go, but commit yourself to nothing further, no matter what they offer.'

'I will not commit myself,' Kaspar said.

'Tell me of the festival, Kaspar,' his aunt said. 'Tell me of Rudolf's girls, and which did you think the prettiest?'

'I do not know. I never thought of it.'

'Nee, you were thinking of your horses and of ivory. Yet they are marriageable, and before long some man will take them. Already I hear that young men are often there. Soon they will opsit with one of them. I wonder which will go first.' Bending over her sewing, she went on. 'If I were a man I should court the dark one. She will be a fine woman.'

'What, Stephanie, who threw the stone?' Kaspar said. 'Nee, Tanta Sybilla, she is one who would take a candle to look into a powder barrel.'

'She will get over all that when she is married and has babies to tend, and perhaps she was angry at something.'

'Why should she be angry?'

'I do not know, but it might be that she was. And she will have a good portion. Letta is penniless, and so quiet. There is nothing in her.'

'I think there is a great deal,' Leendert said. 'Ja, she is

like a little horse, and often you can go farther with a good little horse than with a bad big one.'

'And often a woman marries a big man who is a fool,' his wife said. 'Magtig, you sit for hours saying nothing, and then, when there is no occasion to speak, you say the wrong thing.'

'What have I said now?' Leendert asked.

'Nothing.' His wife looked at Kaspar from under her eyelids. 'Nothing except something that proves all men to be fools. But you may be right about Aletta. Ja, you may be right, but only time will show. But if I were a man I would choose Stephanie.'

Kaspar said nothing, but looked from the one to the other, wondering at his aunt's preference. For the first time since he had left Rudolf's, he thought of the girls as women; and surely there was no comparison between them. He saw Aletta as she had stood facing Coenraad. Thought of how she had helped him with his dog; of how she had borrowed the snake-stone. And suddenly he knew that he would like to see her again. There were things he was not sure of — the exact colour of her eyes; of whether she had one dimple or two; of the way her mouth twisted a little when she smiled. No, certainly his aunt was wrong. But then women were so often wrong about other women, especially if they were small and fair. Now that he came to think of it, he had never heard a small fair woman praised by another woman.

Getting up he went out to look at his wagons.

'I hope he will think of what I said,' Leendert said when he had gone.

'No doubt that is what he went out for,' his wife answered, 'so that he might consider the matter of Coenraad and van Ek under the stars. It is moonlight,' she added.

'Yes, and we will get no rain till the next change of the moon,' Leendert said, wondering at the way his wife's mind jumped from subject to subject.

6

Sybilla understood her husband now. But when he had sold a good farm over her head, collected his cattle, packed her and the children — there had been but two of them then and a third on the way — into the wagons with as much household gear, implements, tools, and seed as they could carry, and had trekked, she had not understood him.

It had been this way:

One day Leendert had said, 'We are going to the Great Fish River.'

'But it is wild,' she had said.

'Ja, it is wild,' Leendert had answered, picking up a saddle and beginning to mend it, stitching it, drawing the thin leather lace tight as he worked and going back on the same seam from underneath so that it was sewn double. It was beautiful work; straight and strong. It had never ceased to astonish her that so big a man could work so finely.

And it was thus that they had come.

What a tedious journey it had been! She had been far gone, and as the wagon rocked forward on creaking axles she had found much time to think. Day after day those wheels had rolled, following the wide road across the veld. Many had driven along that road, and the driver of every wagon, having his own ideas and disdaining to follow in the exact spoor of the others, had made a way of his own. So, red and rutted, dusty, hundreds of yards wide in places, the road dragged its way through the veld. Day after day the riempie bed on which she lay had creaked, sagging beneath her weight. And while they travelled it had come to her: first as an idea as she sat by the fire at night before they slept, watching the light of the flames reddening Leendert's black beard while he sat brooding beside her, and then, later, as the road unwound from beneath the wagon like a ribbon — as a certainty. It was that all men were mad. Not only Leendert her husband, but all men; and this knowledge produced a peace as real as the red dust that settled on her, covering everything.

That was the day that Bokveld had died. He was not the first ox to die on the trek, but he had been a fine beast. He had pulled on the near side in the fourth yoke: a red ox with a line of white marks down his back, a white tail, a white-dashed face, and a belly whose whiteness had spread down the inside of his legs. Before they had started, Bokveld's horns had been sawn off, for, growing downwards, they had been about to penetrate the flesh of his cheeks. If unwatched and running on the veld, such beasts could die. She had seen this happen. Sybilla's face puckered as she thought of Bokveld. He had been one of her own oxen. It was many years ago, but if I saw him today I should know him, she thought. He was not a long ox and rather short on his legs, but very strong. A fine, willing beast. Among a thousand she would know Bokveld. His bones lay on the Karoo with the bones of other beasts; his skin they had taken with them. That night she had tried to persuade Leendert to go back. 'There is no return,' he had said.

And here, she looked out into the night. Where there had been nothing, they had made a home; built a house that was almost a fort, with narrow slits for windows; made lands, a garden, planted the trees they had brought with them, their roots wrapped in straw; reared cattle, sheep, and horses; and here she had borne her children, the first alone, under a tree in the hot sunshine, as a cow might calve.

With her hands folded on her lap she smiled at the simplicity of men and at her early lack of understanding. Kaspar had hardly thought of Aletta till by a dexterous word she had turned his mind that way. She liked Aletta, and it was as easy to turn a man with an idea as an ox by waving a white cloth in his face. But nothing must be direct. They must think the idea their own. If he married Aletta she would feel that she had done it, and when she took their babies on her knee it would give her a pleasant glow as if they were her grandchildren.

Leendert sat opposite to her smoking his pipe. When he drew on it she could see his face. Leendert, who when she was a girl had swept through her heart like a flood through a mealie land. What a courtship that had been! She began to laugh quietly to herself and settled lower in her chair. It was a pleasant memory now; but at the time it had been terrible.

For days he had sat on her father's stoep, saying the same thing over and over again till she could have cried. Each day he had fed his horses with her father's best oat forage and had gone on sitting, staring over the lands; staring, smoking, and following her with his eyes as she moved about. And in the evenings he had talked about his cattle to her father. Two hundred cows there had been then, with six bulls, one to thirty cows, and many calves, heifers, tollies, and young oxen ready to sell.

'Ja,' he would say, 'I should be getting back to see to them. One cannot leave good stock to watchers.'

He kept saying this, but he did not go; and each day his horses grew fatter on her father's oats, putting on flesh till they nearly burst out of their red hides.

'Before God, take this man, Sybilla,' her father had said. 'He is rich and well-spoken of. If you don't, I think he will stay forever. He is that kind.'

From the moment she saw him, she had meant to take him, but he made her angry. He had not courted her. He had given her no chance to show her attractions. He refused even to be jealous of the other men who came to see her. He had just sat stolidly, staring, spitting, smoking, and talking of his cattle; of Roiland, his best bull that every now and then broke out of his kraal to go twenty miles to fight a neighbour's bull.

'Ja,' he had said to her once, 'Roiland went all that way with a gate stuck on his horns, and nearly killed Jan Hoffman's bull. Is that not a great marvel, Sybilla?' he asked.

'Ja,' she had said, 'it is a great marvel.'

But this was not the way to go courting, nor was it seemly to talk of bulls to a maid.

'I am glad you think it is a great marvel,' he had said, 'but he only gets like that sometimes. Once a year or twice a year it comes into his heart to fight, and then nothing will stay him. Then I send a picannin after him and in a week he is home, as gentle as a dog.' Turning to her father, he had said, 'I will give you one of his sons, Oom Hendrik.'

Her father's eyes had glistened. He had heard of Labuschagne's stock.

She had left them then and gone on to the back stoep. She would not stay to be bargained for like a Kaffir maid! Wait while she was sold for a bull calf! Why did he not straightway offer ten cows for her — that was the custom among the Kaffirs: ten cows for a woman — and lead her off?

Next day she had seen him inspanning his red horses, four of them, to a light Cape cart. They were so fat and fresh it took two boys to hold them. Her heart stopped beating. He was inspanning, and he had said nothing. He had not spoken. She watched his big hands fiddling with a new voorslag. Looking up he had seen her and said: 'This is a fine lash. It is made from a blesbok skin. I made it myself.'

His horses were kicking and squealing in their harness, lying back in it and lashing out, for the flies tormented them; and then jumping forward so that the cart rattled on its axle, as they snapped at each other. Leendert had continued to fiddle with his whip, testing the thong between his hands and whistling softly to calm his horses. Then he had turned to her and said, 'Are you ready, Sybilla? It is time we left.'

Never so long as she lived could she forget that moment; or the way she had gone in to get her things. Her father and mother had laughed at her anger and her red face. For, not daring to speak directly to her, Leendert had talked to them; but it made her ashamed to come to him so quickly and without hesitation. But he was that kind of man, very silent save when he talked of cattle.

And the horses would not stand. Soon, if she kept him waiting, they would begin to kick. Her box, a little hide-covered wagon-box ornamented with brass nails, was soon lashed behind the seat and the riems pulled tight about it. She could see him now holding the reins in his hands, the two pairs looking nothing between his fingers.

'You are ready, Sybilla?' he had said.

'Ja, I am ready,' she had answered.

But she had not been ready, for now Leendert, who had been so still, came to life.

'Maak los!' he had shouted.

The Hottentots almost fell as, rising in his seat, he slacked the reins. Twice, like a pistol, the long whip clapped. With the fingers of his left hand guiding the leaders, he clapped the whip again. It was like this that she had left her father's house, driving in a swaying cart behind four bolting horses that galloped with their ears laid back, urged forward by the mad giant who was going to marry her.

'Do you always drive like this?' she shouted.

'When I drive, I drive,' he said. 'My horses know my hand on the reins. With you they will be like children.' He had handed her the reins. And it was so. At once they slowed to a steady canter; and he had laughed. 'You see, Sybilla, I am a quiet man. I do not know the way to court a maid, but with beasts it is different. It is as if I knew what was in their hearts and they knew what was in mine. I can do what I will with a beast. I am a simple man and the beasts are simple, too. They are as God made them.'

Looking into his eyes, she had seen that they were serious. The sparkle of excitement had gone out of them. As he looked at his horses his eyes were moist, so greatly did their beauty move him.

Yes, that was Leendert. That was her husband. A man as simple as a beast, as gentle. Upright and God-fearing, but slow and obstinate in all his undertakings. A good man to be with, and ill to cross.

She was still sitting, lost in thought, when Kaspar came back.

'Is everything all right?' Leendert asked.

'Ja, everything is all right,' Kaspar said. 'But tomorrow I will ride back to Frederik's. I have not enough dogs, and perhaps he would sell me one of his pups if they are weaned.'

'If you are going there, you will pass by Rudolf's. I have a gift for his child,' Sybilla said.

'Of course I will stop at Rudolf's.'

'It would save sending.'

'Do not forget to say that I was sick,' Leendert said; 'that I was in bed when you came.'

CHAPTER VII

THE GREEN DRESS

I

RIDING alone, Kaspar returned to Rudolf's. In the morning light the road was no longer menacing and he marvelled at his previous fears.

Happy with his uncle and aunt, he did not feel so far from home. He must have been tired and more lonely than he had known. But this loneliness was ended now because of his new relations and because Rudolf was his friend. He wondered how Aletta would greet him; if she would be surprised to see him. He thought of how he would explain his presence by saying that he was going to old Frederik's house to get a puppy from him and on his way had brought a gift for the child from Tanta Sybilla.

Witvoet was better, but it would be a good thing to have a young dog — a bitch pup, that he could breed to him. Old Frederik's dogs were good, and the brindle bitch very fine, indeed. A dog did not get those scars for nothing. On a bad dog there was never a mark, for they avoided danger; on a foolish dog there was never a mark either, for they got themselves killed.

The cliffs he rode under were festooned with yellow-flowered creepers. They hung down from every crevice, filling the air with scent. Yesterday in the dusk he had not noticed them, and leaning from his saddle he pulled off a long tendril and wound it round his hat. In the full sunlight the kloof was strangely beautiful. Hot and silent, empty of life, he saw that it was a great fissure in the mountain where some cataclysm had riven it, splitting it in two as a log is split with an iron wedge, a crack through which the silver river wound its way. Once the peaks that towered up on both sides above his head had been joined together. The stained patches of ochre deposit on the cliffs balanced each other; for every mark on one side there was one on the opposite — mark for mark, crack for crack, they corresponded. The rocks in the road seemed friendly now as, rounded and warm with sunshine, they stood upright beside their dark blue shadows.

The brown horse played with his bit, snatching at it and tossing his head as he cantered through the kloof. Kaspar was happy. He was riding towards Aletta with a fresh young horse under him. The kloof was beautiful and the sun bright. He put his horse to a gallop. All his doubts and fears had gone. He was on the verge of achievement.

Coming to a small sluit, he jumped it. As the horse landed, his stirrup leather broke; pulling up, Kaspar dismounted and sat down to mend it while the horse grazed near him. The race must have strained the leather, and it was lucky it had broken now rather than then. He thought of Aletta, of selling his horses, of trading beyond the Great Fish River. Soon he would be a man.

2

When he rode round the sugar-loaf hill, Kaspar saw Rudolf standing with two Kaffirs in the cattle kraal. Hooking his reins on a post, he went in to him.

It would be easier this way — first to pass the time with Rudolf and then to go with him to the house. He had not thought of what he would say to Aletta when he saw her.

He had counted on the words coming to him out of the air, for surely when his heart was so full his mouth would not be empty. There was so much he wished to tell her: of his home at the Cape; of his mother and father; of old Frans; of a dog he had had as a child. He wanted to tell her of the first race he had ridden; of the first buck he had shot. But he did not know how to begin, so instead he must stand high upon the piled dung of the cattle kraal with Rudolf, watching the Kaffirs flay a small red-and-white calf.

'How goes it?' Rudolf asked, holding out his hand.

'It goes well, Oom Rudolf.' Kaspar touched the dead calf with his foot. 'What was the matter with her?' he asked. He could see that she had been slaughtered and had not died, for she was fat and sleek.

'She was crippled,' Rudolf said. 'When they came in last night, her leg was broken. The herder said he did not do it, but I know that he did. Magtig, there is no way to stop them throwing stones at cattle. I have beaten him,' he added, 'but that does not bring me back my versie.'

'It is a lovely skin,' Kaspar said, 'very beautifully marked for a waistcoat.'

'Ja, it will make a waistcoat,' Rudolf said, sighing, 'but it would have been a cow.'

The boys, having severed the skin of the legs at the fetlocks, leaving a little rim of white, blood-stained hair above the hoofs, split it up the inside and peeled it upwards. It came away with a thin, tearing sound as they dragged it from the forelegs, chest, and ribs. The fine powdered dust of the kraal clung to the pale meat. It was strange how pale the flesh of a young calf was — pink, with blue-tinged muscles and white ligaments.

Rudolf cracked his whip at a cow that had come running to the fence of the kraal and stood with her neck outstretched, staring up at them, lowing continuously with long, deep bellows. Starting softly, the bellows ended in a roar.

'That is the mother,' he said. 'She is a fine beast.' He cracked his whip again.

'Ja, she is a fine beast,' Kaspar said.

The calf was flayed now, and with the wet skin folded over his arm Rudolf went towards the house.

Kaspar wondered how he would begin when he met Aletta. It depended on how she received him; on whether she was pleased to see him.

'How is Stephanie?' he asked.

'Stephanie is better, but she cannot go out, for the light hurts her eyes,' Rudolf said, giving him a sharp glance. Was Kaspar going to be another of them? Sometimes he was worried about Stephanie. She was courted by too many and by none formally. Men came to her like bees to a comb. Coming and going and coming back again, but not staying. This was not good and might lead to great harm, not only to his daughter, but to the men themselves, for at such times men were not calm and overready to fight. Yet he was sure Stephanie was a good girl, only overfond of men and unable to choose between them. Yes, that was the way of it; and Aletta never seemed to think of men at all. If only the one thought of them more and the other less, it would have been better, but as they had been made so were they, and to doubt that it was for the best was to doubt the wisdom of God.

'Come and see my pigs, Kaspar,' he said. 'I have a sow with thirteen young ones. They are two days old and so far none are overlaid; but with pigs you never know,' he went on. 'Magtig, you think you have a fine litter, and then one morning you come to see them and behold the sow has lain on several. But this sow is a good mother and most careful of her young. I believe that she looks round and counts them before she lies down to rest.'

Kaspar did not want to look at the pigs. He wanted to see Aletta. He wondered what she would be wearing. He could not remember her face clearly, and again the question of her dimples troubled him: had she one or two? Surely it was very rare for a girl to have only one.

They stood leaning on the rough pole fence that surrounded the pit in which Rudolf kept his pigs. The sow lay extended with her back to the wall grunting happily as her piglings drank. Like their mother they were white spotted with black, but the white part of their skins was very pink and bristled with hairs that shone like silver wires as the sun caught them.

'They are beautiful,' Kaspar said.

'Ja, they are beautiful, Kaspar; and I always think that nothing tastes as good as a sucking pig. You must stay a few days, and we will have one.'

'I will stay with pleasure, Oom Rudolf,' Kaspar said, 'and I have brought a present for the child from my aunt.' He pulled a parcel from his saddle-bag. 'I must take back the cloth,' he said as he undid it. 'My aunt likes it greatly, for it has a border of red and is one of three that she bought at her marriage.'

'Bring it with you,' Rudolf said. 'We will give it to Maria when we go in.' He touched it gently with a thick brown finger. 'She will be pleased with it.'

3

Aletta had seen Kaspar come. He had come with flowers in his hat. She had thought he would return, but wished he had not, or had, at least, delayed his coming. She had been preoccupied by thoughts of him since he left, and now, before she had made up her mind, he was here. Yet she knew she would never have made up her mind if he had not come; knew that he would have gone on drifting pleasantly in and out of her thoughts, getting fainter and fainter as the days passed, till finally he drifted out of them altogether. But he was here talking to Rudolf about his pigs, and he must be faced. She wondered what had brought him here, or at least what excuse he had made; she knew the reason of his return and wished she were more skilled in talk. He must be used to a different kind of woman, to girls who had seen so much more than she, who had even been to Europe, who wore beautiful clothes, who could play the harpsichord or the spinet, do fine embroidery, sing, and paint in water-colours. What, then, could he want with her? She bent lower over the table and wondered how he liked his food; perhaps the bobotee she was making would be too highly seasoned for him. Draining away the milk from the bread, she smoothed out the lumps with a fork. The onions were already fried and she added them to the soaked bread and the meat. Salt, curry, sugar, vinegar, and eggs, all mixed and beaten up in a bowl, she added next, and worked them in with her hands, kneading the meat as though it were dough. Then she put it into a greased earthenware dish, poured over the top the milk she had drained off to begin with, and set it in the oven to bake. It should be good. Her bobotee was good, but she wondered if Kaspar would like it; wished she knew what he ate at home, and that she knew more of towns and the way they lived at the Cape. What was Kaspar's home like? What had his upbringing been? What did he care about and what things did he dislike? What, she sighed, did she know of Kaspar? Nothing, and nothing of the great outside world.

No, she knew nothing of towns, though she had been to Graaf-Reinet and would one day, certainly, go to Cape Town; this all women did with their betrotheds to obtain permission to marry from the Governor. A journey of near two hundred hours by wagon, counting only the time that the wheels rolled. Sometimes it so happened on these journeys, if delayed by floods or insurrection, that the girls became mothers before they were wives, Nature being more powerful by the wayside than law. Perhaps she would make this journey with Kaspar, and at his side see what the greatest town in the land was like. She had heard it said that there were more than a thousand houses under the shadow of the mountain, lying between it and the sea. But this she did not believe. It would mean as many houses as Rudolf had cattle. It was an impossibility. But Kaapstad must be a wonderful place, a house for each beast. She laughed at the idea as she cleaned her hands, scraping the fragments of meat from her fingers with a knife before she washed them. A house for every cow, each ox, tolly, heifer, and bull calf. She saw Oom Rudolf's beasts so housed, each standing with its head out of a window or peering from a door. It must be a fine thing to see the ships come sailing in from over the sea, and it would be interesting to see an Englishman. They were not as other men; they wore no beards, and it would be strange to see a grown man with a face as hairless as a boy's. Strange and indecent, also sinful, for where God made hair it should be allowed to grow.

Stephanie at least would like the bobotee; it was sweet enough to tempt her, though when she was ill she was difficult about her food.

The milk jug was put away, the dishes stacked, and the crumbs and fragments of meat swept onto the floor to be picked up by the fowls that wandered in and out of the open door. Hesitating a moment, she took her kappie from where it hung on the ox-horns nailed to the wall by the door, and went out.

Kaspar and Rudolf were still standing by the pigs, leaning their elbows on the fence of the pit.

'Good-day, meneer,' she said to Kaspar, and, turning to Rudolf, said, 'the coffee is ready.'

4

Through swollen lids Stephanie watched Aletta go out. She saw her greet Kaspar and turn to her father. She could see that she was nervous and Kaspar ill at ease. What cause had Aletta for nervousness? Why was she so forward and eager? And why, if she was, did she show it? Surely now was the time for dissimulation. If she had run back, if she had been cold, he would have followed her as a hound follows on the blood spoor of a wounded buck, with his nose down, whimpering with excitement and blind to everything. But no, instead, she must stand up to him and look into his eyes so that he could see her fears. When the game was hers, she threw it away by her honesty: men must imagine themselves the pursuers. Not a downward look, not a toss of her head: without defiance, without modesty, Aletta was standing as awkward, as tongue-tied as Kaspar. She had not even stopped to fasten the strings of her kappie, so quickly must she have run out.

Staring out of the narrow window, Stephanie thought of what she would have done; of how she would have bridled; have asked him why he had come back so soon. And then she would have capitulated less to his urgency than to his superior strength, pretending that he had his will of her and keeping her hold on him by his sense of obligation to her. If it was me, she thought — and suddenly she determined that it should be she; that she would have Kaspar. She would be well in a few days, and surely, since he had come back, he would stay. It was my life he saved, she thought, and I have a claim on him.

5

Kaspar was glad to talk to Aletta of Stephanie. To speak of her was the first, the only thing, that occurred to him. 'How is she?' he asked.

'I told you she was better,' Rudolf said.

'Ja, she is better,' Aletta repeated.

'I am glad she is better,' Kaspar said, wishing Aletta would walk in front of them so that he could see her, instead of beside them with her arm round his horse's neck.

'How is your dog?' Aletta asked.

'He is better,' Kaspar said.

'I am glad he is better.'

'You like horses?'

'Ja, I like horses.'

'Ja, she likes horses,' Rudolf said, 'and she rides like a boy.
You never saw such a girl with horses either to ride or to
drive. It may be because she was reared on horse's milk by
old Frederik,' he said, laughing.

As if it were but yesterday Aletta remembered how she had
sat in front of Frederik, grasping the rough mane of his horse
between her fingers. When anyone spoke of those days they
seemed very close to her. She could still feel Frederik's hand
on her belly as he steadied her. Once he had tied her to him
with a riem as the commando had fought its way out of an
ambush. She remembered the galloping and the firing of
guns, and being frightened because old Frederik's hands no
longer held her, but were busy firing and reloading his piece.
But how much was actual memory and how much due to
what she had since been told, she would never know. Yet
Oom Rudolf was right. For some reason she did seem to
have some special feeling for horses and they liked her in-
stinctively.

'The coffee will be cold,' she said, looking at Kaspar.

It was over. She had spoken to him directly and he had
answered her. Now she was glad that he had come. It had
only been the idea of meeting him which had distracted her.
The fear that she would not know how to meet him; that she
would appear awkward in his eyes, comparing unfavourably
with the girls he knew at home. But he had not thought so.
And as they went towards the house, he touched her hand.

'Kaspar has brought a frock for the baby from Tanta
Sybilla,' Rudolf said. 'It will be welcome. For a small child a
frock is better than a cow or a sheep. It can be used at once.'

When they went in, Maria was nursing her baby. She
greeted Kaspar.

Kaspar gave her the little dress — he had wrapped it up in
the cloth again.

'My aunt wants the cloth back, Tanta Maria,' he said.
'She values it.'

The frock was passed from hand to hand. Tanta Maria

gave it to Rudolf and he passed it to Aletta. 'Put it away safely, Letta,' he said.

As she held it, running her fingers along the pleats, Aletta heard Rudolf say, 'Then you will stay, Kaspar?'

And his answer: 'Ja, I will stay, Oom Rudolf. I will be glad to stay.'

He was going to stay.

Did his eyes seek hers and rest on them softly, or was it only that she thought they did?

6

Stephanie was going to get up. Her eyes were well. It had taken a week to cure them and Kaspar was still here.

'I must not put on my best, she thought, but there is the green.'

Yes, the green dress was very pleasing, neither too good nor yet shabby. It was a lovely colour, grass-green — and a little tight about the bodice. It had flounces lined with red silk and a little red collar that showed off the knot of her heavy black hair. Tanta Maria would say nothing — she had eyes for nothing but her new baby — and Aletta knew that she often dressed up for no reason. It was not as if it were her best. Nee, it was not her best, but it had been when she was smaller, and it fitted her as a jug fitted water. There remained only the question of the sash and stockings. She rarely wore stockings, and it would be best not to wear them today, for even her stepmother, preoccupied as she was, might remark on them. But could one wear a sash without stockings? She slammed open the chest, found the green dress, and shook out its folds. Below the dress, lying on the other clothes, was the sash. She pulled it out and drew her fingers caressingly along the wide red silk. She loved the feeling of rich material in her hands. It was cool and felt slippery, almost wet. Regretfully she put it back. Changing her mind, she took it out again.

Maria was sitting in a big chair near the window when she went in. Kaspar stood near Aletta by the table.

'Good-day, meneer,' she said. 'I trust that you are well.'

'I am well,' Kaspar said. 'Do your eyes no longer hurt you?'

'My eyes are well.' She looked at him and held out her hand. 'I do not think I have thanked you, meneer. You saved my life.'

'It was nothing,' Kaspar said.

'It was something,' Rudolf said. 'But let us eat.' He sat down.

Stephanie put the coffee on the table. She did not look at Kaspar again, but stood very near as she served him. Her sleeves were rolled up, and as she withdrew her arm from the table, it touched his.

Aletta understood. She knew the expression that would be in the veiled, lowered eyes; understood the raised toe that tapped the ground and the set of Stephanie's hips and shoulders. Stephanie wanted Kaspar. Suddenly she saw that Stephanie had meant this from the beginning; that from the moment she had seen him, she had meant it; that the walk she had taken with her during the festival had been to find Kaspar; that the episode with the snake had been due to her not finding him.

Stephanie's dress shone richly green as she moved, and round her waist, rather low so that it swathed her hips, she wore a sash of cherry red.

Aletta felt her confidence leaving her. Why had she been so certain that it had been she that Kaspar had come back to see? Why could he not have come back for Stephanie? Had anything passed between them when they had all stood near each other listening to old Frederik's speech? It did not take long for Stephanie to attract a man. Without words, with a look only, they were at her feet. She had changed into a dress that was too tight for her; one that showed off her hips and breasts as if she were naked, and clung even to the curve of her thighs. She stood near to Kaspar, watching him from under the dark, lowered lashes that lay so demurely on her cheeks. Aletta had seen her do this before. She knew that from now on she and Stephanie could no longer be companions.

She looked at Rudolf. He would be glad if Kaspar married Stephanie, for Kaspar was a fine young man and well-off beyond the ordinary. Drawing herself up, Aletta stared at Stephanie coldly. Stephanie would hurt Kaspar. No man was the same when she was done with him. She was like a weed that spread over the land; like the rooibloom that was so beautiful, but which lived by sucking the sap from the roots of mealies. She looked from Stephanie to Kaspar. What did he feel? Perhaps nothing at all. Perhaps he cared for neither of them. Perhaps there was a woman in Kaapstad, some girl there that he loved.

CHAPTER VIII

POINTED WITH BIRDS

I

'I MUST see you, Letta,' Kaspar said. He could delay at Rudolf's no longer and must ride on, yet it had taken him two weeks to say these words, to face Aletta and ask her plainly to listen to him.

'I must see you,' he repeated. Since his coming, this was almost the first time he had seen her alone.

'Who? Me?' Aletta asked. 'But you see me continually,' she went on. 'I am always here.'

'I see you,' Kaspar said, 'with your Tanta Maria, with Oom Rudolf, with Kattie, with Stephanie. But I must see you alone before I go.'

'You will come again,' Aletta said. 'You will pass here again on your way back from Oom Frederik's.'

'I will pass here, but only to off-saddle for an hour, and tomorrow I must go.'

'Ja, if you do not go soon, Kaspar, Oom Frederik may have parted with the pups he does not wish to keep, and then you would have had your journey for nothing and regret having stayed here so long. It was to get a puppy that you came, Kaspar?'

'That is what I came for, to get a bitch pup to mate to old

Witvoet, and my aunt asked me to bring a present to Tanta
Maria as I passed this way. Let me speak to you, Letta.'

He was urgent. Any minute they might be interrupted.
Any minute Stephanie might come, for she never left them
alone.

'What are you doing now?' Aletta asked. 'Surely you
are speaking to me and we are alone.' She drew a half-circle
in the dust with her bare toe.

'I may never come back,' Kaspar said.

'What, from Frederik's?' Aletta laughed. 'Nee, you may
never come back, but the day after tomorrow you will be
here with the puppy to show me.' She hesitated. Kaspar
was right; they were never alone, and at any moment someone might come. Was it that she was not ready to be alone
with him? Or, was it because she knew herself to be ready
that she paused? And yet she was happy now and ready to
stay as she was. She liked the tender looks that passed
between them. She liked the gentle touch of his hand on her
arm. She wondered if he thought she would break, so gentle
was he. She liked to feel his eyes on her and to know that
they softened when he looked at her. She liked to feel that
he was by her, watching over her; that he thought her
beautiful in spite of her small size, her crooked smile, and her
one dimple; in spite of the fact that she did not know who she
was and had no marriage portion.

Though she joked about his journey, Kaspar would not be
the first who had crossed the river and had never returned.
Going to Frederik's was nothing, but when he came back he
would be on his way north to Kaffraria. Many wagons
went north and sometimes their spoor led one way only.
They had never come back. She was afraid of everything —
of Stephanie, of the future, of the Kaffirs. Afraid, too, of herself and astonished at her own behaviour. I am behaving
like Stephanie, she thought. I am drawing back and leading
him on. Was this due to fear? To a desire to hold things till
they became clear? She began to understand Stephanie and

the pleasure to be obtained by wielding power over men. When they were like this, a woman could do what she willed with them. And what did she will of Kaspar? She felt herself growing ashamed. This withdrawal of hers was not real, and he looked so unhappy.

'I will see you tomorrow,' she said, 'after we have eaten and before you go.'

'Where?'

'In the shed.'

'You will come? You promise?'

'I will come, Kaspar.' He could hardly hear her, so softly were her words spoken.

She would come. She had said so. There was no trickery in this maiden.

Aletta looked up into his face. As her eyes met his, she smiled shyly. Her mouth was not quite straight; it turned up a little more on one side than the other; it was a sad little smile, and her eyes were gentle. Her hands were crossed in front of her, the fingers of the one grasping the wrist of the other.

2

That night Kaspar hardly slept, and the morning went slowly as he helped Rudolf with his work. He was tired of the beasts he handled; tired of the milling herds of long-horned cattle, and the sheep. Every few minutes he glanced at the sun. It did not seem to move at all, and the shadows of the trees got no shorter. He wondered about Stephanie. Hitherto no device had sufficed to keep her away, but perhaps Aletta would succeed where he had failed. Already he had confidence in Aletta, feeling that much would be safe in her small hands. Ja, much, and more than much, for if she was willing he would lay his life in them.

Riding at a walk he watched the herders collect the sheep. The short-cropped grass was spotted with lambs. Much cleaner than the ewes, they lay flat on their sides or played together, gambolling, standing on their hind legs as they butted their heads together, or, lost, wandered bleating till found by their dams. When his dog approached them, the ewes faced it, swinging outwards with lowered heads and stamping feet. Other flocks were being driven into the kraals. They came from all round. The sheep and the goats were kept separate, but it was strange that the sheep should be so foolish that a big gelded goat should have to lead each flock.

If there was no rain soon, Rudolf would lose most of his lambs, for without young grass the ewes could not make milk. He had burnt off two mountains so that at the first shower the young grass would come away freely. But farming up here was harder than it was at Kaspar's home in the south. There were greater droughts and there were losses from wild beasts — wildcats, wolves and wild dogs, lions, leopards, even vultures, all took their toll. Baboons came down from the mountains and would rip up the young lambs and kids for the milk in their bellies, and beyond this there was a continual leakage due to theft by the Kaffirs and the Bushmen.

Today was to be the end of a great counting. These flocks that were coming in were the last. They had been pastured at some distance on the other side of the Berg in charge of some of Rudolf's best boys. Circling his horse, Kaspar turned towards the house. On his right he could just see Rudolf's head and shoulders and the head of his horse. The legs of both were lost in the low red cloud of dust thrown up by the sheep he drove. Once he heard Rudolf's whip clap and the answering shout of a Kaffir. The flocks were converging on the kraals now, and he saw Rudolf ride forward, swaying on his legless horse, at a canter into the opalescent cloud in front of him. The short, stiff grass was broken, cut into chaff by the thousands of sharp little hoofs that passed over it, the ground speckled with black pellets of dung and the air rank with the reek of sheep. A loose ox, disturbed by the noise, tried to break past Kaspar and get into the kraal. Swinging his horse round, Kaspar galloped beside the ox, clapping his whip. Two of Rudolf's dogs — they were trained to come to the crack of a whip or the report of a gun — joined him and turned it back before it overran the sheep.

They began to count, Kaspar and Rudolf standing side by side and checking their counts with those of the Kaffirs, who slipped a mealie pip from one hand to the other for each ten as the sheep poured out of the gate, halting them at the hundreds, which they marked by a small stone set on the wall of the kraal.

Taking them in fours and sixes, Kaspar counted on, glancing, when he could, at the sun, or, when unable to raise his eyes, watching the shadow of the open gate. It seemed to get no shorter, nor did the flocks get smaller. The sheep ran out like a stream of dirty water. Grey, black, and brown, some horned, some hornless, they ran, pressing against each other, their little hoofs pattering the stone-hard ground, and jumping away like buck as they passed them.

But at last it was done. Soaked with sweat and red with dust, Rudolf and Kaspar went into the house to eat and rest. Kaspar watched Aletta as she ate. There was nothing to show in her manner that she was moved. She was still and calm, small and entirely unperturbed. Her mouth was firm, and her hands, as she helped to serve the men, steady.

The talk turned to old Frederik and to the trouble he had had with his Hottentot.

'He should never have taken him,' Rudolf said. 'He should have known better, for coloured folks are like others; it is not so hard to tell the good from the bad, and it is in my heart that Booy is a skelm and that he stole those twenty sheep and sold them to the wild Kaffirs, though it was never proved.'

'But what will the end be?' Kaspar asked.

Frederik's troubles seemed small and distant to him; as he spoke of them he wondered how Aletta would take his words. For a girl should be courted; it was her right; and yet he had no time to court her now, no time to spend weeks opsitting with her, for he was tied by his promise to take his horses north. There were his goods to be sold, and his duty to his folk, who must be got home to their families. Nee, he must say what it was in his heart to say and leave Aletta to decide.

'You will sleep now,' Rudolf said.

'Ja, I will sleep,' Kaspar said, picking up his hat. 'I will go and lie under the great fig tree.'

3

'So you have come.'

'I have come, Kaspar. I said I would come.'

'Where is Stephanie?'

'Stephanie is busy.' Aletta's eyes were bright with laughter.

'What is she doing?' Kaspar asked.

Aletta began to laugh. 'She is very busy, Kaspar. We have been lucky. All night I planned, but could think of nothing, and then this morning I saw the cat looking for a place in which to have her kittens. So when Stephanie was out, I put the cat in the chest where she keeps her clothes. It was very comfortable there for her. She liked it, Kaspar. She turned round and round to make herself a nest. And is she not lucky to be brought to bed on green silk?' Aletta was almost crying with laughter. 'Ja, Stephanie will be busy for hours. And she is so angry — she has only just found out. There are four kittens, two tortoiseshell like Mina, a red one, and one that is all black, with a white face and white feet. On his nose he has a black spot, and he has one also on his chin, and his stomach is white.' She talked fast. What more could she say about the kittens? About cats? 'It is funny that tortoiseshell cats are always females, is it not, Kaspar?'

'Ja, it is funny, and it is true, but still I do not see why Stephanie will be busy.'

'That is because you are a man and do not know women.

It is not good for clothes when a cat has kittens upon them. The green dress was on top,' she added. 'I am glad it was on top, for it was in my heart to put it there. Do not fear,' she went on. 'Stephanie will not come. She will be busy ironing out her clothes all day. What was it you wanted to say to me?' she asked.

'Only that I am going,' Kaspar said, 'and ——'

'But you said that yesterday.'

'But that is not the only thing. It is that I am coming back. I want you to know that I am coming back.'

'Natuurlik,' she said. 'Of course you will come back.'

She looked down. What did he mean when he spoke like this? And why did he hold her hand so long? He held it gently, but his arm was trembling. 'It is dangerous,' she said, 'but you will not be killed. A friend of Coenraad's is safe.'

'I did not mean that I should be killed,' Kaspar said, wondering what he had meant to say when he began. Of course he would come back. At the moment he had no desire to go.

He took a step forward. 'You are like a small bird,' he said.

The arm about her stopped trembling. It grew hard like an iron band. With his other hand, Kaspar raised her chin, forcing her head back so that he looked into her eyes. Her arms moved upward from his waist to his neck. She felt she must hold on to him. If I do not hold on to him, she thought, I will fall. His shoulders stooped over her. His lips came nearer. He was kissing her, straining her to him. Her body, bent into an arc, fitted into his. He had not said what he had been going to say, but what necessity was there for him to speak? Already it was beyond words. Now there were only feelings. Now there were not even feelings. Now there was nothing but a warm emptiness enclosing her. An emptiness that was Kaspar. In all the world there was nothing but Kaspar.

4

As he rode away, Kaspar could remember nothing of what had happened, and this surprised him. Surely when a man — but no, it was not so, and it hurt him to think of it. Only a few hours ago. He thought of what he had done since then, of what he had done before.

He thought of how he had come upon her in the shed, of how she had stood still waiting for him to come to her. He thought of how he had seen her then and of the beam of light which, coming through a hole in the thatch, had struck the top of her head, making her hair shine like ripe straw; it had run over her, over her body, onto the ground at her feet; golden knife of sunshine in which particles of iridescent dust had danced, mounting up and down, as though alive. All about her had been things he knew: wool ready to be carded; riems, tobacco, biltong hung from the crossbeams of the roof; and there was a calf-skin spread, pegged on the dagga floor. It was the one they had been flaying when he came. Between the pegs the skin curled upward, wrinkling and pulling as it had contracted, drying. He remembered thinking that there should have been more pegs; that had he spread it, there would have been more pegs.

All this he had felt, as he went towards her, with the thick, greasy smell of the sheep's wool in his nostrils, the scent of the tobacco, and the sweet, rancid smell of the riems and drying skins. The sound of his footsteps had been very loud on the earth floor and the distance between them great. He had felt his heart pounding and the blood in him run upward so that he knew that if he must speak he could not.

Aletta had not moved. As a buck that knows itself perceived, she had stood, with only her breasts rising and falling as she breathed. Their moment had come upon them. They knew it, and both had taken it as they were fashioned, as God had created them: she, standing very still, waiting; he, actively pressing forward. It was not his will nor hers. This he had known very clearly. It was like a dam that had been built, that had lasted a long time, and then, when the head of water became too great, had burst. There was no hope, no precept, no morality. Before this nothing had existed; after it all would be different. But it was not different. It was the same.

Something, that time they had been together, had been taken from him. He did not know where it had gone. All he knew was an emptiness, a craving that it should be again; that his turbulence should be subdued by Aletta's acquiescence; that his hardness should melt into her softness, making him nothing. But remember?...nee, he could recall nothing.

Vaguely he knew the joy he had had of her. Of touching, touching, so that he lost himself in a maze of sensation. He looked at his hands, flexing the fingers. He thought of her body where below her ribs it sank into her belly, of her smooth flanks; of her hips that rose steeply when she lay on her side. He had knowledge of her. She had been his and he knew her, knew the change in her eyes before he took her and the way they fluttered open — after.

Before he left, he had looked at Aletta as she stood, with her sleeves rolled up, working the yellow butter on the stone slab of the dairy. The stone was slate, dark and shiny with water. Drops, opalescent with milk, ran over the edge onto her bare feet. She was dressed in faded blue, sun-faded till it was the colour of a washed-out sky.

This was Aletta. This was the woman. But in his heart he knew it was not she; that the woman a man possessed and the woman a man saw with his eyes were not the same; that they never could be the same. It was like a bird perched and a bird flying. What was a bird when it was not flying?

He had continued to watch her; to watch the muscles of her arms moving as she worked the butter, pressing it between her hands, washing it and scattering salt on it with her fingers. What was she thinking of as she bent over her work?

Of him? Of butter? Of a new dress, perhaps, or the children she would bear? What did he know of what went on in her head? Only when he saw her eyes again would he know; or by her carriage, by the thrust of her breasts or the quick catch of her laughter.

Tightening his belt as though he were sick or hungry, he went out into the sunshine, away from the smell of milk and ripe cream; out into the world he knew. She had not seen him. For a moment he stood still, dazzled by the glare. It was strange to have left Aletta. Out here there was only light and brightness. The weight of the sunshine was heavy; it stung him. He could feel it biting into his bare fore-arms. With half-closed eyes he looked at his horse. The brown looked black and white, colourless above his shadow. His head hung low; he stood on three legs resting his off hind leg. As he watched, the horse flicked his tail at the flies, twitched the skin on his shoulder, and looked round. Kaspar saw the mark on the stirrup leather where he had mended it. He had sewed it with rawhide and had moved it from the near side to the off, for it might break in mounting. He knew the feel of the join he had made, and touched it for reassurance.

The sun glinted on the horn of a cow as she raised her head to stare at him. A spreeu dug its beak into some half-dried dung for the fly-worms that were in it and then stood with gaping beak and wings spread away from its body in the heat. Before God, these things were real. The ways of the beasts and the birds were good. On the veld there was a way, a plan for each. There was precedent and knowledge handed down; out here he was a man.

Making loose his horse, he tightened the girth. The brown horse snapped at him. He laughed. Horses often bit when they were being girthed up. He was strong and girthed them hard. Slipping the rein over its head, he mounted. It was not in his heart to say good-bye again. They had parted in the shed and not till he had been alone in the mountains

and slept under the stars at night would he face her again.
He was glad she had not turned as he watched her in the
dairy. What could he have said?

5

To Aletta, Kaspar's coming, his possessing her in the shed,
his going, were at once beyond understanding and beyond
thought; as significant as the dawn, the rising of the sun from
behind the mountains each morning; as inevitable. That it
had taken eighteen years to rise was as nothing compared to
the glory. And God had said, let there be light; and there
was light. And God saw the light, that it was good. And
God divided the light from the darkness.

Now, whatever she did would be Kaspar. He was in the
butter that she worked. He was in the cattle kraals. He was
among the peach trees grouped about the front of the house.
He had seeped into the marrow of her thoughts so that she
was possessed by him, so that she would carry him everywhere with her; not as the man he was, strong, rough, with
clumsy hands, and a voice which broke oddly sometimes,
but as a presence, a warmth that permeated her.

She put her hands up to her breasts. He had cantered
away. The sound of his horse's hoofs had been sharp on the
hard earth; had weakened as, topping the rise, he had
dropped into the drift; had risen again as he rode up the bank
on the other side, and receded finally until it was nothing,
and the faint throb in her ears only the pounding of her own
blood. Till he returned, she would listen for him. Whatever
she did now, wherever she was, she would be listening, her
head turned for the sound of galloping hoofs.

Looking down, she smiled. The front of her dress was
greasy with butter and dark — indigo — with water from
her hands. Stephanie would say ... very well she knew what
her Stephanie would say ... She felt herself blushing, the
colour rising hotly in her cheeks.

She could change her dress. But her eyes — surely all the world would see by her eyes. She had gone straight from Kaspar to the dairy. She had known that he had stood looking at her. She wished now that she had turned her head.

Pulling a red earthenware pot towards her, she crammed the butter into it, wiping the palms of her hands on the lip, and, with clenched fists, forced the butter down. Little bubbles of water rose as she squeezed, and air; and the butter made a small sucking noise as she withdrew her hands. On the butter there was the cast of her knuckles. When the pot was filled, it would be covered with a green pig's bladder. As it dried, it would become as tight as a drum, and the butter would keep till the winter. This pot would stand on the shelf with the others in the cool gloom of the dairy. No one but she would know that it was different. Picking up a knife, Aletta scratched a mark on the pot. There must be no confusion about this thing. It held much more than butter.

6

The strange gentleness of women was new to Kaspar. In his life he had not known it. When Aletta and he had been alone together, alone in the world of their making, she had been like water; she had flowed into him. He thought of her hands again, light, yet urgent and strong, when they had sought him.

His mother had been a fierce, hard woman who gave him much food, few words, and little tenderness after he could walk. There had been others, younger ones, with a call on her milk and lap. Brothers and sisters, following each other, had been nursed, weaned, and turned out like foals to wander in widening circles.

It was not that he had never thought of women. He had. He had been to weddings. He had watched the coloured people. He had lived his life on a farm among sheep and cattle. At

times he had felt strangely; had woken in the night with
a girdle about his loins and a weight pressing on his shoulders;
had got up and walked, going to the river where it ran below
the house to listen to it rippling over the rocks, or to the
kraals, and stood motionless among the sleeping beasts.
Then he had gone back and slept again. But he had seen this
thing in another way, differently, less as a marvel, a beauty,
than as a necessity. He had seen it as a part of life, almost as
a duty.

Between animals there was little love: an association, a
mating, and they went on grazing, cropping the grass after
their desire was slaked. With his parents there had been
nothing like this. There could not have been. It existed for
the first time in the world.

From a clump of matted thorn came the liquid note of the
shrike. Kaspar pulled up his horse. He wished to see the
bright red breast of the bird, more bright than blood, scarlet
against the blackness of its body. Shrikes were not rare.
He often saw them. But today, at this moment, he felt it
would give him pleasure to look at it. Probably there would
be two of them, for it was said that when one called, the other
called too, simultaneously, so that it sounded as though
there were but one. How did they know? he wondered. The
birds came out, black and scarlet, hopping from under the
scrub.

He rode on. He began to sing. A flock of small blue-
breasted finks flew past him with some rooibekkies. A pheasant called. The world was full of life today. The veld pointed
with birds. It was as if everything were a great picture
— all planned and arranged, grouped so that if you
looked carefully no one thing had the advantage over another. There was no difference between the smallest flower
of the veld and its greatest tree; none between the ant and the
elephant. Each was perfection, and in the smallest part of
each was further perfection. The wetted seed bean swollen
and ready to sprout with its shoot curled like a child in

the womb; the streak of colour on the petal of a flower; the stiff hairs each growing from a bulb-like root on the back of a wild pig — were all of one pattern. Each was striving towards an end, towards accomplishment, and that they existed was cause enough for endless wonder; for each was a subtle marvel, each complete in itself, and each part of some greater thing, the great no more perfect than the small, the sum no more marvellous than the integral parts. In six days the Almighty God had done all this, making it from nothing, creating the trees and the beasts and the birds and the flowers: making man out of dust and spittle and woman from a rib out of the man's side. Sitting back in his saddle, Kaspar rode down the slope of the mountain. It was only fourteen days ago that he had ridden up this little padjie to the festival.

CHAPTER IX

THE LETTER

I

SINCE coming back from Rudolf's place, old Frederik had been tired; his gout was worse and his mind disturbed. He wished he had not spoken to the court messenger as he had; that he had tempered his words. But the man had angered him by his questions, by his assumption of importance, by the cheap authority of his small official standing; and his servant had stolen the eggs from under his red hen. Though he had not known this when he had spoken, it now rankled him and made apology impossible.

Sitting on the stoep, his large body hunched together, he smoked and thought.

Near his feet the red hen scratched at the hard ground, clucking to her one chick — very small, pale buff, marbled with brown and black, it pecked in the dust under its mother's shadow. The hen was luckier than he — she did not know what she had lost and was content; whereas he was not content. God, in His wisdom, had given man vision and memory, and his memories were bitter in his mouth. Nothing was left to him; of his family, of the sons and daughters that he had had, none remained. There were no grandchildren, no great-grandchildren. There was only little Frederik, his son by a Bastard slave girl. What would become of him? Rudolf might take in the child, but not the woman; she was too young for Maria to welcome her. Selina would go to some other man. As the waters ran down hill, as surely would this happen; and since she would never give up her child so would it, too, pass into a stranger's hands and be reared among the Bastards that he bred of her. And this would be the end of his blood — himself dead, his son a servant, perhaps not even knowing his father's name, and his herds scattered. That something would happen he was now certain. Events had gone too far and he was caught in the cleft stick of his own pride. For the first time he faced it definitely, not merely as a probability, but as a fact. The administration was not satisfied with the freedom of the Border life, with the independence of the Burgers. They wanted to make an example of someone. Coenraad had laughed at them too long, and then there were the missionaries at Bethelsdorp who clamoured continually against the Boers and their treatment of their servants. He wished now that he had gone at the first summons. But there would have been talk at the courthouse. They would have asked who he was and how he lived. Knowing it, they would still have pressed him. There would have been sniggerings about his coloured concubine and his child; questions about his property and affairs.

Looking back, he tried to think where he had failed... tried to think if there were things that he should have done which he had not done. There were such things, as there were in the life of every man. But what he had done was the best that he could do. In his work, in the taming of his land, he had never spared himself, working with all his strength, without complaint and to the glory of God. Like Job he was being tried; and restless, unable to sit still, he climbed the mountain again.

Each day now he made this pilgrimage, toiling up the mountain-side, painfully conscious of his weakness. Unwilling to think further of the future, he thought of the past

— a past that till now he had not dared to consider. Always he had worked on. Always, whatever had happened, however bad the year, there had been the next one to think of and plan for. Droughts passed, locusts went as they had come, miraculously. When cattle died, more were born.

And there was his son Jannie. He had never got his body back from the Kaffirs. He would have liked to have it back. He wondered what had made him think of Jannie. Jannie would have been forty now. Perhaps it was because of his brother. Jannie had been very like Johannes. Johannes was a bold man and a good brother to him, though he did not like Selina, and had not from the beginning, which had made a breach between them. Yet at a time like this he was ready to help. A hard man, but true to his kin. If things went wrong, he had promised to come from Tarka and not to come alone. This was his word. Gerrit, who lived near-by, would come too, but Gerrit was never ready to take risks unless he saw a profit. But Opperman should have done something. He was his friend and should not have let things go so far, and it was his duty as Veld Kornet to settle such disputes as had arisen between him and Booy. He thought of the correspondence between them. Before God, no man could have been more reasonable than he.

There was the first letter written in June 1813. He remembered that it was June, for it had been very cold in June that year and he lost many sheep. It had all seemed nothing then — just a disagreement about a Hottentot, and on hearing from Opperman he had written direct to the Landdros of Graaf-Reinet explaining the situation. It had been a very simple letter in which he had stated his case, without prejudice or favour. It was the letter of one honest man to another, of a respected Boer to a magistrate detailing the matter of the heifer that he had borrowed from Booy. He had given him another heifer for it which was better than the one he borrowed, and after that he had lent Booy ten rix dollars, and it had been agreed between them that he should keep the heifer for a surety. Then there were the two oxen Booy had borrowed, the sheep he had lost, the spade he had broken, the second one that he had stolen, and the matter of the kitchen iron. It had been a good letter. Looking back on it he thought no one could have expressed the situation more clearly, more justly; and then later in the same year he had written another — to Stockenstroom — telling him that Opperman had said he must send him the hire contract for Booy and take him into his service once more. This he had complained of, saying that Booy teased him too much and tried to seduce the few servants he had left, stirring them up against him. That letter also had been written with the mouth of truth. He had said that, had the Hottentot been soundly thrashed the first time he ran away, he would not have run a second time without cause; and he had added a postscript stating that he would certainly have come himself to explain had he been able to leave his home and ride so far. Later there had been another letter to Opperman asking him again to mediate between him and his servant. By that time the heifer that he had in surety had given birth to a calf, and this also he was holding in pawn till matters could be arranged. Like the other letters it had been respectful and fair; all that he had ever demanded was justice. That was all that he demanded now.

And had it been just of Opperman to send Booy back with a letter demanding the return of his cattle without ever taking into consideration the losses he had suffered by him? Of course he had beaten him. His demands — those which he had added to the letter that he bore — had been impertinent. But now the times had changed. Today one could no longer strike an insolent Hottentot, nor cross the river to trade and hunt without permission. Soon, no doubt, it would also be a crime to shoot a Bushman. But he was too old to change. He could only live one way. It was the way his fathers had lived before him and the way his sons would have lived after him had they not been killed. He thought of his dead children again. Once they had been safe from interference here; now they were not. Selina was right in this, at least. And the English were fools, not knowing the wisdom of letting sleeping lions lie, not appreciating the benefit that he and his like conferred upon them, and refusing them their demands for powder and lead and a predikant to teach the Word of God to their children. The East India Company had been bad enough, but the English were worse — talking a strange tongue, filled with new strange notions, and caring little for the Word of God. A blasphemous, clean-shaven race.

He stared out over the wide landscape, his mind filled with thoughts of flight. It would be so easy. In a few hours he could load up, get away where none could follow him. It was a fine, secret country of bush so heavy as to be impenetrable, and roadless save for the elephant paths and the narrow tunnels made by lesser game. Like a dark, torn cloth, the mantle of the scrub followed the watercourses. And how well he knew it! From the drift where the Little Fish joined the Great Fish River, along Botha's River, the Kowie, the Ecca, the Blau-krans, the Sheshago, the Koosie, the Koonap, to the Kat, this forest of low trees seeped between the high kloofs into other forests, linking Kaffraria with Lower Albany and Oliphant's Hoek; joining the Bushman's River Bush with that of the Zuurberg, and stretching out fingers to Kieskamma's Bush. Ja, the knowledge of it was clear to him, like the lines on the palm of his hand — the great deep lines of the gorges, and the little thin lines of the spruits.

Out of the bush rose the mountains that divided stream from stream, and through this country, at once its lock and key, ran the Great Fish; no river so tortuous, looping and bending, flowing now north, now south, now east, now west, indeterminate in its course, but certain of its end. Overhung by trees, it ran in a mad, swirling torrent thick with mud in the rains; or lay idle, its bed filled with stagnant, stinking pools from which even wild beasts hesitated to drink in the dry season. So close was this country that in many places a man must lead his horses through tunnels half dark on the brightest day; a land where below the high banks of the rivers there were quicksands that would engulf those who did not know them, and drifts so deep that the water reached up to the saddle-flaps. And beyond the river valleys, rolling up in breast-like folds to the great mountains, were the foothills: down land, good sheep-veld of short-cropped, sweet grass, broken by steep krantzes of white-streaked sandstone. Here aloes, good for the blistering of strains, grew among the stones, clinging to the face of the cliffs; gaily flowered, some as tall as a man, they bloomed, flowering like orange-and-red candles on their long stems. But the kloofs were silent, dark with the menace of hidden things, of wild Kaffirs, leopards and snakes that lay concealed in the heavy foliage. Yet he loved this land, this sea of bush which was unchanging, which, in the memory of man, had neither grown nor diminished in size; against which the veld fires that swept over the hills raged in vain; these endless morgen of forest brightened by the light green of the spekboom, darkened by isolated nabooms, its depths scented by wild jasmine, its open hillsides scattered with the yellow and blue spears of strelitzias, its small vleis lit with red amaryllis. He loved the thickets of flat-leaved prickly pear against whose yellow flowers jewelled sugar-birds hung wingless, their long tongues seeking the deep flower-honey. He loved the rank willows that trailed their long tendrils into the sullen watercourses, matting the banks with hairy roots that were like the brown beard of a man, coarse and curly and hard to the touch. He loved the hot dark silence of the day that was broken only by the intermittent calls of michi and diedrik; the swift evenings when roosting guinea fowl and pheasants cried into the purple dusk; the moonlit nights when dikkops and the kievietjes screamed as they flew to water.

There was nothing he did not know of this land. It was his home place.

But if he was not going to run, he must make a plan, and

he must make it quickly. There were but two things left that he could do: he must write once more to Stockenstroom, the Landdros, asking him to send his letter to the Government; and, in case his letter failed, he must get his guns ready. At last he was clear. These two actions — the one for peace and the other for war — were the answers to his quandary; and with either his name was safe; with neither did he give ground or abandon honour. His prayers were answered: no longer did he hesitate between two opinions.

2

Frederik was proud of his writing. It sloped strongly to the right; the letters with tails had fine, long ends; and it was large and legible.

Somewhere in the house there was an ink-horn; also quills and parchment. With infinite pains, the long goose-feather trembling between his fingers as he recut the point, he thought out what he would say. Meneer, or should it be Excellency ...

Excellency [he wrote],

I wish to lay before you this my petition. Many years ago when I was a young man I came to this place and made it. All men as far as the Bokveld know it to be mine, and now the Government questions my title and my treatment of my servants, that of a Hottentot named Booy in particular. We in these parts, Mynheer, are quiet, God-fearing folk; Boers, caring for our land and our herds. But we came far to seek this peace and it is good that such as we should lie between the Kaffirs and the tame folk of the Platteland. I speak for all, Mynheer, when I say that this land is ours, that we are free men. Therefore I request that we be left to go our ways and that we should be sent powder and lead, also that a magistrate should be set over us to administer justice and a predikant to teach the Word of God to our children. Taxes we will not pay. They have been paid by the dead who lie in the kloofs and are buried in the small hills behind our houses.

Frederik was pleased with this letter. It had taken him two hours to write it, and it expressed what he felt; and what those about him felt. Above all they were free men, and this they must learn at Kaapstad, even if men died. That he had said little of Booy and the grievance between them seemed to him of small importance. Stockenstroom and Opperman could send copies of his letters. What he wanted was peace. What he had done was to warn the Government that he and his like wished to be let alone to live the lives they had designed, and if it did no more, it should gain time, and time at this moment seemed significant. If he had time, everything would settle itself.

He looked at a twisted thorn tree. That was where he had outspanned when he came first to this place. The front wheels of his wagons had lain against the trunk and he had sat there leaning against it while he ate. He had known then that he would stay, for land was like a woman: men sought and sought till they found a place which filled their hearts. Even if the farms were not good, men clung to them because they were their choice, because something in that place appealed to them. A man came, outspanned by a certain tree, and said: 'I will dwell here. I will make my home here.' It was his choice.

Suddenly old Frederik thought of the horse he had been riding that day. Bles, a dark bay with a blaze that ran down his face right onto his nose. Bles had been young then; a very wild and nervous horse, but intelligent, with the heart of a lion and the most beautiful feet he had ever seen; hoofs as small and neat as a buck's. Ag, how sure-footed Bles had been; able to gallop through stony kloofs and never falling. Yes, Bles had been a good horse and the father of many good ones. It was years since he had thought of him. Things now seemed to mean so little in themselves, but served only to revive his memories. Perhaps he had reached an age when a tree meant only the thought of the horse he had once tied to it. From that tree he had looked out over the valley, which was now his farm, down at the river, at the bush-clothed slope beyond it, smoking and thinking. And today, at this hour, he knew that with land men were like lovers, savouring it with their eyes, stretching out their hands to touch what their eyes saw, and then going forth to take. A worked farm was like a woman with whom one had lain happily, like a fruitful wife, something a man could not be parted from without blood being shed. A man fought for the sweat he had lost, for the thoughts he had suffered.

In all the world he saw no light; it was dark, and only honour left. He moved so as to be able to look straight down the valley, fixing his eyes unwinkingly on the ridge. He had begun his watch. One day or another they would come. Hans, his Bastard servant, was also watching. He had told him this morning to come at once if he saw anything. It might come soon — before his letter had gone. It might come today or tomorrow. Ja, at any time now there might be scarlet on the hills.

3

Congratulating himself on his good fortune with Aletta, reproaching himself for having taken advantage of her innocence, Kaspar rode slowly towards old Frederik's. Why had she loved him? Why had he loved her? At this moment he was happier than he had ever been and also more unhappy. It seemed to him that the sight of his eyes was clearer and that where he had been deaf he now heard. What had happened was beyond understanding, as much beyond it as the bursting open of the buds in the spring or the fall of the leaf in the autumn. Perhaps there was no giving and taking. Perhaps Aletta had given him nothing. Perhaps he had taken nothing from her. Perhaps it was like night and day, two separate things which were not separate, but bound by the dusk and the dawn into one.

He wanted to go back to Aletta, to turn his horse and

gallop back to where she was; just to be with her, to see her, to know that she was near him. Yet every pace his horse took increased the distance between them. From now on all that he did was for Aletta. Without her the greatest things were without significance, while with her, even the small ones assumed an importance that, a few days ago, he would have believed impossible.

4

Frederik's place was very green. The small orchard behind the house, where, fenced by a loose-packed stone wall and fed by the furrow, peach, apricot, almond, and fig trees grew luxuriantly, was a bright patch, very isolated, pointing the dull olive of the surrounding country. With water Frederik had made the desert bloom. Like a nest against the hillside he had built this place, recessing it into the mountain by the poort through which the river ran. The cliffs behind the house, the rocks even by the kraal, grouped like old men bent in conversation, all added to its look of solid worth and peace.

The old man was on the stoep with his dogs about him when Kaspar came. The brindle bitch stood with her head resting on his knees. His hand was on her head, and against the wall beside him were his sticks and a heavy gun. It was taller than his head as he sat in his chair, and the dying sun was reflected on it. Six puppies, golden as lions, played, rolling at his feet.

Frederik looked at Kaspar without any recognition in his bloodshot eyes. It is not I that he expects, Kaspar thought, as he dismounted and came towards him.

Slowly the old man's bearded mouth parted in a smile that showed his fangs. It was Kaspar van der Berg who had come to visit him, riding his second horse. He looked the boy and the horse over. The brown was good, but not so good as the roan. He was glad he had come; he would show him the letter and speak to him of it. Kaspar was from the south and

knew their ways. He wondered how he would send the letter:
he could not send Hans — he needed him; and a picannin
was uncertain for so serious a mission. Perhaps Kaspar
would advise him. He must decide how he would send it.
No doubt counsel would come with the night, but it was
something that the letter was written, and something that
Kaspar was here. It would be good to talk to someone,
even a boy.

'How goes it?' he asked, 'and how is Leendert?'

'It goes well, Oom Frederik,' Kaspar answered, 'and my
uncle is better. He was hoping to get up when I left him.'

'It is a pity he did not come to the festival,' Frederik said.
'Had he come he would have seen Coenraad and Christiaan,
who are not often present at a gathering.'

'I told him they were there,' Kaspar said, 'and he was
sorry to miss them. But he was too sick to come. He was on
his bed when I came and as weak as a foal, rocking on his legs
when he got up to greet me.'

'It is the fever,' Frederik said. 'Ja, magtig, I know how it
feels. But it is good when you sweat. Did he sweat much?'
he asked.

'Ja, Oom Frederik; he sweated a great deal so that his
blankets must be dried in the sun.'

As they spoke, darkness began to fall. It fell as though it
were palpable, the horizon fading and closing in on them.
The mauve light of the evening became purple. A flight of
dikkops on silent wings flew past them from the hillside to
the vlei; a jackal barked; in the distance another answered
it. The night of Africa was falling fast with its menace.
Man was no longer the master, but a small thing, condemned, till dawn brought freedom, to go within-doors or
huddle, bent over a protecting fire.

Kaspar shivered.

'Put up your horse and come inside.'

'I cannot put him among your horses: he fights, Oom
Frederik.'

'There is the small kraal,' Selina said. She had joined them and stood leaning against the open door.

'Ja, set him in the small kraal, Kaspar. Have you food for him with you?' Frederik asked.

'I have some mealies.'

'Then take him up.' Frederik pointed to the bush behind the house. 'The small kraal is there, away from the others. It is one that I made when I first came. It is a good kraal,' he added, 'but it has become too small.' As Kaspar led the horse away, Frederik fell to thinking of what would happen to his beasts, to his cattle and his sheep if . . . Nee, nothing would happen. He only thought of these things because the spring had gone out of him. Where once he had been as steel he was now as iron. Yet iron was strong. He would see what Kaspar said about the letter. The letter would explain everything, or at any rate delay matters till he had time to explain. He had been a fool not to write to the Governor before, and yet until recently it had not come to him that there was serious danger.

As they ate, Kaspar watched Frederik. He was no longer merely an old man who could speak of nothing but his wrongs or tell stories of the old days on the Border. He was the man who had rescued Aletta: the man who had carried her for weeks on the pommel of his saddle. He was almost her father, more her father in a way than Rudolf, for Rudolf had his own children.

Tomorrow he would see her again. Tomorrow he would be back.

Kaspar looked round the room. It looked different. The guns were no longer resting on their pegs in the wall, but stood leaning in a corner. Without the guns the walls looked bare. They must have just been taken down, for there were flakes of whitewash on the floor. Kaspar wanted to talk of Aletta. He wanted to know all that there was to be known of her, but could not bring himself to ask.

The brindle bitch came in, followed by her pups; with full

bellies they struggled after her, wagging their small tails. They ran up to Frederik, and, standing up against his legs, licked his hanging hand. Sleek and fat, they played and rolled about the floor. There were four dogs and two bitches.

'Will you sell me this one?' Kaspar asked, holding up a little bitch in his hand, her belly warm and soft on his palm as she moved her legs, as though she were trying to swim out of it.

'That is the best one you have chosen,' Frederik said. There seemed to be little point in keeping her now, though when he had put the bitch to Bothma's dog he had intended to keep all the pups. He had lost four dogs in the past year from Bushmen's arrows, and a farm could not be protected at night save by dogs that watched while men slept. In all the district there was no dog as large or as savage as Bothma's; it was a regtig Boer hond of the best strain that had been kept pure and without admixture. Yet he was pleased at Kaspar's choice. The boy knew dogs. It was the one he would have picked himself. 'I will not sell her. I will give her to you, Kaspar,' he said, 'and when she is older, she will make a fine wyfie for your dog. But do not breed from her too young; not in her first season. Wait till she comes on heat for a second time and is more than a year old. Ja, jong,' Frederik went on, 'it is the blood that matters and her blood is good; she must be fairly dealt with. For, as you deal with a beast, so will it deal with you. It is in my heart that this is what the Lord Jesus Christ meant when he said, "Cast your bread upon the waters!"' he cried, getting up. 'Out of dust was man made and to dust he will return. This is so, for the rich or the poor. Even the Governor will one day be dust, and perhaps be better remembered for the horses he has brought here — the ones that you have told me about — than as a ruler of men.'

He spat onto the floor, wiped out the spittle with his foot, and sat down heavily.

'Ja, there is good blood in that little puppy,' Frederik said

again. 'Her great-grandmother was mine, and her grandmother, and her mother' — he put his hand on the old
bitch's head — 'with two others to help her, once killed a
leopard. The other dogs died of their wounds, but she lived.
Kyk daar,' he said; seizing both her legs on the off side and
flinging her onto her back, he pointed to a long scar on her
flank.

'Like your other horse,' Frederik went on, 'she is scratched.
When it happened, I could see her ribs,' he said. 'The skin
hung loose like the flap of a saddle. Magtig Kaspar, in man or
beast it is the blood that tells. Put like to like and breed like
is the law. No matter what they say, nothing good has been
got out of bad stock, and the heart of the son is like the
father's heart — good or bad as the case may be. All my life
has been spent among beasts, breeding them together to the
glory of God, and it is in my heart that the Almighty will
think well of a man who so handles his creatures. To this
end have I laboured, and today my flocks and herds are good.
Ja, I have done what I could with my lands and my beasts.
I have done all that I was able, all that it was in me to do.'

Kaspar felt that he was forgotten. Frederik seemed to be
talking to himself. Getting up, he got a rag, some fat in a
tin plate, and taking a gun on his knees began to grease it,
wiping it down carefully from the muzzle to the stock.

'Put this one back,' he said, 'and give another. But
pas op, they are loaded.'

Selina gave him a frightened look as he spoke and went
out to the back.

The brindle bitch had stopped licking herself and sat on
her haunches, staring at her master. She understood guns
and their use.

On the rafters above Kaspar's head a hen moved as a cock
outside crowed.

It was bright moonlight. The cock crowed again and
another answered it. Its challenge was faint and thin in the
distance of the night.

CHAPTER X

SO DIED BEZUIDENHOUT

I

IN THE morning Kaspar prepared to go. The weather had changed. There was a high wind that rattled the shutters and might bring rain. It was of rain that Frederik spoke as they drank coffee.

'It may come, Kaspar,' he said, looking out of the window at the clouds, lead-coloured and heavy, that were building up against the wind. 'It may come, and we need it badly.'

'Yes, it is needed,' Kaspar answered, thinking of Rudolf's sheep and the mountains that he had burned off. In a few hours he would be back there, and if the rains were heavy, he might be held up and forced to remain till the floods ran down. He wanted to remain there and yet wanted time to think first. If Aletta was going to be his wife, he must speak to Rudolf. Rudolf was his friend; he would be glad. But he was not ready to speak yet. The puppy, in a bag at his feet, was whimpering a little and trying, with small, ineffective teeth, to tear the holes he had made in the leather, while her mother, sniffing and pawing at it, looked anxiously from Kaspar to her master.

'I must be on my way, Oom Frederik,' Kaspar said, picking

up the bag. 'And thank you. She will be well looked after, as you know.'

'That I know, Kaspar, or you would not have had her,' Frederik said, taking his hand. 'And remember that when you pass this way I shall be glad to see you. It is good to see a visitor now and again, and we are cousins, since Rudolf is my sister's husband and kin to Leendert who married your mother's sister. Ja, we are very near together, knitted by relationship and blood.'

The door swung open. Wind and dust filled the room as Hans, his eyes starting from his head, ran in.

'Baas, they come!'

Frederik sprang to his feet. 'How many?' he asked. 'How many come?'

'Many, Baas. Ek weet nee, how many. But they come fast,' he gasped. 'Their coats are red and green on the hillside. You said I was to watch, Baas,' he chattered. 'I have watched well and they come in hundreds. Ja, magtig, they come.' He was dancing up and down, twisting his hands together.

'Quiet, fool!'

So it had come. The letter was too late. Vragtig, the impossible had happened. Frederik's mind went back to the day that he had cursed the court messenger. On that day he had made a compact with death. On that day he had sown the wind and today would reap the whirlwind. Selina had been right; they had dared to do this thing; to send soldiers for him. Soldiers to take a free Burger from his place! Red and green, Hans said. They had then sent coloured soldiers, too. Hottentots. A mist of blood clouded his eyes as he grasped his guns.

'Take guns!' he shouted, pushing one into Kaspar's hand. 'Take a gun, Hans!' Seizing one in each hand, he ran out to the rocks by the dung-kraal.

The soldiers were close now. 'Stand back!' he shouted. 'Stand back, you fools, or I fire!'

The wind caught up his words and flung them into the

hillside behind him. 'Fools...fools...' the mountains echoed.

They had sent soldiers, white soldiers in red coats and coloured soldiers in green — Hottentot troops against a white man!

The soldiers continued to advance. Dropping on one knee, Frederik fired over their heads. That should halt them. Once they saw he was in earnest, they would stop. They did stop. The officers drew their swords. The halted men lined up.

'Fix,' came the order...'bayonets!' And precisely as if the fourteen men were one, each bayonet sprang from its scabbard, flashed as it turned, paused, and went home.

The clockwork action of the trained soldiers struck Frederik hard. There was another order. The soldiers spread out and began to run forward. Kaspar made a movement towards them.

'Sit down!' Frederik pointed his gun at him. 'Sit. If you move, jong, as sure as there is a God above us, I will shoot you dead.'

He could see the gold lace on the officers' uniforms and the shining buttons on their tunics. 'Stop!' he shouted once more, and, picking up the other gun, fired again. 'Shoot, Hans! Shoot, Kaspar! But fire over them.' Surely they would stop now. He hid behind a small outcrop of granite that he had cursed many times because it made the turning of a wagon difficult. The soldiers, kneeling, answered with a volley, their balls splattering the rocks all around them. He heard Kaspar cry out, 'I am hit, Frederik!'

Kaspar's face was streaming with blood. As Frederik looked at him, he raised his gun. 'For God's sake, shoot high, Kaspar!' he cried. He was too late...one of the soldiers dropped his gun, grasped his belly, and fell forward. It was a white soldier. His red coat had drawn Kaspar's fire. The others closed in, filling the gap. The officers waved their swords, and changing direction, they moved at a run towards the kraal in an effort to outflank them.

'Come!' Frederik shouted, jumping up and running towards the river. On the other side of it, near the spring, there was a small krantz. Here they would stand again. Kaspar and Hans followed at his heels. Barking angrily, the dogs ran with them. From the ledge on the cliff, Frederik, resting his gun on a big stone, fired once more, putting his bullet into the ant-heap from which one of the officers was directing operations. The officer jumped down and looked round. Though he still presented an easy mark, Frederik was unwilling to shoot him. All he wanted to do was to hold them at a distance; to keep them away. If they took him, they would lay their hands on him. No man could do this. He was ready to die before a Hottentot laid hands on him.

The blood had spread from Kaspar's face over his shoulders, staining his shirt, and was smeared over his face where he had rubbed it with his hands.

'Is it bad, Kaspar? Are you badly hurt?'

'It is nothing, Oom Frederik,' Kaspar said.

The soldiers, who had been hidden, reappeared. They were casting about like hounds at fault, but, hampered by their accoutrements, made little progress in the heavy bush till the green-coated sergeant gave a shout.

'That verdomde Hottentot has found our spoor in the river-bed,' Frederik said.

'Round to the left!' the sergeant cried, and running clumsily, the soldiers ploughed through the heavy sand and up the bank. Two, more agile than the rest, began to climb a tree. When they reached the fork, they would be above the ridge and able to shoot down upon them.

Frederik raised his gun. 'If you climb higher, I will fire to kill!' he shouted.

The men hesitated, looked down, and then went on climbing. As one of them, bracing himself against a limb, put his gun up to fire, Frederik shot it from his hand. The shock of the heavy bullet on the stock caused him to fall. Thinking their comrade hit, the others opened a ragged fire from all round, and, following the sergeant, streamed up to attack the krantz.

Hours seemed to have passed since Hans had run into the house. And where were the others who had said they would come? Where was Gerrit? He was near enough to have heard the firing. Where were Johannes and the men from Tarka, from Baviaan's River, and Bruintjeshoogte? This attack on Frederik must have been well planned and swiftly carried out, or they would have had news of it. News went fast on the Border. It was shouted from hill to hill by Kaffirs, and carried swiftly on horseback or by running men.

If I had known that so many would attack me, I would have driven off my beasts and hidden, Frederik thought. But his friends must be coming. The noise of the battle must have been heard as the sound of volleys went crashing through the mountain valleys. Already there were vultures in the sky, sailing in wide circles, as they waited and watched. Men would see the vultures. All he need do was to hold off the troops till they came, and when they saw the whole Border was against them, the soldiers would withdraw. Ja, it was one thing to take an old man alone; another to face armed Burgers called from their homes in the defence of one of their number.

'Be of good courage, Kaspar,' he said. 'Soon help will come. All we must do is to hold them off. Keep shooting near them so that they fear to approach.'

As he spoke Frederik saw a flash of red and the light of a shining bayonet near them.

'Come!' he whispered. 'We will go back over the river again into the cleft where the honey-hole is.'

His gout was forgotten as he scrambled down the bank. Crouching low among the reeds he crossed the river, and swung himself up to the cave, clinging to the overhanging branches of the trees and shrubs that grew out of the cracks in the rock. His hands were torn by the thorns, but he did not feel them. Behind him he heard Kaspar and Hans breathing heavily as they climbed after him. He held one gun in his hand, the other was slung over his shoulder. On the far side of the river the soldiers were calling to each other. They had reached the ledge and found them gone. Time was being gained; time was what they needed. It was only a matter of time before help came.

2

Kaspar had lost all sense of time or space. This could not be the farm he had approached so happily sure of a welcome yesterday. As he had ridden up, he had looked at the krantz where they were now fighting. Nothing was real. It could not be. He still had the bag with the puppy. Each time they moved he had clutched it. The shots fired from inside the cave echoed and re-echoed. Over his shoulder the dogs barked and growled as they peered into the bush. Below him was a dark pool of water and, on a patch of sand beside it, he saw Selina's spoor and that of the child where it had crawled about on its hands and knees. He was thirsty. Before God, he had never known real thirst before. Some blood had got into his mouth and it was salt; some had coagulated on the small hairs of his moustache and beard. It came away in blackish flakes as he touched it.

The sun was high now, and, though the back of the cave was cool, the ledge on which they lay was hot and the kloof airless. The high wind had fallen and the sky had cleared. Below them there was only silence. He wondered where the soldiers were; what they were doing. He searched the bush for movement, watching for the flash of a bayonet or a glimpse of scarlet in the undergrowth; straining his eyes to see, his ears to listen; watching, hardly daring to blink, till he felt as if his eyes would burst from their sockets.

After the firing the silence was oppressive. What was being planned? And all the time the buzzing of the bees went on; the drowsy buzzing that took him back to the orchards of his home, to the summer days when he had lain under the blossoming trees, thinking of the great things he would accomplish when he was a man.

To and fro the bees went, flying swiftly as though drawn along by a thousand threads, into the crevice above his head, and leaving it: a continuous stream of life, the noise of their vibrating wings filling the empty silence. It was intolerable, endless, and whatever happened the bees would go on, unperturbed, working, building their six-sided cells against the cold stone of the rock. If he died they would go on. If he lived they would go on. Their activity was increasing, and he wondered if the change in weather and firing had induced them to swarm.

In the breathless heat everything shimmered; the sun beating directly down on the rocks sent up the heat in waves till the whole mountain became incandescent, till it shone so brightly that it burnt the eyes; and in this oven-like stillness, that was spread as heavily as a blanket over them, Kaspar lay waiting for he knew not what. It was hard to breathe, hard to see, hard to believe himself alive.

Every minute more bees, heavy with honey, gilded with pollen, swept into the crevice, while others flew lightly out. The buzzing never stopped. Again he thought of his boyhood. Was it possible that he and the boy he thought of were one? It was as if he stood apart and watched this scene. It was all outside of himself. It was a dream. Soon he would wake up, saddle his horse, and go back to Aletta. He had killed a man. No, he had not killed a man. You could not kill a man like that, not so easily. Why, all he had done when he was wounded was to point his gun and pull the trigger. And how could I help it? he thought. I was hurt, the gun was in my hand. Surely it must be harder than this. Surely that little thing he had aimed at, no bigger than a bird at a hundred paces, had not been a man. The soldiers had looked like toys, little red-and-green manikins, of painted wood, as they ran across the veld. He wiped the

blood and sweat from his face and found himself trembling.
He was hot, yet his teeth chattered. He looked at Hans.
He was muttering to himself, the saliva running in bubbles
from the corners of his mouth. Frederik was calm. He must
have been ready for this: expecting it. Of course he was
ready for it. The speech he had made at the festival, the
letter he had shown him the previous night, the loaded guns
in the corner, Selina's frightened looks — why, even the fact
that he had given him the pup so easily — all pointed to it.
But he had been too busy thinking of his own affairs, of his
trading, and his love for Aletta to see it. And if he had,
would it have occurred to him that things could go so far?
That the grumblings of this old man would lead to this?
To war; to armed rebellion? This was treason. Kaspar
felt as if he would vomit. What would happen now? Here
was the end to all his fine plans. How would he see Aletta?
They would never beat off the soldiers. There were too many
of them.

From below them a voice called up, shattering the silence
as though it were a fragile ornament of glass — time which
had stopped began again.

'Come out, old Frederik! If you come out we will not
shoot.'

3

Frederik raised himself onto his elbows. So they were
calling him to come out. They were afraid. Cupping his
hands round his mouth, he shouted: 'If you want me, come
and take me. I will be damned if I come out. Ja, take me if
you can.'

There was no answer. Not a branch moved.

'They are afraid, Kaspar,' he said. 'They are afraid of an
old man, a boy, and a Bastard Hottentot.'

'Come out and no harm will befall you!' It was the same
voice, this time from above. 'You can take your horses or
inspan your wagon.'

'Let us give ourselves up, Oom Frederik.' Kaspar had taken hold of his arm.

'Nee, Kaspar; they are afraid and we gain time. The others will soon be here. If we go out now, we shall all be hanged.' Standing up, he shouted, 'Shoot me dead; then only will you get me into your hands.'

There was a sound near the mouth of the cave, to the side of it.

'Halt! Wie gaan?' Frederik advanced, his gun ready.

'Master, it is me, Joseph, a sergeant of the Cape Regiment. Can I come near?'

'Keep away.'

The dogs had sprung forward. Kaspar and Hans were holding them.

'Let go the dogs. Put the dogs onto him!'

But they cuffed them back.

'Master Frederik, put down your gun. I will put mine down; and let us talk together.'

'Master, let me go out,' Hans pleaded, 'and I will talk to him.'

Frederik dropped onto one knee and prepared to shoot. 'I will talk no more. Only with bullets will I talk; so keep away from me.' This time, if anyone came, he would kill him. Before God, the man who showed himself at the mouth of the cave would die. He lowered his gun slowly; yes, it might be best to talk. Every moment spent talking was a moment gained. His friends were coming. In his heart he saw them, galloping over the mountain roads, their guns in their hands, raising the people as they came.

'I will come out,' he said, 'but you must all go to one side, beyond the dung-kraal. Then I will have my horses fetched and ride with the gentlemen as far as Labuschagne's place.'

'Let me go and fetch the horses, master,' Hans implored.

'Stay where you are. Move one step and I shoot.'

'Will you swear to ride with us?' Joseph asked.

'Ja, I swear to God Almighty that I will ride as far as

Frans Labuschagne's, the cousin of Leendert, and from thence to Graaf-Reinet in the company of these gentlemen, taking with me two Burgers to testify as to my character; but the gentlemen must not apprehend me.'

Frederik's voice was firm. If they guaranteed this, he would go with them. He stood leaning on the muzzle of his gun while they consulted together. First one voice, then another was raised.

'By our souls, we will do this,' one of the officers shouted.

'"By my soul" is no oath to me,' Frederik said.

'We swear by our souls that no harm will come to you.'

Frederik now saw the officer clearly as he stood out from under the trees. A passion of anger swept over him. Smashing the butt of his gun down onto the ground he shouted: 'Nee, I see it! It is a plan to verneuk me, to take me safely, without risk. Before God, I shall not come out. Shoot me dead and then fetch me, for I will speak no more.'

So they had thought to trick him, to lure the old lion out by a ruse. Ja, magtig, they had sought to do this and they had failed. 'By my soul' was no oath. Choking with rage, he turned back into the cave.

'What are you doing here?' Frederik looked at Selina in astonishment.

'I brought you these.' She put down a bag of bullets and powder. His eyes took her in slowly. Her hair, covered with dirt and cobwebs, was down, hanging to her waist, her arms were torn by thorns and roots. Selina's dark eyes widely distended, like those of a frightened buck, as she stared back at him.

'How did you get here?' he asked. 'How did you pass the soldiers? God damn them!' he shouted. 'God damn their souls! Why could they not leave me in my place?'

'How did I come?' Selina repeated after him, as if she were a child saying a lesson. 'Why did I come? I came because you are my master; because you have been good to me, and it seemed to me that you would need what I brought.'

'Did you bring me water?' he asked.

'Water? Nee, I brought no water. Did you need it?'

'Ja, we need it. But how did you come? Tell me that.'

'I know this cave.' She made a gesture towards the pool. 'Once I saw a koodoo there,' she said. She paused and went on. 'And there is a hole daar agter.' She pointed with her thumb behind her. 'You could not get through it' — her eyes were on his shoulders — 'but Kaspar could.' She turned to him: 'Why don't you go while there is yet time?' she asked.

'You would have him go, Selina? Have him leave me?' Frederik asked.

'Ja, Frederik; this is the end. Long ago I foresaw it and I will not wait. But why should he die too?' she went on passionately. 'Your horse is watered and saddled, Kaspar; I did it before I came. Come with me, and I will show you the hidden roads.'

'I cannot come,' Kaspar said. 'I stand by old Frederik.' Yet he knew that he stood, not by Frederik, but by the man whom Aletta loved as a father, the man who had brought her from the Kaffirs. Later they would say that he had stood by him till the end, and she would hear of it.

'I am going to my son,' Selina said. 'I left him only to bring you powder. Good-bye, Frederik. If you had listened to me, this would not have been, but you were too proud to listen to a Bastard girl; too proud to run.' Her eyes grew glassy. Kaspar, who was beside her, staring into them, saw himself reflected, saw Frederik, and Hans crouching at his feet with his long gun held in his hands. Scarcely opening her lips, Selina went on. 'This is the end, old lion, of you and of your place. But it will not be forgotten; men will come to see it. They will come into this cave, with their hats in their hands, as though it were a place of weeping. You are an old man. Your death is a small thing, Frederik Bezuidenhout. But it is the little beginning of a great one, for when many come against an old, solitary man, a seed is sown. Ja, the seed of a bitter crop that your son's sons will harvest. Yea, they, and their sons after them.' She put out her hand for support and then said in her own voice: 'Good-bye, Oom Frederik. I go to my child. If you come out alive, ride to Coenraad's. I will be there.'

'Selina!' Frederik said. But she was gone.

Kaspar reloaded his gun. His horse was saddled and stood ready in the small kraal. His horse had not been found, and there was a way out of the cave. All round them now there was the sound of movement; rustlings, the clash of accoutrements, the flash of sunlight on bayonets, and curses from the soldiery as they manoeuvred through the bush. They were being surrounded. Kaspar felt the weight of the men closing round him; the trap was closing in. There were more sounds from above. A shout. Some orders rapped out that he could not distinguish. Frederik went out, followed by Hans. A shower of rocks came down. One fell on Hans, pinning him under it. Frederik fell, but got up again and levelled his gun. There were two reports. Frederik fell, his gun clattering on the ground.

'Boy, my arm is off.' He raised himself on his elbow, swaying back and forth on the edge of the krantz, seeking to recover his balance and get back to safety. The bullet had taken him in the left arm and, pulverizing it, had come out at his right shoulder. He made a last effort to crawl back, dragging himself along on his stump, the fingers of his other hand clawing at the stones, sticky with his own blood. It was flowing from him as from a leaking bag. He gasped, swayed for a moment on the very edge of the cliff, cried out, and fell.

Kaspar heard his body smash as it struck the rocks and a dull splash as, rolling from them, it fell into the water. From all sides came the cries of the soldiers as they ran down.

Scarcely knowing what he did, Kaspar dropped his gun and, picking up the puppy in the bag, ran down the cave. It was over. Old Frederik was dead. The cave narrowed into a slit. In the dim light he saw a great root, like the leg of an elephant. Clinging to it, he looked up and saw the sky. A piece of Selina's dress was caught on a sharp point of rock. It was this way that she had come and gone. Making himself as small as he could, he began to climb.

4

The crack up which Kaspar clambered led to the top of the great rock that was balanced like a ball on the kopje. It was flat, and hot beyond belief. Scorched by the sun from above and by the heat of the stone from underneath, he lay panting, crouched like a bird beneath a stooping hawk. His arms and legs were torn, his eyes were filled with earth; the wound on his cheek had reopened and was bleeding fast. His tongue was so swollen in his parched mouth that he could not swallow, and all the skin of his body cried for moisture. Water. If only he had water! There was no more water in him, and as he sweated, it seemed to him that he was sweating the water out of his very blood; that he could feel it getting thicker. Below him there was water. Below him was the dark, shaded pool into which old Frederik had fallen.

Slowly, with infinite precaution, he crawled to the edge of the rock and peered down. From here, hidden by a fringe of harsh grass, he saw the soldiers searching for him. They seemed to think he had escaped down the river-bed, but after beating the bush on the banks and looking among the high reeds, they gave up and came back. Old Frederik had been dragged out of the water and lay wet and bedraggled on the sand. Someone had thrown a dirty rag over his face, but he lay oddly with one leg twisted under him. They might have straightened his legs, Kaspar thought, when they put him down.

The puppy moved in the bag. He was astonished that he still had it. How had he climbed the narrow passage carrying the bag? He did not remember bringing it with him. He let her out. Little the worse for her adventures, she wagged her tail, staggered into the shade of his body, and clambering over him with small sharp nails, licked his bare chest and neck.

Cradling the puppy against him, Kaspar went on thinking of water. He must have water. The puppy must have water.

Almost lethargically, as if it were no concern of his, he watched the soldiers pile arms and, sitting down, begin to eat the food they pulled from their haversacks. He was not hungry, only thirsty — if what he felt now was thirst; if it was not something that went a long way beyond mere thirst. But his horse was safe. They had not found his horse and were not likely to, unless someone picked up his spoor and followed it, for the small kraal was at some distance from the house and well hidden among the rocks and trees. When the soldiers went, he would get his horse. When they went, he would get water. That was the only thing that mattered now — that the soldiers should go. Eventually they would go. Eventually he would be able to come down. A man did not die of thirst in a day, or at least he had never heard of it happening.

One of the officers drank from a flask and handed it to the other. They were laughing together. Kaspar wondered what they were laughing at. He wondered when he would laugh again. I used to laugh a lot, he thought, but that was when I was a boy. That was when I was at home. Why had he not stayed at home in safety? Why had he wanted to be different? What had driven him into this and what part had he in it? The scene below was irrelevant. It had nothing to do with him. What could he have to do with the soldiers sitting by their arms, eating with jackets loosened; or with the officers drinking and joking together in the shade of a big stinkwood tree; or with the crumpled man that lay with a dirty lappie over his broken face? The brindle bitch was dead too; she lay beside old Frederik as though she were asleep. She must have tried to defend her master's body. He wondered where the other dogs were. Perhaps they had gone with Selina. And where was she? Running through the little hidden paths of the forest, he supposed, with her child on her back, its head nodding as she ran.

Bewildering thoughts ran through his head, chasing each other, superimposing themselves one over the other, a second coming before the first was clear. His childhood, his home, the long sweep of oaks that led up to his father's house. Aletta. Frederik. But Frederik was dead. There was no Frederik. Yet only this morning Frederik had said there would be rain if the wind held. This morning was a year ago. Yesterday was ten years ago. Aletta was in his arms. His gun was raised and pointed at a little scarlet figure that had thrown up its arms and fallen. In those ten years he had made and killed a man. Made; for the first time the significance of what he had done with Aletta flashed into his mind. By that act he might be a father, and by the killing of the soldier he was parted from her.... Once more he was in the kitchen at home, smelling sassaties as they roasted on bamboo skewers. His mind went back to Aletta and the soldier. In twenty-four hours he had made and killed a man. Neither should be so easy to do.

A bugle sounded. Crisp and clear, the notes rang out over the veld and rose into the hills as the bugler, his cheeks as fat and scarlet as apples, blew into the brass. The officers were straightening their clothes, buttoning them, and fastening their white sword belts and crimson sashes.

Hans, his hands tied behind him, was mounted on a horse. He sat sagging over its neck while a trooper lashed his feet beneath its belly. Kaspar felt no sorrow for Hans. Only relief that they were going. Two men picked up old Frederik, one by his shoulders and another by his feet, and carried him toward the house. The men sprang to attention at an order: sloped arms, formed fours, turned to the right, and moved off. He saw them stop to pick up the dead man — that is the man I shot, he thought — tie him onto the horse in front of Hans, and go on.

He counted them carefully lest some should be left, but none were left. Their work was done. They grew smaller, marching away as they had come — triumphant, with bayonets fixed, a little green-and-scarlet snake spiked with shining steel.

The kloof was silent. The Baviaan's River empty.

CHAPTER XI

A MAN PURSUED

KASPAR climbed down and drank. Kneeling like a Kaffir, resting his forearms on the rock basin, he lowered his face into the water and sucked it up. Careless of all else, he drank, breathed deeply, and drank again. Then he splashed the water up onto his face and neck, over his chest, and into his armpits so that it ran down his ribs onto his belly. The wound on his cheek smarted as, holding the edges together with one hand, he cleaned it with the other. Reflected in the shadowed mirror of the pool he saw it clearly — a deep gash, running from below his eye almost to his right ear. It might have blinded me, he thought. Before God, he had wanted to be a man, but his manhood was being thrust upon him too fast.

At his side, her body against his thigh, the puppy drank, lapping the water with a long pink tongue till she was so swollen that she could not walk, but sat on the sand, staring up at him. Suddenly she climbed onto his knee and licked the wound on his face.

From the pool Kaspar followed the track to the house; as he came to the shoulder of the mountain, he paused. The house still squatted against the hillside. The whitewashed walls were very bright where the sunlight caught them, and the shadow from the wide eaves black over the deep-set windows. The baboon sat on the top of his pole. He looked like a man silhouetted sharply against the sky. From the kraal came the lowing of cattle and the bleating of sheep. They were unmilked and thirsty. When he came near, the baboon left his pole and came to grasp his legs. The dogs lay dead in the yard. One of them had been sabred.

The door of the house was open. On the stoep the red hen that Frederik had brought in so carefully the night before searched with her single chick for grubs in one of the butter-barrels of blue lilies that had been overturned. The broken flowers lay wilting, half in and half out of the earth, while the hen pecked and scratched between the fibrous roots.

Kaspar hesitated to cross the broken threshold. He was afraid. But he was hungry. Before he left he must get food. Straightening his shoulders, he went in.

The room which Selina had kept so neat was in disorder. Everything was flung about, the floor cut by heavy boots. They had laid Frederik on the table. Too small for so big a man, his legs hung from it, his feet just clear of the ground. His blood, staining the white wood, had run into a thickened puddle beneath it. The hen and chick had walked through it. Their footprints made an odd glutinous design across the dagga. Flies in hundreds were clustered over the corpse, covering it with a black fur that thickened on the wounded arm and breast. As Kaspar went nearer, they rose about him. There was a little stone grasped between Frederik's fingers, and a tuft of broken grass. Cups and plates had been swept aside when they had laid Frederik down, but the Bible had not fallen; it lay near his head beside a beaker half full of coffee and dead flies.

Seizing a strip of biltong that hung from the rafters, Kaspar ran to the door. There was nothing he could do. A feeling of terror came over him. Unable to resist, he looked again. He had not seen violent death before. He tried to feel respectful in the presence of death, but could not. There was no grandeur in such a death. There was only the thing which, this morning, had been an old man, the thing on which the flies — black, blue, and metallic green — now hastened to lay their eggs. He closed his eyes and held on to the wall. His hunger had gone. He felt ill. But he could not leave Frederik like that. He went back into the house. There was a cupboard in the back room. There must be something in the cupboard that would do. There were many things that would do. He found himself selecting something suitable. There were Selina's dooks — they were too bright. I want something white, he thought; a sheet, a handkerchief. On the second shelf he found what he wanted: a white cloth embroidered with blue flowers. He wondered who had worked them. Going up to the body, he opened the cloth and spread it over Frederik's face: he looked almost worse now with his face covered.

Kaspar picked up the puppy and ran to the hidden kraal. Suppose they came back? Now that he had given away to fear, he was possessed by it. It sat like a monkey on his shoulder, chattering into his ear. Hearing him come, the brown neighed: Selina had tied him to a ring. Pushing the puppy deep into his shirt-front, he buttoned it, tightened the girth, and swung into the saddle.

2

There was a way back to Leendert's over the mountains, a short way that did not go near Rudolf's. He must get back to his servants and decide what he would do about them. Then he must send news to Aletta. Frederik had indicated the path he was taking to him yesterday. It began near a giant naboom and went almost vertically up the mountain.

He saw six mounted men in the valley. They were riding for Frederik's. Had they been sent by the military? He set spurs to his horse. He rode without consideration for his horse, without caring, provided he got back, whether he foundered him or not. Bent over the horse's neck, he galloped, thanking God for the quality of his father's stock. The brown would gallop till he died.

Sometimes the track went straight up the mountain, and the horse, with his quarters gathered under him, had to climb with rearing forelegs; at others he had to spring like a buck from rock to rock or to slide almost on his hocks as they slithered down a slope. Kaspar thought of Aletta, of the man he had killed, and the absurd simplicity of his death. He kept thinking that it ought to be much harder to kill a man. He had fired, heard the bullet strike, and watched him fall: a scarlet doll that had thrown up its hands and, clasping them to its belly, had fallen grotesquely and lain still. That was killing. Because of the pressure of his finger on the trigger, and his will to hurt because he had been hurt, he was a fugitive. He would never see his parents again. He was frightened, not at what he had done — for he seemed to have done nothing — but at the effects of his action. He was not sorry. What had happened was inevitable. There had been no choice. He felt as he had felt as a child; as he had felt the day he had driven in the bung of a vat of wine and been unable to stop its running out in a purple stream over the floor. Only this time it was blood that ran unstoppered over the veld. He still could not believe that he could not tell someone what he had done and have it put right.

As he rode, pressing his horse harder and harder, he was overcome by a savage anger that this should have happened to him.

Loose stones slipped from beneath the horse's hoofs. Stumbling and recovering from his stumbles, lathered with sweat and foam, the brown picked his way between fallen trees, past boulders, scrambled up soft banks and down stony sluits. Kaspar's mind went back to old Frederik, to the peace of yesterday, to Frederik's pleasure in his dogs. What was justice when it could send troops to take an old man like Frederik from his place? There had been no harm in Frederik Bezuidenhout, and there had been much good that more than outweighed his obstinate simplicity.

After he had seen Letta he must find Coenraad and van Ek. The thought of van Ek gave him confidence. He pulled up his blowing horse and dismounted to rest and eat. He had reached the top of the Berg. Bathed in the evening light, the country was extended below him — a carcass whose bones stood up out of the bush; ranges as jagged as vertebrae; long smooth neks, like legs and arms, ran out of them; and through the grass-covered slopes of the foothills, the flesh that covered the bones, came little hasty streams, veins, that fed the great artery of the river.

Beautiful and uncaring, the country was unveiled, its hidden places voluptuously open and tempting. It lay waiting for him. It seemed to him that the evening breeze whispered: You belong here now, Kaspar van der Berg. See me now, as I am. Know me. Know the life that I hold, adventure, and success for those who dare to take it. What is the timid south compared to me? You may die here, but first you will live.

The puppy sat beside him. He and that small puppy were alone. He ate slowly, feeding the puppy with pieces from his hand, cutting into slivers the dry meat he had taken, alternately one for himself and one for her.

The lilac light was changing to purple. From purple it turned to grey, to dark blue, to indigo. The trees on the slope appeared to move. They took up fantastic shapes, becoming mounted men, giants, dwarfs, lions, as they crept towards him. Everything was strange and ghostly. Bushes and rocks no longer stood separate, but merged into the heavy masses of the mountain. The beauty of the early evening had gone, the map was rolled up into a solid, thickening blackness. His horse came up to him trembling and snorting. The puppy barked shrilly and backed into his legs. He felt her hackles rise as she growled, baring her milk teeth at some hidden danger. From the krantz above him came the scream of a baboon and the low, purring snarl of a leopard. Kaspar shivered. He had no gun. He should have taken one of Frederik's. He had no tinder to light a fire. He was even uncertain of the road. Like a fool, he had sat thinking and dreaming while the night fell heavily upon him. His horse started again, nearly pulling the reins from his hand. Kaspar got up, but he could see nothing. In two or three hours, when the moon rose, he would go on. He must put more miles between himself and Frederik's place. A cold mist came up from the valley. The dew was heavy. He put the puppy back into his shirt for warmth and waited, listening to the night sounds, terrified and unable to identify them. He was new to this life and to this land, alien and unarmed.

The moon began to rise. The serrated edge of the Berg behind him flamed with fire. Then the first great curve of the moon appeared; bright orange and enormous, it rose slowly, flooding everything with light. But it was a different world. One that was cold and sharp, with hard, white edges and deep, impenetrable shadows. Everything was very still in the flaring light of the high moon. White flowers were suspended, stalkless, or hung separate from the trees. The slab-like leaves of the cactus plants reflected the light, shining like cold steel mirrors, or were black. The valley below him was filled to the edge with floating mist. It hung level as water.

Mounting his horse, Kaspar began the descent, but abandoned it as the brown stumbled and fell. He should never have stopped and allowed the horse to stiffen. He should have ridden him straight on. He would have got farther and the end would have been no worse. Dismounting, he off-saddled and took off the bridle. He felt his horse's legs: his knees were not cut, but he could not get up, and lay on his side. Now he must go on on foot. Staggering as though drunk, he fought his way along the track, tearing his hands and clothes on the thorns, driven by the fear of pursuit and the horror of the scene he had left behind him. 'They should not have done it,' he kept saying. 'They should not have done it.' He felt his cracked lips moving as he talked to himself: 'It was a wicked thing to do, wicked to kill an old man like that.' He saw Frederik lying as he had left him on the table. Aletta, Selina, the brindle bitch, the red hen with her chick that had scratched in the old man's blood, were all confused in his mind, mixed up with the scarlet and green jackets of the soldiers, the sound of the guns and his brown horse's despairing neigh as he left him. He thought he was back at home. He was with Aletta in the shed. He laughed hysterically at the way she had got rid of Stephanie. He saw the snake writhing round old Witvoet and Stephanie falling. In a daze he forced himself to put one foot in front of the other, driving himself towards the glimmer of light he saw in the distance. Sometimes he lost it and woke, panic-stricken, to reality. Then finding it again, sank back into his swaying march.

He should never have let his horse stiffen. I should have known it, he thought, but how could I? — since only when pursued did a man ride a horse to a standstill. Pursued! He was a man pursued. From now on he would always be pursued. A fugitive, with a price set on his head. When you committed a murder, you became valuable. They put a price on you, dead or alive. This was a new thought — that it would be for always. That wherever he went men would be ready to kill him as though he were vermin. The light was nearer. He was advancing. He was astonished at his progress. He knew himself to be too tired to move, and yet he was moving.

3

The barking of the dogs brought Leendert from the house with his gun in his hand. 'Halt!' he shouted. 'Halt, or I shoot.'

'It is me — Kaspar.' He had got back. He was back among his people.

'It's Kaspar,' he heard his uncle say to Tanta Sybilla. 'It is Kaspar who has come back. He is on foot.'

'On foot! Why is he on foot?'

'Why are you on foot?' his uncle shouted as he came nearer.

The dogs were quiet now and fawned against him. More men came up. Some of his own people, and a truculent-looking, cross-eyed man.

'Baas, you are hurt.' Frans touched the bandage on his face.

Kaspar tried to smile. There was something funny about the bandage. It was the cloth with the red border that Tanta Sybilla had told him to bring back. He had brought it back. He began to laugh.

Leendert took hold of him. 'Sybilla!' he shouted. 'Kaspar is hurt.'

Kaspar pulled the puppy out of his shirt. 'I have got the puppy,' he said. He had gone to get a puppy. He had got her. There seemed to him nothing to explain.

'What has happened?' Leendert asked. 'Magtig, what in God's name has befallen?'

Why did no one take the puppy? If no one took her, soon he would drop her. She was very small. She might hurt herself if she fell. He held the puppy out to Frans. The old Hottentot took her. His hands were trembling. The young Baas was hurt.

'Where is the brown horse?' he asked.

Tanta Sybilla came out. She had a cup in her hand. 'Drink this,' she said.

Kaspar drank.

Tanta Sybilla turned on her husband. 'Get him in,' she said. 'Before God, will you stand there questioning while he bleeds to death?'

'He is not bleeding now,' Leendert said.

'What has happened, Baas? Where is the horse?' Frans was in tears.

The brandy had revived Kaspar. His head was clear and he felt stronger.

'The horse is on the road, Frans. I foundered him ... and I have killed a man — an Englishman.'

'Magtig, then it is good that Coenraad's folk are here,' Leendert said. 'They came soon after you left.'

'The brown horse foundered and you have killed a white man!' Frans wrung his hands. This is what came of letting his young master out alone. And what would he tell the old Baas?

Sybilla led the way into the house. She must get hot water, bandages. Kaspar must be fed, put to bed, and rested. She believed in putting people to bed. When they were in bed, you knew where they were. He had gone to get a puppy. If he had stayed in bed, this would not have happened. Of course it was Aletta. Again a bed. That was where everything ended and most things began. She poured water into a basin and set it on the table.

'Give him food,' Leendert said. Sybilla would try to put Kaspar to bed, but he must be got away at once. They might come after him. Sybilla could only see that he was wounded and tired.

Kaspar sat down. Coenraad's people had come. He wondered where they were.

The cross-eyed man came over to him. 'Is it true that you have killed a man?' Not quite white, smiling, and powerfully built, he stood with his arms folded across his chest. His elbows rested on the butts of the pistols in his belt.

'I have killed a man,' Kaspar said. 'There was a fight at Frederik's, and he is dead.' What right had this man to question him, to treat him as an equal?

'I am Afrikander'; the man smiled more widely. 'I am Jan Afrikander.' His tone carried the implication that his name alone answered every question. 'And Coenraad sent me for you.' He moved the candle, stuck his thumbs into his belt, and looked Kaspar up and down. 'So the little trader is now a man,' he said, and went off into silent laughter. 'Ja, magtig, he is now a man like us.'

A man like them. Kaspar started to get up. It was ridiculous that he should have suddenly become a man like this.

'Did you not know,' Afrikander went on, poking a finger into Kaspar's ribs, 'that to be a man you must kill one?' Going to the door, he whistled. A moment later there was the sound of running feet. Kaspar found himself surrounded by men; Bastards, armed and savage, who stood staring at their leader. The room was filled with the acrid scent of their sweat — an animal smell, like that of Kaffirs — but more bitter, flavoured with stale dop, wood smoke, tobacco, and sour food.

Afrikander pointed to Kaspar. 'We have got a little game-cock,' he said. 'He has killed his first man today.' More kindly and with his hand on Kaspar's shoulder, he went on: 'You are frightened and upset. Ja, that I understand. I have been through it. That first man one kills!' He sighed deeply. 'It is like a girl who has a man for the first time. The thing that puzzles you is that it was so easy. Is that not it?' Then he asked: 'Did you shoot him or was it with a knife? Nee, what does it matter? He is dead, and we must go. Get the horses,' he said to his men, 'and have the wagons in-spanned. Eat and rest, meneer. In an hour we will go, and with the river behind us you are safe. Ja, magtig, you are safe now, but I do not want to fight here. It would be bad for Leendert. But do not worry. When you have killed ten men, you will laugh at tonight. When you have killed twenty, you will hardly remember it. To kill is nix. Shoot fast and first. But we will teach you. I like you, Kaspar. Jan Afrikander is your friend and you are one of us. Ja, from this hour you are one of us.'

So this was the bond. Killing a man made you one with the killers. Kaspar rubbed his hand across his eyes. He had never thought of it before, but men could be divided into those who had killed and those who had not.

The men laughed at their leader and came forward one after the other to take his hand before they went out to get ready. Kaspar could not believe himself to be a friend of Griqua Bastards, slaves and deserters. Time, this particular time, was detached from the rest of his life. It was like a bead cut from a string. He could look neither back nor forward. It was like a bead rolling. His life was now without continuity. He was tired and they said he must go on. The Great Fish River was the division between the lawful and the lawless; over the river there was safety; over the river he could plan. But he must see his people first. He must ask his servants what they wished to do. 'Give me more coffee,' he said. 'I must go to my wagons. I must see Frans.'

The past, his old plans, belonged to another man, someone he had known well, but with whom he was no longer concerned. The present had become normal. There was nothing strange in it — neither in his exhaustion, nor in the day he had passed, nor in his going on with Afrikander. So much had happened that anything might happen. His thoughts of Aletta had faded into a desire to see her again, but it was without urgency. Tanta Sybilla's food in his belly felt good, pressing it out against his belt. He was sore and sleepy, but he must go on. To what end, and where, was in the hands of Afrikander. No matter how tired he was, he would go on. He had come far; with food and rest he could go farther. There was no end to human endurance — while a man lived he could go on. Had they been white, he might have acknowledged his exhaustion.

Getting up stiffly, he went to the wagons. They had nearly finished inspanning and were knotting the riems of the last pair of oxen. Frans came up to him.

'Baas,' he said, 'it is in my heart that after this there is no return.'

'There is no return, Frans.'

The old Hottentot scratched his head thoughtfully. 'What will the Baas do about us?' he asked.

'It is of that I would speak,' Kaspar said. 'Once we are over the river, I must get new people and you must go back.'

'Ja, we must go back,' the old man said, 'but has the Baas ever seen a man out with a hunting dog that he commands to go home? He can command him and throw stones at him so that he runs into the bush with his tail between his legs, and yet at the end of the day when he makes his camp the dog is still there and comes to his fire.'

'What do you mean?'

'I mean, Baas, that your fire is our fire, that some of us are coming with you. I am coming, and Klein Johnny that your father bought from the English captain is coming. I, because I am old and have a wife who speaks too much, and Klein Johnny because he is young and would see the world. Lazarus is coming too, and Klaas. The others wish to go back if the Baas will let them, for they pine for their women who are still young and fat. I have told them that there are young, fat women everywhere, but they wish for these special ones to whom they have grown accustomed. So my counsel is to let them go, for if a man wants a certain woman there is no sense in him. I have talked to those Bastards' — he indicated Coenraad's men, who stood holding their horses near the fire; 'they say their orders are to lead us across the river, through the Bushman country to Baas Coenraad's camp. Let us all go there and then, when the horses are safe and the wagons loaded with ivory, let those who wish to go back return here to Baas Leendert and from here to the old Baas, your father. Then with the wagons richly loaded he will see that you have accomplished something, even if in hot blood you killed a man.' He paused. It was the longest speech Kaspar had ever heard Frans make. He was moved by the devotion of his people and wondered what he had done to inspire it. 'Ja,' Frans went on, 'whatever you say the four of us will come with you, so it would be better to

command us to come, then we shall not be guilty of disobedience.'

'You can come,' Kaspar said. 'Bring me Tigernek.'

4

Two of Coenraad's men went in front. Then came Kaspar,
riding with his uncle, then the wagons and the horses and
spare cattle, and at the rear, Afrikander with the rest of his
men. It was behind them that danger lay. Though as yet
it was too soon to expect attack, Afrikander was prepared for
it. 'They may not be ready to follow you,' he said to Kaspar,
'but there are soldiers about and they would like to get me.
They know me well, for I have done much of Coenraad's
work.'

Silently, the convoy followed the guides. There was only
the sound of the horses' hoofs on the road, the shuffling of the
oxen, the creak of the gear, and the heavy rumblings of the
wagons as they rolled. There was no shouting or singing, no
clapping of whips. Where the way was sandy, it was like the
passing of a company of ghosts between the trees.

The night was paling into dawn. Everything was opalescent, changing slowly from grey to milky pink, and the distance a soft blue.

Overhanging trees tore at the wagon tents, scraping them
with rasping, thorny branches that flicked back as they went
by. Sometimes an ox lowed or a man cursed as his horse
stumbled.

The river was in front of them. Afrikander closed up his
men. One after another the wagons laboured through the
drift and up the opposite bank. 'We will stop here,' Afrikander said. 'Outspan your beasts.'

It was morning. Last night's moon hung a faint and pale
disk in the blue sky. Kaspar slipped from his horse. He
thought of yesterday morning. Yesterday he had been at
Frederik's.

Leendert turned to him. 'Good-bye, Kaspar,' he said. 'I will recover the brown if he still lives. Send me news,' he added, 'and I will get it to your father.' He turned his horse and rode back, splashing through the water.

The Great Fish River was crossed. They were outspanned in Kaffraria. Kaspar lay down and slept.

CHAPTER XII

MY BROTHER'S BLOOD

I

ON THE day of the fight Gerrit Bezuidenhout had been leading water.

He cut little furrows in the red soil, dammed them, and turned the water onto the land. He worked with bare feet and trousers rolled to the knee. The fall of the land was steep, and many of the little dams broke so that he had to be perpetually running back to rebuild them, his feet splashing and slipping in the mud. He had a slave with him at whom he shouted. The head of water was too big; too small. But the slave only laughed. He liked to lead water and to play like a child in the mud. The crop was good. The young oats were coming up like green assegais, one close to the other without gaps; dark green and healthy, thick as mealies, and it was pleasant, when the sweat ran from under one's arms and down one's legs, to have cool water on one's hands and feet. Sometimes he stopped working and splashed it over his naked body, thumping his feet and wriggling gently to the chant he hummed. He was happy, and when he was happy he sang and wriggled his stern like a tailless dog. He had eaten meat — a sheep that had died — and there was more of it, pleasantly rotten, hanging in a tree; and there was a woman. A fine hot day, a dead sheep, and a woman. Suddenly he stiffened, braced like a pointer. His master had stopped work too and looked towards the mountains.

'Did you hear anything, Petrus?' Gerrit asked.

'I heard guns, Baas.'

Again it came. Faintly echoing through the hills — a little popping sound.

'Get the horses!' Gerrit shouted as the echo of another volley came from the hills. Driving his spade into the ground, the Hottentot ran towards the veld where the horses grazed.

Gerrit closed the furrow at the outlet of the dam with a plank and some sods and went into the house. He came out with his saddle on his arm and two headstalls in his hand. He went in again and brought guns, powder-horns, and two bandoliers of slugs and bullets.

Before God, life was difficult. No sooner did you start doing something than you had to stop. Somebody murdered. Somebody's cattle driven off. And there was his brother's trouble. The sounds came from that direction. It was strange the fears Frederik had — as if one need fear the Government up here; but that some Kaffirs had attacked him was possible. As soon as the horses came, he would collect his sons and ride over. He thought with pride of his sons, the four tall men who farmed round him. They were strong like himself and the fathers of twenty children. Poor Frederik, with his wife and children dead. But he should not have taken a Bastard girl into his house. If he had married a good woman and had the girl as well, it would have been different. He could have had Stoffel Fourie's widow for the asking; she had a fine herd which, to a sensible man, more than offset the hairs on her face. Surely a man could put up with a hairy woman if she had ten cows to every hair, and Lena Fourie had much hair. It spread over her chin along her upper lip onto her cheeks.

The horses clattered past. They were followed by Petrus,

who shouted and leapt into the air as he chased them into
the kraal.

'Which, Baas?' he shouted; 'which do you want?'

'Bosboi for me, and you can ride the Skimmel.'

Gerrit clapped the saddle onto his horse. Petrus jumped
onto his own, riding barebacked. The other horses ran out
again, kicking and squealing.

With his gun in his hand, Gerrit set off at a canter to call
his sons. As like as not they would have heard the firing and
be ready. There was no peace in this land, and only half
the oats were wetted. Anger filled his heart and with it some
joy. It was a long time, at least a year, since he had shot a
cattle-thief. And it was something to ride out with four sons
at your back; four men with twenty children between them.
Twenty alive, that was, and more to come. He watched his
daughters-in-law like cows and liked to see them heavy.

2

Before they got to Frederik's, they saw a mounted soldier
and rode up to him. He was riding away from the house.
The firing had stopped.

'What was the firing?' Gerrit asked.

'It was nothing,' the soldier said, and rode on.

'Nothing,' Gerrit said. 'All that firing nothing with
powder at the price it is!' Suddenly he was frightened for
his brother. Shots, a dragoon riding heavily, in marching
order, and his brother's fears all fitted, like teeth, into the
jaws of real disaster. 'Ride, kerels!' he shouted. 'Something
is not right.'

Sitting down in their saddles, they pressed up the valley.
Behind Gerrit, Petrus clung to the mane of his Skimmel,
riding with his head bent to avoid the stones thrown up by
his master's horse.

Before they got to the drift, they saw another man on
the mountain-side; he was on a brown horse, and galloped

like a madman without a greeting or a shout as they came near. Gerrit raised his hand and they slowed up. Without a word they separated, extending to the right and left in a semicircle. With their guns across their thighs, ready for use, they closed in on the farm at a walk, riding from tree to tree, halting at each to look and listen.

Gerrit was in the centre with his servant behind him. Two of his sons were on his right and two on his left. First one advanced, then another, while the others watched. At a signal they halted, and Gerrit rode forward alone. He was uneasy. Everything was too still; quite silent except for the lowing of the cattle and the bleating of the sheep. It was unnatural that they should be kraaled and calling at such a time. The calves were bellowing for their mothers. The mothers were answering them. And by now the dogs should have been barking. Never before had he come so near without the brindle bitch running out, barking savagely until she recognised him.

He tightened his hold on the reins and pushed his heels into his horse's flanks. He had him in hand. The horse cocked his ears and whisked his tail as he walked, half-trippling, with his legs well under him, showing the whites of his eyes as he looked back at the shining barrel of the gun that lay across his neck.

The young men watched their father. Almost invisible in the shadow of the trees, they waited, listening uneasily to the sounds made by the beasts.

Gerrit changed the gun from his left hand to his right and pulled up. Sitting forward in the saddle and shading his eyes, he stared at the house. There was no smoke coming from the chimney. The dogs were lying in front of the house, but they did not move. Only the baboon moved, and he was behaving strangely, walking round and round, his chain fully extended as he strained, pulling and jumping against it. And there was something else — the barrel of upset lilies. He knew how his brother tended the flowers. They had belonged to his wife — and the dogs were dead.

The young men saw their father lower his hand from his eyes. His horse broke from a stand into a gallop. At full speed, from all round, they followed him, charging inward like spokes of a wheel running towards the hub. The ground shook as their horses closed in. Each instant they expected to see something: Kaffirs run out, or a Bushman break cover. At the white walls they pulled up. The baboon had climbed to the top of his pole and was chattering with terror. There was nothing to attack but the silence and the stillness and the heat that lay over the land. They saw the broken flowers, the dead hounds, the hanging door, the spoor of horses and of booted men. 'The soldiers!' they said. The damned soldiers.

Jacob, Gerrit's youngest son, spat.

'We are too late,' he said.

Gerrit dismounted and went in.

'Magtig!' he shouted. 'Come here and see!'

He stood at the doorway again, bareheaded. 'Come here,' he said. 'They have killed him.'

3

The five Boers, hatless, standing with the butts of their guns on the ground, filled the room. Behind them, at the door, Petrus waited, trembling.

None of the young men spoke. They waited for their father.

'So it has come.' Gerrit ran his hand through his beard. Old Frederik had been right. He pulled his pipe from his pocket, looked at his dead brother, and went out, followed by his sons.

'There are things to be done,' he said after a long silence. 'Off-saddle the horses and let them graze.'

His sons stared at him.

'The cattle have not had water.' Gerrit looked towards the kraal. 'This must have begun early or they would have been out.'

'Why did we not hear the firing sooner?' Herman asked.

'Ja, why did we not?' the others said. 'We started as soon as we heard guns.'

'There was a high wind this morning,' Gerrit said. 'No doubt what we heard was the end. That was when they killed him.'

'Ja, that is why we did not hear, Pa — because of the wind.'

'Ja, there was a high wind.' Gerrit was thinking of Selina and the child. 'Get those cattle out, Herman,' he said, 'you and Martinus. Water them. And' — he paused — 'it is in my heart that they would be better at home running with our beasts till matters are settled.' His mouth was compressed. In the eyes of the law a bastard was without rights. 'Go and water those cattle and sheep,' he said again. The two young men moved off. 'Count them, and take them home,' he went on. If they were not got away, they might be confiscated.

His brother was dead. But it was likely that some of the beasts were unmarked so that in the division that would follow . . . Frederik had let things go. When a man took a coloured woman to live with him . . . He opened his mouth, and then closed it. The less said the better, and his sons would know what to do. He watched them lead their horses to the kraals. They flung open the gates and rode down to the river behind the cattle.

'Send back a wagon!' he shouted.

Martinus raised his hand. He had heard.

'Who are his heirs?' Jacob asked.

'His heirs are his brothers and his brothers' sons,' Gerrit said.

'What of the child by the Bastard woman?'

'Who is the father of the child?' Gerrit asked, looking from one to the other. 'Did we see him lie with her? How do we know who is the father of a Bastard woman's child? He may have many fathers.'

'What of Frederik's wishes?' Jacob said. 'Would it not be according to his wishes that his child should inherit?'

'I say that it is not his child. That in law the child has no rights. Magtig, who are we to cross the laws of God and man? Are we to blame that Frederik went a-whoring? And there are some who will say this is a judgment on him.'

Herman came back at a gallop. 'There are forty-eight head of cattle,' he said, 'and five hundred sheep.'

'I thought there were more,' Gerrit said. 'Forty-eight head of horned stock and only five hundred sheep. Get them back quickly,' he ordered. 'Spread them among our herds and come back with a wagon for the gear.' He tightened his belt and, turning to the others, said, 'Come, we have work to do.'

4

Gerrit did not like the look in his brother's eyes as Johannes sat on his sweat-streaked horse with the men of Tarka behind him and looked at the goods piled up outside the house. Johannes' eyes went from the feather mattress to the stools and chairs. They took in the bright tinware, the guns and the powder-horns, the saddles, bridles, yokes, trek-tous, and tools, all stacked neatly on the short grass outside the house. Everything that Frederik had was here, even his milk-pail and a box of copper nails.

Gerrit and his sons were not the only ones who had come to Frederik's. By the afternoon there were twenty men round the house. Faber had come with his brother-in-law. The two Mullers, young Fourie, Big Joachim, and a party of strangers who were looking for new grazing. Rudolf was there. Angry Boers, fathers of families, who felt the death of the old man who had been their friend, and who, beyond his death, felt their own peace menaced. They had brought food, and one had shot a buck. Most had servants with them, agterryers. They talked together in monotonous, chanting voices and kept looking towards their masters, who stood or sat round their separate fires. A white man shot by white men. This was a new thing. White men killed by Kaffirs they had seen, and white men killed by Bushman arrows, but not this. Their voices rose, keyed by the excitement of the event, and died down as their masters shouted at them.

The talk of the Boers was of the funeral, of the English, of Opperman who had betrayed Frederik, of life into which a new factor had entered — this threat of soldiers in a land that they had deemed, because of its difficulties, entirely their own. Soldiers that could not be spared to help them attack Kaffirs, or to recover stolen stock, could be sent against one of their number to kill him in his home as a jackal is killed at the mouth of his earth. They looked at Johannes; he had just come in with the men from Tarka. They had started on the previous day, having heard that there were soldiers on the road.

'Where are the cattle, Gerrit?' Johannes asked.

'I sent them away.'

Johannes looked up at the sky, searching it.

'What are you looking for up there?' Gerrit followed his brother's gaze.

'Aasvoels, brother. Where there is death there are vultures, jackals, and wolves that, smelling carrion, come.'

'It is too dark for vultures.'

'Nee, Gerrit, there are many sorts of vultures. Some are without wings and come on horseback.'

The Boers laughed.

'What do you mean?' Gerrit demanded angrily. 'Do you think that I ... that I ...' He hesitated.

'I think nothing, Gerrit. My heart is too sore to think. And where are the woman and the child?' He looked round.

'She is gone,' someone said.

'So she is gone, and while she is gone my brother takes the cattle and the gear.'

'We are his heirs,' Gerrit said. 'You share with us.'

'His son is his heir.'

'His bastard, you mean. And who knows that he is Frederik's son? Perhaps he is your son.' Gerrit laughed. 'You are so interested in him.'

'He is Frederik's son. That all men know, and the goods are his.' Johannes dismounted and went into the house. It was still hot from the heat of the day, fetid with death and the stale smell of sweating men. 'Give me a candle,' he said. With trembling hands he lit it. The room was empty but for Frederik. He lay on the table with his legs hanging over its end. Johannes had seen enough. He turned away. In the morning he would see more. Picking up the reins of his horse, he led him away from the others, knee-haltered him, and prepared his camp. He chose a little ridge far from everyone. One brother was dead, another a thief. He wanted to think.

5

By the light of the moon and a lantern hung in a tree, Joachim Prinsloo worked at the coffin. All Boers were good carpenters, but he was considered above them in the making of coffins. It was a speciality of his and he was proud of his skill. But it was hard to work hastily like this and without sufficient light. There was only one who could rival him in this art, Willemse Prinsloo, but he was a doctor as well and had greater opportunities. Joachim worked silently except when the saw bit against a nail; then he swore, pulled the saw clear of the wood, and held it, like a gun, pointed up at the lantern to see if the teeth were damaged. It was old Frederik's saw. It needed setting.

On the ground a Hottentot knelt, his back golden-red in the firelight, boring holes with an awl for the pegs that would hold the box together. Planks were scarce. The doors of the house had gone into it... It was not what Joachim would have liked; with new planks he could have made a fine coffin, but there was no time to get planks. It was hot, and he, like the others, wanted to get away. There was something evil here, but he worked carefully. The coffin was strong. Pegged down, lashed tight with riems, it would hold old Frederik. He thought of the last time he had seen him; of how they had sat side by side eating and drinking at Rudolf's. If he had said then, 'Oom Frederik, soon I will be making you a coffin,' how old Frederik would have laughed! And now he was making it. Life was strange. It made him sad. He wanted to be with his wife. I ought to be in bed with her now, he thought, instead of making a coffin for my friend Frederik. Life was not strange when one was in bed with one's wife. It was simple and beautiful. No other man had a wife like his. He was sorry for other men.

6

As soon as it was light, Johannes Bezuidenhout got up. Today he would learn the story of his brother's death. Like an old hound, he worked round the farm, he quartered the kopje, he went to the spring. This was where they had picked him up. Here they had run. He bent down and touched the deep toe-marks of his brother's spoor in the mud of the river-bed. They were big feet, and the impress of the left foot light and dragging where he had saved it. 'Old and lame,' he muttered. 'Ja, a poor lame old kerel.' Frederik's exploits came to his mind. He thought of the things they had done together, of their boyhood, young manhood; of Frederik's marriage; of the birth of his children; of the death of his children. He went to the krantz, to the cave; he saw the loosened stones where they had climbed into it; he saw how Kaspar had escaped. The blood on the ledge was black and dry. It was his brother's blood. There was a torn tussock on the edge of the krantz that Frederik had gripped in an effort to save himself as he fell, and there were the marks of his nails on the stones.

As Johannes stared down at the pool below him, the bees

swarmed. The cave was filled with bees. It throbbed like a drum with the beating of their wings. For a moment the sky at the entrance was darkened by them, and then with a swirling roar they flew out. He followed the swarm with his eyes till it disappeared.

It might be enough for the others to know that old Frederik was dead, but to him it was not enough; he must know every detail. The story of Frederik's last fight must be passed on. His death must not be still-born. When he had traced every footmark, seen every getting up and every lying down written clearly in the dust, it was not over. These were but the words. The writing would take time to read; to build up and put together. He sat down and lit his pipe. An hour later he got up. Now he knew more than all the others, save the Bastard Hans and young Kaspar.

When he came back to the house, they were putting Frederik into his coffin. But he would not go. His legs were stiff. He lay on his back with his legs up, resting on his shoulders and his heels; his stomach, his thighs, and knees were raised.

Joachim stood beside the coffin, scratching his head in despair. It was a fine coffin, but he should have thought of this and made it less long and much higher at the lower end. He kept saying, 'I could have made it so, but it would not have been a nice coffin. It would not be respectful to make such a coffin.'

Johannes turned on his brother. 'You were here first, Gerrit,' he said, 'and you never thought to put your brother on his bed. You never thought to lay him out decently because you wanted a clean bed, not one spotted with your brother's blood. It is in my heart that you never liked old Frederik. I think you were afraid of him.'

'We came to his aid,' Gerrit said.

'You came towards the sound of firing as you were in duty bound. Stand back now, stand back,' he said. 'Give me the lid, Joachim.'

'It will not go, Johannes. We have tried it, and he is stiff.'

'Give it me, I say.' He took it from him. 'Good-bye, Frederik,' Johannes said. 'You are my good brother and I mean no disrespect.' He fitted the top of the coffin over his brother's face. It fitted neatly. The end of the lid lay along the dead man's thighs. Johannes set his foot over his brother's head. 'Now sit on it,' he said. 'Ja, you, you great fool, Joachim, and you, and you' — he pointed to the biggest of those who clustered round him.

Reluctantly they sat down on the coffin, as men sit on an over-full trunk; and slowly beneath their weight, old Frederik's rigid muscles and tendons collapsed, first slowly, and then quickly, so that his feet hit the bottom of the coffin with a thud.

'Make him fast,' Johannes told them.

'Magtig, I do not like this,' Joachim said, wiping the sweat from his brow. 'It is not decent.'

'Make him fast,' said Johannes, 'and we will make an end.' The pegs were driven home.

'Do you see the way I have put his name upon the top?' Joachim pointed proudly to the F.C.B. that he had written with nails upon the lid.

Pushing him aside, Johannes said:

'Listen to me. My brother Gerrit has taken the cattle, the sheep, and the gear. In the sight of God, they belong to my brother's son; in the sight of the law, they belong to his brothers, I among them, unless the Government claims them. But you have seen that there is no law now, for it is not lawful to kill an old man in his place, nor if there was such a law would I profit by it to take my share of his goods. I have enough, and am not one that would seethe the kid in its mother's milk. But listen, friends: I claim the right to my brother's body and the right to name the place where it will lie.' He looked round angrily. His head was lowered into his shoulders; his hands, hanging at his sides, twitched as he went on. 'He did not die as others die,' he shouted;

'not naturally by a spear or an arrow; not by the mauling of a wild beast or the thrust of a bull's horn; not of old age or of sickness. Therefore his burial must be a special thing. And he will lie here ... at the threshold of the house.' He pointed to the big stone that was let into the ground.

'But he wished to lie with Paulina,' Gerrit said.

'Ja, he wished to lie with Paulina,' Johannes repeated. 'But this is a greater thing, that he should lie where we found him. Listen, kerels' — he raised his voice. 'What is it that a man should lie in his own little graveyard with his wife and his children? Who passing by will give his grave more than a glance? It is one among many, perhaps overgrown and forgotten. Nee, before God I swear that this will be something else.' He wiped the sweat from his bloodshot eyes and went on. 'They say make little weeping for the dead, they are at rest. But I say that my brother is dead, but not at rest. I say that he will never rest until he is avenged. I say that my brother's blood crieth from the ground. I say that the harvest is past, the summer is ended, and we are not saved. I say that we who were free have become tributary, and woe be to the fearful hearts and faint hands and the sinner who goeth both ways. Vragtig, truly, I say, if we be men, those who have done this will reap what they have sown. Dig, and dig deep. A thousand times old Frederik has walked on that stone. Ten thousand times a thousand will his blood cry out from under it. Dig deep, I say, and lay my brother down.'

The servants began to raise the stone, levering it up with a bar rested on a log and throwing stones beneath it to hold it up. There were things that ran out from under the stone: a centipede; a blue-breasted lizard that had lost its tail, leaving it in the hands of the tame Bushman who tried to catch it. And there were things that could not run: fat, white, brown-headed grubs with thick, segmented bodies that lay encurled with their tails touching their brown heads.

'Pause, white men!'

The Boers looked round and saw no one.

'Pause, I say.'

Then they saw him, a little crouching figure in their midst, almost black, crusted with dirt and festooned with bladders, dried snakes and bones threaded onto strings.

'Who are you, Kaffir?' Johannes said.

The man turned his eyes upward. They were unblinking as a snake's. 'I am called by many names. Ringhals is one of them. Little Flower is another.' His lips writhed back in a grin. 'Ai ... I am the Little Flower of Love ... the Little Flower of Death.' He shook with laughter till the teeth of beasts and men, the dried toads and snakes and bones that hung like a cloak over his ribs, rattled against each other. 'Hold, white men,' he said again, 'before you bury the dead man there. Think well, for he will not be at peace, and as the seed corn brings forth a thousand fold, so shall his spirit breed hate in the land. Bury him with his woman and children. Bury him, mourn him, and forget him!'

Crouching, he stared up, turning his slit eyes inward and making his voice come from first one place and another so that the Boers kept turning their heads to listen. 'Today there were shots in the mountains and the aasvoels flew down,' he went on. 'Bullets,' he droned, 'round like seeds, like the seeds on the heads of the Kaffir corn. Plant them' — his voice was shrill — 'and they will bear a crop. The spear is broken. Would you forge a thousand spears from one that is broken? Would you lay a burden of death on your children's children? Ai ... ai ...' His voice broke into a wail. 'I see it. There is death in what you do ... death ... But bury him where you will, white men. What is it to me, who know more dead than quick, who walk with the impis of death about me — to me, who know all the dead? Ai ... on every little pathway I meet the warriors who have died there, and they give me the salute of kings. Ai ... the morani of the Masai, the drinkers of blood and milk in the north that you have never seen, salute me. Ringed Amazulu hold aloft their

spears, saying, "Bayete, Little Flower of Death, we salute
you." But do what you will. Let the sons of kings be kings if
they can kings be. Once this old man whom you put away
befriended me, therefore I say that you are fools and the sons
of fools. Therefore I lay a curse upon you.'

A Boer near him stepped forward. The witch doctor
sprang up.

'Strike,' he said; 'raise your hand to strike me, if you dare.
Ai...white man, strike the mamba with your open hand!'
He laughed again.

The Boer dropped his hand.

'I am leaving you, but the man in the box should lie with
his woman. How can he rest in peace alone?' Like a bat
folding his wings, the witch doctor wrapped his worn
kaross about himself and raised his hand. 'Farewell, white
men. The Little Flower gives you greeting. The lost ones
give you greeting.' He opened his arms as if he would take
flight. The Boers fell back from him. He passed between
them and was gone.

Some then called for their horses. They would take no
further part in this. Frederik Bezuidenhout was dead.
This talk against Rousseau, Opperman, and Stockenstroom
was madness. Frederik lying dead was a proof of how mad
resistance was. But others stood by Johannes. They were
thinking of their old freedom, of the little republic they had
once made. Perhaps the time would come when they could
make another.

CHAPTER XIII

TO THE NORTH

I

ALETTA was outside when Rudolf came back. He rode slumped in the saddle.

'What is it?' she asked.

'Times are bad, child. The Devil is loosed in the land.'

'What is it? Tell me, oupa. Is it Kaspar?' She went up to his horse; her hand was on its neck, her fingers twisted into its dusty mane.

'Old Frederik Bezuidenhout is dead,' Rudolf said, dismounting.

'Dead? Was it the Kaffirs?' she asked.

'It was the English. They came for him. They have shot him dead.' He dismounted heavily. 'You must tell Maria,' he said.

'The English? Up here? Old Frederik dead!' Aletta repeated, unable to take it in. The words, when she said them, meant nothing to her. They sounded strangely. 'Dead,' she said again.

'Ja, dead.'

Somewhere behind the house two coloured maids were chattering. One of them, Rosina, began to sing. Generally Aletta liked to hear her sing, but today she put her hands up to her ears. Frederik was dead and Kaspar had gone to Frederik's. He had gone to get a puppy. They had laughed about it. That was yesterday. It was unbelievable that this should have happened to her — that it should have happened since yesterday.

A heron flew with slow wings across the vlei. Its neck was folded back, its legs outstretched behind it. She watched it carefully, as if she had never seen a heron before, till it was hidden by the big fig tree. Why had it gone? Why, just when she must have something to watch, was the world empty? She looked at the sky where it had been. Rosina's singing was louder. Plaintively wailing, it rose and fell. She sang as though her heart would break. But Aletta knew that Rosina's heart was not breaking. She knew that Rosina only sang when she was happy. It was April who made her sing. She had seen them together. She knew that at night Rosina crept out to April.

'Where is Kaspar, Oom Rudolf?' she asked. 'Is he dead, too? Is it that he is dead and you dare not tell me? Before God, I am a woman. I can be told.'

'What is Kaspar to you, little one?' Rudolf looked at his foster daughter. She stood away from his horse. Her mouth was firm, her eyes were fixed on his. What was Kaspar to her? By the way she stood watching him he knew what Kaspar was to her.

'I think Kaspar is everything to me,' she said. If only Rosina would stop. If only everything would stop and it could be yesterday. Had he got his puppy? He had been going to bring it back to show her. She had been looking forward to seeing it — to seeing him bring it to her — to holding it after he had held it. But what was the good of thinking of all this now? He might be dead. In a minute she would know. Rudolf would tell her. She did not want to know. She prayed that something would happen to delay the answer she demanded. If only Rosina would stop singing; if only another heron would fly across the empty sky.

'So it has come to you, little one.' Rudolf's voice was tender. Love had come to his little Aletta. It had come very swiftly and was hurting her. 'I have no news of Kaspar, but Johannes says he got away.'

'He will cross the Border.' Aletta sighed. It did not matter now if Rosina sang. Kaspar was safe.

'Ja, he will be safe if he gets to Coenraad,' Rudolf said.

'Were many there?' Aletta asked. She thought of the men who must have ridden towards the firing from all round; of the way news of it came to Rudolf, cried from a hilltop by a herder; and of how, taking his gun, he had mounted and gone off.

'Ja, many,' Rudolf said. 'They rode in from all round. Gerrit has taken Frederik's cattle and gear. Johannes has gone mad. He swears vengeance against Opperman and called his brother Gerrit an aasvoel. He had them lay Frederik under the big stone at his door. You know the stone,' he said.

Aletta nodded her head. She knew the stone.

'And out of the earth at our feet, as we stood round, an old witch doctor sprang up and prophesied.' Rudolf ran his hands over his eyes. 'And he was right. Ja, he was right when he said a seed of hate was planted. He said that a dead man should lie with his wife. Take my horse, Letta. I am going away till you tell Maria.'

In his heart Rudolf was afraid. Frederik was dead. And though many had left at Johannes' outburst, others had been roused. Things were afoot. In the old days there had been leaders. But who was there now? The best men were dead, and he mistrusted the younger. Perhaps Leendert was right when he kept out of everything. But how was anyone to have known the English would do this? That their troops could strike so far and fast? Aletta would tell Maria. He could count on Aletta. Surely a man should be able to tell his wife such things and not put the burden on a girl. Once he could have told her. But not now. He was too tired and she was ill. Something was wrong with her leg. The hot cow-dung he plastered upon it at night did no good. The decoctions of stewed willow leaves that invariably eased lameness did no good, and she scarcely ate. Nee, he thought, she does not eat enough to keep a bird alive. And her milk was making the child ill; it did not thrive, but grew thinner every day, its face more wizened and monkey-like.

2

'So the old fool is dead and the young one fled.' Stephanie laughed contemptuously. 'Magtig, why did Kaspar not give himself up at once? What will his riches avail him now?' she asked. 'What will he do with them in Kaffirland? He should have left the old man,' she said passionately. 'Ja, it would have served him right with his gluttony and his concubinage and his bastards. It is a judgment; a judgment of the Almighty.'

Aletta looked at her coldly. 'Ja, he could have run sooner or have given himself up,' she said, 'but what would his name have been? Nee, Stephanie, Kaspar did right to stand by his friend, and perhaps he remembered that it was old Frederik who took me from the Kaffirs.'

'You!' Stephanie said. 'What have you to do with it? Perhaps you think it is you he looks at? Do you think that?' she asked, coming nearer. 'Would you still think that if I told you that he —— '

'Stop, Stephanie! Before you say too much. Stop before I call you the whore that you are: a harlot with seeking eyes and hands. Do you think I do not know your tricks? The wiles that you think so hidden! Ja, Stephanie, they are as hidden, as secret as those of a female cat. Nee, I will say nothing but this, and listen well. Kaspar is my affair, and the others' — she paused — 'you can have them all, since you need so many.'

'So you want him,' Stephanie sneered. 'A boy!' She

tossed her head. 'And did you think I wanted him for more than an hour or two? I like men, not boys.'

'You like men,' Aletta broke in bitterly. 'This is news, indeed. Ach, sis Stephanie, even the cattle are decent; they come into season and go out of it again.'

'Ja, it is news that I like men. Welcome news' — Stephanie paused — 'to the men. And as for old Frederik, I am glad he is dead. Glad,' she repeated. 'A man who lived with a coloured woman openly and without shame.'

She spat contemptuously and turned away. Aletta watched her go into the house and close the door.

Kaspar was a fugitive. How could he come to see her? Nearly all the Border Boers had killed men. But they had been Kaffirs or Bushmen. To kill a white man was murder. To kill a soldier was worse. And in a way it is my fault, she thought. If it had not been for me he would not have come back. The puppy was only an excuse. Her life was going to be changed by a puppy. A litter of pups had been born, and because of them, Kaspar was running. He does not know this country, she thought, suddenly afraid. Anyone else, once he got clear, would be safe, but Kaspar might get lost. He might come to harm. When would she know? This was what it was to be a woman. It was never to know. It was never to be able to find out for oneself.

Now she must tell Tanta Maria that her brother was dead. How did one break news like this? She went in softly. Maria was resting on her bed. She did this only when Rudolf was out. She did not want him to know how ill she was.

'What is it, Letta?' Maria said.

'It is bad news,' Aletta said. As she spoke, she knew how much worse the news could have been. Suppose Kaspar had been killed. But if Kaspar had been killed, it would have been nothing to Maria. She would have been sorry because he had seemed a pleasant young man, and in a week she would have forgotten.

'I can see it's bad news.' Maria sat up.

'It is Oom Frederik.'

'Is he sick? If he's sick, he must come here.'

'He is dead,' Aletta said. 'There has been an accident...
He was shot.' She came up to her foster mother and put
her arms round her. 'You have been good to me, Tanta
Maria,' she said.

'What kind of accident... how was he shot?'

'It was the soldiers,' Aletta said, and began to cry.

She loved old Frederik. He had saved her from the Kaffirs.
But it might have been Kaspar.

Tanta Maria held her close and patted her shoulder. 'Poor
Frederik,' she said. 'Where is Rudolf?' she asked. 'He is not
hurt?'

'He is outside... he told me to tell you.' It had not been
hard to tell. It was much easier to give other people pain
than to bear pain oneself. She thought of how Frederik had
found her.... All the time the battle raged she had hidden
crouched behind some great pots in the kraal. When
Frederik had picked her up, she had kicked and screamed.
She had not wanted to go. She had forgotten white people.
Frederik's hands had been hard and rough and he smelt
differently. But later she had got used to him, and her
fear was that if she slept and fell off the saddle he would
leave her. She remembered her fear of falling asleep and
waking to find herself alone in the veld. And then she had
come to love him and had cried when he left her with Rudolf and Maria... kicking and screaming and shouting in
Kaffir when he left her. Rudolf and Maria had often spoken
of it.

3

When Kaspar woke, it was late afternoon. He was fully
rested and some of his courage had returned. He stared
moodily over the river — the past lay there. The bank of
the river was the boundary of his life; on this side he must

begin it again. He began to plan. When the goods and horses were sold and the wagons returned to his father, he would be free. Too free. Only the north lay open to him and he must make his way there. Then there was Aletta. I must see her before I go, he thought.

In the daylight Afrikander looked more villainous than ever. His good eye looked out at the world savagely; his bad one, half closed, leered. On his head he wore a flat red cap of dirty velvet; the upper part of his body was clothed in what looked like a woman's blouse of white, pink-striped brocade, his legs in skin-tight, leather small-clothes. He was still fully armed with a pair of pistols and a hanger on his belt. A long elephant gun, bound with brass rings, hung over his left shoulder.

'So you are awake, Kaspar,' he said, coming towards him. 'You slept well, meneer, I hope?'

'I slept well,' Kaspar replied.

'That is good. Ja, to eat and to sleep are good, though it is better not to sleep alone. I never sleep well alone. Without a woman at my side, I am nervous. Ja, magtig, without a woman I am like a child — I have dreams. Last night I dreamed of red elephants. Magtig, it was terrible. One of them, a great bull, sat upon my chest. Think of it — a red elephant on your chest!'

'I do not dream,' Kaspar said.

'You do not dream!' Afrikander looked surprised. 'But you will. And when you do, get a woman. With a woman you get so tired that you cannot dream, and if one woman is not enough, get two. Get three, then there are no elephants. The worst dream that a man can have,' he said again, 'is that of elephants, of red elephants that sit upon your chest.' He looked round as if he expected to see a red elephant.

'What are you going to do?' Kaspar asked.

'To do?' Afrikander said. 'We will stay here till we hear if your uncle has regained the horse you lost. I was told to bring you in with your horses, and before God I will do it.'

'Are we safe here?' asked Kaspar.

'Safe?' Afrikander paused as though he were considering the question. 'We are never safe, but we are safer than those who would come against us.' He began to laugh. His lips went back, showing his pink gums and great eye teeth. The barrels of the pistols in his belt rattled together, but no sound came from his gaping mouth. 'Look,' pointing to the drift. Behind the rocks, almost hidden, Kaspar saw six men lying. 'Let them come,' Afrikander said.

'If we are going to stay, I would go to Rudolf's. I have business with Rudolf.'

'Ja, business,' Afrikander said. His half-eye closed entirely in a wink. 'I understand that business; I will give you two men.'

'I wish to go alone.'

'You cannot go alone. You must be protected till you learn our ways. Two men will be enough. They will watch over you while you do your — business. How long will it take you?' he asked. 'Can you finish in an hour? That should be enough.' Ja, magtig, enough for them both. Again he went off into silent laughter. 'I will give you good men,' he said, 'and you had better ride one of our horses in case you get shot.'

4

Johannes Bezuidenhout remained at his brother's house after the others had gone. His brother was dead. He had been betrayed, and his blood, the same blood that ran in his own veins, was spilt.

He had watched the horsemen go. Some had been afraid of his words: afraid of his threats. Only a few had stood by him. The others, unwilling to become embroiled with the authorities, had ridden off earlier. Even Gerrit, having taken what he could, had ridden off. Johannes laughed: the house was stripped of everything. They have taken the substance, but I have the shadow, and today the shadow is worth more than the substance, he thought. He had old Frederik's silver-mounted powder-horn, his great gun, the one that took four balls to the pound, and the Bible stained with his blood. These would suffice. With these he would raise the Border. 'These are enough!' he shouted to the empty hills. 'Genoeg...genoeg...' And falling on his knees, he began to pray.

'Almighty God,' he prayed, 'give me strength. Give me my dead brother's strength, his skill as a leader. Let his mantle fall upon me that I may free our people from the yoke that is upon them. Let us be free, as once we were free. Lead us out of Egypt, deliver us, O God.'

His gun was on the ground at his side. His brother's gun and his silver-mounted powder-horn were slung round him.

There was one more thing to be done. Johannes looked down the valley and up it. He was alone. His horse was grazing its way down to the river; cropping the grass, walking a few steps, and cropping again.

Bending over his dying fire, he pushed two charred logs together and blew upon them. They burnt up. He added more wood, and then, testing the breeze with a wet finger, picked up a flaming branch. Walking deliberately, with the brand in his hand, he went up to the house.

Without hesitating he brought the flame under the eaves. The dry thatch began to smoulder; a gust of wind caught it and swept it upward. Frederik's house was burning. Nothing could stop it now. Johannes was driven back by the heat as the flames ran over the roof, covered it, and leapt into the sky. There was a crash as the rooftree fell. A great column of smoke went up. For miles round they would see this, a black pall of rolling smoke.

Frederik's house was burnt again...burnt for the last time. It was the end of the house and the beginning of something else.

He must get men to help him. Men would help him and God would help him.

The baboon was screaming. He loosed him, undoing the chain from his belly. When he mounted, the baboon followed him.

5

Kaspar and his two companions camped on the road. It was a path that none but men trained on the Border could have found. It was one of the thousand little paths, scarcely more than a foot wide, which join all Africa together by their intricate network; that run from village to village, join water-hole to water-hole, link river to river. East and west, north and south, there was nowhere a man could not go did he but know the way. Not a village that was not tied by some hidden, devious path to every other village throughout the vastness of all Africa. Before God, he thought, I believe that there are roads from this very spot where we stand to Arabia and to the posts of the Portuguese on the eastern and western seas.

This land held gold and elephants. He had meant to visit it, to see its wonders, but now, owing to the circumstances which had befallen him, he must live here. Instead of a few months he must spend his life in these wilds. He looked at his companions with some distaste. He must learn to live as these men did. Swift and sure they had ridden their small horses at a canter through the mountains — halting, advancing, swinging this way and that, following signs that were all but invisible to him. Could he learn what they knew, without sinking as low as they? Could one develop the faculties of a wild beast without becoming one? Crouched over their fire, they sat roasting meat on the points of their knives. Griquas, men of Hottentot, white, and Eastern blood. Links, leader of the two, was much whiter than the other and had blue eyes that looked strangely pale in his leather-coloured face. His clothes were the tattered, dressed-leather clothes of the Border, but, like all Coenraad's men, there was something rakish about them. Under his hat he wore a knotted yellow silk kerchief, and a single gold earring in his left ear.

As soon as they had eaten they got up. 'Come,' Links said.

'Come!' Kaspar repeated. 'Are we going on?'

'Nee, but we never sleep by our fires.' He made a wide sweep with his hand. 'How do we know who has marked the fire? When we have eaten, we always move.' His companion threw more wood on the fire, building it up. 'Anyone who would follow us will come up to the fire,' he said, 'and while we are away from it we can see him. Ja, it is easy to shoot a man as he stands against a flame.'

'How would you know who he was — that he was an enemy?' Kaspar asked.

'Any man who comes to our fire is an enemy. We will lie up there.' Links pointed to the mountain. 'From there we can see and, even if we move, will not be seen with the Berg behind us.'

With the three knee-haltered horses grazing round him and the two renegades beside him, Kaspar lay down. He felt safe. These men slept with one ear cocked and only one eye closed. Twice he saw them start up and put their hands on their guns. He had heard nothing. Only the cropping of the horses and the sound of their uneven steps as they moved.

Before dawn, without waiting to eat, they saddled up, and as the sun stood halfway up in the sky, they came to the sugar-loaf hill. Here, with the house in sight, they halted.

'We will wait,' Links said. 'Pierre can go down and see that there is no one about. Of all our men he is the best at this. He is half a Bushman and can hide so that unless he is walked on no one can see him.

'Go, Pierre,' he said.

The little man grinned and began to slip off his clothes. For a moment he stood naked. Then he stretched, raising his arms above his head, a slight yellow-brown figure that blended into the surrounding foliage. Kaspar saw him bend down for his belt and gun. When he looked again, he was no longer there.

'Where is he?' Kaspar asked.

'He is gone.' Links clicked his fingers. 'He is like that. At any time he can disappear. Ja, magtig, in a laagte of short grass, grass no higher than that' — he held his thumb and forefinger apart — 'he can disappear. Soon he will be there' — Links pointed downward — 'and not even the dogs will know it.'

Kaspar sat down to wait. Beside him there was the pit of an ant lion, a little hole half an inch deep and an inch across. It was cone-shaped, its sides covered with loose sand. As he looked, an ant blundered into the hole. It tried to climb up the loose sides of the pit, but the sand collapsed under it. There was a little spurt of engulfing sand from the bottom of the pit. Desperately the ant avoided it and made another rush for the wall. It gave way beneath it. There was another spurt of sand and the ant was dragged down. Like a crocodile in the depths of the river the ant lion lay in wait for anything that fell into its pit, ready with ever-voracious jaws for any insect that came its way. The bodies of the victims when sucked dry were thrown out. Kaspar dropped a fragment of grass into the pit. Again the spurt of sand. It was dragged down. He threw another, but the lion was not deceived again. Kaspar wondered what preyed on the ant lions. He was certain that something did, for so were things arranged — each beast had another which lived upon it. Even lions and leopards in the end became food for vultures and jackals.

Moving forward, he looked down at the farm below him. The big fig tree was a dark blot against which the whiteness of the house stood out, and there in front of it were the peach trees where he had tied his horse. The farm looked like a child's toy, like the Noah's Ark which had been given him when he was a little boy. It had come from Europe and was considered too good for him to play with, but he had enjoyed looking at it. He could see the dogs lying outside and small black spots that he knew to be poultry.

A woman came out of the house carrying a child. It must be Tanta Maria. A coloured maid standing at the doorway emptied a bucket onto the ground — a signal for the chickens to run towards her. Kaspar searched for Aletta. If only he could see her. It would be something to lie here on his stomach in the mountain and watch her coming and going, but he saw neither Aletta nor Stephanie. Rudolf came out onto the stoep and sat down with his feet on the rail. He does not know we are here, Kaspar thought, or that Pierre is creeping, like a snake, within a few yards of the house. No wonder Boers lost sheep and cattle. There was cover not for one, but for a hundred men round these mountain farms. And then, as noiselessly as he had gone, Pierre reappeared. His belly was scratched with stones; sweat ran down his flanks and stood out in beads along his forehead.

'There is no one,' he said, 'and the klein meisie is by the kraal.' He grinned. 'If that is the one you want,' he said to Kaspar. 'She is alone — go and take her. If any come we will shoot them.'

'Whom are you going to shoot?' Kaspar said.

'Ek weet nee,' Pierre said. 'Anyone who comes. We do not mind. Or do you want to carry her off?' he asked. 'We could do that, though it would be better if there were more of us.'

'I want to speak to her,' Kaspar said.

'To speak to her! Have we come all this way so that you can speak to her?' He shrugged his shoulders in disgust. 'Goot, then, if you want to speak to her, go on, while we watch. If you hear a shot, stop speaking and come back. I will have the horses ready. And take no gun; it will cumber you if you have to run. The shooting you can leave to us.'

6

When Kaspar got to Rudolf's, he found Aletta sitting on the wall of the kraal with her knees drawn up to her chin, her legs clasped in her arms. She was above him, and he could see the sky between her arms and legs . . . a diamond of blue sky broken by the quick curve of her breast. His heart beat faster as he looked at the soft curve of her body outlined against the sky. It looked as it would feel. It was strange how from the look of a thing one knew how it would be to touch it. It was as if one had eyes in one's hands. Some things he never tired of touching; other things he hated to touch.

Aletta moved uncomfortably. Kaspar stood still. To look at her was enough. When he had looked more, he would go forward and take her in his arms. He wanted to hold her high, to toss her up like a child, to kiss her bare feet and her breasts. He would have liked to possess her, yet the thought of possessing her made him sick in the pit of the stomach. It was impossible that she had ever lain in his arms. It was impossible that this girl sitting so composed and thoughtful on the wall of Rudolf's kraal had allowed him to love her. Was there everything between them, or was there nothing? A great doubt swept over him.

'Letta!' he called gently. 'Letta!'

She slipped off the wall and faced him.

'Kaspar!' she said. 'How did you get here? What are you doing?' She looked round. 'Is it safe?'

'I had to see you before I left,' he said.

'I knew if you were not hurt, you would come back,' Aletta said.

Kaspar turned his head.

'But you are hurt' — she touched his cheek with her finger. It was black-scabbed and inflamed and swollen. He would carry the mark of his wound till he died.

'I have come back,' he said.

'Did you get the puppy?' she asked. The puppy meant nothing. He had gone to get a puppy. It was something to say. Her mind was busy with his wound. He might have been killed, she thought. 'Father Frederik dead!' she said. 'In two days everything is changed.'

He put his arms round her. 'Ja, Letta, all is changed.'

'Nee, Kaspar, not all.'

'You still love me?' Kaspar asked. 'I am no longer rich. I am no longer free to come and go. I have killed a man. I am hunted. There will be money on my head.'

Aletta put her arms round him. 'I have not changed,' she said.

Aletta said she had not changed, but everything else was changed. Today if a bird rose suddenly from a bush, he must feel for his gun. Today had no connection with yesterday, and there might be no tomorrow. This surely was what his life would be from now on, an endeavour to secure the uncertainties of each tomorrow, the life of a vagabond living from hand to mouth, from hour to hour. His arms were round Aletta, his hands on her breasts.

'What are you going to do?' she asked.

'I came to say good-bye. I felt that I must see you again. I did not know ...' he stammered.

'You did not know? What was it you did not know?'

'That you would still ...' He hesitated. What had he thought? Had he really thought she would give him up? 'I do not know,' he said. 'All that I know is that I had to see you before I went.'

She swung round in his arms, hiding her face in his shirt. 'Oh, Kaspar, why did this happen?' she sobbed. Her courage had gone. Her body shook with sobs as she clung to him. 'Everything was so beautiful,' she gasped.

'Ja, it was beautiful,' Kaspar said, stroking the hair on her neck upward. On her neck her golden hair was darker. But his eyes were not on her hair. He was looking up at the mountain. Links was up there, and somewhere near-by Pierre was lying hidden, covering him with his gun.

'I must go,' he said. He held her face in his hands, tilting it up so that he could look into her eyes. 'You are sure that nothing is changed between us, Letta?'

She nodded her head. 'Nothing is changed. Nothing will ever change.'

He bent over her, pulling her in to him. Like two bows they fitted into each other, against each other, the one bent forward, the other back.

'I am going now,' Kaspar said. 'I will send news when I can. I am going to take my wagons and horses to the north. They are already over the river. When I have sold my goods for gold and ivory, I will send them back to my father. They will pass this way. After that ... after that, I do not know. But I will come back, and we are young, Letta. Before, it was opening like a flower. Now it is something that I must break open. But I will do it. Ja, Letta, I will make something of it, something for us both, if you will wait.'

'I will wait,' she said, and bent to touch her foot so that Kaspar should not see her cry again. I am a Boer woman, she thought fiercely, biting her lip. Boer women do not cry.

Kaspar felt awkward. He did not know how to go. As she stooped in front of him, he looked at the parting of her hair. The skin showed very white where the hair was pulled away from it. The parting was a thin white line drawn down the centre of her head. He touched it with his finger and she stood up. This woman was flesh of his flesh, bone of his bone. They had been one. How could he leave her? 'I cannot go,' he said. His lip began to tremble. Magtig, he was going to cry. A man of twenty years going to cry in front of a woman!

Now it was Aletta who had to persuade him.

'You must go, Kaspar,' she said. 'You must go.' She spoke gently as though he were a child, as though she were asking him to go into the garden and bring in some earth apples. She was surprised at the effect her words had on him — at the way he became calm and stopped trembling. His arm closed round her, crushing her to him savagely; his shoulders went back, he swung her off her feet as his mouth found hers, pressing it. She could not breathe. She did not care if she could not breathe, if she were broken in his grasp. Kaspar was holding her. He loved her. He lowered her to the ground. 'I will go now,' he said.

7

Stephanie had watched Kaspar come. She was angry. What did he see in Aletta? It was no good saying he was only a boy, that he was stupid. She hated seeing him with Aletta. No one had ever noticed Aletta before. And Kaspar was rich; he still had his horses and his wagons loaded with goods. If he would take me with him, she thought. If only I could make him take me with him. Hiding herself, she waited for him.

'Kaspar!' she said.

'Stephanie! What are you doing here?'

'I was waiting for you. I wanted to see you. I had to see you before you left,' she whispered, coming closer to him. 'Don't you understand?'

'I do not understand,' Kaspar said, trying to shake her off. 'I must get on. I must go, Stephanie. They are waiting for me.'

'You had time for Letta.'

'It was Letta I came to see.'

'And me? Am I nothing?'

Kaspar looked at her angrily. 'What is it you want?' he asked.

'What does a woman want of a man, Kaspar? You are a man now,' she whispered, putting her mouth up to his ear. 'Take me with you, Kaspar.' She clung to him, thrusting herself against him. 'Take me, Kaspar. I will do anything you want, only take me.' Her hands strayed over him as he held her. Suddenly he kissed her, not as he had kissed Aletta, but hard, bearing down on her mouth as if it were a fruit. Stephanie lay still in his arms. She had known she could do this with him. I can do this to any man, she thought, closing her eyes. He slackened his hold, pulling his arms back so that she almost fell. 'What is it?' she asked. 'Is someone coming?'

'Ja, what is it?' he asked. 'What was it you almost made me do?'

'Made you do?' she laughed. 'And didn't you want to? Was I wrong when I said you were a man?'

'You were wrong if that is what you think of men.'

'Nee, I am not wrong when I speak of men, only of boys. I do not understand boys. Boys whose eyes are full of tears. Boys who are afraid.' She still held him.

'Let me go, Stephanie.'

'Let you go! Do you think I would try to hold you? Did you think I was serious? Why, it was just a joke. A joke between me and Letta. It was a wager we had between us.' Stephanie laughed again. 'You cannot know how dull life is here, and if we did not have our little jokes, how would we live? We drew lots, Kaspar, as to which of us should have you first, and Letta won. We pulled straws and you were the short straw that Letta pulled.'

'Harlot!'

'Ja, Kaspar. Both harlots. There is nothing to choose between us, except that one is fair and the other dark. So, go on your way and come back when you are grown up.'

He forced his way past her. 'Pierre!' he shouted. 'Pierre, where are you?'

Stephanie stared after him. Surely he had not believed her? Surely he had seen into her heart and known that her words were lies, spoken only for contradiction. It was all Aletta's fault. She hated Aletta. Kaspar could have taken her away.

CHAPTER XIV

A BOW DRAWN

I

AGAIN Kaspar slept in the hills, saw the horses silhouetted against the sky, listened to them cropping the grass and to their sudden starts. He lay on his back staring at the stars. He tried to reconstruct the patterns of the constellations in the sky. There was a book at home in which they were joined by thin white lines into the figures they were named after, but he could see nothing. He could only think of Aletta. He rolled over on his side. The ground was hard and stony. Sleep would not come. It would be weeks before he saw her again, and Stephanie had spoilt their parting. The silken cord of his love, that had drawn him back to Rudolf's, that had sent him to Frederik's, that had, by his being there, caused a British soldier to die of his bullet, was smirched.

Suddenly he wondered what the man's name was. That was something he would never know. Nothing was left him now but his belief in God, and the knowledge that God was trying him beyond his strength. Perhaps God was back in Cape Town. Up here He seemed distant; a strange, inscrutable God. Why had He caused old Frederik and the soldier to be killed? And why had he, when he had come to get a puppy, been thrown into the battle? He thought of the ant struggling in the slippery sand of the ant lion's hole: of its slipping, of its final engulfment. He felt himself an ant that struggled in the sliding sands of a pit. But he would get out. These people, to whom he was now tied, had knowledge of many things. He would learn from them all, even from the meanest slave. If he must live this life, he would live it fully. He had not wanted this. It had been thrust upon him.

When dawn broke, he had not slept, but he was no longer tired. He was consumed with energy. He would go on into the very heart of whatever life might bring. He was young and strong. He had wagons, goods, and horses. He had men who would stand by him and strange wild friends. His back was turned to the south forever. What remained for him was to be found beyond the mountains, beyond the plains they were going to cross. He had new courage, begotten of his despair.

2

When they came to the camp by the river, Kaspar had not spoken to Links or to Pierre. Their bawdy jokes had been received with such a look of anger that they had attempted no further familiarities. His anxious, dreamy expression of yesterday had gone. His eyes were sombre. 'Before God,' Links said to Pierre, 'I do not know what happened down there, but he even sits differently upon his horse.' It was true, there was now no sympathy between Kaspar and his borrowed mount. He rode him hard, with a heavy hand on the bit. He was possessed by a new passion for mastery, by a desire to get on, to see what there was to see and to ride through anything that opposed him.

Kaspar pulled his horse onto its haunches as he came to the wagons.

'What is it, Baas?' Frans asked.

'What is it?' Kaspar said. 'It is nothing, Frans, save that we will move on at once. Where is Afrikander?'

'I am here. So the little cock is growing his spurs.' Afrikander's mouth opened, splitting his face into two as he smiled. His yellow teeth were set like beans into his pink gums, and he laughed till he rocked on his bow legs. 'So we move,' he said. 'The little cock says we move.' He came nearer. 'Listen, little cock, crow as loud as you will on your own dunghill — it lies there.' He pointed back across the river. 'Crow there, and your neck will soon be wrung. This' — he made a gesture — 'is my dunghill. But all the same, I like to hear you. It is a good sign, and if you want to go, we can. The brown horse is in. He is not hurt. Inspan!' he shouted. 'We trek at once.'

Afrikander's men began to saddle their horses. The oxen were brought in, water-bottles filled, and the priming of the guns looked to.

'Ride in front, Pierre, with Links,' Afrikander said.

They cantered forward. When they had gone four hundred yards, they slowed to a walk. 'Now, you!' Afrikander sent a pair of men to the right flank, another to the left. 'We will go with the wagons,' he said to Kaspar; 'the horses and spare oxen will follow with your men and the rest of mine in the rear.'

Kaspar was interested in the way Afrikander's men took up their stations, unslinging their guns and riding with them across their thighs. These folk knew their business. If they could neither read nor write, they knew their work as soldiers and hunters. He wondered what they had been. Behind each of them was a past which had led them, step by step, to the life that they now led. These, except for Afrikander and Links, were ordinary Griqua Bastards, but others, from what he had heard, were white men — soldiers and sailors, deserters, criminals and adventurers. He would meet them later.

A thousand thoughts occupied his mind as they drifted north over the mountains towards the desert plains. Every day was the same. They advanced over the same kind of country, in the same formation, at the same speed. He found himself caught up in the routine, in the slow rhythm of their marching, halting, outspanning, and inspanning. It was like what he had known all the way up from the Cape, but it was not the same, for this was not a peaceful country that they rode through so quietly, and the men who rode were not farmers visiting or travelling; they were the offscourings of Africa, the scum of it that had risen to the Border.

3

The mountains were behind them. They were now riding deeper and deeper into a land forbidden to white men. No trade, no intercourse was allowed here, but the law was distant and weak and great ranges lay between the seats of the lawgivers and those to whom it was given. The Governor had said that the roving of the Boers must be checked and that there must be an end to this infiltration; and so, on paper, by a legislative device it had been ended, stopped, by a line drawn on a map. The river was the boundary. But those born and reared on the Border continued to move forward and to trade and to hunt, as they had always done.

Kaspar tried not to look back at the mountains that lay along the horizon behind him. He had come to know them and to realise their significance. Across them, hazardously, came the few comforts from the coast. Across them with equal hazard, and only upon occasion, came the voice of authority. Till the death of Frederik Bezuidenhout, the Berg had been a division between two kinds of men, two kinds of life, at once a menace and a comfort to those that inhabited them.

With prayers and curses the heavy wagons, double-spanned, lumbered over the passes, outward bound, with hides, butter, soap, and biltong. Over them again they lumbered back, with as many prayers and curses, homeward bound, with lead, powder, and wrought goods that the Boers were unable to manufacture. What could not come from the coast on the wagons did not come. Hard mountains, a strain equally to man and beast, but on the whole a welcome barrier, an insurance of privacy, and here, between and beyond the ranges, a life was led by farmers enured to hardship, that they called free. What had they asked of the Government? They had asked that it should appoint local officials, issue them ammunition, and leave them free to attend to their vast inland frontier. This was all they asked: that they might be allowed to lead a quiet life free from taxation and the petty worries of an administration that was unsympathetic to their interests, that thought of them as wild, uncultured folk in need of discipline. And what had they received? A check to their freedom: the death of one of their number and the threat of the enforcement of new taxes. Kaspar was done with the south and the law. It was behind him. Now he was beyond even the land of the border Boers.

4

The sparse trees stood almost leafless, twisted as though warped by the heat of the sun; the grass was harsh and tus-socky, burnt up by perpetual drought. Yet, as they went on, Kaspar was astonished at the amount of game he saw and at the excellence of his companions' shooting. They only shot what they needed and did it casually, without dismounting. They made long marches, from water to water. To the west, Afrikander said, there was no water at all, and the only buck that could live there were those which could go waterless for long periods — springbok, hartebeeste, eland, and gemsbok.

This was the Bushman country. It had a life of its own, a static, indestructible, untameable life. The plains stretched away into the horizon — a sea of yellow grass, limitless, undulating in vast, gentle waves, spotted and blotched by the herds of game that drifted over them — wildebeeste, quagga, blesbok, and springbok: springbok in unbelievable, countless numbers which suddenly, for no apparent reason, began to pronk, leaping with arched backs into the air. In the sunlight they were white as they jumped, like bucking horses, with their noses tucked in, almost touching their hoofs, and the long white hair of their maned backs extended in a wide fan. Each buck as he leaped, with his feet drawn together, turned into a bounding disk, and there were hundreds of such disks. One would start, and the others follow, till the plain was full of them, all bounding up, landing, and leaping again almost before their small hoofs touched the ground — jumping straight or sideways, swinging about, swaying this way and that, like dancers independent of the ground. Sometimes the game was still, grazing as peacefully as herds of cattle; at others it was as if they were infected by a madness. The swart wildebeeste would gallop like squadrons of wild horses, their long white tails flowing as they wheeled and charged. Prancing, they swept in all directions, striking fiercely at each other with their curved horns, or drop to their knees in mimic combat, scattering the herds of quagga that ran with them. From absolute calm, the veld, as this happened, would become a swirl of moving beasts, of charging wildebeeste, leaping springbok, snorting quagga; of ostriches with fluffed plumes, trotting as fast as a horse could gallop; of herds of white-faced blesbok, their bodies a metallic purple, galloping with their heads low into the wind. And nowhere, even when the game was still, was there any rest for the eyes, nothing on which to focus them in this trembling immensity. The air quivered with heat above the parched, cracked soil on which the game came and went, moving in an orderless, endless pattern, distorted by continuous mirage, till they resembled the fabulous monsters of which one read.

Kaspar's head ached. His eyeballs felt as if they would burst from their sockets. At intervals he rose in his stirrups to disengage his trousers that were stuck to his legs with

sweat. Coenraad's men were used to it. They rode un-
complainingly, with their heads drooping over their horses'
necks. The heat was something to push against. It had a
malignant power. It struck from above and rose up again, in
waves, from below. Day after day it went on. The only
change was that the men slung their guns. The barrels were
too hot to hold. The dogs walked behind the wagons with
extended tongues. The draft oxen pulled with glazed eyes.

Kaspar saw Pierre pull up his horse and reach for his gun.
Everyone halted and unslung his gun.

Afrikander leant over to Kaspar. 'He has seen something,
or he has smelt it.'

The lumbering wagons drew up and some of the oxen lay
down in the yoke. For what seemed an hour the little caravan
was frozen into utter stillness. Then Pierre swung his horse
and raised his gun. He hesitated, brought the gun to his
shoulder, and bent his head over the butt. He is going to fire,
Kaspar thought. He could see nothing. A herd of wildebeeste cantered by in a cloud of dust. They turned suddenly,
wheeling into the cloud they had raised. A puff of smoke
came from Pierre's gun. As the shot shattered the stillness
of the veld, two Bushmen broke cover, a man carrying a
small bow, and a woman with a child on her hip; they had
been lying flat in the grass and ran, twisting and turning like
duikers. Links fired and the woman came down. Two others
fired, but missed. Witvoet and Wolf dashed in pursuit.

'Call off your dogs!' Afrikander shouted. 'Call them off
or they will be killed.'

Kaspar saw the running man fit an arrow to his bow.
His dogs returned reluctantly.

'Why do we not chase them?' Kaspar asked.

'It is not our business to chase them,' Afrikander said.
'And how do we know how many there are?' He looked
worried. 'Never chase a Bushman,' he said, 'especially if
you are alone.'

Pierre had ridden up to the tuft of grass at which he had

fired. He laughed and pointed downward. 'He has got one,'
Afrikander said. Links rode towards the woman he had shot.
The heavy bullet had gone through the child and, smashing
the woman's back, had come out between her breasts. He dismounted. His horse smelt the body and backed away. Links
dragged him forward, bent over the dead woman, took a necklace of ostrich-egg beads from her neck, and turned her over
with his foot. 'She was a young woman,' he said. 'It is
a pity we did not get her alive.' He swung the necklace round
and round on his finger. 'Here,' he said to Kaspar, who had
ridden up, 'you can have it.' He tossed it to him. Kaspar
caught it. The crumpled figure was no larger than a child,
and the child, that still clung with tiny hands to its mother's
back, no bigger than a monkey. Its eyes were closed. Its
little mouth was open, drooling blood. The woman's feet
were only a little longer than a man's finger. Kaspar turned
his horse and cantered over to Pierre. The man he had shot
lay in a pool of blood; half his head was blown away. He
was naked except for a loincloth of skin and a short cloak of
springbok hide. Over his shoulder he had a bag; it had contained his weapons, fire-sticks, and trinkets. These were
scattered. And on his belt, attached to it by thongs, were
five pots made from the outer core of springbok horns.

Kaspar dismounted to examine them. They contained
pigments — red, brown, yellow, white, and black. The man
had been an artist. Links had told him that among the
Bushmen there were many painters.

Pierre reloaded his gun and stroked it caressingly. 'I saw
his eyes,' he said to Kaspar. 'I saw them shine through the
grass, and I shot between them.'

'I do not like it,' Afrikander said. 'We are at peace with
the Bushmen. I do not like it at all. Now we shall have to
pas op; they will want revenge.' He stared to the north. 'We
are going to have to hurry. Ride with your guns ready,' he
said to his men, 'and you' — he turned to Kaspar — 'issue
guns to your people. Keep the horses nearer' — he looked

at the little herd grazing behind them — 'and your boys are going to have to drive. If we kill some oxen, we kill them. There are plenty of oxen in the world. Ja, vragtig, the world is full of oxen. Now trek!'

Kaspar was astonished at the concern he saw on the faces round him. 'What can they do?' he asked. 'What can little men like that do against us, and why do you fear them when you cared nothing for the soldiers?'

'Soldiers!' Afrikander spat contemptuously. 'What are soldiers? But these people are different; they do not know fear, and this country' — he swept his arm around — 'is full of them. Come back, Martinus!' he shouted. 'Come back, you fool!'

Martinus had ridden forward to do a little scouting on his own. He was not more than five hundred yards away.

'Come back!' Afrikander shouted again. 'Before God, it is as I thought. It has begun.'

As Martinus turned his horse, two little figures sprang up between him and the commando. He swerved and galloped hard. Coenraad's men started towards him. 'Stop!' Afrikander said. 'He must manage for himself.'

Kaspar could not understand his anxiety. Martinus was armed and mounted; he was swinging out in an arc that would bring him back to them after a gallop of half a mile. But he did not seem able to pull away from his pursuers. They clung, like dogs, to his horse's heels. Just as Martinus began to gain, another Bushman sprang out of the grass. Kaspar saw him bend his little bow. Martinus turned his horse again; swinging it round, he raised his gun and fired. The Bushman flung up his arms and fell.

'That was a fine shot,' Kaspar said.

Afrikander said nothing, but his thick lips were tightly compressed. 'Look, jong,' he said suddenly, 'and learn. It is the end.'

Martinus was reloading frantically, galloping with slack reins, as he poured powder into the barrel of his gun. Kaspar

saw his hand moving up and down as he rammed it. He was
feeling for a bullet now. And then Kaspar saw what Afrikander meant: the Bushmen behind him had increased their
speed. They were running up on either side of him. With
his gun unloaded, Martinus was at their mercy. It was
incredible that men could move so fast — faster than a horse
could gallop. They were overhauling him. Halting suddenly,
they raised their bows. Martinus clapped his hand to his
cheek and pulled up.

'He is dead,' Afrikander said.

The Bushmen, completely at their ease, shot again, and
then, without another look, trotted away.

Martinus turned his head to stare after them. Then he
rode slowly back. The arrow had fallen from his cheek, but
the poisoned barb was in it. His face was the colour of dirty
paper.

'I am a dead man,' he said.

His companions nodded their heads. 'Ja, you are dead,'
they said.

'Is there nothing we can do?' Kaspar asked, as he watched
Afrikander pull out the barb. 'Can you not cut the flesh?'

'There's nothing to do,' Afrikander said. 'He will die in
an hour. Get into the wagon, Martinus. You will be better
there.'

In an hour Martinus was dead. His horse died in the
night.

CHAPTER XV

A TOOTH FOR A TOOTH

I

THE days that followed were a nightmare of driving by day and of watching, with the horses tied to the wagon-wheels, by night. Everyone was nervous. They felt themselves watched, but saw nothing. Afrikander raged in vain. He had lost one of his best men, but could do nothing to avenge him. Nor did he know how Coenraad would receive him. Coenraad did not like having his men killed and would be angry at having trouble with the Bushmen, with whom he had been at some pains to remain at peace. Talking to Kaspar, Afrikander fluctuated between long tales of his own exploits, ill-concealed fears of what Coenraad would say, and terrifying stories of the Bushmen. He told Kaspar of a big drive against them farther south, and of how they had driven them out of that country into the mountains and killed them. He told of their cruelties, their powers of endurance, and of how, above all others, they hated the tame Bushmen that the Boers had among them. For all his boasting, Kaspar knew him to be afraid of these little people, who, unconquerable, clung to their hunting grounds until they died.

Half asleep, he rode at Afrikander's side, listening to

his voice and watching, with strained, bloodshot eyes, every rock or clump of grass that might conceal an enemy. Tired as he was, he knew himself to be ready to fight. The part of him that was asleep was the human part. The man in him was all but dead from exhaustion, but the animal was awake. His nervousness was communicated to his horse. Tigernek, refusing to walk, crab-stepped unceasingly, tossed his head, and kept reaching for his bit. Finer drawn, his eyes more prominent in his lean head, his ears quicker to move as he cocked them, his mane and tail longer and more unkempt, Tigernek was no longer a race-horse but a horse of war.

Man and horse were one. The days they had spent to-gether had made them very close to each other. The young stallion now followed Kaspar when he dismounted, walking behind him and nuzzling his back. He came like a dog to a whistle, and at night would stand over him, touching his face with soft lips. The saddle had become Kaspar's home. He sat on it all day. He slept with his head on it at night.

Twice Afrikander showed him where Bushmen had slept, nests made in low bushes. They had pulled down the branches in the centre, weaving them, as birds did, and lining them with grass.

Kaspar had lost all count of time when Afrikander pointed to a thin film of smoke to the north. It was scarcely visible against the sky.

'Is it the camp?' Kaspar asked.

Afrikander nodded. 'Ja, we are nearly home.'

The men straightened themselves in their saddles and set their hats sideways. The trek was almost over.

'Magtig, I am glad,' Afrikander said. He sighed with relief.

The column closed in on the wagons, the men riding in pairs round it, before and behind. Links and Pierre remained in front. Then came Kaspar with Afrikander.

They had been seen, and soon a party of mounted men cantered towards them, firing their guns in salutation.

Afrikander's men fired their pieces in return as the new-comers, increasing their speed, galloped past, wheeled, and joined them. They were led by a white man who rode up to Kaspar and swept off his hat. He was very small, gaudily dressed, and overmounted on a big black horse that he only succeeded in managing by means of a heavy bit.

'Welcome, meneer. Welcome.' Leaning out of the saddle, he extended his hand. 'I am Kaptein Alexander,' he said. His hand was small and cold. 'We have been expecting you for some days. It is an honour to meet you, meneer. You may have heard men speak of me,' he went on. 'Did you hear my name? It is Alexander: Caesar Alexander. Both famous names, meneer, and apt.' He relapsed into silence while Kaspar looked at him in astonishment. Perhaps he was considering how aptly he was named, for till they got to the camp he was silent, sitting perched on his great black horse.

Kaspar had never thought of what Coenraad's camp would be like: events had pressed too hardly, one upon the heels of the other, for this. It had been an objective; a place where he would be able to rest. The village was concealed by a fold in the ground, so that until you rode into it it was invisible. It consisted of one long straggling street of huts and cottages, built of unburnt brick, with small kraals behind them. As the wagons rolled down the wide road between the houses, people ran out shouting. Children trotted beside them, dogs barked. Afrikander's men and those who had joined them fired their guns, and the oxen, excited by the noise, shied from one side of the road to the other. A woman dived almost under Tigernek's hoofs to snatch up a naked child who, ignoring everyone, still played in the road. Kaptein Alexander rode in front of the procession, making his horse prance as he spurred and held it. His plumed hat was over one eye, his right hand was on his hip. In the middle of the village the road opened out into a wide outspan or parade ground. Here Kaptein Alexander wheeled his men, and the wagons, following him, swung into line and pulled up.

There was a shout as Coenraad and van Ek rode up.

'Welcome, Kaspar!' Coenraad shouted. 'I am glad to see you.' His eyes swept over the assembled crowd. He smiled. 'We are all brothers here,' he said.

Van Ek dismounted from his dun and took Kaspar's hand. 'So what I feared has happened,' he said. 'You are caught up in the tide.'

Coenraad looked at Kaspar's cheek. 'You are wounded.' He looked closer. 'Before God, I was right,' he said; 'you are lucky. A little lower and your jaw would have been shattered. A little higher and you would have lost an eye.'

'It was at Frederik's,' Kaspar said. 'He is killed.'

'We heard about it,' Coenraad said.

'How did you hear?'

'We have ways.' Coenraad looked at the convoy and the commando beside it. 'You are a man short, Andries,' he said. 'Where is Martinus?'

'Martinus is dead.'

'Dead? How did he die?'

'He was killed by a Bushman.'

'A Bushman!' Coenraad roared. 'Before God, it is enough. This time it is finished.' He jerked his chestnut into a rear. Up and down it plunged, bucketing and jumping under him while he swore and shouted: 'Allemain ... Where is Allemain? Magtig, what is this place that no man is ever ready when I call? Allemain! Allemain! By the living God, where is he?'

From a near-by house a man came running. Without putting his foot in the stirrup he leapt onto a waiting horse. 'You called me?' he said. On his back, fastened by a tattered silken rope, he carried a long silver trumpet.

'Ja, I called! Sound the alarm! Sound it till you burst your lungs, and we'll see if the whole world sleeps or if they can be stirred into some semblance of life. Sound it till the devils of hell come running.'

Kaptein Alexander, drawing his sword, formed up his

men. Without haste, Allemain turned his horse, looked at the reed of his trumpet, moistened it, and fitted it to his lips.

Shrill and clear, heart-breakingly sweet, the call rang out. Like a bird taking flight the sound swung over the thatched roofs of the village. The call, a pause, the call again. Shattering all lesser noise, it rose and fell, cutting the clear air with a silver blade. The man was a trained trumpeter. Somewhere he had served with mounted troops. Kaspar had never heard a dragoon at the Cape sound a better call. A little drum began to tap slowly, then faster, into a roll and rattle. Come-come-come, it cried. A big native drum boomed heavily.

The village was an ant-heap disturbed. Men dashed out of their houses carrying saddles. Women brought food and ammunition as they girthed their horses. Guns were fired to clear them. Women screamed, horses neighed, oxen bellowed as they were inspanned. A troop of spare horses galloped down the street. Natives, armed with long shields and spears, appearing from nowhere, gathered in groups. Tame Bushmen scouts and trackers stood ready with their bows. Ten minutes after the first call, Coenraad's men were ready: of every colour, of every nationality, variously mounted on every kind of horse, variously armed and accoutred, they surged in rough squadrons about their leaders.

Coenraad raised his hand. There was silence. The only sound was the clink of metal on metal, the trampling of the restless horses, and the wailing of Martinus' woman. She stood outside her house, crying and wringing her hands.

'Martinus is dead,' Coenraad said. 'He has been killed by Bushmen. This time we will make a clean sweep. This time we will smoke the hornets from their nest. It is said that an eye should pay for an eye, but I say a hundred eyes will not be enough. We start tomorrow. Be ready.'

The men disbanded. Coenraad turned in his saddle. 'I am glad you lost no horses, Kaspar,' he said. 'There are more good men than good horses here' — he shrugged his shoulders. 'But we will talk later when this is over. You had best come with us. You will learn something of war and the ways of those who live beyond the river.' Raising his hand, he drove his spurs into his horse.

2

During the afternoon Kaspar had time to consider the village. The women were more numerous than the men; no doubt Coenraad had seen to this. In such a place all must have women or none must, and he found promiscuity to be punished, not for moral reasons, but because of the discord created when one man interfered with another's woman. A few of the men were white, but the women were Griqua Bastards, Malays from the Cape, Bushwomen, and Kaffirs. Most of them were young, most had children or were with child; but it was the men that interested him most. Scarred in mind or body, they were blemished men who, unable to hide their disfigurements, bragged of them. Some had their backs furrowed with the calluses of old floggings; some had the galls of manacles on their wrists or ankles which, festering, had never wholly healed. Tousled, or dangerously clean, they stood about the camp in groups as they cleaned their arms, mended saddlery, and packed such things as they needed for the expedition, while their women carried water, cooked, nursed their children, and quarrelled with high-pitched voices.

These were the folk he had heard spoken of. Evil folk, all wanted by the Government on one charge or another: murderers, runaways, deserters. Men who, if they were taken, would be hanged. But they would not be taken. About them all, slinking or arrogant, there was an air of savage intractability. Under such a leader as Coenraad and living as they did near mountains filled with native allies, nothing less than an army could subdue them. By the very severity of the measures it had taken against them, the Law had created this force against itself. A man must be hard-pressed to join them. Kaspar thought of Coenraad's smile when he had said, 'We are all brothers here.' Brothers in desperation. His presence was accepted. They had evidently heard of him. To them, he thought, I am not Kaspar van der Berg. I am the young man who has killed a soldier.

There was no refinement here; no tempering of angers that flamed up furiously in simple arguments whose conclusion was often a shot. Men talked with their hands on the butts of the horse pistols in their belts, sat down to eat with knives that were daggers; yet they were competent in all that they did, as close-knit as a pack of hounds, as ready as hounds to combine in running down their prey, and only quarrelling over the kill. They were as suited to the lives they led as lions or as leopards to theirs. There was little feeling of colour among them, and Kaspar realised what the white men must have gone through before they lived on terms of equality with black. Men ruined by an accident or some chance injustice. These were the worst, nursing their vengeance like venom within them. Kaspar thought of Aletta. As long as he clung to her, he would be safe. She was an anchor for his thoughts. It was not Aletta but circumstance that had betrayed him.

He watched a man splicing a broken saddle-tree with green hide. He worked beautifully, whipping the thin strip round and round evenly, and finishing it so neatly that there was no sign of a joint. When he had done, he looked up and held out his hand.

'I am Jim Jeffries,' he said.

'You are English?' Kaspar asked.

'Yes, I am English. I am a sailor.'

This was a strange place to find a sailor. It was strange, too, to talk English again. The last time he had spoken it was to Lord Charles Somerset, the Governor. His Excellency had asked him about one of his father's horses that was for sale.

'You are coming with us?' Jeffries asked.

'Yes,' said Kaspar.

'Then I will see you tomorrow. Perhaps you will talk with me. It is good to talk English again.'

As Kaspar passed one of the houses, someone called his name: 'Meneer van der Berg.'

It was Selina. She was standing at the door of a hut. She looked well and the child was fat and smiling.

'So you are here too, meneer,' she said.

'Ja, I am here.'

She seemed pleased to see him, and he was glad to see a familiar face.

'It is good that you are safe,' he said.

'I am safe, but it was a hard journey, meneer, and it would have been easier if you had come with me. I nearly stole your horse,' she added, laughing.

'I could not come. I had to wait to see the end.'

'The end is not yet come,' said Selina. 'Nee, it is in my heart that my old Frederik's spirit walks. He is not at peace. He should have been laid with his wife. We have had word about the burial. He brought it' — she pointed to an old Kaffir who squatted in the shade.

He looked up. 'Greeting, young man. Yes, it was I who brought the word. It was I who prophesied to the white men, giving them the fruits of my wisdom for nothing. I am Ringhals, whom some call the Little Flower. I am the clash of spear against shield, the forerunner of the rushing wings. I come before the aasvoels.' He turned his eyes on Selina. 'I have taken her under my wing. She is a small bird over which I crouch. She is the little bird of the Little Flower.'

He was a very small old man, and very dirty.

'I do not understand what he says, but he is very wise,' Selina said. 'We came on the road together. Without him I might have died; and he has found me a man.' Her face lit up. 'Ja, meneer, he has found me a young man who is very beautiful and kind. It is a pity that he is so silent.'

'Silent?' Kaspar said.

'Ja, meneer, he never speaks. They call him "Silent Willem."'

Ringhals looked up. 'It is better to speak too little than too much,' he said. 'Can the moon speak, or the stars?' he added. 'If he becomes angry he will beat her, but he will say nothing. She will forget her bruises. Words are not forgotten. Words bruise the soul. They are burnt into the heart forever. A woman's back is fat; it heals quickly and her cries die in the air. Have you a big coat, young man?' he asked.

'Ja, I have a big coat,' Kaspar said.

'Then take it with you tomorrow when you ride out.'

'It is hot,' Kaspar said. 'My horse blanket is enough.'

'It is better to be hot than dead. Ai . . . the dead are very cold. They never grow warm again. I am tired, and would sleep.' He leant back against the wall and waved them away.

'I will see you again,' Kaspar said to Selina.

'Ja, meneer, you will see me. This is my place.'

Ringhals opened his eyes. 'You will see me also,' he said. 'If you give me tobacco, I will watch over you.'

Kaspar gave him tobacco.

'The lost ones will watch over you. And take your coat — the biggest one you have.' His chin dropped onto his chest and he closed his eyes.

Selina and Kaspar looked at each other. 'He is very wise,' she said. 'He is a great wizard.'

The old man opened his eyes. 'I am the greatest wizard,' he said, 'the father of a multitude of wizards. I am a herd of elephants. I am a buffalo, a black-maned lion, a . . .' His chin dropped and he began to snore.

'I think he is tired,' said Selina. 'He has drunk much beer and it makes him tired.'

As Kaspar went back to his wagons, he saw a herd of fat oxen being driven south by two mounted men. One of them was Jeffries. They waved to each other. Kaspar wondered where they were going. It seemed odd that with the Bushmen disturbed they should be sent towards their country with so small an escort, and he would miss the Englishman tomorrow. He had been looking forward to talking to him.

Van Ek was waiting for him at the wagons. He sat on a stool while the puppy, rolling at his feet, tugged at his trousers.

'In a little while you have seen much, Kaspar van der Berg,' he said.

'I have seen much, Oom Christiaan,' Kaspar said bitterly. 'Seen much, done much, lost much.' He was pleased to see the old man. He had thought of him a great deal and he needed counsel. He sat down on the ground and the puppy came over to him. He turned her over and scratched her belly with his finger.

'What is she called?' van Ek asked.

'Nothing as yet,' Kaspar said. 'I have found no name for her.'

'That is good. Never be in haste to name a dog or a horse — their names come by themselves. One day or another a name will come. Neither be in haste to name an event as good or bad. For the outcome of any event is uncertain.'

'And what of God?' Kaspar asked. 'Do you not believe in God?'

'I do not believe in God, Kaspar. Why should I? What has God done for me that I should believe?'

Kaspar was astonished that van Ek was not struck down for such a blasphemy. How could one doubt God and live? And surely good could be told from evil.

'But you must believe in something.'

'Ja, I believe in life everlasting,' van Ek said. 'I believe in it, for I have seen it. I see it all the time before my eyes. Look there'—he pointed to a bone lying near the wheel of the wagon. 'That is the leg bone of a buck. The meat has been eaten off it by men. In the night a wolf may come and crack it for the marrow it contains, and the ants will finish the fragments he leaves. In the end all of that bone will go back into the ground, causing grass to grow. A buck will eat the grass, a man shoot the buck, or it will be killed by a lion, and then it all begins again. That is life everlasting.' He knocked out his pipe on the side of the stool and refilled it.

'And what of justice?' Kaspar asked.

'What is justice? And to whom? I know nothing of justice. I know blind chance. I know accident. I have seen the good perish and the evil flourish as green bay trees. How can a God who is concerned with all things equally favour one to the detriment of another? How can He care equally for the destroyed and the destroyer? — the buck and the leopard?'

Kaspar was perturbed. 'Then what is the reason of it all?' he asked. 'Why are we here?'

'I do not know. Surely it is enough that we are here. Nee, I think the causes are beyond the understanding of men, and such explanations as men have they have invented. They are toys well fitted to the littleness of those who believe them, but meaningless in reality — if indeed there be reality. Thoughts and explanations are all tricks of the mind whereby we gull ourselves into calmness, lull ourselves into thinking that all is for the best, that all will come right in the end. It is of those things of which men know least that they are most certain, Kaspar, and to these straws they cling with all their might.'

Some men came up carrying guns. 'Are you ready, Oom Christiaan?' they asked.

'Ja, I am ready. Set up the bones.'

From a carcass near-by a Kaffir collected the rib bones of an ox. One of the newcomers paced out a hundred yards and the Kaffir drove the bones into the ground with a stone. They stood up like a line of thin white ninepins. Taking a gun from the man nearest to him, van Ek loaded it and fired.

'High and left,' he said. Pulling a small file from his pocket, he adjusted the sight and fired again.

Satisfied, he reloaded and went on firing. Each bullet hit a rib bone fair and square till, of the ten set up, not one remained standing. He gave the gun back to its owner.

'Is that good enough?' he asked.

'Before God, it is good enough,' the man said.

Van Ek took another gun; more ribs were fetched. Quietly and precisely the old man checked the sights of each gun handed to him and shot down the bones as fast as they were set up. No one expressed surprise. They were accustomed to his skill.

'It is wonderful,' Kaspar said when van Ek put the last gun down.

'It is nothing,' the old man said. 'It is something that I have learnt to do. I have shot much,' he added. 'Come, let us go to Coenraad and see what he is doing.'

Coenraad was busy. No longer blustering, he sat with a map and a small book in front of him, talking quietly, explaining and planning the details of the raid to Kaptein Alexander and Andries Afrikander. He spoke calmly of what they would do, spoke as if he were discussing the operations of a farm — a harvest or a reaping. There were questions of arms, of reserves, of cattle to be driven on the hoof, of water supplies. Sometimes Afrikander offered a suggestion, but for the most part he stood silent, watching Coenraad. What was he thinking? Kaspar wondered. What were they all thinking, these men who planned the extermination of a tribe so coldly? His ways were set among strange people. What had the old witch doctor meant when he said, 'Take a big coat, young man'? Pondering on all that he had seen and heard, Kaspar said good-night and left them.

His people were grouped round their fire, but instead of going to them he went straight to his wagon. Tomorrow he was going to war. To go to war seemed a natural thing to do. He was even curious about it, wondering if he would be afraid. He had little feeling one way or the other against those whom they would fight. The Bushmen were scarcely human. They stood, intermediate, between men and beasts.

He wanted Aletta. If it had not been for that dead soldier, I would be there now, he thought. But one day he would go back, no matter what happened. Each day since he had left her, new things struck at his heart. Each day some sound or scent, some sight, brought her back to him, reminding him of her till it seemed that she stood beside him so near that by stretching forth his hand he could touch her dress.

In the morning, mounted on Tigernek and accompanied by Lazarus, Kaspar fell in with others. Today there were no trumpet calls. The men sat still on their horses, their saddles loaded with food, water, and blankets. They waited coldly, with their long guns slung behind them. There were spare horses, pack-horses, and a small herd of oxen. On the flanks the Kaffir auxiliaries squatted, waiting under their captains. Coenraad and van Ek rode up. Coenraad was met by Kaptein Caesar Alexander and Afrikander.

'Is everything ready?' Coenraad asked.

'It is ready,' Alexander said.

Coenraad looked over the men and gave the order to advance. He turned his horse southwest. Riding easily and in no particular formation, the men followed him.

That night they camped twenty miles away. Kaspar was surprised that they moved so slowly. Travelling as they were without wagons, they could have covered fifty or sixty miles. He asked Afrikander why they went so slowly.

'Ja, we could have gone sixty or seventy miles,' he answered.

'That is what I am saying,' Kaspar said. 'Why do we not go faster?'

'Why? Nee, ek weet nee. But there is a reason. No doubt soon, tomorrow perhaps, we shall know it.' More than that he would not say, but smiled contentedly. 'You had better rest,' he said. 'Before we are done you will see how we can march. And tomorrow ride with me.' For three days they moved easily, but on the fourth the formation changed.

They now rode in a long single line as if they were driving game — a few horsemen, some Kaffirs armed with spears and kerries, then more horsemen and more Kaffirs; while all along the front tame Bushmen trotted, weaving back and forth with their eyes on the ground, working like spaniels as they cast this way and that.

Kaspar looked at Coenraad who was near him. He rode his big chestnut. Paying no attention to what went on, he sat loosely with his black beard sunk into his chest.

Suddenly a Bushman, who had been scouting far ahead, came running back. Coenraad galloped towards him, followed by three others. The little Bushman ran with them, keeping up easily. They pulled up. Allemain sounded a call and the line swung in a new direction. They were now going due west.

Afrikander began to laugh. 'Magtig, what a man!' he said to Kaspar. 'Look!' He pointed down.

'That is cattle spoor,' Kaspar said. 'What are cattle doing here? The only cattle...' The significance of what he saw struck him. 'Why, they must be the ones that Jeffries took.'

'Ja, they are the ones that were sent off,' Afrikander said. 'The Bushmen have got them and the trap is sprung. Did you notice the way the cattle went?' he asked.

'They went south.'

'And we went southwest to cut off their spoor.'

'They were fat cattle,' Kaspar said. 'Surely if he was going to throw them away, Coenraad would have sent the worst and not the best.'

'That is what a fool would have done. Thin cattle would have been allowed to pass through. They would have been suspect. But who would suspect fat cattle? Nee, Kaspar, you have much to learn of war and stratagem.'

'And the men who went with them?' Kaspar thought of the English sailor.

Afrikander shrugged his shoulders. 'They may be dead or

they may be back at the camp, but most likely they have waited a while and will follow the spoor when they are certain we are in front of them.'

Kaspar nodded his head. So that was it. It was not a mission he would have cared for.

Coenraad was moving his men faster now. They put up all manner of game which ran in front of them — lumbering eland, gemsbok with horns like spears, ostrich, springbok.

'Watch out, Kaspar,' Afrikander said. 'There are Bushmen all round us here.'

'I have seen nothing,' Kaspar said.

'You have seen nothing, but they are here. Look!' He showed Kaspar a depression filled with stones in the ground. 'That is a Bushman water-hole.'

'I can see no water.'

'No, but it is there.'

As they watched, one of the tame Bushmen ran up. Pulling a reed from his bag, he pushed it down into the sand between the stones and then, lying on his belly, began to suck.

'And there' — Afrikander pointed to a blur in the distance — 'is where we are going. I have heard it spoken of.'

As they rode, the blur changed from a formless mass into a rampart of granite that rose straight out of the plain.

'That,' Afrikander went on, 'is the Bushman stronghold, and they will gather round it to fight.'

'But if Coenraad knew it, why trouble with the cattle?' Kaspar asked.

'Without the cattle it might have been empty. As it is they will have assembled there to feast; it is their custom, and we shall catch them, gorged and tired from making merry.'

So this was the reason for their lack of speed. Coenraad had spread a feast for their undoing.

That night they slept fireless with double sentries. Next day they still followed the spoor of the cattle, which did not lead straight to their objective, but wound from one waterhole to another.

'By God, Coenraad is slim,' Afrikander said. 'His trick has made them lead us to water. Do you know, Kaspar,' he went on, 'that no man has been as far as we are now? And many have perished on this road for lack of water. Thin cattle, if they had taken them, they might have driven through waterless, not caring how many died, but these were too fat to go far without drinking and too good to destroy. For Bushmen love fat above all things. It was a fine plan to verneuk them.'

They marched on. There was still no great haste. But Coenraad had passed the word that if a Bushman was seen, he wanted him alive. The granite kopje was now clearly visible in its entirety. It looked like those pictures Kaspar had seen of mediaeval castles. An impregnable mass of dull-reddish rocks piled one onto the other. Coenraad sent a party of horsemen round to cut off their retreat in case the Bushmen should decide to abandon it. Then he gave the order to charge. This last stretch was covered at a hard gallop, the wide line of attackers closing in on the hill. The Kaffirs, running between them, clung to the stirrup leathers of the horsemen. Two Bushmen who had been lying on the ground sprang up in front of them. One, believing he had no chance of escape, stood up and faced them, waiting bow in hand; the other ran, but both were brought down by the Kaffirs' kerries. Leaving the prisoners to be brought up more slowly, the commando swept on. More Bushmen ran from them and were fired at, but none were hit. They reached the hill and ran like monkeys into the rocks, scrambling up them, appearing and disappearing as they threaded the face of the cliff. At the bottom of the kopje Coenraad's men drew up. There they found what was left of the cattle that had been captured. Some had been slaughtered and eaten, but many were still alive. Horribly mutilated, they milled and bellowed. Their entrails protruding from their torn bellies, hamstrung, with tails and ears cut off, eyes gouged out, they presented a terrible spectacle.

'That is true Bushmen's work,' Afrikander said. 'They are like devils.'

The wounded beasts were despatched and camp was made. Coenraad was satisfied. The Bushmen, as the spoor indicated, had come in from all round. The charge on the hill had driven more in, and they were now invested. Their stronghold was really a heap of gigantic rocks not more than a hundred yards in diameter and easy to watch. Coenraad disposed his men round it. They lit fires, and soon the smell of fat beef cooking rose into the air. Against the pale green evening sky the kopje stood out dark, ringed by fire.

The prisoners remained tied and guarded by the Kaffirs who had taken them. They had received neither food nor water. To Kaspar there had been something terrifying in this methodical advance. It was no adventure. It was like the navigation of a ship in which the actions of men were calculated and weighed like the strength of the wind or the running of a tide. With his head on his saddle he stared at the rampart of rock in front of him. How many Bushmen were up there? How would they defend themselves? The noise they made was terrible. They were dancing and shouting. Sometimes he saw one of them silhouetted against the skyline for an instant, a tiny baboon-like figure that leapt high into the air and disappeared.

'They are still feasting,' Afrikander said.

Near him, by the light of the fire, a big Kaffir whetted his spear, rubbing it against a flat stone that he moistened with spittle. Kaspar watched him rub, stop rubbing to test the blade against his thumb, and rub again.

CHAPTER XVI

THE THIRSTY SPEAK

I

THE morning attack that Kaspar had anticipated did not take place. Horses and cattle were watered and taken out to graze. Men sat round smoking and talking, or slept with hats pulled over their eyes. Had there been women and children with them, it would have looked like a picnic. Kaptein Alexander employed the time rearranging the plume in his hat which had become loose, while Andries Afrikander, sitting beside him, offered advice.

'What are we going to do?' Kaspar asked as he came up to them.

'I don't know.' Afrikander took his pipe out of his mouth, spat, and pointed towards Coenraad and van Ek. 'They are making a plan.'

'It was a mistake, meneer, to bring my best hat,' Alexander said, looking up. The feather was in place. Pulling a small brush from his pocket, he began to brush the dust from his clothes.

Afrikander got up. 'Coenraad has sent for the prisoners. Let us go over.'

Van Ek did not greet them. He was sitting with his gun across his arm, watching the kopje. The prisoners stood between their guards. With them was a tame Bushman interpreter. They looked sullen and defiant.

'Will they talk?' Coenraad asked the interpreter.

'Nee, Baas, they will say nothing.'

'They will talk later,' Coenraad said. 'Bring ashes from the fire, and salt.'

Kaspar watched them mix the ashes with rough salt.

'Put it in their mouths,' Coenraad ordered, 'and peg them out.'

The Bushmen's mouths were forced open with sticks and filled with the mixture. It was rubbed into their gums and forced into their cheeks. They were then flung down, spread-eagled, and lashed to pegs driven into the ground.

'They will speak soon,' Coenraad said. 'The thirsty always speak.' He paid no further attention to them and examined the hill in front of him with a small spyglass. 'It is a strong position, but it can be taken. Did you bring your coat, Kaspar?' he asked.

'Yes, I brought it. The old wizard said, "Take your coat," so I did, though it is not cold.'

Coenraad laughed. 'He is a wise old man. It was something I had not thought of.'

'He told you, too?' Kaspar asked.

'Ja, he told me. With much mystery and casting of bones. And to the coats I added goatskins.'

'I do not understand ——' Kaspar began.

'You do not understand, but you will,' Coenraad said.

2

The Bushmen spoke at last through swollen lips. All their people were in, to the last man and his woman. Their mountain stronghold, they asserted, could not be taken. There was a spring of water on the top. There was only one way up. They were well supplied with food.

Having told what they knew, they were killed. It was the

simplest thing to do. Coenraad went back to his plans. His men returned to their pastimes: they continued to clean their weapons, repair clothes and gear, to gamble with dice, to play cards, and to sleep. The sun climbed higher. Vultures came sailing out of the sky to feast on the slaughtered oxen. Pied crows joined them. More and more birds came till there were hundreds. Kaspar had never hated vultures before, but now they seemed to be an accompaniment to his life. They came majestically, to gorge themselves till, even running clumsily with outstretched, thrashing wings, they were unable to rise from the ground, and sat huddled, their bare necks sunk between their shoulders, waiting till they had digested the offal they had eaten. The sun sank. The night, like the preceding one, was eventless.

High up on the kopje the Bushmen were still feasting and dancing. Below, the vultures slept, but the wolves, hyaenas, and jackals were at work, and the night was ugly with their howling, barks, and laughter. Unable to sleep, Kaspar lay first on one side and then on the other. Soft as a dark blue velvet cloak, the night was spread over him, a lovely star-spotted covering for evil. A lion roared, silencing the scavengers. It roared again. To his right, against the sky, a sentry stood leaning on his gun. Tigernek, frightened by the lion, came nearer to Kaspar. The horse's warm breath was on his face and the occasional movement of his legs, as he changed his weight, was the only sound that savoured of security. At Kaspar's side Lazarus slept soundly, lying on his belly with his head pillowed in his arms. Kaspar envied his servant. The attack would take place tomorrow; everything was prepared. Each man had been supplied with a goatskin mask that, covering his face, hung down onto his chest.

3

The beginning was easy. When they had eaten, they advanced to the base of the hill and met no opposition. Here

Coenraad detached van Ek with six picked shots, posting them to cover his advance, while the Kaffirs, their plumes waving, their weapons shining in the sunshine, skirmished forward.

Kaspar watched them spring from rock to rock, hissing between their teeth and rattling their spears against their shields. Naked but for their swinging kilts of catskin, agile as buck, they ran up the slope.

'Put on your coats and masks,' Coenraad ordered.

Wearing their coats, their faces hidden by masks of breyed goatskin through which their eyes gleamed, and carrying shields of blankets spread over thin withes, Coenraad's men forced their way through the thick bush. The heat was intense. The coats and shields caught on every thorny branch. There were three heights to be carried, the first which they were now reaching, and two others where there was no cover.

A honey-bird, recognising Kaspar as a man despite his strange apparel, flew twittering and calling in front of him; angry that he took no notice of its call, it came nearer and nearer in its efforts to divert him. As he reached the first plateau, he saw a Kaffir raise his shield and throw his spear. There was a cry as another clapped his hand to his throat and fell back dead, his weapons clattering on the rocks beside him. Coenraad, shouting to the Kaffirs to fall back, led his men on. A shower of arrows fell among them, and now Kaspar saw the use of the coats and masks. The heavy duffle held the small arrows. They stuck there like the quills on the back of a porcupine. Van Ek's people were firing. It made Kaspar feel safer to know that the old man was there watching over them. He thought of the way he had sighted the guns at the camp. He would pick off any Bushman who showed himself with the same cold precision.

The honey-bird, now furious, refused to leave him. It flew in front of him, perching on rocks and shrubs for an instant and flying back to him. In the middle of a battle he was alone with a bird. Sweat ran into his eyes, his clothes stuck to his body, his gun was heavy in his hand, and he panted for breath.

They were in action. Bushmen sprang up in front of them. Little yellow figures that bent their bows and fired their poisoned arrows, plucking them from the fillets round their heads. Variously painted, utterly unafraid, they continued to expose themselves, though many fell beneath the bullets that were being poured into them. Van Ek had succeeded in scaling another cliff and was now enfilading the Bushmen from the flank. The bird was still with Kaspar. It interfered with his shooting.

The Kaffirs who had been sent back broke through the attackers and flung themselves at the rampart in front of them. It was like watching a battle between red and black ants. Often as a boy he had staged such battles. It seemed utterly without relation to himself. It had been like this with Frederik. Was a battle always like this? Was a fight, which should be the most real thing in the world, the most unreal? He found himself more and more occupied by the bird, wondering where the bees' nest was that it wished to lead him to and almost sympathetic with its anger. For generations men had followed its progenitors to open the nests they found. He heard Lazarus shout, 'Look at the bird, Baas!' He nodded his head.

A low cliff was in front of him. A dead Kaffir lay at its foot; he had a short Bushman spear in his belly and a dead Bushman grasped between his hands. Setting his foot on the corpse, Kaspar dragged himself up, breaking a fingernail as he did so. He was completely without fear. Kaspar van der Berg was not in the battle at all, but stood, as it were, at a distance from it, watching this little man who bore his name, grotesquely wrapped, struggling on, pausing to fire, load, and fire again. He had shot four Bushmen. The third had been a very fine shot; the man had been running, and had rolled over when he hit him.

With a certain sardonic amusement, he watched his own

progress critically. In war man was evidently split within himself. There were many Kaspars: one Kaspar, the little one that climbed, was aware of the other Kaspar that watched him. There was also a third man who, terrified, longed for his home; a fourth, mad with a lust to get on and kill, one who was swearing, whose fingers bled, whose knees were torn; and a fifth who thought only of a honey-bird.

That men were killed to his right and left was nothing — these things happened to other people. He was safe, since he was not personally engaged and only a spectator who watched a comedy of killing. He saw Coenraad close with a Bushman. He raised him, struggling in his arms, and hurled him off the cliff. Shots, cries, and the screams of the wounded rose and fell as the battle surged round him. They were now near the top. Stones and rocks began to roll down on them as the women joined in. Even smaller than their men, like little yellow dolls they moved swiftly among them, shouting encouragement as they sent rocks thundering and leaping down. Some, twisting themselves up, hurled stones with their hands. They did this with such force that one striking the forehead of a Kaffir at Kaspar's side penetrated it, sinking through the bone.

Leading his men forward with a rush, Coenraad succeeded in splitting the Bushmen, driving one party into the cave that opened out behind them, and the others back to the very top of the hill. Leaving some men to hold the entrance of the cave, the others went on. The Bushmen were getting short of arrows and shot less frequently. This device of Coenraad's, the use of blanket shields and coats, had rendered them all but helpless.

They closed in on their chief — a man a little larger than the rest — and prepared to die round him. Massed as they were, the bullets of the attackers wounded several at a time. The chief fell with a bullet in the groin. Clustering over his body, the others fought on. There was a volley from close quarters that cut them to pieces, and the Kaffirs swept in with their spears. For a moment there was a tossing heap of black and yellow bodies, savage cries, screams; assegais rose and fell, plumes and shields tossed, and the Kaffirs fell back. It was finished.

Smeared with blood, they leapt into the air as they looked for more men to kill. Coenraad shouted to their captain that he wanted the women and children brought in. None of them were to be hurt.

Following the example of the others, Kaspar reloaded his gun and watched the Kaffirs run through the little huts. They ran like dogs hunting rats, dragging out the women and children who had taken shelter at the last stand. Thirty women and children were caught. Surrounded by Kaffirs, they looked very small. The world they knew had crumbled about them. Their men were dead; their homes broken.

Coenraad's men took off their masks and coats and sat down. Word was sent to those who held the cave that the fight was over and that Coenraad was coming down.

'When we have eaten, we will smoke them out,' he said.

Kaptein Alexander, having lost his plume, took a long white feather from the head-dress of a dead Kaffir and fastened it on his hat, first pulling out the arrow barbs which stuck in the thick felt. He looked ruefully at his velvet trousers, which were torn, and sighed. 'When fighting one should wear old clothes, Kaspar,' he said; 'but it comes hard, for I do not like to wear old clothes.'

4

Unable to eat, Kaspar went round the huts with Lazarus. They were very small, only four feet in diameter, and were made of mats sewn with buck sinews to bent willow branches; round the base of each was a ring of stones. The huts were grouped about that of the chief, which was a little larger. All had openings to the east. Beyond the central ring there were a few isolated huts that Kaspar supposed belonged to the guards, for these were so placed as to command an extensive view over the plains that stretched out to the horizon on all sides. Here, land and sky were one. It was a world of eagles, of buzzards and wild beasts. An ageless immensity that confused all man-made concepts, where the pattern of God's plan was worked out to the end. This surely was an answer to Oom Christiaan's cynicism; or was his cynicism the outcome of such places, since they showed the utter insignificance of man and all his works?

Today they had done a great thing. Today, by means of gunfire, they had demonstrated the power of civilisation. The gun he held was an example of its superiority; the dead at his feet the result of that superiority. To live, others must die. Because Martinus had died, these men were dead, for now he recognised the Bushmen as men. He turned over a body. A man, he judged, of twenty years, beautifully formed, with small hands and feet, slim wrists and ankles: a little warrior who had died with his weapons in his hands. He was painted in chevrons of red and yellow that, beginning at his navel, ran upward over his breast and spread over his shoulders. His hair was dressed with fat and red ochre powdered with mica. Round his legs he wore little bells made of dried skin, each with a bean in it. Kaspar, picking up his leg, shook it so that the bells rattled. Last night they had rattled as he feasted and danced.

They were gay little people. Cruel — Kaspar thought of the mutilated cattle — before God, that was true; but did not cruelty come out of cruelty? White men came and hunted game which was as much to them as their cattle to the whites. White men raided them, took their women for their own, raised their young children into slavery and castrated the older boys to render them more docile. Kaspar looked at the girls and women. No doubt this young man had possessed one of them. No doubt, even now, she was wondering which of the tumbled bodies was his.

Kaspar had come to the north because he had thought

that in the wilds he would find freedom. Instead, he had found carnage. Devoid even of its trappings, injustice and cruelty reigned here also. Perhaps it reigned everywhere. Perhaps it was a natural law that such things should be. He thought of the honey-bird again. What had it wanted but destruction? What had its call been but a demand that he should follow it to the bees' nest it had found so that he should break it open — the honey to him, the grubs in the comb to the bird?

The captured women and children were tied together, coupled like animals. Small and helpless, they stood waiting. They seemed dazed and beyond feeling. Their eyes, dull and lustreless, were sunk into their flat faces. Coenraad's men jested and talked. They touched the women, who recoiled from their hands. Soon they would be apportioned and become servants, slaves. Concubines to be beaten, illused, and treated worse than dogs.

Kaspar watched them being driven down the hill. Coenraad was going to the cave to finish the business. He is going to smoke them out like bees, Kaspar thought. To ravish their combs and to throw the grubs to the birds, to the wolves and the jackals . . . but this time the grubs were men. Let them go. He had had enough for one day. He wanted to think. At old Frederik's, without meaning to, stung by his wound, he had killed a British soldier. Today he had killed four Bushmen deliberately. His old astonishment that it should be so easy returned. Soon, he supposed, as Afrikander said, it would come naturally. Soon he would be able to kill without a qualm.

He thought of his hatred of slavery. And yet what was this but a slave raid? The captured women and children were just so much meat to their new owners; something to use, abuse, or neglect, as they willed.

He was with renegades. But he had learnt that many of the Border Boers made just such forays for slaves and boasted of them. In some way he had confused the wilds with simplicity and freedom.

Moving slowly over the flat top of the hill, he examined the things that lay about: the scattered untidiness of a battlefield; the painted corpses, the weapons, the broken and unbroken pots and vessels; all the small equipment by means of which these people lived. He found water-bottles made of ostrich eggs, beautifully engraved with pictures of beasts, and stoppered with wild bees' wax; karosses and mantles of springbok skin; necklaces made of ostrich-egg disks strung on sinew; bags of dressed hide and bark fibre; small stone mortars and pestles; horn tobacco pipes; drinking cups made of tortoiseshells; bottles of wildebeeste paunch closed with wildebeeste's tails; arrowheads; receptacles full of poison; stored meal made of powdered locusts; ants' eggs ready to eat; digging-sticks, fire-sticks, stone knives; flat grooved stones that they used for working poison into their weapons; bone arrow-points fitted into reeds; arrow quivers; jackal-skin caps; and many dried bulbs and roots whose use he did not know. He found and drank from their spring, and saw the place where they danced, a smooth piece of ground beyond the huts. By such things as he saw lying about had these little hunters lived for hundreds of years. With such simple things had they existed in an inhospitable, almost waterless desert: generation after generation breeding and dying, hunting game, feasting and dancing by moonlight. There was something very wonderful in this.

Looking up, he saw van Ek sitting on a rock at the edge of the krantz. The old man had not seen him. He pulled a small flute from his pocket. It was in two parts and he screwed them together slowly, blew a tentative note, another, and then, settling himself on his haunches, began to play. With his elbows raised, his eyes fixed on his moving fingers, he threw the thin stream of his melody over the cliff into the plain.

At first Kaspar almost laughed. This was not music — it was not loud enough. Why, at fifty paces it would be inaudible. It was brittle, a small sound like the crawling of an ant, yet there were pictures in it: pictures of battle, of despair; not the despair of the vanquished but that of the victors. Was this the same van Ek who had lain concealed, picking off with such unfailing precision the Bushmen who exposed themselves? His gun lay by him, but why should he come up here alone, to empty the notes of his little flute into the wilderness? Afraid to move, Kaspar remained hidden, vaguely ashamed at watching the old man, who sat at the edge of the cliff making music. Privacy was the right of all men when they demanded it.

From below him came some shots. A volley fired quickly, and then a trickle of shots that, following the volley, fell like drops of water — one, two, or three, another, a silence, and another, the last. Kaspar rose — van Ek turned and saw him.

'So you were here,' he said.

'I stayed here,' Kaspar answered. 'I had seen enough.'

The old man unscrewed his flute and, wrapping it up in a piece of soft skin, put it back into his pocket.

He lit his pipe. 'I also have seen enough for one day,' he said. He picked up his gun. 'It may only be that I am getting old; that I have seen too much.' He put his hand on Kaspar's shoulder. 'Yet I think I see the end of the road,' he said. 'The long trek is all but done. There is but one thing left to do. But Coenraad will never do it alone. He is too young and too hot, but he is a good leader, and it is a fine weapon that we have forged.'

He pointed to the corpses. 'You think this is sad,' he said. 'I think it is sad, too. I have nothing against them ... but that scum' — he looked down at the men crowded round the mouth of the cave below them — 'must be kept sharp, and the grindstone to sharpen them is war. What was Martinus to us?' he went on. 'A nothing. But the men are like hounds: one must hunt the pack, Kaspar, and when the day comes we will set them against great game. Ja, one day, if all goes well, they will bay up the British lion.' His whole face had changed. He was no longer the old dreamer, the philosopher that Kaspar knew, but a man who lived for his hate. 'When that is done,' he said, 'I will depart. But it is good to have a man like you with us. If you are not killed, you will make a leader, for you learn fast.'

Scattered about the mouth of the cave were the bodies of six Bushmen. A big fire still smouldered in its mouth. They had been smoked out like rats and shot like dogs as they ran out. Inside the cavern, lit up by the flames, Kaspar could see their paintings. In the flickering light giraffe, wildebeeste, lion, and eland, painted in white, black, grey, red, and yellow pigment, seemed to move along the walls.

'It is over,' Coenraad said. 'We will lie here tonight and tomorrow march back. Give the prisoners food. They will be distributed later. I will have no fighting over them, and the first man to quarrel, or any man who touches a woman before they are drawn for, will be shot.'

They marched back by the same route, the prisoners being herded by the Kaffirs. Three of Coenraad's men had been killed and were buried. The dead Kaffirs, some fifteen in all, were, according to the custom of their people, left for the wild beasts and birds to dispose of. There were no wounded; a poisoned scratch was fatal.

5

The men who had been on the expedition stood round Coenraad. A table had been placed in the centre of the parade ground; he sat at it with a pack of greasy cards in his hand. Van Ek, Kaptein Alexander, and Afrikander were behind him. Pierre and Links were with Kaspar. The prisoners were lined up. Coenraad dealt the cards. As he dealt, a man stepped up to the table and took the card. When he had done, a number remained in his hands. He set them down and began to call:

'Ace of hearts.' No one had it. 'Ace of diamonds.'

A man stepped forward. It was his pick. He put his card face up on the table and walked along the line of prisoners. The boys, who were at the end of the row, he ignored. Suddenly bending forward, he seized a girl by the wrist and pulled her to her feet. Springing up, she fastened her teeth into his bare forearm, holding it with both hands on each side of her face. When he struck her she did not let go, but went on pulling and worrying at it like a dog. As he strove to shake her loose, he lifted her clear of the ground. He was a big man and she was no larger than a child. Roars of laughter went up from the crowd as she held on. He swung her as a bull swings a dog at a baiting. Shouting with rage and pain, he tried to loosen her grip, and only succeeded when the skin she was holding parted. She had bitten a piece out of his arm. She spat it out onto the ground and abandoned all further struggle. Pulling a riem from his pocket, he secured her wrist and led her off.

'Ace of spades!' Coenraad shouted.

Another man went forward and took his pick. Card after card was called. Man after man claimed his reward, and all the prisoners, except for the first, went peacefully enough. Kaspar held a ten of diamonds. By the time his name was called, he had torn the card almost beyond recognition. Not to take a woman would brand him as different from the others, yet he wanted no woman. Old Frans and Lazarus, who stood behind him, eyed him with astonishment. Kaspar knew what was passing through their minds: that the young Baas should be here with these men and engaged in drawing lots for captured women.

The women sat with lowered heads, their hands clasped over their breasts, as he walked down the line. He wanted none of them. It did not matter which he picked, and still he hesitated. Coming to the end, he walked back. He could have taken a boy, but that would have seemed stranger and only one construction would have been put upon it. Unable to decide, he saw one of the girls look up; she was almost the smallest there, perhaps eleven or twelve years old. In her face he saw such a look of pleading that, without knowing what he did, he pointed to her. She got up and came to him. Taking no further notice of her, he walked back to his place. The child followed him like a dog and settled herself at his feet.

'Are you not going to tie her?' Links said, giving him a riem. 'We always tie them for a week or two till they get tame.'

'I am not going to tie her,' Kaspar said. 'I do not think she will run away.' If she ran, he thought, it would be a fine solution. What would he do with her? He knew what the others would do with their women. But this one did not seem a woman to him; she was something he had acquired. In his mind he bracketed her with his puppy. She would have to be fed and looked after. Like the puppy, he would have to find a name for her.

The women were finished and the boys were drawn. Van Ek chose one, and coming over to Kaspar gave him to him. 'I do not want a servant,' he said. 'I have enough and cannot be troubled to train another.'

Two might be easier than one, Kaspar thought, as he accepted him. They would be less lonely together. He was now thinking of getting away; his horses, except the two he was keeping — Tigernek and the brown — were sold. Such goods as Coenraad's people needed they had bought. The rest — beads, blankets, copper and brass wire, axe-heads, and mirrors — he would take north, loading only one wagon and leaving the others here till his return.

When Coenraad got up he went over to him.

'I am going to trek on,' he said.

Coenraad nodded. 'You had better take a couple of men from here. I will lend you two who are accustomed to hunting elephants and who know the country to the north. When are you going?' he asked.

'Tomorrow,' Kaspar said. All he wanted now was to get

away. Perhaps farther north there would be peace. It might be that one found it only among wild beasts. He would also be farther from Aletta. He could not be too far away from her. He was going to try to forget her. What was the good of thinking of her? Of thinking that he could make a home and live as other men lived? It was not fair to ask her to come with him. At any time if he ventured near the river he might be taken. If she went with him, she would be cut off from her foster parents, from her friends. He must forget her, and the way to forget was to place distance between one-self and one's memories; to adventure so that the adventures when they were passed formed new memories. Thus the past became overlaid with a lacquer of more recent events which sealed it down so that it no longer lived and breathed; so that it no longer pulsed in one's heart.

Links and another Bastard, Willem — the silent one that had taken Selina — were to go with him. As he left Coen-raad, Ringhals shuffled after him. 'The young lord is pro-ceeding to the north,' he said, 'to hunt for the teeth of elephants and the ivory of the sea cow. To barter for gold. Ai... ai... and that is all he seeks? It is not that he seeks peace in his hunting? It is not that he hopes to forget many things among the dangers that he will encounter?' He laughed, hugging his kaross to his shoulders.

Kaspar turned on him angrily. 'You know too much,' he said. 'Have you been spying on me?'

'Why should I spy? Are not all things known to me? And how does one young man differ from another? Ai... ai... they differ. They differ as two grains of sand differ, as two mealie pips. They differ so much that no man can tell the one from the other.' He grasped Kaspar's arm. 'You are going north,' he said. 'I also go north, so it may be that we will meet there.'

'Why do you go north?' Kaspar asked.

'I go where the lost ones call me. Also mayhap I have business in the north. There is a man there with whom I would deal. A man calling himself a wizard who has made mock of me, who has dared to say that I cannot make rain and have no control over the storms. That man shall see whereof I am made. That man is a child. When he still sucked at his mother's dugs, I was an old man and wise. It is said that he challenges me, and it is in my heart that you will be there when we meet, for our ways are twisted like two cords together; therefore it would be well to remain my friend.'

'I am your friend,' Kaspar said.

'A friend is one who gives gifts,' the old man said.

Kaspar laughed. 'Is tobacco a gift?' he asked.

'Tobacco is a gift.'

CHAPTER XVII

STRANGERS COME

I

THE news of Frederik's death had travelled fast. Before Kaspar had reached Coenraad's, it was known all over the land, the tale of it in all men's mouths. From Kaffraria to Stellenbosch, over the Platteland, the Roggeveld, the Zuurveld, it was a subject for discussion, for anger — an old Boer shot down in his place.

Johannes Bezuidenhout was back in Tarka, nursing his anger in the Winterberg, talking, as it seemed to most, futilely, of driving the English into the sea, of revenge against Lieutenant Rousseau, Opperman, and Stockenstroom. His brother's death weighed heavily upon him.

Always gloomy and passionate, he was warped by his hatred. His talk was of nothing else; his prolonged silences no more than a further manifestation of it too deep for words. His brother's blood cried to him perpetually from the ground. His Bible was always open at the passage. He read it to his wife Martha, to his brother-in-law Faber, to the Muller brothers: 'There it is,' he said, 'in God's word, in the Book of Genesis, written for all to see . . .

'"The voice of thy brother's blood crieth unto me from the ground. And now art thou cursed from the earth, which hath opened her mouth to receive thy brother's blood from thy hand. When thou tillest the ground, it shall not henceforth yield unto thee her strength; a fugitive and a vagabond shalt thou be in the earth"; and then, turning the pages, he said, "Woe unto them that join house to house, that lay field to field, till there be no place."'

The wrongs done to his brother were his wrongs. The wrongs done to his people were his wrongs. God willing, and if he lived, he would revenge his brother and free his people. Old Frederik should not have died in vain. He needed help, and help would come. Those who would not listen he damned as men of little faith, as worshippers of false Gods, as cowards. The very trees and the mountains, the valleys, plains, and vleis of his country all called to him. This was 'onse land,' the land of the Boers over whom the jurisdiction of the English was arbitrary and without reason.

Plan after plan occurred to him, only to be dismissed as impracticable. Before God, there must be a way! If only he could find it! His prayers, night and morning, were that the Almighty should show him a path whereby he should achieve his heart's desire — the liberation of his people from the yoke of the Egyptians and revenge for his brother's death.

2

'Are you Johannes Bezuidenhout?' A stranger, dismounting from a dusty horse, extended his hand. 'I am Hendrik Prinsloo,' he said.

Johannes looked at him distrustfully. 'Prinsloo?' he repeated. 'What Prinsloo? Where are you from?'

'I am the son of Martinus Prinsloo, and I come from the Bosch Berg.'

'That is good,' Johannes said. 'I know you. You were imprisoned in the Castle and your father was with van Jaarsveld.'

'So you have heard of me. Ja, I was imprisoned and de Mist released me. Also' — he lowered his voice — 'I am the son of my father.'

'Come in, meneer.' Johannes led the way to the house. This was the answer to his prayers. 'I am the son of my father,' he had said. His father had been a rebel. 'What has brought you so far?' he asked.

'Perhaps I am visiting,' Prinsloo said.

'You have ridden hard to visit.' Johannes looked at the horse. 'And do men now visit without their wives and children?'

'I did not say I was visiting. I said that I might be visiting.'

Johannes made him known to the others: to Diedrik and Christiaan Muller on whose farm he lived; to Cornelis Faber, his brother-in-law; and to his wife and son.

Once in the house Prinsloo's manner changed. His eyes holding them, his arms folded across his chest, he said:

'I have come far and what do I see? Ja, magtig, what is this? Folk who sit still while innocent men are shot. It was not thus in my father's day. Before God, in those days there were men in Africa. They did not have to be beaten from their beds by women with sticks. I see now that I should have come with my wife and children, but I had thought to find men in the Baviaan's River and at Tarka. Ja, I should have brought my wagon and my family, then we could have sat smoking and talking while the children played.' He turned from them contemptuously.

'Stop!' Johannes said, grasping his arm. 'I am ready, but what can we do? Have you a plan? The Almighty knows how I have tried, how I have prayed. I have talked, but none will listen. I am a voice that cries in the wilderness.' There were tears in his eyes. 'No one is with me.'

'I say that you have preached to the baboons, Johannes Bezuidenhout, and if you want a congregation, let me call in also the apes from the hills and the dogs that lie before the door. But you are not alone. Put a saddle on your horse and come with me. We will find men and a way.'

'Do not go, Johannes,' Diedrik said. 'It is no good. We are all with you, but they are too strong.'

'Have you no faith, Diedrik Muller?' Prinsloo turned on him savagely. 'Is there not a God above us, and do you not know that he that observeth the wind shall not sow, and that he who regardeth the clouds shall not reap? Come, Johannes. Let us go forth.'

Johannes went out to get his horse. 'Where are we going?' he asked.

'We ride to Stephanus Bothma at Paling Kloof. He is of one mind with us.'

'Why are you with me, meneer? You are not related to us.' Johannes became doubtful. There must be a reason for all things, and that a man not known to him should throw in his hand with him needed some explanation. It was what he had prayed for, but he had prayed for many things and never before had had so direct and quick an answer.

'Why am I with you? I am with you because I am against the English; because I hate them and will fight them as my father did; because, above all else, I care for the freedom of our folk.'

So it was true. God was unwilling to let such a sin go unpunished and had sent Prinsloo to him. He had sent him like an angel with a flaming sword. The English would be driven from the garden of Africa. He was no longer alone. He had Hendrik Prinsloo, and behind Hendrik stood the might of Heaven. 'Whoso sheddeth man's blood, by man shall his blood be shed,' Johannes said. 'And let them say what they will, it was not we who began it.'

At Bothma's they found some Kaffirs. They were making him a friendly visit and had been given a sheep.

Filled with new confidence, Johannes spoke to them. 'Are your people ready to rise?' he asked.

'We are always ready,' their leader said. Pulling a rib

from the sheep, he gnawed it in silence. Wiping his hand
on his hair, he went on: 'But why does not Bezuidenhout or
another Dutchman go into Kaffirland to speak with Gaika?
Our chiefs place little reliance on messages sent by their
people.'

There was truth in this. A white man should go to Kaffirland. But who could go? Who would go?

'Is it safe to send?' he asked. 'Would the messenger not
be killed?'

'Why should he be killed?' The Kaffir's eyes were crafty.
'Are messengers bearing good news ever killed?'

That night Johannes and Prinsloo went back to the Mullers' farm. 'Be of good cheer, Johannes,' Prinsloo said; 'the
people of Bruintjes Hooghte and the Zuurveld are united
with us.'

'You are mad if you go farther in this matter, Johannes.'
Diedrik Muller spoke vehemently. 'If you have a grievance, take it to the courts of justice.'

'The courts of justice!' Prinsloo said. 'Where are they?
Ja, there are courts, but there is no justice to be found in
them; no justice for Burgers, only for the Kaffirs, Bastards,
and Hottentots. Before God, to get justice now a man must
be black.'

Two days later the expedition to Gaika set out: Faber,
a boy called Engelbregt, and the Hungarian, Frans Marais.
With them went Bambeloe, a Hottentot gun-bearer.

3

When they came back the Border began to change. Strange
horses were often beneath the peach trees at Rudolf's; strange
men sat at his table, men who talked of their grievances, of
perpetual quit-rent tenure of land, of farms made so small
'that the cattle eat one another dead.' 'And what do they
say when we tell them? They say, sell some and make them
fewer.' Old Frederik Bezuidenhout was spoken of as a martyr;

Johannes Bezuidenhout spoken of as a saviour. One who would lead them out of captivity. A month ago few had noticed Johannes or had listened to him. Hendrik Prinsloo, whom they called Kasteel Hendrik because of his imprisonment in the Castle, was spoken of as being with Johannes; and old Martinus, Kasteel's father. Memories of the dead van Jaarsveld were revived. Men spoke with confidence of what they would do, and to all who came Rudolf was friendly. Many meals were served them. Much coffee was drunk. Rudolf was hospitable, for while he talked and listened he could stop thinking; stop worrying. So much was going wrong. His wife was not mending. Her baby was sick. In his heart he knew what was coming to pass. The Lord had given, the Lord would take away. But what had this to do with the hospitality he extended? What had his private misery to do with his public life?

Stephanie was more than ever a worry since there were so many men about, folk of whom he knew little; and she seemed harder, and sometimes he thought that, beneath her outward politeness to Aletta, he saw hatred. Before God, what had he done that his house should be like this, divided against itself, his wife and child ill? Aletta was absent-minded, doing her work in a dream, scarcely noticing what he said to her and ignoring Stephanie's hidden gibes. Only Kattie remained the same — a laughing child who ran about, played, and shouted. Nee, there was little peace to be found these days. His friend, old Frederik, dead; Kaspar van der Berg, whom he liked and who he had hoped would take one of his girls, a fugitive from justice; and over all the land a threat of war.

They talked of vengeance, but what ever came of vengeance? Old Frederik had been shot, but had he gone to court when summoned he would not have been killed. As for Stockenstroom, Opperman, and Rousseau, they had had their duty to do and had done it. All this arose from Booy, old Frederik's Hottentot. His carelessness, his petty thieving, were responsible for all that had happened and all that would happen. Rudolf wanted peace and quiet. He wanted things as they used to be with Frederik alive, with Maria and her baby well and his two girls happy. He thought of them as they used to be — children who played and ran out to him when he came home. He thought of them when they were like Klein Kattie, little children who rode on his knee. He sighed.

Without meaning it, little by little he was becoming involved with Hendrik Prinsloo. Such things were contrary to his nature. He was a farmer. He loved his wife, his children, his home, his cattle, his sheep and horses. He went out to look at a mare that had just foaled, but it gave him no pleasure. He saw the foal standing on trembling legs beside his dam as she nuzzled him. A colt. He wished he had a son to break him. He remembered how he had loved training young horses. How he had liked to handle them, to clap a saddle on their backs as they stood with one foreleg tied up; and of how, when they were used to the saddle and a weight on their backs, he had mounted and told the boy to take the wrappings off their eyes. He thought of how they stood motionless, dazed and trembling, and how life suddenly came back to them and they sprang away in great bounds over the veld. Magtig, that had been good. To feel the lift of a young horse plunging, to hear the pounding hoofs and have the wind roaring in one's ears. It was good, but it was over. Those days had gone. He gave another look at the foal; he had a heart-shaped mark on his forehead. He would call him Heart. That was a fine name for a horse. Ja, Heart — and he would have a great heart, too. His mother was a good mare and the sire was Coenraad's chestnut. It would be something to tell Maria. Later, when he was steady on his legs he would have him driven down. And there was the new calf, too. Rudolf regained some measure of happiness. It was good to see young things. It was the Lord's will that they should be born and that man should rejoice in their birth.

4

In the house Maria sat with the baby on her knee. 'You must drink, mie kleinkie,' she said, holding it near her. 'Ja, you must drink and grow into a fine woman, one whom men will ride from far to seek. They will come from very far,' she went on softly, 'mounted on their best horses, to court a mooi meisie like you, and I shall sit on the stoep and laugh, for once your father came like that, riding a fine black horse that he made dance when he saw me. And he was only one of many: some were richer than he with wide farms and big herds of cattle, but my heart went out to your father. On that first day he swept through my heart like a flood through a crop planted in a valley and one day it will be like that with you. A man will come riding; he will tie his horse to the stoep pole and will not leave without you. When he goes, you will be on his saddle with your arms about him. He will be your man and you will belong.'

Maria rocked the child, swinging her back and forth. One day, if the Lord willed it, the child in her arms would sit as she sat now, rocking her own child, and dreaming of its marriage. If it was a boy, she would think of her own mating and wonder about the woman he would take into his arms, possessing her. If it was a girl, she would think of the man who would come courting her, of the man she would marry and of the children she would bear. If I live, Maria thought, I may see her children. I may watch her nursing them and hold them myself. Her heart was filled with tenderness for her baby's unborn children. The child was delicate, but many young children were delicate, and God was good.

So, since the beginning of time, had women thought and pondered about their children's children. Life was a woman's business, an endless filling and emptying of wombs. It was women who held life in their bellies, who nourished it under their hearts. On and on and on it went, an endless cycle, to the glory of God. And by the time the mother's stream was dry, the daughter's had begun to flow. She thought of her age. She was thirty-five. She wondered if her time of bearing lusty children to her man was done. Kattie was three, and since her birth she had had one still-born child and one who had lived only a short time. But they had not been cast in the accustomed mould. Even the one who had lived a month, who had lived long enough to be baptised Hans Christiaan, had never clutched at her as the others had done; a weakling without the courage to attack his mother's breasts. She thought of Jacob, her first-born; he had flung himself upon her as if she had been an enemy. Long before he was weaned she had seen his father in him. But Jacob was dead. He had grown from a baby into a child and from a child into a boy, and then, before his voice had changed, he had died. She thought of his illness. Perhaps with doctors he could have been saved. She had often thought that with doctors he might have been saved. Kattie was a strong child standing firmly on her legs. But everything was not right with the baby. She did not thrive. Maria wondered if it was her milk. It might be that, or it might be something else. It might be so many things. She sighed.

The door burst open.

'Voertsek, Wildman, voertsek, Witbooi, Jakkal!' The dogs were all round her, trying to lick the child in her arms. Magtig, the house was no place for hounds. They belonged outside. She closed the door behind them and bent down, her thick legs apart, to throw a pinch of salt into the coffee that cooked in the brass pot on the fire. Rudolf would be back soon. Ag, men! One could not understand them. Neither young nor old could one know what went on inside their heads. The Almighty had made them that way, so it must be right. But it was difficult for women. And one could have children by a man one did not understand. In this matter as in many others, as far as she could see, understanding was of no importance. It was without significance, and, willing or unwilling, with or without understanding, children came. To white folk, to Hottentots, and to the beasts of the field.

She put down the child and, taking up a knife, cut some meat from the flank of the springbok hanging from a beam. It was dry outside, with a crust; the ribs clung to the backbone, coming away reluctantly so that she had to twist her knife and pull at the flesh with her hands. Then it came with a jerk, a little tearing sound that was good in her ears. There had not always been meat in their home, not even wild meat that was so flat and dry — she thought of the great drought that had driven all the game away and killed most of the stock — and there had been little fat and no vegetables. How could one rear children without fat? With fat Jacob might have lived. But that was over. Now they had big flocks of sheep and a fine garden. She looked round to see if the dogs were back in the room. Dogs stole meat. If there was a dog about, almost before you put it down they had it. One would think they could reason as did Christian people.

Rudolf would shout for food as soon as he came in. The necessity of providing pressed on her even in a period of plenty. It was her responsibility. Many times she had dreamed of food, not for herself but for the others, for her man and her children who looked to her. Food ... men ... before God, food was what men wanted from a woman when it was not something else. Ja, the demands of men on their women were without number — something to be sewn or made, a wound to be dressed. They wanted you to lie down because you were a woman. They wanted you to get up again because they were hungry.

She threw the meat into a pot and sat down. Men were like children: they were always wanting, always asking, always taking, and then suddenly they would cease to be children and become men. That was why you could not understand them. Then they lost the sweet reasonableness of children and were more foolish, less predictable than beasts.

And it came upon them suddenly without rhyme, like a sickness. They would be as good as gold, slow to anger and patient in disaster, very gentle and tender, and then an idea would occur to them and they would be like mad things. She nodded her head sadly at the vagaries of men. The way to understand them was not to understand them. Ja, for a peaceful life one must accept them; they were just something that happened to a woman.

It might even be that women were also just something that happened to men, and once women accepted this, the storm of man's love, the fury of his strange angers, and his needs — which were as great as, though different from, those of a child — life became simple. Ag, ja, one must take men as one found them; take them as one took the weather, and God knows the weather was never right: too dry, too wet, too hot or too cold. Men were without reason, and capricious, but if they demanded much, they also gave generously. And if men were made one way and women another, what then? The nature of a cow was different from that of a bull, though both might be red and both ate grass. Man and woman had been created on the sixth day, created alike, but not the same. So it was, and so it would be. But to try to understand? That would indeed be impious, for the Lord's ways were strange and beyond all understanding, nor, to a woman, was it necessary.

She heard the chickens cry out as they scattered, heard the flutter of their wings as a horse, ridden fast, pulled up with scraping hoofs at the door. Rudolf was back. When he came in there would be news. He always had news. He would tell her how the crops were looking, about the cattle, the sheep, or the horses. He would say what he had seen, talk of riems stolen by the servants, of what he was going to do next year; speaking with his mouth full, and reaching with big hands for food across the table. With Rudolf came the breath of life, the scent of fresh cow-dung from the kraals, of goats or sheep, the acrid smell of horse sweat mixed with his own, and the smell of tobacco from his beard. With his coming the house was filled. Ja, one was aware of Rudolf, strong and clumsy as a bull in the house, but a man of great subtlety and very dexterous with horse and gun. Outside these matters he was a child. If she could keep him talking, he would not notice how ill she was. Her heart was soft for Rudolf, he was so big and stupid.

'I am hungry, Maria,' he said as he came in.

'I knew you would be hungry,' she said. 'The food is nearly ready now. Will you have coffee and rusks while you wait?'

'Ja, I will have coffee and rusks.'

Maria poured out the coffee and stood with her hands on her hips, watching him soak the rusks in the cup before he ate them. It made her very happy to watch him eat. She took his gun from the table and hung it up by its sling to the wall. It had a long barrel, and both barrel and butt were bound with bands of brass.

'How is the child?' he asked, looking towards her.

'She is better, I think,' she said. 'Have you any news?'

'Ja, I have fine news,' he said, laughing. He pointed with a wet rusk to the sleeping child. 'She will be a rich woman — already she has her first calf. And is it not a fine thing that a little girl should have a calf born before she herself is weaned?'

'What cow has calved?' Maria asked.

'Our cow that we sold to your brother Frederik,' he said. 'The black one that we sold to him and that he brought back as a birth-gift for the child because she would not stay. It is a bull calf. And that is not all, Maria. The mare that Coenraad's red horse served has foaled. He is a beautiful foal — a colt with a mark like a heart on his face.'

'Like a heart,' Maria said. 'I have never seen a horse with a mark like a heart on his face.'

'Tomorrow you shall see him, and I have named him. I have called him Heart.'

Maria looked at her husband. He was dressed in a shirt of breyed skin, with breyed skin trousers that fitted tightly to his legs. His bare feet were covered with velskoen that he had made himself. The Kaffirs had breyed the skins of which his clothes were made from the hides of buck that he had shot. Round his waist he wore a heavy belt in which hung a long sheath-knife. He was a fine man in his full vigour. It was not his fault that her children were not what they should be. But life was like that — a man wore out several women before he died. She wondered if she should tell him of the pain in her leg. Men were so foolish about pain. Wounds they could see and understand, but anything else, any hidden malady, a sickness that lay under an unbroken skin, frightened them. If she told him she would have to comfort him about herself, an added burden that she felt unable to face. One day she might have to tell him. One day it might become apparent that she was ill. Or she might get well. She was going to have another child. This he knew, and she could attribute her illness to her pregnancy, and if he said, 'You were never like this before,' she could answer: 'Yes, but this is so soon. Perhaps I am still tired.' Ach, God, how tired she was! What an effort it was to get about, and what strange thoughts filled her head, not only in her dreams at night as she slept beside Rudolf, but in the daytime too.

I must be careful not to fall, she thought. She had fallen that morning; her leg had suddenly not been there. At least that was what it had felt like: as if suddenly she had only one leg. I must not fall, she thought; it will frighten him.

Also she found herself worried by the disturbance on the Border. More and more she thought of old Frederik, her brother. More and more she became convinced that Johannes was being made use of; had become no more than a tool in the hands of Prinsloo and others. And how much was Rudolf involved? Perhaps not at all; he never spoke of it, but there were too many people pausing here now on their way to the north or coming back from it. When things were going well, men were not so restless; they did not ride their horses so hard. She busied herself with the food.

'You will eat, Rudolf?' she asked. 'You are hungry?'

'Ja, I am hungry,' he said.

She smiled. He was hungry. She would feed him as she had fed him a thousand times. It gave her pleasure to prepare his food and to watch him eat. Stephanie and Aletta came in. The baby was asleep. Klein Kattie played with the kittens on the floor. It was home. Maria was happy; her fears had gone. As to being ill, she had been ill before. It would pass off. Rudolf gave thanks and began to eat. He drank more coffee with great noisy gulps. When he had done, she and the girls would eat while he sat and smoked. They were all in the hands of God, and whatever happened was for the best. She would soon be well.

Rudolf forced himself to eat. He had always been a heavy eater, and to make Maria content he must finish the food on his plate. He thought it would choke him. Before God, how could a man eat at such a time! He tried not to look at Maria. How was it, he wondered, that she thought she could deceive him? As if a man brought up with stock could not tell lameness by her footsteps and know by his ears alone that she was worse! But she was doing this to save him pain, and he must pretend to know nothing; he, a farmer who could pick out sick beasts at a glance, must pretend that he did not see that she was thinner, the baby worse. It might be that Maria's milk did not suit the child. It was not that she had no milk. She had plenty, but she was making it out of her own flesh and falling away to nothing. He wondered if he could suggest fostering the baby onto a tame Kaffir woman. Would it not be better that they both acknowledged their fears and prayed to the Almighty together instead of singly about their troubles? He wiped his mouth on his wrist. It was over till tonight. If only she would not pretend! If only she would stay in bed! But she would not rest. When he asked her, she said, 'It is nothing, Rudolf,' and looked away. When he asked her about the child, she said the same. Tears came into his eyes as he thought of her courage, and she had said nothing when she found herself with child again. It was rare that a woman became pregnant while she still suckled. Ja, it was rare, but it had happened, and there was nothing he could do.

5

But Maria did not get better. Her leg swelled and she had no use of it. Sensation had gone out of it. If she pricked it with a needle, she felt nothing. She had done this under the bedclothes, trying it all the way up from her ankle to her thigh. She could pretend no longer. From where she lay she could look into the other room, could see the furniture in it. The black stinkwood table, marked with yellow ribbons of lighter grain; the chairs, the tinware on the sideboard. These things went on. They would last longer than she. Long after she was dead would they go on. Her children would use them, the men her daughters married, the women her sons married, and their children. But she had no son; her sons were dead. This was the only injustice she had done her husband. A man had the right to sons.

Her mind went back to her furniture, to the tin cups and plates that gleamed dimly from the other room. Men had made these things. Her father had made the furniture, and others, whom she had never seen — skilled tinsmiths — had fashioned the beakers and the plates; made them with loving hands, turning them round and round, holding them up to the light, searching for defects and proud of achievement when they found none. As now, for the first time, she thought of these others, so in the future might some think of her. Is this not a plate that came from your mother — from your grandmother? Then for an instant they might think of her as they used them.

She wondered if those who got the things would keep them as she did, treasuring them, or if they would not care. Perhaps they would feed dogs from her platters, putting them on the floor filled with scraped leavings.

She knew she was dying, and her revolt against her illness grew less as she got weaker. She suffered the attentions of Aletta gratefully; she talked to Rudolf, admiring the mare and foal he brought to show her daily, but wondered as she did it how she succeeded in speaking so clearly on subjects that had ceased, long ceased, to matter. Rudolf must never know how bad she was. He must not guess. She always said, when he asked, that she was better. 'Ja, Rudolf, I am better. I am only a little weak. Perhaps tomorrow I shall get up,' and she would move her good leg. Aletta knew how sick she was. She had to know, but there was a conspiracy between them. They were women protecting a man. Sometimes she thought he did know, but it was better when things were not spoken of. Words made reality. Once a thing was said, once it was spoken of, it existed as a living thing.

Her mind, when she was not talking to Rudolf, was far away, lost in the past: in the days when she played on the floor in her father's house, in the days she had spent as a bride, in the hopes and disappointments of the past. She remembered worrying about Rudolf's first wife, Stephanie's mother, and wondering if he compared them, wondering which he loved the most. He had always been good to her, but sometimes she had found him staring into the fire, thinking. Was he thinking of the other woman? Had she failed him in any way?

Those days were so much clearer than the present. Old Frederik was often with her; she remembered a thousand incidents of her girlhood, of her mother and father, of Gerrit and Johannes. She thought of Klein Kattie, whom she would soon have to leave. Of her baby she thought less, for they would not be long separated. Poor Rudolf! He had been a good husband, a good father, but he would do quite well without her. She had seen it so many times. Only young hearts could break; with older folk it was a different thing. They recognised the feeling of despair and emptiness because they had suffered it before; they knew that it would pass. Aletta would look after Rudolf and Kattie, and when she married, he would still manage by marrying another wife himself or by taking a coloured woman into his house. It seemed so unimportant now. Perhaps it was even the greatest compliment a man could pay to a dead wife. If he had given her all that was in him, if he was afraid of suffering again, then to take a coloured woman was a solution, for even if he could love no more, he was still a man. This was what had happened to Frederik. Ja, it was what had happened, only she had never seen it that way. Rudolf had not loved his first wife, the mother of Stephanie. She knew this now, and smiled at the way she had been jealous of the dead woman. Poor Augusta! Rudolf had been young when he married her. She had been beautiful; but beauty was not enough for a man like Rudolf. She thought of the girls. Aletta would be safe. Stephanie was another thing, but she had done what she could for Stephanie. It was too late now to do more.

Rudolf was beside her. He had brought down the horses again. 'Look, Maria,' he said, 'how beautiful they are.'

Maria looked at the mare, and foal. 'Ja, they are beautiful together,' she said. The old mare, quiet, heavy-barrelled; the foal, so gay, trotted lightly beside his mother. His little short-haired tail was never still. Half afraid, half curious, he ran forward, and back to stand finally under his mother's neck. His legs were strong now; he no longer rocked on them. Maria wondered what colour he would be. You were never certain with a foal: they changed so much, and she would never know. Rudolf was like a child, bringing them down each day to please her. He was always trying to please her, doing little things, bringing her a flower, bringing in something he had grown — a big onion, a strangely shaped potato. At least it gave them something to talk about. She could say: 'That is a fine onion. It is the finest you have ever grown,' and he would go away as pleased as a boy, confident that she was better.

6

With Maria's illness most of the work fell to Aletta. There were Maria and the baby to attend to. There was Klein Kattie, who never left her side, but, clinging to her skirts, followed her wherever she went. Stephanie would have nothing to do with Kattie. Kattie was only her half sister, and from the beginning she had resented her father's remarriage. Nor would Stephanie help with Maria or the new baby. Both were ailing, and she hated illness. She had never been ill, and illness roused her anger. People had no business to be ill. The fact that her stepmother was again with child made her feel quite sick. Her father was old, Maria was old, and the thought of them making love disgusted her. Love, of which she knew something and thought a great deal, was permissible, was understandable and natural, only when people were young.

Her mind was occupied continually by the thoughts of Kaspar and Aletta. She loved and hated him. Sometimes she did the one, sometimes the other. Sometimes she did both together. Her feelings for him were like two fruits, one sweet and one sour, growing side by side on the same bough. She longed to hurt him and then to assuage his hurt. Why had he loved Aletta? What had Aletta done to make him love her? 'And why did I act like that,' she wondered, 'throwing the stone at the ringhals and lying to him about Letta?'

Because Kaspar loved Aletta, she hated Aletta. Her mind was full of plans to make him notice her. She wondered where he was. There was no direct news of him. She had heard rumours, through Coenraad's messengers who came and went, that he had gone north to trade and hunt. He might be killed. For a moment she hoped savagely that this would happen, and then turned faint at the thought of Kaspar dead. If he was dead, it would be finished. As long as he lived, he would come back one day. No one knew how she longed to see him. Each man that came down the road from the north she watched till he was near enough to recognise.

Aletta watched the north road too. Why had Kaspar sent no message? He had promised to send messages, to write. She had nothing of his. If only she had one letter in his hand that she could keep in the bosom of her dress by day and under her pillow at night! When she washed, she looked down at her breasts. There between them was the place where his letter would lie when it came. Perhaps it would come tomorrow, perhaps the day after. That it would come, she was assured. That he would one day follow his letter, she was certain. On this she based her life, her faith in the God who had sent Kaspar to her. When she thought of him, she went singing about her work so that the Kaffirs laughed and nudged each other. The meisie was in love. The meisie was happy. Sometimes she cried, and the Kaffirs still laughed and nudged each other. It was right that sometimes she should cry, from emptiness.

The marked pot of butter still stood unused in the dairy. She often went to look at it, to touch its cool sides with her hands, to lean her forehead against it. The trees where he had tied his horse still stood in front of the house. And sometimes she went into the shed — it still smelt of wool, of riems and tobacco, of skins — but she went there seldom. Why need she when the knowledge of it was always in her heart, when the scent of it never left her nostrils?

She had long talks with Maria, taking in her sewing to sit beside her as she mended clothes. Only as Maria was failing did she come to know her. Only in these long, quiet hours did she learn what had been in Maria's heart for years.

It seemed to her that even Maria had not known before many of the things she spoke of so confidently. Her words and her thoughts were so clear. She spoke with such certainty. She listened with such patience. It reminded Aletta of the wool she used, to hear Maria unravelling the strings of her life. It was as if, now that it was drawing to a close, she at last had time to do it — to search it for reasons. With the tentative, tired fingers of her mind she seemed to pick at her past, pulling out pieces of it and joining them with infinite patience. It was as if a spider having woven its web began suddenly to undo it, knot by knot, spoke by spoke; for life was like that — a wheel-like net that was tied together by great events, by chance meetings, by births and deaths, by small fortuitous incidents, which in the end became as significant as acts of God.

Aletta told Maria of Kaspar and what she felt for him; told her of how he had taken her: told it without shame, even with a kind of pride. Maria had smiled softly. 'So you are a woman,' she had said. No more than that. No reproach. No comment. After that Aletta's heart had been opened. Perhaps only the very old or the very ill could understand. Perhaps you had to be almost done with life before you could take it as it came, without regret or remark, accepting it at last for what it was.

Aletta understood what Maria felt; of how the death of her brother had told upon her. She understood why she sat propped up with pillows, staring for hours out of the window towards the mountains where he had lived. She understood why she had seen little of him in late years. It was because of Selina. But it had not occurred to Maria that her brother would die, that he would be killed, suffering a martyr's death. Johannes with his threats and his shoutings bore her down. What had happened was God's will, and what could Johannes do against it? Gerrit's silence, the way he had profited by Frederik's death, hurt her as much as his brother's raging. Too much had happened before she was well from bearing her child. She was fading away slowly, becoming less and less active and brooding more and more. Little things lost their meaning. She spoke of the great truths, of the things that could not be changed: the taking in of food, the lying of a man with a woman. These things — conception, birth, puberty, sleep, and death — were all beyond understanding and veiled in mystery, for these acts and the satisfaction of these desires were according to the law of God, and by them was life circumscribed. It seemed to her that men lived, as it were, in a little kraal and the posts of it were the years of their lives.

7

There was talk at Rudolf's of a raid Coenraad had made into Bushman's land for women and of unrest among the Kaffirs, and it was said that Kaspar, before going hunting, had possessed himself of a Bushman girl. There had been some laughter at this, for the Burgers of the south were bitter against such things. 'Ja, they are bitter, but no sooner has one of them come north than he succumbs to our customs. Ag, ja, a little bread is better than no cake, and a little yellow girl better than no woman,' Stephanie said.

It was she who made the most of this. It was a story that amused her, and she repeated it to all comers, asserting it as the truth. Stephanie was in a strange state of mind: more irresponsible than usual. Gay and reckless, she continued to take no notice of her stepmother's illness. Nor did the illness of the baby or her father's sorrow affect her. She had contracted a friendship with a man who was one of Lieutenant Rousseau's intimates. Aletta was not clear about his business in these parts. She was not satisfied with the story he gave out — that he was making a map of the Great Fish River boundary. No, Meneer van Zyl was not what he said he was. And she did not like him. She did not like his appearance. Tall and slight, with eyes that looked past you when he spoke and a small mouth that was like a blister in his long thin face. And why should they at Rudolf's truckle to those who were allied to the military? In God's name, had they not suffered enough already? But van Zyl dressed well. He had seen the world, was generous with small gifts and large compliments, and as such was enough for Stephanie.

But Aletta had little time to dream: there was too much to do. Day followed day. Work followed work — the interminable work of women in which nothing permanent was achieved. A meal was made and eaten. Soiled dishes were washed and resoiled. Dirty clothes were laundered only to be dirtied again. Sometimes she thought enviously of men's work. When a man made a dam or planted a valley orchard, something was done. Something that after he died would remain. That bank of earth and stones, that copse of trees, would forever be a sign that he had lived. When Maria died, what would be left of her? There was no question now of her living. Each day brought death nearer. Her baby would die too, and all that would be left of her would be a few clothes hanging on the wall, her best dress in her chest, and Klein Kattie. A woman would have lived, loved, and suffered, and at the end what was left? Nothing but a small girl child to repeat in her life her mother's. More fortunate or less fortunate, it would in its major issues resemble it. And yet there was beauty all round: beauty that hurt Aletta by its perfection; beauty in the foal that Rudolf brought to the house each day; beauty in the potato creeper that flowered on the stoep poles, in the flight and song of birds, in the shadows of the trees; and above all beauty in her memories of what had been. Her worries and her work were nothing to her when they were associated with those memories. On that slender thread of the past, on those few days that Kaspar had spent with her, did she build her hopes of the future. He would come back. The rumours were lies. One day she would hear from him. That she had not heard was due to some unforeseen circumstances, to some accident.

CHAPTER XVIII

THE HEIFER OF THE KING

I

ALMOST as soon as they left Coenraad's camp, Kaspar asked about the silence of Selina's man.

'Why does he not talk?' he asked.

Links began to laugh. Silent Willem smiled, opened his mouth and pointed to it with his finger. Where his tongue should have been there was nothing. His mouth looked enormous, a great pink cavern in which a thick stump moved.

'They cut it out,' Links said.

'But who did this?' Kaspar asked.

'That no one knows. He was like that when he came to us. We call him "the Silent One."' Links laughed. 'But there are worse things to lose than a tongue,' he said. 'He is still a man.'

The Silent One nodded his head in agreement and gave a grunt.

'Can he not talk at all?'

'He cannot talk,' Links said. 'But he is a good man. And not to talk to people makes life very simple for him, Kaspar; men like him greatly because he is always ready to listen to their words and cannot argue. Before God, in all the camp I doubt if there is a more liked man.'

As they advanced, Kaspar learnt much of wild beasts and their ways. He learnt that lions are most dangerous on wet, stormy nights; that the furious galloping of the wildebeeste is due to a worm in their brains; that the river horse gives birth and suck under water; that a water tortoise smells like a lion to a horse and will make it shy. Night after night as they sat over their fire, day after day as they rode over the veld, Links talked of animals, birds, and snakes. He told him of one snake that, in order to proceed more rapidly down a hill, would take its tail into its mouth and roll down it like a hoop.

'I never saw this myself, Kaspar,' he said, 'but I have heard it spoken of.' He said puff-adders died when they brought forth their living young, the little snakes, already full of venom, biting their way out of their mothers' bellies.

The Bushman boy and girl became slowly tame, used to the sound of firearms and accustomed to the horses. Kaspar had called them Adam and Eve, for it seemed to him that the mother and father of mankind must have resembled them, living as they did freely, off the beasts and fruits of the earth. He began, too, to doubt much of what had been told him of the Bushmen; to doubt that they were not human, that they were cruel, savage, and intractable. He found Adam and Eve grateful and devoted servants, skilled hunters and brave beyond the ordinary.

Moving without haste, the wagon made its way into this northern and forbidden country. There was no hurry. There was water in plenty, good grass for the oxen, and much game. Days passed to the sound of the turning wheels and creaking gear. They saw neither man nor domestic beast. This country had been swept bare, and was empty of mankind. Rivers and mountains were crossed, sometimes hazardously, but, under the skilled guidance of Links, always successfully; and then they came into Mziligazi's country, into a land interspersed with kraals. Gourds of sour milk, baskets of sweet potatoes, and beef obtained from the headmen made a pleasant change of diet. The King had heard of their coming and they received gifts of cattle. These, at each halt, were skilfully slaughtered by a single stab from a spear, delivered behind the shoulder. As soon as the ox fell, its tail was severed and fought over. The beast was then skinned with spears, and the entrails, instead of being thrown to the dogs, were divided among the people and consumed with great eagerness. The bones were the property of the boys. Everything here was new and strange to Kaspar; but everything was governed by a convention as rigid as any in more civilized parts, more rigid, since for disobedience there was only one penalty, that of death. Bred to the spear under Tshaka, Mziligazi ruled by it. Son of Matshobane, he had become a captain and was put in charge of a military kraal called Bulawayo — Pick Off the Old Men. It was in this kraal, Links said, that Tshaka had ordered his old warriors to be killed because they were eating his beef and making no return for it. But Mziligazi had broken away from Tshaka and come here, bringing twenty thousand Zulus with him.

When they reached the King's kraal, Kaspar was surprised at its size. About three miles in circumference, it contained fully fifteen hundred huts. Links pointed out the royal palace; situated on a slight eminence, it comprised a hundred huts which were, he said, inhabited by the King's women. No man was allowed to enter it.

Links had been here before. 'We cannot ride straight in,' he said, 'so we will camp till the King sends for us.'

'How long will he make us wait?' Kaspar asked.

'A day or two days.'

Links pointed to some thorn trees. 'That is where I went last time. Let us go there.'

When they reached the trees, they halted the wagon, outspanned the oxen, and went to bathe in the stream that ran down the centre of the valley. Kaspar then got out his best clothes: a very large dark brown felt hat, it had a beautiful nap and was nearly a yard in diameter; a clean white cambric shirt that his father had given him; a silk neckcloth of dark blue, elegantly spotted with small white dots; dark green velvet small-clothes, and a new, bright blue cloth coat somewhat military in cut with large horn buttons; white silk stockings, and shoes with silver buckles. He also prepared the presents he had brought for the King: twelve brass bangles, a roll of scarlet cloth, a bottle of sweet oil for the healing of sores, a large mother-of-pearl-handled pocket-knife with folding blades, and a white china cup with a coloured picture of King George the Third painted on its side.

From the moment of their arrival they were visited by women and girls. These commented freely on the whiteness of Kaspar's skin, on the quality of his clothes, and the peculiar texture of his hair, which they removed his hat to feel. Nor were they abashed by his bathing, but, on the contrary, pressed nearer, eagerly, married women and maidens alike. They seemed surprised when they saw he was made as other men. Satisfied on this point, they either left or went to call their friends. In Links and the Silent One they showed little interest; in Adam and Eve a certain amount, and only with difficulty could they be restrained from killing them. The young women were well and gracefully formed. They seemed cheerful and ready to laugh. Naked, except for small aprons of skins, some of which were beautifully embroidered with beads, they stood about, chattering like birds. As darkness fell, they moved off, still chattering and gesticulating.

As he sat over his fire Kaspar talked to Links about the women. They had differed a great deal from each other in size, colour, and shape.

'They are all captured women,' Links said. 'When the Zulus came here they brought no women or cattle. They brought only their spears and shields. Mziligazi is breeding a new nation from them. Already they have a new name. They are no longer the Amazulu, but the Matabele, the people of the long shields.'

Kaspar passed an uneasy night. After the silence of the veld, the sound of the shouting, the singing, and the strumming of the native drums and stringed instruments disturbed him. It continued till the dawn, when it was interrupted by the crowing of a thousand cocks, each challenging its neighbour.

The sun was hardly up when the King's messenger came. With Links and the Silent One, accompanied by his servants carrying the gifts, Kaspar went to the palace.

2

Mziligazi was a man of medium height, with a powerful chest and thick neck. He was younger than Kaspar had expected, and his voice was soft, almost effeminate. Round his shorn head he wore a wax ring decorated with three feathers from the tail of a parroquet. They were placed horizontally, one in front and two behind. Round his neck he wore a single string of bright blue beads; a bunch of twisted sinews encompassed his left ankle, and round his waist was a girdle of leopards' tails.

'I wish to trade. And to hunt.'

Kaspar paused while Links translated his words to the King, who smiled, nodded his head, and spoke to the old induna who stood on his right hand. The induna laughed. The King's women, kneeling on mats before him, laughed. The laughter was taken up by those behind the King. It swept round the royal circle and away from it till everyone was laughing and looking at Kaspar.

'Tell him I wish to hunt,' Kaspar said again. 'Ask him if he gives his permission.' He felt himself getting angry. The King's women, great chocolate-coloured masses of fat, heavy as river horses, rolled about on their hams in sycophantic laughter at their master's jokes. One, passing her breast under her arm, gave the child on her back suck. Their laughter was without humour. Whatever the King said would be funny to them if they thought he intended it that way. Though he used Links to interpret, Kaspar could understand much of what was said.

Except for the King, over whom one of his attendants held an ox-hide shield, there was no shade, and the warriors and women shone with sweat and grease.

Mziligazi sat in front of his hut. He paid no attention to the presents Kaspar had brought him. They looked paltry arranged in a pattern on a koodoo skin at his feet. Kaspar remembered buying them in Cape Town. 'So you are going trading in the wilds,' the merchant had said.

Above all things, he must show no fear. Coenraad had warned him. 'You take a risk, Kaspar,' he had said. 'But you will come back a man, or you will not come back. Before God, it is in my heart that a man is twice weaned, once away from milk and once to blood.' Kaspar folded his arms across his chest. With his fingers he pinched the muscles of his arms. They were hard. If they killed him, those muscles would go on quivering ... the muscles of his arms, of his legs, of his belly would go on twitching after he was dead. Relaxed, his bowels and bladder would empty themselves and he, Kaspar, would be nothing. Under the spears and the kerries he would have become offal. He made himself think of Aletta. The thought of her was like the taste of honey in his mouth. For her he wanted to live. Because of her he did not dare to die. She might be going to have his child. She might be cast out or forced to marry another. He must finish here and get back to her. In a few months the hue and cry would have died down.

He thought of Rudolf's house — he could almost see it — of his parting with Aletta, of their coming together wordlessly in the shed. What would happen to her? There was no saying what a man like Rudolf, good-natured and friendly as he was, might do under such circumstances. Kaspar was appalled at the thought. 'I should have stayed,' he thought. For a woman to have a child before marriage was not rare, but then the man was with her and their betrothal a bond tantamount to marriage. But this looked like seduction. He knew that it was not. Aletta knew that it was not. But that was what it would seem to others, and his name would be damned with hers, a seducer and a harlot. If only his mind had been at rest about this matter! If only he was certain! And if he had been? Suppose he had got her with child and had known it; then, unable to leave and unable to go, he would have stayed in the vicinity. He would have kept going back and forth between Rudolf's place and Coenraad's, and because of this would without doubt in the end have been taken by those who sought him. Dead, how could he help Aletta? And alive up here, how could he help her?

The King, the women, and the warriors seemed insignificant now. He hardly saw them. A man and woman came together. They loved without thinking of the future. How could they think at such a time? There was no future, no past; no present, even. When one loved, time itself was obliterated and irrelevant. A child and the act of love were as little related as a lightning stroke and a clap of thunder. They were one, the one caused by the other, a part of it, but different. He looked at the picture of King George the Third on the cup. He had shot one of his soldiers. That was why he could not go back. Before God, if he could not go back, all that was alive in him was dead already. What was the nest when the bird had flown? He stepped forward. A warrior, his tippet of white and black ostrich plumes waving, sprang out with his spear raised. The King thrust him back.

Kaspar stood still. Now was his chance. He had learnt the greeting phrases from Links.

'Oh, Black Bull,' he said, 'oh, father of a multitude; oh, sire of lions; oh, Chief who bestrides the storm-clouds as though they were riding oxen; oh, Black Elephant, of whom all maidens dream, I wish to trade with you and your people. I wish also to hunt on your hills, your valleys; and along the mighty rivers of your land.'

'Your wishes are small,' the King said. 'Truly, your wishes are like those of the little ant that says: "Master, can I dwell in the timber of your house?" And then in the night brings all his friends, and behold, that house falls. I say that the white men are as ants. They come slowly. One here and one there. Then one day many will come. You can trade. But I will have no hunting. No white men among my elephants. No white men looking for gold along my rivers.'

His eyes narrowed. Kaspar waited.

'I shall not kill you,' the King said. 'I shall keep you by me, for you make me laugh. Hunt? What do you come to hunt? Is it steenboks you would hunt? Is it dassies in the mountains?'

'I hunt elephants,' Kaspar said.

'Elephants!' the King said. 'What are elephants? Would you know one if you saw one?'

'I should know one,' Kaspar said.

'Elephants!' The King, laughing loudly, stood up.

Everyone shouted 'How! How!' They looked surprised as if they had seen something of surprising beauty; as if a vision had burst upon them.

'Elephants,' Kaspar repeated.

'Have you ever killed one?'

'No.'

'Have you ever seen one?' the King asked again.

'No.'

The King laughed louder. His mood had changed.

'Then you can hunt them. You can hunt them till they drive you out of the land, or kill you, flinging you into the air with their trunks and flattening you beneath their knees. But before they kill you, you must eat and drink. Bring beer' — he spat upon his palm. 'Have it here before the spittle is dry upon my hand.'

A slave sprang away and returned, followed by three women with pots on their heads.

'We will feast and sing and dance,' the King said. 'Take

heed, my children' — he raised his voice — 'the white boy
is as a calf to the Black Bull. He lives in my shadow. My
breath is upon him.' He spoke rapidly to the induna beside
him, who repeated the King's remark.

Laughter swept over them again.

'What is it?' Kaspar said to Links. 'What does he say?'

'He says you are like a little drum that makes a big
noise. He is willing to see if the drum is empty or full of
meat.'

'He will see,' Kaspar said.

3

Again Kaspar slept badly. The beer he had drunk, the
mass of meat that the King had pressed upon him, feeding
him with it from his own hand, lay heavily in his stomach.
His fears for Aletta kept recurring. Since he could do nothing,
why could he not put her out of his head? Thoughts of a
woman emasculated a man. Only so long as he kept away
from the Border and moved here and there without plan
or regularity was he safe. Only by never sleeping two nights
in one place and never frequenting one area could a man in
his pass hope to keep alive. He tried to think of elephants,
but in his mind he saw one of the girls who had brought beer
to the feast. She was one of Mziligazi's concubines, that
were ironically, it seemed to him, known as the King's sisters.
She had been light in colour, with a small straight nose and
oblique, hot, brown eyes. She had walked beautifully, swaying like a reed, with her breasts thrust upward, and her body
braced from the loins against the weight of the great pot
upon her head. He thought of the line of her arm and
breast as, kneeling, she raised her hand to put down the pot.
The pink palms of her hands and the soles of her feet looked
soft. Like the others, she had been naked but for a little
fringe of bead-embroidered apron that hung in front of her
waist. Behind she wore nothing.

Kaspar dreamed of Aletta. She was wearing blue. Suddenly she was naked and her skin changed, darkening to golden brown. She carried an earthen jar upon her head. She pursued him, mixed up with herds of elephants that rushed at him trumpeting with raised trunks. He woke ... a Kaffir woman! Surely it had not come to that? Yet what else was there for him? He was a renegade, a man classed as a murderer, with a price upon his head. If he wanted a woman, the King, in his present mood, would give him one; or more than one if he asked for them, and they would be as much his as the cattle the King had sent him; as much his as the cows to milk, the oxen to kill. But he did not want them.

He saw the brown girl again. He could not get her out of his mind. He saw her going out of the kraal with the empty pot balanced on her head, her croup swaying. She had been conscious that he was looking at her; conscious that she was woman and desirable; conscious of her power to tempt men. She was one of the King's women, and to tamper with her would mean death for both. But did death matter now? His life was no longer a matter of sincere endeavour. It had become something to hate with, to gamble with; a thing with which to make a parody and a laughing-stock of the thing men called love. Since he could not have it, he would destroy it. There was no love. There was only pleasure: the pleasure of loving, of eating, of drinking, of fighting, of hunting; the pleasure of living till you were killed.

He rolled about, cursing the rats which infested the hut the King had put at his disposal. As soon as he was settled, one would run across him. His dogs were at the wagon; he had not brought them with him for fear they would fight with the village curs. And this would go on for days. Today had been no more than a prelude. There would be more dancing, more mock battles, and smelling out, while oxen were roasted whole and strings of women brought fresh beer. He thought of the brown girl again, of her looking at him, manoeuvring

to be near him. It was not a pretty death to have your
bones broken with kerries and be left to die.

What would happen to his people if he was killed?...
But what would happen to them if he was killed hunting?
At Coenraad's camp there had been a faint flavour of justice. It had been savage, but its savagery had been super-
imposed on a past, less savage life. It had taken all old
van Ek's sophistry to justify it and all Coenraad's flamboy-
ance to disguise it. It had a reason. It rose out of hatred
for the English. It was a revolt against itself, a seeking
of revenge against those who had brought it about. Among
Coenraad's folk, if there were questions there were also
answers. Here there were only men who, knowing neither
right nor wrong, understood nothing but the swift blow of a
spear and the swift parry of a stick or a shield; who served
unthinkingly a king that was at once a child and a man;
a king who took women as a child takes sweetmeats; who
made blood flow because he liked its colour; who killed
for a whim; who tore the arms from men as a child pulls
the wings out of a fly. A world of fighting men who thought
of cattle and women as rewards, and of women who, regarding themselves as cattle, were ready to be used, purchased,
and sold, conquered into servitude and bred like mares to
any master.

Kaspar slept fitfully, no sooner asleep than he was woken
by the rats that gnawed at his toe-nails till they bled. He
sat up. How much had he dreamt and how much was fact?
Had the girl really looked at him like that? Perhaps it was
just that he was overtired, that he had overeaten and over-
drunk, that he was excited by the fact that he had at last
arrived. Try as he would, he could not separate reality from
nightmare. The girl was real enough. But had she singled
him out? Had her coquetries been directed at him? Had
she wished him to notice her? He got up, put on his velskoen, and went out. He wished he had spent the night in
his wagon, but Links had said that he must use the hut.

Links had not mentioned the rats. He went back and lay down. He might be able to sleep with his shoes on his feet.

4

'I have been waiting for you to wake, lord.'

Kaspar looked down. Outside his hut, sitting against it, was Ringhals, the old witch doctor. He was closely wrapped in his kaross.

'The young sleep long,' he said. 'They are not like the old who need little sleep, little food. Ai . . . the old need only sunlight and a small gourd of milk to live. It is strange that the old, like the young, should crave milk; that the very old like the very young should seek women only for the warmth they can get from their bodies. When a man is strong and full of fire, he seeks a woman's body for other things. He seeks her out of the pride of his manhood. Ai, to a young man a woman is the answer to all questions; he adds woman to woman in his heart, as a maid adds beads to her embroideries. But young men should be careful in their choice. Young men sleep long.' He looked at the sun reproachfully. 'Yet they do not sleep forever. To sleep forever is a long sleep' — he paused; 'and only when the moon is green can a man drink from another's pot without that man's consent. Ai, and particularly is this so if he thinks to drink secretly in the night. Suppose that while he drinks the other should want the pot? Should wake and stretch out his hand for it? There might even be some who would wake him; who would say: "Oh, Black Bull, oh, Elephant who rides the storm-clouds as though they were riding oxen, you have a beautiful new pot that it were well to savour."'

'What are you doing here?' Kaspar asked. 'Have you news from Coenraad?' he asked.

'I have no news from Coenraad. I cannot tell you why I am here unless it is that the lost ones called me to refute Toolah, the false wizard. But you are the man who killed the soldier. I saw that fight. I saw also the old man die and witnessed the burial of his body. It was only the body that was buried, for his spirit is abroad. It walks,' he said. He pulled his kaross closer and sighed.

'What do you mean by your words? Are they a warning?'

'Words, oh, white man, what words? What have I said? Behold the grass.' He pointed to a tall tuft near him. 'Can you see the dew upon it?'

'I can see the dew,' Kaspar said.

The old man raised his hand to the sky. 'When the sun is there' — he pointed straight overhead — 'will there be dew on the grass?'

'There will be no dew,' Kaspar said.

'There were no words. There was no warning. I am old. I crave only for sunshine and a little milk. But it is in my heart that a man who has drunk heavily drinks no more. It is in my heart that if another man who would drink and was thirsty stood by a tree' — he was staring out at a solitary tree on the veld — 'he might find dew upon it if the hour was propitious.'

'At what hour does the dew fall, old man?'

'It falls when the moon goes down, lord; in the hour before the dawn when the world is grey, and still, and cold.'

'Why do you tell me this? Why do you bear me her message? What have you to gain?'

'I bring no message. And as to gain, my ways are strange. Perhaps there is a bull elephant that I love not. Perhaps a maid that I would pleasure. Perhaps I would betray the drinker of dew and profit by it. Who knows? My ways are wonderful. Even I do not understand my own ways. Even I am surprised and abashed at my great powers.' He closed his eyes. 'It is warm enough to sleep now.' He opened his eyes. 'The girl is named N'tembi,' he said.

So it had not been a dream. The King's sister had sent him a message.

'Explain more fully,' Kaspar said.

The wizard did not answer. The kaross had slipped, his thin ribs rose and fell as he slept.

Kaspar ate his breakfast slowly. 'I should go now,' he thought. 'I should go before more befalls. But the King will not let me go, and since he will not let me go the girl will have her way.' It was simple enough. Suppose he refused her. Then she could, without difficulty, incriminate him and have him destroyed. Thus, only by falling in with her wishes could he close her mouth, for then, with her life as well as his own at stake, she would be careful and bound to him as much by self-interest as by desire. Thus, if matters went as it seemed they must, the dangerous course was the safest. He was surprised at his own decision, surprised to see how little morality or feeling entered into it. The girl wanted him, but no doubt she wanted more than that. If she only wanted a man there were plenty ready to risk death for the pleasure of possessing her. And as to the wizard's motives: no doubt time would show them.

5

An attendant of the King's came requesting Kaspar's presence at the great kraal. Mziligazi was sitting on a rolled mat in front of his house. He was talkative.

'What are the clouds?' he asked. 'Are they not like sheep's wool?'

'The clouds are vapour, O King,' Kaspar said. 'They are like the steam that rises from a cooking-vessel.'

'Where is the vessel, white boy?' the King asked.

'There is no vessel.'

'Then there is no vapour. Now, tell me,' he went on, 'why do the white men have only one wife? Or is this a lie that I have been told?'

'It is not a lie,' Kaspar said. 'It is the law.'

'Why is it the law? Is it so that they shall not tire themselves with women and therefore be more fitted for war?

Before battle, men should not lie with women; they should exercise with their arms. They should eat much meat. Is this what the white men do?'

'They have one wife because it is the law,' Kaspar repeated.

'That I do not believe,' the King said. 'If it is not for war, then it is because they can use no more than one wife, and if this be so, either the women must be insatiable as wolves, or the men as weak as children. I have heard that even the white King has but one wife and no sisters.' He laughed. 'Before the sun goes down, you will see the might of a nation. Ai, you shall see it. Fetch the doctors!' he cried. 'Bring them here. Bring also the visiting one who calls himself the Little Flower. I would test his powers.'

A messenger ran out. 'The King calls for the doctors! The Black Elephant, the Black Bull cries for the doctors!'

Soon they came. Old men masked, hung with bladders, bones, beads, dried beetles, snakes, and toads; ornamented with the tails of wild beasts, their thin ribs bedaubed with paint. Two only were unmasked: Ringhals and a young girl naked but for a live snake coiled round her neck and a girdle that ended in a small apron of white beads. When the others abased themselves before the King, she stood erect, staring past him at the hills.

'I see you, doctors,' the King said.

'We see you, Lord of the Heavens. Do you want rain, Black Bull? Do you want your enemies smelt out?' They writhed so that the bones and ornaments they wore rattled together. 'Do you want us to prophesy?' They crept forward, hopping like baboons on the knuckles of their clenched hands, grovelling their shrunken limbs in the dust, sniffing at it like hounds. The one nearest to Kaspar began to writhe faster, wriggling a stern decorated with a fringe of zebra mane. 'Blood ... blood ... blood,' he chanted. 'I smell blood. I see it running hot and scarlet. I see the vultures tearing the entrails of men with their beaks. I see them

plucking out their eyes.' Great bubbles of spittle burst
from the corners of his mouth as he scuttled in and out of
the assembled warriors. Each one as he neared him blenched
and turned pale. Not a man moved. Of all the doctors,
this was the one they most feared. He was the most dangerous, the most blood-thirsty, the most rapacious in his demands. Suddenly Ringhals rose, and, pointing to the wriggling
figure with both outstretched, leathery arms, began to laugh.

'Behold Toolah,' he said. 'Behold the great doctor sniffing
the ground like a dog. What is it, Toolah?' he asked. 'Do
you seek a bitch in season? In this place you need not seek
far. Why leave your own old kraal? Have you not twenty-
one wives selected for their youth and beauty? Is even one
of them satisfied? What do you do when you hold them in
your arms? Is it not said that while they work in your
fields they speak together and wait for the return of the
impis; and that as the spears of the young men are hungry
for blood, so are your women hungry for men?' He began to
shuffle sideways, putting one leg across the other. 'I am
the Little Flower of All the World. I am the Little Cloud
that Precedes the Storm. I am Ringhals; I am Mamba.'

He had reached the girl with the snake.

Again he raised his hands.

'Come, small one ... Come, spirit of evil. Come, beauty
that goes on its belly. Come, death that strikes swiftly.'

The snake uncoiled slowly, slipping round the girl's neck,
rearing up till its head was above hers. Weaving slowly back
and forth, it stared at him. He raised his arms farther
towards it.

'See, it will strike,' the people whispered. 'See, its head is
going back to strike the impostor.'

Like a thick rope, the snake unwound, dropped forward,
sliding its head round his neck and staring into his eyes.
Its darting tongue was against his lips. He opened his
toothless mouth. The snake put its head into his mouth and
withdrew it. For a moment the old man and the young

woman stood bound together by the snake. Its forepart was round the neck of the one, its tail grasped the neck of the other. Then it advanced. It was round Ringhals' neck. Coil after coil was round it. Its belly hung down over his chest, its tail, beyond his shrunken loins, almost touched the ground. Undoing the snake as though it were a scarf, Ringhals reached for its head, opened its mouth, spat into it, and then, winding it round and round his stomach, began to dance. At first it was a strange, tottering dance, the dance of an old man; then it became stolid like the dance of a solemn child, his feet going flat upon the ground, his knees bent; then it changed again, becoming swift and lissom. It was seductive, the dance of a girl. It changed again. It was the dance of a young man, of a warrior.

'Ai, Toolah, smeller-out of men,' he shrieked, 'can you do this? Can you charm the snake from the snake-woman? Can you dance with it? See, I dance with it.' Putting the snake on the ground, he sat down. 'Go back, snake,' he said. 'Go back, evil one. Go back to where you belong.' As it crawled away, even the doctors fell back. This way and that it went, till, finding the girl, it climbed her as though she were a tree.

Ringhals closed his eyes. 'I would rest,' he said. 'The lost ones are coming to me.' Opening his eyes he looked at the King. 'Is it the custom to give beer to strangers?' he asked. 'My heart is cold in my body. I am older than the world and need much beer. The hosts of the lost ones suck it from me.'

'Give him beer,' the King said. 'Bring much beer and meat.'

Among the carriers of beer was the girl. Her eyes met Kaspar's and he looked away.

The King passed him the rib of an ox he had been biting. 'Eat, white boy,' he said. Kaspar ate. The witch doctors were clustered together in the shade of a hut. The snake-girl had gone. Ringhals sat alone in the bare space in front of the

King. He had emptied his bag of bones out in front of him. They lay between his legs. Like an ancient and shrunken child, he played with them. Muttering to himself, he moved them back and forth, rolling them with clawlike hands, picking them up, examining them, holding them close to his face, and replacing them.

'He makes medicine,' the King said.

'I make strong medicine,' Ringhals said. He could not have heard the King speak; he was too far away.

'So the King wishes to test me,' Ringhals went on; 'to test the Little Cloud. Does the Black Bull know that I put that thought into his head? That I wish to be tested? That it is in my heart to prove Toolah impotent? Ai ... ai ...' He laughed. 'Like an assegai my words are sharp, cutting on both edges. Today I made snake moutie. Today I played gently with death, cradling it in my arms as a woman cradles a suckling child.' He drank more beer. 'But what I have done is nothing. When I have rested I will perform marvels. I will show the King, the Black Elephant, that he and his warriors are cattle being herded by false doctors. Ai ... ai ... before the sun sets, I will have them broken like reeds under a herd of buffalo. Who smelt out Masild? Who smelt out Kari and Tauwana and the others who loved the King? Who seeks, one by one, to kill all those who love the Black Bull best? Who culls the greatest of his captains, whispering against them?' He peered down at his bones. He turned his ear to them as though he were listening. 'What do I see?' he asked. 'What do I hear? I see Toolah. I hear the name of Toolah. I see him waxing like a woman great with child. But I say that he is not great with child. I say that he is great with wind: that he is blown up like a bladder. I say that the spear of my mind is sharply pointed against the bladder of his intelligence. I say that I threaten Toolah. I say that the vultures that will pluck out his eyes are already on the wing.' He looked upward and pointed. 'That one and that one. Those are but two of the multitude that will pick his bones. The lost ones cry for Toolah, the evil one: the one who has taken their name in vain.' He drank more beer, and then, gathering his bones into their bag, he put his head upon it and slept.

More food was brought and regiment after regiment came into the kraal. At a given signal they began to march, greeting the King as they passed him. They were all boys. They carried spears and vari-coloured shields. One regiment wore caps like the Malays with a peak six inches high, ornamented with a bunch of feathers. Another wore small turbans of otter skin with crane's feathers at the side. A third wore bunches of feathers all over their heads, fastened by a network of small ties. They ran, trotting lightly on their toes, but so great was their number that they shook the ground. As they passed in front of the King, they saluted him, crying 'Bayete,' and then under their captains they began to run, weaving in and out, shouting, whistling, and hissing between their teeth, leaping, beating their kerries against their shields, each trying to excel the other in the feats of agility that they performed. Clouds of red dust rose. As they leapt, they loomed up out of it, holding their shields and shining spears high in the air. There was no sound but their hissing, the stamping of their feet; nothing visible but the slim black bodies glistening with sweat that showed vaguely through the opaque red dust. With a final shout, they ran out as they had run in.

The King was smiling. 'Those were but boys,' he said. 'They are the lion cubs that one day will be men. Then I will give them wives. But first they must earn them.' His eyes lit up. 'But here be men,' he said.

A new regiment came in. They were men of thirty years or more, veterans, scarred and torn by war. They carried white shields and were armed with short, wide-bladed assegais, and kerries. Over their shoulders hung cloaks of white cows' tails. On their heads they wore tufts of white cows' tails and ornaments of white cows' tails round their

arms above the elbow and below the knee. The regiment
that followed them was dressed in thick capes of black
ostrich feathers. On their heads they wore heavy caps, also
of black ostrich feathers. Their shields were black, pointed
at each end, and stiffened with rawhide plaited vertically.
They carried the same short, broad-bladed assegais that
Tshaka had introduced and knob-kerries made of rhinoceros
horn. With these they were said to be able to bring down a
running buck or a bird on the wing. The sound of their
running was like rolling thunder, for they were strong, heavy
men with deep chests. Great muscles ran rippling over their
backs and down their thighs and calves.

Stacking their shields, they danced, while the women and
girls clapped their hands and chanted. The clapping girls
looked like willow slips against a forest of oaks. The King
clapped his hands, keeping time for the girls.

'They are my children,' he said to Kaspar. 'They are the
fathers of the cubs.'

Toolah had crept forward. He was crouching at the King's
feet. 'Oh, Black Bull,' he whispered, 'look towards the river.'

The King looked.

'Do you not see a river horse on the bank?'

'I see it.'

Toolah smiled. 'Would it not please the King that his
children should bring it to him?'

'They shall bring it.' He called to the captain of the Black
Shields and pointed.

The old warrior stiffened. 'It shall be done,' he said. 'It
shall be done as the King commands, with men's bare hands
alone.'

He raised his arm and the dancing ceased. 'We go, lord,'
he said. He turned and, followed by his men, ran bare-
handed out of the kraal.

To Kaspar's amazement he saw the regiment divide and
race to the bank of the river. Before the hippopotamus could
get back to the water, they were upon it. He saw it charge,

saw one man cut in two by its jaws, and then saw no more
as the warriors swarmed over it. It was the King's command
that they bring him the river horse, and slowly, like men
dragging a living mountain, they brought it to him. The
way from the river was strewn with men; men who lay still,
men who tried to rise; but it came nearer and nearer. It
came, dragged, forced, overpowered by the sheer weight of
men upon it through the gates of the great kraal. Bellowing,
roaring, biting with jaws that could engulf a barrel, it was
forced in.

'Kill!' the King cried. 'Let the boys kill.'

The boys sprang forward, whistling. The men, their own
fathers, flung themselves down as they came so that their
sons could pass over them. The hippopotamus lay on its side.
It looked like a giant pincushion, so full was it stuck with
spears. The boys fell back.

The regiment of Black Shields, depleted, covered with
blood, ran up to where the King sat. Its captain, a man of
fifty, was in front of them. A string of rawhide was tied
fast above his wrist; his hand was gone.

'The King's will is done,' he said. 'Is one enough?' he
asked. 'Shall we go into the river and drive more out?'

'It was well done,' the King said. 'Kill your wounded and
throw them into the river.'

Kaspar felt cold. He thought he was going to faint. He
recovered himself, and Ringhals began to laugh, holding his
naked flanks with clawlike hands.

The King's smile of pleasure turned to a frown. 'Why do
you laugh, wizard?' he asked.

'Laugh, O King? What is laughter? Laughter'—his
voice was pitched high—'is but the tribute of the foolish
to the exhibitions of the wise, or sometimes of the wise
to the exhibitions of the foolish. Is it wise or foolish, great
one, for the lion to sever his own veins and watch his red
blood flow?' He pointed towards the river. 'Behold the
King's blood flowing,' he said. 'I know. All the world knows

that the King has much blood, but even elephants can die from the loss of blood. A bloodless elephant is meat for wolves and jackals. Fine warriors lie dead, O King, and to what purpose? And at whose suggestion? Next time, lord, let Toolah charm the river horse. Let him cast his spells upon it. And if by some accident the great doctor were killed, who would mourn him?'

Facing the King, Ringhals sat on his hams, cross-legged, and went on speaking softly as if for the King's ear alone. 'I am a great doctor, a great wizard, and I say your doctors are small men who disgrace their name as doctors. Men with maggots in their hearts and worms in their intestines. Ai, they are suckers of blood, ravishers of virgins. All day I have sat here insulting them, and they do nothing. They have no powers. All they can do is to scratch their vermin while they plot. Think back, O King; think of the brave men who have died because of them. Think forward, O King, to the day when, because of them, you have no brave men left to die; to the day you stand alone with the jackals round you. What does one do with a flea, O King? One crushes it between the nails of one's thumbs so that it goes click and is no more. What does one do with a louse, O lord? With a tick? With a biting fly? What does one do,' he cried out loud, 'O people, with the suckers of blood? With smellers-out who know so little of their craft that they must work by day when they can read the faces of men?'

'Be silent, stranger,' the King said. 'You talk too much. Your words are big, but what do we know of you?'

'Shall we kill him?' a chief behind the King said.

'Kill me?' Ringhals said, surprised. 'Why would you kill me? How would you kill me?'

'You shall not be killed,' the King said, 'but you and my doctors shall compete in magic.'

'When they are ready, let them come, lord,' Ringhals said. 'I am content.'

Setting a child's skull on his knees, he stared into its eyeless sockets. More beer was brought. N'tembi took Kaspar's calabash to fill it. Her hand touched his.

'Bring on the dancers,' the King said.

They came, and with them came the trained oxen, their horns twisted into fantastic shapes — bent like lyres, curled like the horns of a koodoo, or downward like pot-hooks.

'Bring meat. Make music.'

On into the night the feast continued, with beer and dancing and meat. Great fires blazed. Drums beat continuously. Kaspar's eyes were blurred by the figures that leapt and jumped, his ears deafened by the clapping of hands, by the never-ending stamp of thousands of feet, by the scream of instruments. There were to be days of this — days of bloodshed, of smellings-out, of debauchery. The King's eyes were bloodshot and his speech thick with beer when he called for his women and prepared to retire.

'Tomorrow,' he said, 'the wizards will contend. Tomorrow more men will be here and you shall see more of the might of my nation, white boy.'

He drank from the china cup that Kaspar had given him.

Back in his hut Kaspar waited till it was time to go. He thought of a thousand justifications for going, but the blood that pounded in his veins as he waited was the reason. He had to see N'tembi. It was as if she had put a spell upon him. He had not undressed. Getting up, he looked out. The moon had gone. The night was dark blue, pierced by stars. Round him the world slept: the King with his women, the warriors with their spears beside them. He buckled on his belt. Not a dog barked; nothing moved. The world was drunk with beer and sleep, even the dogs were heavy with meat, and except for the throb of one distant drum everything was silent. Would the girl be there? Moving carefully, he walked past the huts. They looked like great beehives black against the sky. His legs were wet with dew. Running down his trousers, it filled his shoes. Away to the left, he saw the dying fire at his wagon. Near it his people would be

sleeping. Had that wagon ever been at home? Had he once
watched it loaded up at his father's house? Months? It
was not months ago, it was years ago. It had been in
another life. The tree loomed up before him. His hand felt
for the knife in his belt, the feel of its horn-hilt gave him
comfort.

She was waiting for him. He stretched out his hand and
touched her breasts. The whites of her eyes and her teeth
glinted within a few inches of his face. Her scent, that of a
musky animal, was in his nostrils. She was soft to touch,
soft and silky in his arms, and as he held her he thought of
Aletta; thought, This is Kaspar holding a Kaffir girl in his
arms. Then he forgot Aletta.

CHAPTER XIX

RINGHALS MAKES MEDICINE

I

WHEN Kaspar came back, he found Ringhals asleep in the doorway of his hut.

'What do you want?' he said.

'I, lord? I want nothing. What should I want, who can command the cohorts of the dead, who can call up whole regiments of lost ones? I want nothing unless it be your company for an hour and, perhaps, a mouthful of beer. Have you beer?' he asked.

Kaspar brought out a pot of beer from his hut. 'Here is beer,' he said. 'And now I would sleep, for I am tired.'

'Why are you tired, lord?' Ringhals asked. 'You are young, and was not the dew on the tree refreshing?' Before Kaspar could answer him, he went on: 'Something has come into my mind, lord. It is a small matter, but one in which you can help me. It has to do with Toolah. It were well that this matter of Toolah were finished, for it is in my heart that he, too, thinks of the dew. That he, too, would shake it from the branch. And it is in my heart that he knows something of what has passed.' He took snuff from the small metal box suspended round his neck. Tears of pleasure rolled down his cheeks.

Kaspar shivered. 'What is in your mind?' he asked.

'A small thing, lord. Near here there is a thicket where a mamba lurks. I would have you come with me and take it.'

'A mamba,' Kaspar echoed. 'Who is mad enough to take a mamba?'

'Let the lord come with me and he will see.'

Ringhals got up. 'Come,' he said. 'It is not far. Do you fear a mamba more than Toolah?' he asked. 'Besides, I have the mamba. I need only help.'

'Shall I bring my gun?' Kaspar asked.

'Bring no gun.'

Kaspar had trouble in keeping up with Ringhals as he shuffled through the dark. When they had gone a mile, he stopped and gave Kaspar the forked stick he was carrying.

'The snake is trapped,' he said. 'When we get to him put the fork over his neck behind his head and hold him fast. After that I will do what is necessary. I have strong snake medicine, so be not afraid. You saw today how I charm serpents,' he added.

'It was not a mamba,' Kaspar said.

They went on into the thicket. Here, squatting on his haunches, Ringhals made a small fire and, lighting a torch, told Kaspar to follow him. They came to a ruined hut. 'Now act quickly while I hold the light,' he said.

They went in, and there, in a small wicker cage, Kaspar saw the snake. Coil upon coil of it. As it saw them, it hissed and tried to get out, but could not: its body was swollen with the dove it had swallowed.

'Quickly!' Ringhals whispered. 'Quickly, before it vomits up the bird and strikes.'

Kaspar jumped forward and pinned the small, wicked head to the ground. Ringhals knelt beside the snake and drove a long thorn into its skull. The wicker cage leapt and rolled as the snake lashed about. A moment later it was dead. Pulling a string of rawhide from round his waist, Ringhals looped it round the snake's head. 'Make loose,' he said.

Handling the dead snake carefully, Ringhals pushed its head back into the cage, forced the dead dove out of its mouth, and, turning, left the hut, dragging the snake along the ground behind him.

'Come quickly,' he said.

'Where are you going?' Kaspar asked.

'To Toolah. Should not one doctor make gifts to another? But come fast, lord, for just now we are in danger.'

'It is dead,' Kaspar said.

'Ai . . . it is dead; but is the other dead?' Ringhals asked. 'Is his wife dead?'

They went back to the town and stopped by a large hut that stood somewhat apart from the others. Here Ringhals halted, and with his knife cut a small hole through the wall of reeds and mud. A woman's hand came out to meet his. It took the rawhide string. And slowly, as though it were alive, the snake was drawn inside. Giving the hole a last look and satisfied that it did not show, Ringhals went back with Kaspar.

'Toolah is a fool,' Ringhals said. 'If he must make a concubine of the snake-woman, he should have done it after another fashion. Ai, lord . . .' he said, 'for the old there is only one way with women. They must pay for them with gifts, flatter them with words, and, upon occasion, sleep soundly. What does it matter being deceived, provided one knows of it? And by allowing oneself to be deceived one gets complacent service. Ai . . . the women laugh in their hearts when they deceive an old man, and give him what he wishes. But the old men laugh most, for the young men take the fire out of women and leave them docile. What is woman to an old man who has had many?' he asked. 'She is nothing. She is a memory brought nearer. She is like a lily he has once smelt. Ai . . . she is a perfume from the past. And Toolah was a fool, and more than a fool, to let the snake-girl have access to the hut where he keeps his mysteries.'

'You seem content,' Kaspar said.

'I am content,' Ringhals answered. 'I am content when I consider the effect of woman upon man and of man upon woman. In this lies the key to their management. By this knowledge can they be raised up and by it can they be flung down. Rest now, and when you wake you will see my power.'

2

More regiments had come in during the night. As Kaspar proceeded to the great kraal next day, he saw them standing by their cooking-fires, adjusting their finery while they waited. The spectators, too, were more numerous. They squatted round the open space where the spectacle would take place. In hundreds, men, women, and children, boys and girls, all waited for the King. Twice a wave of excitement passed over them; it was like a wind passing over a field of black corn. 'He comes!' they whispered, making ready to spring up.

The witch doctors were clustered like vultures together. Ringhals was there, sitting apart, with his black eyes flickering under half-closed lids.

Kaspar felt himself keyed up; as expectant as the others, he watched the gates of the King's palace. He marvelled at Ringhals' calm. Both strangers among these people, he felt himself tied to the old man by some strange bond. What would be the outcome of last night's adventure? That there would be an outcome, he did not doubt. Under that shrivelled skull there was a plan. His thoughts were dispelled by the cries of the people. This time the King was coming. Heralds dressed in monkey skins and carrying short wands were crying out his praises as they capered and pranced in front of him.

'Bayete ... Bayete ... Great One ... Father of Heaven ... King of Heaven!' the crowd roared.

Taking no notice of them, the King sat down. 'Let them begin,' he said.

The first regiment to come in wore kilts of red ox-tails. They carried assegais and knob-kerries; their long shields were red and white. The performance resembled that of yesterday as they marched, counter-marched, chanted and sang, clapping their thighs and beating their weapons against their shields. They were followed by another regiment, and another. Kaspar lost count of them. They were all big men and their head-dresses made them look gigantic. They were veterans, mature and seasoned killers. Men who many years ago had earned their right to wives.

After them came the women, who danced more slowly, clapped their hands, and sang. To them the King paid no attention. Beer was brought, boiled beef and blood in great baskets, sour milk; and then a space was cleared for the contest of the wizards.

Ringhals was called for. He came forward slowly, greeted the King, and squatted down in front of him.

'Now let us see your powers,' the King said.

'My powers, Lord of Heaven?' Ringhals countered; 'I have no powers. I am an old man. Such powers as I have are not mine, but those of the lost ones that are vested in me, and woe to those that question the lost ones! Woe to the tricksters, the hucksters, the traffickers in human blood! Ai... woe to Toolah, who is like a little child among crocodiles! One that toys with things beyond his understanding. Ai... he is like a child that deems crocodiles to be lizards. Behold!' he said. 'I make ready.'

Kaspar saw his hands moving under his kaross. It covered him up to his neck. With a final wriggle, he stood up. The kaross was on the ground. Except for a strip of soft hide twisted about his loins, Ringhals was naked. In the burning sunlight his every bone, every muscle, and every ligament stood out. He was oiled from head to foot and shone. He no longer looked old. Only his wrinkled face was old. Kaspar saw how he had once received the name of Little Flower. Standing fully erect before the King, he was not more than five feet high. He raised himself on his toes and turned so that all could see him. 'Behold!' he cried, 'I am naked. Look well and see that I am naked. I carry no weapon. There is no medicine under my armpits. Thus, and with power of the lost ones alone, will I conquer Toolah. Let Toolah go, O King, and fetch his medicines. Let him fetch his skulls, his bones, his dried scorpions, his roots and stones. Let him bring the big pot in which he makes his medicine; the pot that he says contains the lost ones. Ai . . . and if the lost ones are contained in Toolah's pot, how is it that I see them round me?'

Toolah ran forward. 'Impostor!' he cried, shaking with rage till the ornaments that he wore strung all over him rattled. 'Today the vultures shall eat you: today the rocks in the place of death shall be smeared with your entrails and the grass about the rocks spattered with your blood.'

One of Toolah's eyelids was painted scarlet, the other white.

'What is it I see?' Ringhals closed his eyes. 'Is it a doctor? Or is it a foolish old man hung with bladders, festooned with the entrails of a fresh-killed bat, draped with the lips of a hyaena? Ai . . . and what is the tail of a gnu to the powerful ones?' he asked. 'Do they care for the tuft from a lion's elbow? Do they fear the skull of an unborn child?' He paused and raised his hand to his ear as though he were listening. 'They do not care,' he said.

'I will contest with you, little stranger that will soon die,' Toolah snarled. His lips were foaming. 'Ai . . . soon we shall see who is the stronger.'

'I am ready to contest with you, but only if you fetch the pot you use: the pot that you consult when you smell out. Too many have died in that pot . . . If you do not bring it you will say that you failed because you had it not.'

Kaspar saw a glance pass between Ringhals and the snake-girl. She nodded her head.

'I will get the pot,' Toolah said.

'I will await you,' Ringhals answered, and sat down.

Toolah moved away. A great silence fell over the people. Their eyes were on Ringhals, sitting immovable on his kaross. Kaspar saw Toolah stoop to enter the hut. He heard him cry out and spring back.

'A mamba!' he cried, 'a mamba!'

Ringhals never raised his head.

Outside the hut, as Toolah turned to run, Kaspar saw the mamba rise. It struck so hard that Toolah fell. It struck again and again; like a long black whip it struck at him; and then faster than the eyes could follow it, it disappeared.

Ringhals did not move. 'I am waiting for Toolah,' he said.

'Mamba . . . a mamba!' the people cried.

The noise died down.

'Some call me Little Cloud,' Ringhals said. 'Some call me Little Flower. I have many names. Ringhals is one. Mamba is another.' Picking up his kaross, he wrapped it about him and went away.

Now were the mysterious proceedings of the night made clear to Kaspar. Ringhals had known that the dead mamba's mate would follow it. He had seen too much and heard too much of witchcraft to be able to dismiss it, but here was one reason for the success of the witch doctors — a vast knowledge of the ways of wild animals and the courage to use them.

That night he met N'tembi by the tree again, and on succeeding nights. Like Delilah, she had shorn his strength from him; he was a man bewildered. It seemed to him that in different bodies women were an everlasting power, as certain in their tides as the sea itself. No process could hurry their slow gestation; none retard it. The tide rose, creeping forward, its waves uncurling along the strand; it fell back, leaving the sand wet with the sea, and the sea heavy with a detritus of sand. It seemed to him that men and women came together like this: and in this lay the power of women; that in possessing them man was possessed; that having drunk he must drink again; the servant of an unknown rhythm, to the ebb and flow of lust. This was what van Ek meant when he said that all life sprang from death, from what man called waste, from cataclysm: birth from blood and broken tissue; life from decomposition, endlessly repetitious and without exception, the very mountains being riven by storms, the very rivers torn from their courses; man and bird and beast and plant and stone, all subject to change; all life interrelated in a pattern at once destructive and constructive; all servants of chance, of circumstance, with annihilation the end of the old, the beginning of the new.

His desire for N'tembi was like an illness. To obtain her he was taking fantastic risks. He thought of the relations of man to man, of man to woman, of woman to woman. What did any man know of another? Life was like a shower of pebbles thrown into still water. Your circle was intersected by those of others. How did you know who was approaching you? Or how close they would come? Or how long would they stay? Was it chance? Or was it more than chance that determined such things? He thought of God, of all that he had learnt at home, of all that his mother and father believed. But how did God fit in with such things as the beating of the slave girl, with the destruction of the Bushmen, with the savagery he had been forced to witness here? How did He fit in with his desire for N'tembi, and the power that forced him to her? Was it as old Christiaan van Ek had said: that God did not care? What then of his feelings for Aletta? He still had them. He still had memories, dreams of what might have been. His feelings for her had been different from those he had for N'tembi, and yet the end had been the same. The culmination the same, save that from Aletta he had obtained release. From N'tembi there was none, only a fury for more, a feeling akin to destruction, as though continuous possession was a justification of his desire to press that smooth, dark body till it flowed wine. The end? **Before God,** there could only be one end if he did not get away.

Getting down on his knees, he prayed for strength. He had been tempted. He had not been able to resist temptation. The forces of his own body had been arrayed against him. His own hands had betrayed him. The lust of his eyes, the lure of his most secret thoughts. His memories of Aletta had betrayed him. Tomorrow, or as soon as he could, he would go. He had finished trading. Would there never be an end to this running away? First from his home, then from the Border, then from Coenraad, and now from Mziligazi's kraal. Was a man never at rest, never able to be at peace? A man was always alone, van Ek said, and always torn by the terror of it. Because of his terror he mated, so that a woman should help to bear the burden of his solitude. Because of it he bred children so that the frail spark of his life should go on, and each man was himself the product of such thoughts, of such feelings, in the endless number of men and women who had come together and had bred and died to make him. They had known nothing of him and he knew nothing of them, but their seed was in his loins and the urge of his thousand progenitors was upon him. It was for this that they had lived. Increase was the will of a God who, if a thousand must be born for one to live, caused a thousand to be born. A God who caused all things to spawn that others might live upon that which they spawned. Life was an endless cycle of reproduction and destruction, of eating or being eaten. And how did this fit in with the new knowledge from France; with the brotherhood of man; with the teaching of Jesus Christ? These were the things he must find out alone. No one could help him.

3

But it was not easy to go.
From dislike, Mziligazi's feeling for Kaspar changed sud-

denly to a liking that was embarrassing. Convinced that he would soon be killed, nothing was too good for him. He was the Black Bull's white calf. He felt like a sacrifice being fattened for slaughter. Food, beer, gifts were thrust upon him. As he was going to be killed, it did not matter what he was given, for the King, he felt, expected to get them back.

'When can I go?' Kaspar asked.

'Go, white boy? Tomorrow is a day, and when tomorrow is done, the sun will rise again. You are in a hurry to die. You are like my young men, hasty to prove yourself. Why go at all? You have traded for much ivory here, and who is to know that you did not kill it? Stay, white boy, and then later, when you are a man, come back and hunt.'

'The Black Bull was once a boy,' Kaspar said. 'Did he sit drinking beer and watching dances? Was it thus that he became the lord of heaven?'

The King laughed. 'One day I will tell you of my boyhood,' he said. 'But it was not like that. It could not be like that since I had no black bull in whose shadow I could stand. I was always the Black Bull. I was born a calf with horns.'

'Ai . . . he was born with horns,' his people echoed. 'Born with horns . . . with horns.'

'Bring beer,' the King shouted, 'and let the young men dance.'

'Then I can go,' Kaspar said.

'You can go,' the King answered, laughing; 'and when you return we will feast again. Where is that wizard?' he asked.

'I am here, O King.'

'I do not like you, Ringhals,' the King said. 'You appear too quickly.'

'What is the will of the Black Elephant?' Ringhals asked.

'That you throw the bones for the white boy; that you find out if he will return; that you set the lost ones over him, if it be in your power.'

'He will return, O Chief. I have seen his return. But I will make medicine for him. Come,' he said to Kaspar, 'and I will make a circle of the lost ones about you.'

Kaspar followed Ringhals to the hut where he slept. A maiden whom the King had given him tended the fire.

'Begone,' Ringhals said to the girl. 'Hide your eyes and close your ears, lest you see or hear the great ones. To see them is to be struck blind; to hear them is to become deaf.'

The girl ran away.

Sitting down, Ringhals put a pinch of powder from the bag he wore round his neck on the fire. He was silent, staring into the flames. They burnt green. He looked like a dead man. At last he spoke.

'I see men,' he said. 'I see death. I see you walking through the valley of death, but I do not see you dead. No, not till you are old will you die, yet round you there will be much death. I see men hanging by riems from a tree. I see a wagon. You are with it; and I see also a woman and a child, an old man and a man who is wounded.'

Sweat was standing out on his forehead. It ran in little beads down the furrows of his cheeks as he stared into the heart of the fire. Suddenly he looked up. 'Your heart is sore,' he said. 'Ai, your heart is sore, like that of a wounded buffalo that goes round seeking whom it may gore with its horns. Ai ... your shoulders are galled with spears, but I say that the wounds will heal. A fever must burn hot before it burns out. I am old and have seen all things. Go now, young man; hunt and let this fever die. Then leave the rising sun on your left hand and go back. It is in my heart that there, though you will be troubled, you will find peace.'

Kaspar gave him snuff and left him still staring into the fire.

What had he meant by men hanging from trees? But he would not die. He would go back to Aletta.

Kaspar went to his wagon. It was ready. Tomorrow he would be gone. Once more his wagon-wheels would turn.

CHAPTER XX

ELEPHANTS

I

THE country they passed through was uninhabited — rich pastoral land that no longer supported cattle. The warriors who accompanied Kaspar showed him proudly the ruin of kraal after kraal that they had destroyed, hills and valleys where the frames of huts and the stumps of cattle kraals pointed charred fingers to the sky. The ground about them was littered with fragments of bone, with skulls and abandoned weapons. Shattered rusty spears lay beside broken pots and shields which had been gnawed by the wild beasts and furrowed by the ants. 'Ai,' the warriors said, 'the land is cleaned of the dogs that dwelt here. We are as lions. We are as hard as stones. Nothing can break us.' The sight of the ruined villages inflamed them. They spoke of the young men they had killed in battle and of the old men and women they had put to the spear when it was done and of the girls they had carried off.

Twice they passed through military stations where soldiers were quartered and the King's cattle grazed. At both there were women belonging to the King. They were there for his use when he came and to act as spies in his absence.

As they went on, the country changed. Great blue ranges of mountains were hung to the horizons; the rolling plains gave way to bush, trees becoming thicker and more numerous each day. It grew hotter, and there were patches of palms matted along the river-beds. Game was abundant: eland, giraffe, wildebeeste, zebra, swart witpenz, rooibok, reedbok, bastard gemsbok, ostrich, and innumerable rhinoceros. There seemed to be a rhinoceros behind each bush. It was strange to see these big beasts cropping grass like sheep. When they charged, their long horns ploughed up the ground. Creatures of habit, they slept in one place each night, voided their excrement in one place each day till it was heaped up, and grazed always in a circle that would, by dark, bring them home.

Soon, Links said, they would meet elephants. It was of this Kaspar had dreamed when he had seen the piled ivory on the docks in Cape Town. Ivory went from here to the ends of the earth. Hundreds of years ago elephants had been hunted here for King Solomon, and from here ivory had found its way into the hands of the merchants of Carthage and been carried to Rome and Athens. Now it went to the capitals of Europe, where it was put to a thousand uses: fashioned into the backs of brushes and glove-stretchers for fine ladies, into trinket-boxes, into knife-handles, the tops of walking-sticks, carved into ornaments, made into back-scratchers shaped like a human hand, used for the hilts of swords and daggers. Did those who used ivory ever think of whose hands it passed through, of the traders, hunters, ships' captains, dealers, craftsmen, and shopkeepers? Or of the years that the elephants from whom it was taken had carried their tusks through the wilds?

It was much hotter in the low country. There were more flowers, more insects, and the lions were a perpetual menace, necessitating the building of strong skerms each night. And here Kaspar took the ague, being shaken by fever till his teeth chattered.

It was Kaspar's illness that caused Links to halt. Also they were on the edge of the elephant country, and a semi-permanent camp could be erected here that would prove useful to them as a base from which to hunt. The grass was good, there were fine shade trees and ample water. The wagon was drawn up under a great tambouti; near it a clump of pale-grey wild olives perfumed the air. Below the camp the ground fell away in rolling folds, through which a wide river wound its way. Lesser mountains and hills pierced the flats erratically; some stark and bare, others tree-clad, they stood like rocks above the sea of bush. Behind the camp a fountain ran strongly, pouring over the stones in a small cascade.

The warriors were much disturbed at Kaspar's illness. First, because they would probably suffer for it if he died; and secondly, because they believed all illness due to witchcraft. Someone had bewitched the white man, but, lacking a witch doctor, they were at a loss to know the culprit. Meanwhile there was nothing for them to do but wait. Links and Silent Willem brought in plenty of game, which they ate under protest. Game was the food of slaves. They wanted beef.

2

Strange thoughts came to Kaspar as he lay ill. He thought of old Frederik. He thought of his Uncle Leendert, of Selina, of his father and mother, of his home; of Aletta, N'tembi, of Christiaan van Ek, of Ringhals, of everyone he had ever known. Every event of his life was confused into one composite and continually changing picture. At one time he thought he was riding up to his father's house with Aletta on his saddle, her arms about him, when red-coated soldiers attacked him; at another that the vineyards of his home were being damaged by a herd of elephants and that Ringhals, standing beside his mother, conjured them away. He held Aletta in his arms and as soon as he held her she turned into

N'tembi. He dreamed that his little bitch was mated to a lion and that her pups were uncontrollable. He dreamed of Afrikander's red elephants, not in ones and twos, but in hundreds that ran after him. And then sometimes, out of this confusion which, as he dreamed, he knew to be a dream, he saw the whole pattern and principle of life as though it were written on a printed page. There, before him, was all the knowledge of the world, all the wisdom of the ages, if he could but grasp it. Something that transcended all that van Ek knew, all that anyone knew, was there, ready to be held, as a child holds a ball in its hand, if he could but reach it.

Ringhals appeared to him in a dream. He saw him clearly, sitting at the foot of his bed. 'Listen,' he said; 'when a man's heart calls him to go to a certain place, so that he gets no respite from his desire, so that it gnaws at him continually, eating him away as the ants eat the thatch of a dwelling, then he should go. For though there be some who say that it is not so, a man's heart can break ... and a man's body can pine as a caged beast pines, with his body confined in one place while his spirit is in another. Ai ... though he may bear with his pain for a great space, he will one day arise and go. He will do this when his pain is too great; suddenly, in the twinkling of an eye, will he get up and go. Go, even empty-handed and at night, speaking to no one. And in the morning those who come will find him gone.'

Ringhals faded, becoming transparent so that Kaspar could see the stars in the sky shine through him, and disappeared. Then he woke, sweating profusely with his mind clear. 'I will finish my hunt,' he thought, 'and then go back to Aletta.' N'tembi was nothing. The sickness of his body had burnt her out of his mind.

3

The puppy was growing. Through Kaspar's illness she had sat by his bed, watching him and touching him tentatively with her paws. She had golden-yellow eyes like her mother and her coat was darkening from golden-fawn into brindle.

It was very pleasant to lie there feeling himself getting better and stronger each day. It was a rest, the only one he had had for many months. Lying still, he had time to ponder over much that had happened and to see how event fitted into event; to see himself an arrow shot by circumstance into the air. Looking back, he saw that he had acted as he had to act; that circumstance was the master of event. It seemed to him that life had a strange way of taking men and fashioning them to its own purpose. 'It must be because I have been ill,' he thought. Only illness could account for what he now felt and thought, for his quick perceptions.

Unable to do much, he took small things into account; small sights and sounds. He saw that there was not just one world, but a hundred worlds all living beside and inside each other. There was a hoopoe's nest in an ant-heap near the camp from which he derived much pleasure by watching the birds dive down carrying grubs and caterpillars in their beaks; he loved to see them fly on white-barred wings; to watch them raise and lower their crests of feathers. Yes, there was a hoopoe's world which had nothing to do with men, that was complete in itself. There was a world of ants, too. He watched them harvesting the grass, cutting it into small sections and carrying it away: ant following ant in a long line, each intent on delivering its burden. One string going loaded, another returning empty for more. One could hear the sharp rustle of their jaws as they cut the grass.

And so for each and every kind of beast there was a world. Perhaps one for each individual beast. Perhaps one also for each human being. A world of his own thoughts and hopes which in no way resembled those of any other man. He thought, too, about movement. Being unable to move, it became something remarkable in itself; something that was in its way almost as great as the difference between life and death. He thought of a buck standing still. How different it was when it moved! He thought of springbok galloping, leaping, with arched backs, their manes erect, twenty and thirty feet at a time, and so numerous that they touched each other; so numerous that the veld looked like a cloth raised by puffs of wind as they rose and fell; of wildebeeste twisting and turning as they ran, a sea of tossing manes and whirling, horse-like tails; of eland, where the cows, so much faster than the bulls, were able to jump over each other as they escaped; and of rooibok. It was said that no man knew how high a rooibok could jump when pressed. With snakes, too, whom God had caused to crawl on their bellies, it was the same. From being still as sticks, they could strike so quickly that the eye could not follow their movements.

He never tired of watching birds fly or of examining dead birds, trying to find the magic of their wings, looking at the perfection of their joints, at the minutely serrated feathers that fitted so perfectly into each other. All movement was a wonder, all life. He thought of butterflies whose colours came off in a blur on your fingers when you touched them, and how strange it was that they should grow from worms, or that birds should come from eggs. Why should this be? Why should a tree burst into leaf, a plant into flower?

He was surprised at what he had learnt of the wild things and their ways. He laughed a little. It was as well, for he was near to becoming one himself. But it was interesting, and as you went on you found beasts predictable, each according to its kind. You got to know, not what they would do, but what they were likely to do. As he got better, he hid by the water and watched for the coming of the birds in the evening. First came the pheasants, neat and trim with bare red heads, tripping down singly; then, as the sun was about to sink, the guinea fowls in flocks, marching down like soldiers, running swiftly, crouched so low on their legs that they looked like lice. And after them the doves, very swiftly, in pairs: they would land near the edge of the water, take two or three sips, and fly away as quickly as they had come. After the doves, when the sun was down, the sand grouse came, three or four together. They made no haste to drink, but chased each other in a kind of game, or squatted on the bank, settling themselves down like stones. The cock birds made a little song of seven notes, while the hens crooned happily and continuously. After a little while they would begin to drink, one or two going down to the water, then more; and then each pair, when it had drunk, flew off. By this time it was so dark that they could not be seen; their going was marked only by the whirring of their wings.

And all the time there were the frogs. The booming of the bullfrogs and the high fluting of the little frogs that inhabited the vlei. They always began suddenly. Out of the cool evening their song went up — a thousand little strings of sound that blended into a rope which strangled thought. His evenings were happy; he longed for them — the birds, the frogs, and perhaps the sight of a buck stepping down to the water on dainty, hesitant hoofs. A nightjar would swoop past him with a cry. An owl would hoot. It was night, and he would turn to the fires that burnt at the camp.

4

As soon as Kaspar had recovered his strength, they began to hunt. As they were in elephant country and might expect to see them at any time, they proceeded by easy stages. Links told him how the Matabele killed elephants without guns. The bravest of them, he said, crept up behind the great beasts while they slept, and with a wide-bladed axe struck them on the back of the hind foot, endeavouring to sever the Achilles tendon with a single blow. If successful, the elephant stood helpless and was easily killed by the spears they flung at it. If unsuccessful, there was little danger, for the animal, woken thus suddenly, invariably fled without pausing to see what had struck it.

'Does it always run?' Kaspar asked.

'It runs,' the warriors said. 'At least, if it does not run, we have never heard.... If it does not run, then the hunter cannot tell the tale.' They slapped their thighs and shouted with laughter.

They also killed elephants by posting men in trees under which a herd was likely to pass, and driving heavy spears between their shoulders. These spears had blades three feet long and three inches wide, and were fitted with short thick hafts. Held in both hands, they inflicted terrible wounds.

The country beyond the camp was mountainous and hard to traverse with the wagon, so they left it and planned to hunt in a circle round the camp.

Almost immediately they came to an area which had been dug into holes and ploughed up in all directions by elephants as they sought for roots. According to Links and the Bushman boy, several days had gone by since they had been there, but the herd was a big one and seemed to be moving slowly. Their spoor led towards cliffs that were apparently unscalable by anything less agile than a baboon or leopard, but when they got there Kaspar was astonished to see it zigzagged with elephant paths that, following the contours of the mountain, twisted back on themselves, rising and falling in hairpin bends. In some places great blocks of stone had been displaced and rearranged to give a more secure foothold.

These hills were rugged, with deep ravines and precipitous cliffs on which great masses of rock, that seemed ready to slip at any moment, tottered precariously. Though devoid of soil, trees found a hold for their roots on some of the krantzes and clung there, distorted and wrung, above the cracks and fissures in the rock, and here and there in the small valleys a gigantic baobab, fantastically shaped and bastioned, reared long leafless limbs.

Climbing swiftly, they followed the spoor, camping on it at night, and pressing on again as soon as it was light. As they crossed the range they found chewed leaves and flattened bark strewn on the ground. Adam reckoned, from the condition of the bruised leaves, that the elephants were near.

Suddenly Kaspar felt Adam's hand on his arm. He pointed to a thick group of mopani. In the middle of the trees was a large ant-heap. The ant-heap moved. It was an elephant. Unless it had been pointed out to him, Kaspar would have walked right into it. As he watched, the elephant broke off a large branch, tearing it down with its trunk, and reached for the young shoots above it. He flapped his ears; they were as large as tables. His tusks were very white, and though short were thick. As Kaspar raised his gun, the great beast moved; silently, like a grey ghost, he came out of the bush. Two other bulls, that had been invisible, followed him, and slowly, with incredible dignity, swinging their trunks, they walked in single file towards the open. Kaspar could hear the rumbling of their stomachs as they passed him. Towering over everything, dwarfing even the trees, they went to the base of the hill, and, going round it, disappeared.

Links threw up a handful of dust to test the wind, and then, advancing slowly, they followed the elephants. The hill had been cut off sheer, as if it had been cut by an axe, and beyond it the forest was completely crushed. Trees were pulled down, saplings uprooted or broken off, their stumps standing jaggedly among the branches, which stripped of their bark lay like white bones on the trampled grass. Although he could see no elephants, Kaspar could hear the crash of falling trees and the sound of branches being ripped down. His hands trembled with excitement. Lazarus, carrying his other gun, was behind him; Adam was at his side; Links was on his left. The bush thinned and the whole valley became visible. It was filled with elephants. They were there in hundreds; every ridge was black with them, while on the bottom, in the flat, they stood so thick that they touched each other. An elephant came out of a thicket near him. He had a branch in his trunk with which he switched the flies.

Large bulls with enormous tusks, cows, calves of all ages, moved ponderously in front of him, and a small calf with long sparse hairs scattered over its skin began to drink from under its mother's shoulders. They were so near that he could see her udder between her forelegs as the calf, with its small trunk folded back, sucked at her. To his right a big bull was washing. He stood up to his belly in a pan. Filling his trunk with water, he sprayed it in great jets over his back and shoulders. Then he sat down, like a dog, on his haunches and rolled over. As he swung, first to one side and then the other, grunting with pleasure, the mud squirted away and left a pressed-down space that refilled with water. When he had done, he got up, and going into deeper water washed off the mud. Kaspar crept nearer, and resting his gun fired at the elephant's eye. He staggered with the impact of the bullet, and then with raised trunk crashed through the bush, trumpeting wildly. Lazarus put a bullet into his hip as he ran, and, following as quickly as they could, both fired again, bringing him down. There were shots all round them now. Links and Willem were shooting fast and the herd was stampeding. Wounded elephants screamed. There were more shots and cries from the warriors. As he ran past him, Kaspar saw Links bring down a cow; she had a small calf with her. It looked like the one he had seen drinking. The elephants which had been running forward began to come back, turned by the scent of the warriors who had gone round them on the flank. A shouting warrior flung himself on a wounded bull and severed his hamstring with his spear.

Finding men all round them, the herd galloped, trumpeting and screaming in a wild, disordered circle. Kaspar fired and wounded another bull; he hit him hard, but he went on. Kaspar followed, firing shot after shot as fast as he could reload. Suddenly the bull turned, and, with trunk raised and ears extended, charged. Standing fast, Kaspar fired at his throat. He still came on. Kaspar turned and ran. He could feel the trunk waving only a few feet behind him. But the elephant's strength gave out and he fell in full career, crashing down behind him. Kaspar found himself wet with blood that had been blown over him from the lungs of the wounded beast.

The herd, hard-pressed now, were inserting their trunks into their mouths and spraying water over themselves as they ran, while some, picking up sand, scattered it over their backs. All at once, under the leadership of an old cow, they formed up and broke out of the valley. Their charge shook the ground and cut a path a hundred yards wide through bush.

The hunt was done. Twelve elephants lay dead. There were others wounded that could be followed later. From nowhere natives appeared. They came from all sides with their women and children. Throwing off their karosses, the men attacked the elephants with their assegais. First they chopped out the tusks; then, removing the rough outer skin in large sheets, they cut away the inner skin, taking care not to split it, and gave it to the women, who, fastening the corners with sticks to form water-bags, took them to the vlei to fill. Great slabs of meat were removed from the ribs, and then, attacking the colossal ribs with axes, they exposed the bowels. It was around and behind these that the fat was found. The enormous guts billowed out as, shouting and singing, the natives forced their way past them into the cavity of the body, coming out covered with blood and offal, but carrying the fat they sought.

Cutting more strips of hide from the flanks, they rolled them back like carpets, and, plunging into the entrails, dragged them out in great coiled piles. As they worked, they covered themselves with blood from the burst intestines, smearing each other over their heads and shoulders. With shouts and cries of pleasure, they plastered the clotted blood into their hair. Friends, taking great double handfuls of blood and offal, poured it over each other's back, spreading it over their flanks and buttocks. Elbowing, fighting, crawling, slippery with blood, they forced their way back to the meat, swarming like ants over the mountainous bodies;

working from within and without the carcasses, they hacked the meat away from the flanks, frequently cutting each other with their sharp assegais as they quarrelled, snatching at choice morsels. As soon as a piece of meat was detached, the man who had got it would run to his woman who was waiting, throw it to her, and return for more. The women piled the meat on the bushes and trees till they were festooned with chunks and sheets of flesh.

Fires were lit round which the Kaffirs, sucking marrow from the bones, gorged themselves to the throat before they went back to work, while their lean curs scavenged in the grass. On the trees vultures sat waiting till the men were done.

As it grew dark, more Kaffirs arrived. Wood was collected and the fires beside each beast sprang higher and higher. Stripped of skin, the dead elephants looked like great scarlet rocks round which the blood-smeared men, orange and scarlet in the firelight, danced, fought, and shouted. Untiring, insatiably hungry, the blood-plastered Kaffirs attacked the meat, some of them grasping it between their teeth so that they could use both hands to cut it clear of the carcass. From the distance came the roar of a lion and the cries of hyaenas and jackals attracted by the killing, a background of sound to the shouts and screams of the Kaffirs.

At their own camp Kaspar found the fleshy part of a trunk being cooked in a pit filled with ashes under the direction of Links, this, with the heart roasted on a forked stick over a slow fire, the meat from the cavity over the eye, and the foot, being the greatest delicacies. Next day the work went on, the more distant bodies being dealt with. Beside the cow that Links had killed, the calf stood, bleating piteously and trying with its small trunk to raise its mother. The vultures had been at the cow. They had taken what they could from the end of her trunk and udder. They had picked out her eyes, and, unable to tear her hide, were waiting for the great beast to rot. At intervals, one or two would flap down, landing on her back, and these, screaming with rage, the calf kept charging and driving off. When it saw the men approach, it came towards them as though expecting help. When the tusks were cut out and the carcass left for the Kaffirs, it followed them. They had no milk to feed it, so Kaspar had it shot.

5

The hunting went on. More elephants were killed. The tusks hacked from their skulls were buried for later collection or carried back to camp. Kaspar had no more fever and was all but content. By working and hunting, by trekking, by forcing himself, he had killed thought and memory. Dead weeks, dead days, dead hours fell as dead leaves and were forgotten. He lived for the day only, neither considering the past nor hoping for the future. It came to him that a man was happy in action; by galloping, with the spring of a horse under him, or swimming in warm pools or in the arms of a woman. Thus only did a man obtain forgetfulness and achieve that nothingness for which his spirit yearned. By hunting and killing he felt he would grow hard and strong. It was as if he had plunged into deep water and was swimming under it: soon he knew he would come up, make for the shore, and shake all this from him. During the day he forgot, but at other times, in the sadness of the evening, he would still remember.

The truth was hard to find; it always lay beyond: each answer opening up fresh questions; each question more difficult than the last. After the first trial by water, the little drops of question that wore away the rock and attacked faith, came the trial of the great water where a man must swim alone without the help of God; and then the trial by fire. So was man chastened and tempered, turned from ore into iron, from iron into steel; turned from dogma and its petty conception into a wider one that, embracing all humanity, came near to God, to a belief in his design and the pattern of creation, to the certainty that man was not an end but a part, and that, because he mattered so little, he mattered greatly. Dimly in the evenings and the nights it came to him. Dimly he saw himself as he was, and began to understand. As a beast sometimes left its accustomed place to seek herbs at a distance, because it was sick for lack of them, did he need Aletta. So would he seek her. In this hour he needed her as a beast needed water, as it needed salt. To live he must get near her. If he died by the wayside, he would die with his head turned in her direction, with his hands outstretched towards her. He spoke to Links. 'We will go back now,' he said. 'We have killed enough.'

They picked up the buried ivory and turned the wagon. Kaspar had learnt that killing was a matter of willing; that there must be something in your mind, some certainty without which you could do nothing. It was as if inside you there was a will for death which at the precise moment of killing you loosed with a feeling of complete certainty. It was less what you did than what you were. And when you fired you knew. Something of yourself was behind the bullet, projecting it more fatally than powder.

It was necessity that drove him back to Aletta; the same law that had driven the little elephant to stay by its mother and then to follow them. It was the pressure that was upon all things to live out their lives, and, caught in the net of his necessity, Kaspar pressed back.

CHAPTER XXI

HE CALLED MARIA

I

WITH his head Rudolf was aware that he toyed with treason. With his head he knew that evil would be done, and that out of evil only evil could spring; but he blamed the English for the illness of his wife; chose to think that she fretted for her brother and was inconsolable over the manner of his death. Hendrik Prinsloo in particular promised revenge and was very definite about the ends they would achieve. It was only when Rudolf found they were raising the Kaffirs that he tried to turn from them, and when he tried found he could not. He was held in a cleft stick. 'You are with us, Rudolf,' Prinsloo said, 'or you are against us. If you are not with us, I will shoot you dead. Only those who are with us are safe; and we will give the cattle of the others to the Kaffirs as their reward.'

'Boer cattle a reward for Kaffirs,' Rudolf said.

Maria woke to the sound of his voice. It was raised. Rudolf was rarely angry. She turned her head to listen.

'Before God, Hendrik, you know not what you do,' she heard him shout.

Ja, that was her Rudolf, her husband: a good man; a courageous man. Then came the other voice: that of Hendrik Prinsloo.

'You have seen Kaffir wars,' he said, 'and they are as nothing to what we will do. If the Kaffirs have chastised with whips, we will chastise with scorpions. Men, women, and children who are not with us will die.'

'Die by the spear!' Rudolf gasped; 'die under the Kaffirs' assegais!'

'Ja, under their spears and the guns of our folk also. We are at one in this matter: that those who are not with us are against us, and those who are against us are worse than the English, for they betray their own blood, and their blood is on their own heads. Nee, I tell you I shall not hesitate, nor will Johannes Bezuidenhout. Coenraad de Buys is with us, Gaika is with us. Other Kaffirs are coming from the north. The Amazulu are coming in their thousands; the Griqua Bastards, mounted and armed like white men, are coming. It is the end, I say. It is the last day of the tyrants. Like ants before a herd of elephants they will be trampled, driven, till the last one is in the sea, till the sea itself and the sea beaches and the strands of our country are red with blood. Once and for all we will cast off this yoke. Yea, we will smash this yoke that has galled us till not even the splinters of its memory are left. So, see to it that you are with us, Oom Rudolf.'

'See to it that you are with us,' Maria muttered. So while she had been ill they had caught Rudolf in a trap. He was so good and stupid. If I had been well, if I had been able to watch, if he had spoken to me of that which was in his heart instead of treating me as a sick child, this would not have happened, she thought, and now I am able to do nothing. Rudolf, who had never managed anything alone, was going to have to manage alone. She tried to move. She could not move. She could move nothing, neither hand nor foot. But her head was very clear. Never, it seemed to her, had it been so clear. This, she thought, is death. I am dying. It was strange to be dying; strange that she was not afraid. She did not want Rudolf. She felt that Rudolf, when he came, would be unhappy that she had died alone, but it was better to die alone. No one could do anything when a man or a woman was dying. People, even those nearest to you, could only be a distraction. To die was very important, very interesting, and, this surprised her, very restful. For the first time in her life she was at peace; for the first time for many months her body felt nothing. It was a wonderful relief to be without pain and to find that nothing mattered. She need no longer think about food; no longer worry about what her family and her servants would eat.

A woman had so much to do with food. Sassaties, bobotee, snysels — how fond the children had been of her snysels! She remembered teaching Aletta to make them: flour mixed with well-beaten egg till it was a stiff dough; a little salt. Then you had to roll the paste, lifting it as you rolled, sprinkling it with dry flour. You rolled it like a carpet and then you cut it lengthwise into strips, and then you rolled the strips between your hands. And melk snysels, cooked with milk, sugar, and cinnamon! Tripe and trotters; mock venison made from mutton! The leg must soak in vinegar for two or three days; if it was hot, you had to turn it often. You poked cloves and fat bacon into the meat, and then you cooked it in the vinegar that it had been soaked in. She thought of geel rys, of klapper tert, of sourkleuitjes, of curries, of preserves and konfyts.

Food; always food; always hungry mouths to feed. A woman was like a mother bird: in all her life a woman had no rest from making food, from carrying it and serving it. And how happy she had been! Only now that it was over did she know how happy she had been to see her food eaten. To see her children take what she gave them and put it into their small red mouths. How happy when there had been plenty, when the children's bellies had been like drums; when Rudolf had sighed and rubbed his mouth with his hand; when the dogs, coming to the table, had cracked the bones thrown to them, and the servants had been sleek and good-tempered with food. And it had all depended on her. I did it, she thought. Before God, I did it for many years. Yes, she had done the work that the Lord God had set in front of her — bearing children and ministering to them, without sparing herself: never wanting to, for a woman's children were a part of her.

And how strange it was to lie here thinking of all that had happened in her life, seeing events as pictures that came and went. They came without sequence: the picture of her brother Frederik riding in with Aletta on his saddle. What a dirty little girl she had been! How she had cried when he left her! Pictures of Stephanie learning to cook; of Aletta trying to sweep with a little broom made out of stiff grass. Pictures of herself as a girl; of her mother when she had said good-bye and gone off with Rudolf; of Rudolf as a young man. Pictures; just pictures and thoughts. Just words spoken many years ago that still rang in her ears: the voices of the dead: even the singing of dead birds; birds that she had known at home. And scents: the scent of geraniums, of lilies from the vlei where she had played as a child; so sweet was their scent that it was sickly; a heavy, lingering perfume; she smelt it now.

It was all very real, much more real than the things about her; they were faint and thin. It was like when one was dreaming and knew it. You said to yourself: This is a dream; soon I shall wake up. And now she was saying: This is death. I am alive, but soon I shall be dead. Soon I shall be gathered to my fathers, to my dead children. Soon I shall rest. It was as if her life were spinning backward; she was getting younger and lighter; her mind was spinning like a top in space.

She tried to think of the present, to worry, but could not. Others would have to think now. She tried to smile. Her face would not move. She felt that she smiled only inside her mind. To die was rather like being drunk. She had never been drunk, but men had told her what being drunk was like. She was very free: very high: above everything. She was a child again; a bride again; a young mother with her young children round her. Those children were not dead. She wondered that she had ever thought of them as dead. They were round her. She put out her hand to touch them.

That was how Rudolf found her: with her hand out-stretched. Her hand was outstretched to me, he thought, and I was only in the other room.

Hendrik Prinsloo had ridden off, and Rudolf had come in to see if the shouting had disturbed Maria. He took her hand. There was no life in it. He looked into her eyes. They were opened, very wide, with the pupils large and sunk. Maria was dead. There was no doubt now that she was dead. Per-haps she had cried out to him and he had not heard. Perhaps she had wanted him and he had failed her. Taking off his hat, he knelt by the bed in prayer. He prayed for Maria, but his heart cried out in its loneliness: What shall I do? What shall I do now that I am alone?

2

At first Rudolf could do nothing, could believe nothing, least of all in Maria's death. He ate the food Aletta set in front of him. He was even hungry, but the food had no savour. He slept. He could not weep. He lived, if eating, breathing, and walking helplessly round the house were life. He felt himself enclosed, like a beast in the kraal of his own misery. It was as if Maria had made reality for him. With-out her everything was flat. He built, as in a dream, her coffin of planks. He supervised, as in a dream, the digging of her grave beside the other graves, beside his first wife, beside the dead children. He spoke gently and seriously to the few who, hearing of her death, had come to see her buried; but he knew not what he said. When Klein Kattie climbed onto his knee and pulled his beard, he took no notice. His dogs followed him with their tails low and sat down to watch him when he stopped walking, but he never spoke to them.

Rudolf was beyond pain. He knew that he had expected Maria to die, but because he had hoped so much that she would live he had refused to believe that she could die. It was not until April, two days after Maria's death, drove the mare and foal down to the house that he realised she had gone forever. It was like a Hottentot to do that: to forget for two days and then suddenly to remember.

'Take them away!' he shouted. 'Take them away!'

His mouth twitched, tears came into his eyes, great sobs tore upwards from his belly, sobs that hurt him, splitting him in two, shaking his heavy shoulders. Bent over the table, he sat crying, driving his big horny knuckles into his eyes. It had taken the mare and foal to do it, to bring it home. Maria had thought them beautiful.

His grief turned to anger. What was there for him to live for now? What was there to show for his life, for his work? A dead wife, a dying child, and the Border stewing like a pot, a pot under which crackled the laughter of mad fools like Prinsloo. He saw it now, but now was too late. Maria could have advised him, but she was dead. He was alone. Before God, had ever a man been so alone with two wives and eight children dead? Stephanie and Klein Kattie he ignored. He wanted his dead sons. The land was cursed and he would hesitate no longer between two opinions. Now he was with Prinsloo. If Prinsloo was mad, then he too was mad; then there was nothing but madness in a mad world. If it was madness to avenge old Frederik, it had been madness to slay him, and at the back of all this misery were the English. Before they came there had been peace in the land. Peace; that is, except for the Kaffirs, but they were used to Kaffirs.

3

Aletta had little time to grieve. She grieved, but as a woman, differently from a man. She had never deceived herself about her stepmother's illness. She knew that Maria

counted on her to watch over Rudolf and Kattie, to tend the
new baby and to do what she could for Stephanie. She would
do it all, and she did it all, managing everything. But it was
Kaspar she thought of. Where was he? What was he doing?
More news of him had come in. He was supposed to be on
his way back to Coenraad's. When he got there, she would
hear from him. She wondered what had kept him silent.
She was certain he had written: he had promised to write.
Were his letters lost? Perhaps he had been ill. The thought
of him ill made her feel faint. Ill, far away, with no one to
take care of him. And she had no one to speak to now. She
could not speak to Stephanie: Stephanie was occupied with
Jacobus van Zyl, a man who seemed to Aletta thoroughly
untrustworthy. Perhaps it was that she did not understand
him; but there was something strange about him and about
his business. She did not like secret people, and van Zyl was
secret and devious. He was like a highly trained monkey,
full of tricks; but behind those tricks she detected something
else. He was a man who wore his manners and mannerisms
as a mask. He was so smooth that he made her afraid. He
hardly ever came to the house, though sometimes she saw
him in the vicinity with his instruments, and sometimes saw
the flags he had set up on the surrounding hills. Stephanie
saw him often, going out to meet him.

He had come to Maria's funeral, a stranger among them.
He had spoken smoothly of being near-by and wishing to pay
his respect to the dead. He had stood hatless beside the
others, brightly clothed, brilliant as a fink among sparrows.
But where there had been a certain majesty about the heavy
Boers who stood with bowed heads like great oxen, there had
been a slim resistance about van Zyl. He was like a blade
directed against those oxen. She felt he despised them.
Aletta had heard that there were countries where men com-
peted with bulls, slaying them with a slender sword. Van
Zyl was like that sword — cold, pointed, and watchful.

And then afterwards he had asked her when she was born.

The date, the place, the hour. 'If you tell me,' he said, 'I will cast your horoscope. Everything is written in the stars. By the movements of the planets, by the position of the constellations, is the destiny of man governed immutably.'

'I do not know, meneer,' she had answered.

'Nee,' Stephanie said, 'she does not know who she is. She was found by my step-uncle among the Kaffirs.' She had laughed, shrugging her shoulders contemptuously.

'Then perhaps you are a princess,' van Zyl said. 'But it is a pity, because I should have liked to look into your future. I could have given you good counsel.'

A strange and blasphemous man: a dangerous man: as cold and controlled as his own stars. He made her afraid. I need no stars, she thought, to warn me against him. She prayed that he would leave these parts.

More and more was put upon her. Rudolf was away a great deal. He went about the Border and into Kaffirland. The direction of the farm as well as of the house was falling upon Aletta.

The baby died while Rudolf was away. She had it buried in a small grave beside its mother. She laid it in a small painted wagon-box, upon a bed of fragrant herbs that she had picked and covered with a cloth of white linen. The child's foster mother had brought it in. 'The child is dead,' she said. No one was very sorry. It had not been long enough alive to be much loved. It had been too sick for anyone to have great hopes of its future. It had come into the world and had passed out of it. The candle of its life, scarcely lit, had been snuffed out.

'The baby is dead,' she told Rudolf when he came back. 'I buried it beside Maria.'

'You did right.' Rudolf put his arm about her. 'I do not know what I should do without you, Letta,' he said. 'Only you and Stephanie and Kattie are left now. Nee, Letta, I seem to have lived to no great purpose. All that I hoped for is undone.' He hung up his saddle and went in.

Always now either he sat inside, brooding over the great Bible on the table; or he was abroad, riding no man knew whither.

4

Jacobus van Zyl had appeared at the right time for Stephanie. She was angry with Aletta and tired of the Border; and he was something more than bored. Accustomed to Europe, to cities, to the fluttering of skirts and arch glances over the tops of painted fans, he was ready for an adventure, and in this case desire walked hand in hand with policy.

His survey was accurate, for he loved figures, sine and cosine. He loved to calculate, to see things work out; and yet it was not for this, or at least not entirely for this, that he had been sent up to the Border. Stephanie intrigued him, and the story of her conquest would bring him further triumphs when he got home. 'A shepherdess! Oh, la, you have no idea!' He saw himself saying it, repeating her words, acting his own seductive gestures. That would make the ladies laugh. Once you had them laughing, the rest was easy. A mathematician, a man interested in astronomy and its sister art astrology, there was little he did not know of women. There were principles for dealing with the fair sex, rules that worked with the precision of the multiplication table; there were precepts, aphorisms, proverbs. Sometimes he laughed at what people considered the diversity of his tastes. Diversity, indeed! How stupid they were! What was there in life that could not be represented by an equation? What situation that could not be expressed by a graph? And for women the rules were as simple as the rules for baking a cake. He merely complimented a beauty on her brains, a serving-maid on her breeding. Poor dears, all they wanted was a change. The countess was so tired of respect; the street woman, of neglect. With women, as with men, all that was necessary was to give them what they wanted, but it must be served with some subtlety: the insult must contain a compliment and the compliment a barb. Life was simple: just a series of problems, and all could be solved by the same method or variations of that method.

Women were a relaxation. It was the stars that he loved. You could lose yourself for a few moments in a woman, but for real peace one sought the heavenly bodies. There, in the infinity of space, in the majesty of the night skies, was real rest. Much as he missed London, Paris, and Amsterdam, there were compensations here. The southern hemisphere interested him vastly. He wished he could get into contact with the Arabs and Portuguese on the east coast, with Indians, with the Egyptians. There was so much to learn, and as much as the women at home did he miss his books, his library, and the libraries to which he had access.

Astrology was an exact science; of this he was assured. Man was subject to the heavenly bodies. Time and again he had proved it. Meanwhile ... he could not find the stockings he wanted. His body-slave said they had been destroyed by white ants. He put on another pair. He was going to meet Stephanie. 'My shepherdess,' he called her. He wished he understood her foster sister, but so far he had found no equation that solved her, unless it were another man. He buckled on his sword and adjusted the ruffles at his neck. With a shepherdess one must be finely dressed. That was a pretty thought: one day he would write a sonnet expressing it, or make some neat little phrase: in French, perhaps: these things were better said in French; a language that lent itself to such purposes.

He looked at himself in the mirror that hung from the tent pole. It had been said of him that he resembled a very fine weasel. He always thought of this when he looked at himself. A weasel, by God! but a beauty, and there was some truth in it. His face was sharp and pointed. His eyes black and set a little too close together. It was only by an effort that he could make them expressive. But he knew his defects, and because he knew them he turned them into assets. He was tall and slim, almost over-slim, and supple, like a weasel. It became his affectation to accentuate those qualities, that cold eye, that serpentine grace, that swiftness of movement, that poise, which distinguished the Mustelidae from every other species. He was admired by women, as fascinating to them as a weasel to a rabbit; and feared by men, for he was a courageous duellist and as fast to strike as a weasel. 'A weasel, by God!' he said aloud.

Well, most people resembled some animal. Stephanie was like a cat, sleek and perpetually lascivious. Was there such a thing as a chaste cat? One day he would write a little fantasy: 'The Chaste Cat' would be a good title. People were like animals, he reflected, but most of them were herbivores.

He called for his horse.

Nothing would make him love again, not the most perfect woman. Time and experience had freed him from that; he had become, as it were, an atheist in emotion. He would weep no more. That part of him was broken beyond repair. A weeping weasel was a contradiction, an anomaly. Something possible, perhaps, but mathematically improbable.

5

For Stephanie all that had happened and was happening about her meant little. Jacobus van Zyl excited her. His love-making, his appearance, his strange tales of countries across the sea, of wars, of the duels he had fought, of the great folk he knew, all opened up a new world to her. Jacobus was like a fairy prince talking of a fairyland where everyone was rich and beautiful. She never tired of his descriptions of clothes, of ornaments, of furnishings. He had seen everything: he had been everywhere, and was ready to tell of all he had seen and done. With a few words, sitting in the shade of a tree, he could make the veld disappear and bring up in its place the brilliant scenes to which he was accustomed. His love-making, too, was different. It was in no way urgent. He took her casually, as one would nibble at a ripe fruit. It was only when he spoke of the stars that she grew tired. She was not interested in the stars: they were too far away.

Meanwhile, it was very pleasant to see him. Very pleasant to be admired, flattered, and given small presents; to be likened to a flower for fragrance, to silk for softness, to a deer for grace.

Standing by the big tree where they always met, she tapped the ground with her toe. She thought of her new lover, of the beautiful clothes he wore, of his grace, of the compliments he paid her, a shepherdess, a wild rose, a cool spring set in a wilderness. She touched the brooch he had given her. It was heart-shaped, and contained a flower made out of his hair. He was different. She had not known there were men like that: the way he walked, the way he spoke, slowly and softly. The way he bent over her hand and kissed it. Why, I might be a great lady, she thought. She was excited by his composure, by his reflective manner, by the play of his long slim hands when he took snuff and shook back the ruffles from his wrists. She had never seen such white hands before. She had, when she came to think of it, never seen white hands before or a man who wore gloves. His hands were softer than her own and as white as her body. They fascinated her, soft but steely with muscles beneath the thin white skin.

And side by side with her thoughts of Jacobus went thoughts of Kaspar. How was it that he loved Aletta?

6

'And the good Rudolf,' van Zyl said, 'is away again on his travels?'

He dismounted, tied his horse to a tree, and kissed Stephanie's hand.

'Ja, he is away,' Stephanie said. It amused her to hear her father spoken of as the 'good Rudolf.'

They sat down. 'What a man he is!' Jacobus said: 'a man of iron. And I have never understood why the Government has forbidden men to cross the river.'

'It does not stop my father. It stops no one. Besides, what can the Government do? It is so far away. How even should they know what we do?'

'How indeed? I am a servant of the Government, but what men do is nothing to me. I am here to survey these cursed mountains.'

'You do not like mountains, meneer?'

'I do not. I come from a flat country and I hate mountains. They cramp me. What can one do with mountains? One cannot push them down: one cannot draw them towards one: one cannot make love to them. There they remain static, enormous, a perpetual temptation to climb onto their breasts and see more mountains. No, it is the stars I love. It is wonderful to watch the stars,' he said.

He thought of the ancient shepherds, the Greeks, who had named the stars. 'That is the way to freedom,' he went on. He was speaking very softly, as though to himself, but Stephanie knew that he was aware of her. . . . 'By watching the stars one regains perspective,' he went on. 'They are so distant, and by thinking of one's own insignificance one gains a kind of anonymity like that of an ant in an ant-hill, and nothing matters greatly any more.'

Stephanie had not come so far to meet him in order to talk of the stars, nor of anonymity.

'Kiss me, Jacob,' she said.

He kissed her and made slow love to her, while the insects hummed in the heat drowsily, and an occasional bird drew a black line across the sky. Van Zyl smiled as he thought of other women to whom he had made love; of other places where he had made love; of how those women would laugh if they could see him now. But he was happy, well content with his sylvan idyll. And Rudolf was over the river. The good Rudolf, weaving himself a hempen collar. And there were others, many others, concerned in this. There was also the boy, Kaspar van der Berg, who had killed the British soldier. Jacobus did not care for the soldiery: they were too rough and coarse. They understood none of the finer things. They cared neither for literature nor art. They knew nothing of the stars. But it was nevertheless a crime to shoot one, or it was said to be a crime. And his work was going well: his survey was good: the maps accurate and beautifully drawn, some of them in colour. He wondered, as he held Stephanie, why no one had thought of making those maps before. With maps one could calculate. With maps one could move those ridiculous soldiers here and there, like pawns, defeating all who opposed you: with maps, supplemented by other information.

'I must go, Stephanie,' he said. 'I have a long ride back, and I will send you word when we can meet again. One day I, too, would like to go over the river and to map the other side.'

'You, Jacob, you could not go. You would be killed. Only those that are known, those of our people, can go.'

He mounted. Only those who are known, those of our people, he thought.

'Good-bye, my shepherdess!' he cried, sweeping off his hat. 'Farewell, wood sprite, sylvan spirit! Soon we will meet again under the auspices of Venus and the protection of the great god Pan.'

He put his heels to his horse and left her.

They called him 'The Weasel.' He laughed. 'The Ferret' would be a good name, too, but less polite, and the man who called him that would be in some danger, but it was true; and like all libels, the more dangerous because of its truth.

CHAPTER XXII

COMPANY FOR THE ROAD

I

NOTHING remarkable occurred on Kaspar's return journey. The hidden ivory was picked up and packed on the wagon. Kaspar had no more fever. They returned on their own spoor, and even the oxen seemed joyful at having their moist noses turned south. To everyone, save to himself, the wagon was homeward bound. Even to Adam and Eve all were jubilant. Adam and Eve had no cares. Kaspar had become their father and mother and they shared him with his dogs, with whom they had effected a strange alliance. Adam had, to the fright of all, built himself a new little bow and had made arrows which he poisoned after the manner of his people. His joy was to hunt with his bow and arrows, running with the big Boer hounds beside him. He spoke to them, and it seemed to Kaspar that these little yellow folk and his dogs understood each other as if they were of one family. At night they would sleep in a heap, the dogs, the boy, and the girl, all inextricably mixed; Wit-voet's nose on Adam's breast, Wolf at his side, and the puppy curled on Eve's stomach. It kept them warm, they said, and made them happy. In his dogs and his Bushmen Kaspar had servants who knew no fear, but only loyalty.

He could not move without them. When he sent them away, when he said, 'I wish to be alone,' they left him, but stayed hidden behind rocks and trees, never taking their eyes from him. They showed him some of their secrets. He learnt how they made one poison from the entrails of a certain caterpillar; another from the milk of the naboom; and for some they extracted venom from spiders, snakes, and scorpions. He was continually astonished by their agility, their speed in running, and by their capacity for following a spoor when even his dogs were at fault.

The life of all centred round the wagon. It was a republic which he governed, but one in which all filled some special function. By their hunting, their dangers and experiences, his company had been welded into a society. Even the savage warriors had become included, though they were no less savage and no less arrogant.

Links put this matter into words: 'Kaspar,' he said, 'this is a strange thing. You are a boy, but you have done something that I have never seen before. Here are we two Bastards, your coloured slaves, your yellow Bushmen, and these black warriors, all friends. It is that you, without knowing it, have the quality of a leader. Ja, you have changed much since the day we found you, a frightened boy who had killed a man, on the Border. I would follow you, Kaspar.' He held out his hand. 'That is the greatest thing I could say to any man.'

The Silent One took his hand, too. The warriors smiled, showing their teeth. They did not fully understand, but were in accord. If this was a demonstration of affection for their master, they were ready to agree that they liked him.

On his way Kaspar traded for gold which the Kaffirs caught in sheepskins set in the bottoms of sluices made in the mountain streams. As it was carried down in the water, the gold was held by the wool. The dust was packed into vultures' quills stoppered with plugs of wood. A rhinoceros was shot for meat, its hump being roasted, and once Kaspar stopped Links from killing a female that ran with a young one in front of her. She ran with her long horn on its tiny rump, guiding it this way, even at a gallop.

Kaspar's mind was made up. He would return to the King's kraal. From there he would go to Coenraad's, and from Coenraad's to Aletta. What happened after that depended on Aletta: upon Aletta and upon God.

2

At the great kraal Ringhals met them. He came accompanied by two warriors and the snake-maiden.

'Greetings!' he said, and sat down.

'Greetings, wizard!' Kaspar said.

'I have come with these' — Ringhals indicated his attendants — 'to greet you.'

'That is something I shall never forget. To come back and be greeted by a friend is a fine thing.'

'The King makes them accompany me,' Ringhals said. He looked at the warriors with distaste. 'As if I needed protection!'

'And the maiden, is she also here to protect you?' Kaspar asked.

'On the contrary. She is here to comfort me. At night my spirit grows lonely and my bones are chilled.'

'No doubt you came for some purpose,' Kaspar said.

'Am I a butterfly, to drift without purpose from bloom to bloom? I came to bring news, but it escapes me. I am old. I forget. Certainly I came with a great purpose, but exhaustion has taken it from me. It may be that I am tired, or thirsty.' He looked at Kaspar hopefully. Kaspar gave him his flask. Ringhals drank. 'That is fine medicine, lord. It clears the brain. It warms the belly. It makes the old young. Since you left things have happened. A stranger has come: a white trader — bend your ears to my mouth — and the girl has gone to him. It is that which I came to tell you: that women are faithless. Ai ... ai, even to me, the Little Flower in the fullness of my beauty, have women been faithless. But what are women? What are they but a dream symbolic of accomplishment? I tell you, lord, there is nothing in a woman but an emptiness. Only the thoughts of women are significant. This one learns with age, lord. At my age one cares no longer for women. That I like to have young women about me is nothing and in no way a contradiction; it is merely a habit that I contracted in my youth. They no longer interest me. Indeed, except as carriers of beer and other comforts, I despise them.' He paused to rub his stomach. 'There is a nice little fire in my belly, but it burns low,' he said.

Kaspar gave him the flask again.

'And more has happened,' Ringhals went on. 'I am now a very great wizard. I have always been great, but now I am recognised among these people; so, fear not. I will hold you safe ... ai, under my wing you are safe. As safe as a jewel hidden in my armpit. I would sleep now,' he said, 'and to-morrow you will see how they acclaim me. I am the father of a nation.'

He curled up against the wheel of the wagon and closed his eyes. The snake-maiden came to sit beside him. She waved an ostrich feather over his face to keep the flies from it and the two warriors stood on guard over him.

Truly Ringhals had gone far.

3

The other white man had made his camp near Kaspar's own. He had only one wagon, a very fine one, and was engaged in training some oxen that he had bought to replace those lost upon the road. The stranger's name was Adriaan Fourie. His greeting was very friendly. He was young, not more than twenty-five; big and shambling, with a mat of light-coloured hair, and eyes that were neither blue nor green, but something between the two. They did not change when he smiled. His explanation of his presence was quickly given. It was like a story that, having been made up, must be told quickly lest the teller lose the thread of his tale. Still, a white man was a white man; and Kaspar felt friendly towards him. He and this other were alone among thousands of Kaffirs.

Fourie had bought much of the King's ivory and was preparing to go south. He had come in partnership with another man, one Jan Neithling, who had died of a wasting fever on the way. Fourie was going to sell the ivory and divide the money obtained with his widow.

'It would be safer,' he said, 'if we went south together, and besides we should have the pleasure of one another's company.' To this Kaspar agreed. He was tired of his own company, tired of his thoughts, and very willing to have a companion on the road.

From N'tembi there was no sign, though he saw her once. Before he left he must see the King, to thank him for his permission to hunt and to bid him farewell.

'So, white boy, you are yet alive!' Mziligazi said.

'I live, O King. And that I live is because I was under the shadow of the Black Bull. I have hunted, and I crave leave to go. My heart calls for my people.'

'It is right that a man's heart should crave for his people,' the King said; 'therefore you may go. But come back. Come again and bring me more gifts.'

'I will return with great gifts, Elephant whose tread shakes the world,' Kaspar said.

'Come back with gifts,' the King repeated; 'we will feast again and you shall slay more elephants. The meat of elephants has fattened you,' he said, smiling. 'You set out a bull calf and return a small bull. You have horns now; one day they will thicken. But see to it that they grow not too heavy for your head. See to it that they stay pointed with use. Farewell, and return!'

'Farewell, O King!' Kaspar left the kraal.

Outside it Ringhals met him. 'Send them away,' he said, pointing to Links and Adam.

Kaspar sent them on.

'You are going,' Ringhals said.

'I am going.'

'You are going with the stranger.'

'Yes, I go with him.'

'Then pay heed to my words, for there is wisdom in them. Two days after leaving here there is a parting in the ways — one road leading to the right and one to the left.'

'That is so,' Kaspar said.

'Then, when you come to the parting of the ways, let the stranger go one road and take the other yourself.'

Kaspar opened his mouth to speak.

'Ask no more. Do what I tell you, and the lost ones will guard you. Do what I say, and you will come to no harm. Listen, lord: the surface of a piece of water may be smooth; it may be surrounded with short grass that is speckled with flowers; trees may droop their branches into that water; but what do you know of what there is beneath that smooth surface? Ai . . . under the surface of smooth events are many rough things hidden. These things, being a wizard, I know, and, being your friend, I warn you. Walk gently, lord; step fearfully. Only the lion can afford to move without discretion. I have taken you to my heart. Fear not, the might of my wisdom is spread over you.' Ringhals fiddled with a small bag that hung at his waist. It was tightly knotted and his fingers had trouble with it. At last it was detached. 'Take this, lord,' he said.

'What is it?' Kaspar asked. The contents of the little bag felt hard.

'They are small stones: very sparkling and beautiful. They were given to me by a man as he died: a man to whom I had done a small service.'

Kaspar opened the bag and shook out the pebbles. They

were red, green, some were striped black and white like
zebras, and some were white and crystal clear. 'They are
pretty,' he said.

'Ai ... they are pretty and there is much magic in them.
In the hour of your unhappiness contemplate them, lord.
They are old ... as old as the world; and long after you are
dead they will endure. When a man's heart is sick, it is
good to think of stones that are everlasting and indestructible; therefore, take them and hold them in your hand when
the world is black. Now farewell!' Ringhals raised his hand.
'We shall meet again: our paths are twisted together. Ai ...
like two cords are they twisted.'

4

Kaspar and Fourie rode their horses in front of the wagons,
which, heavily laden, creaked and groaned behind them.
Kaspar's heart was full; he was going back to Aletta. What
he would do after that remained uncertain. He would not
throw in his lot with Coenraad. That was not his kind of life:
it was free, but with the freedom of piracy. He knew that
he wanted a place of his own. He saw it in his mind: a valley,
well watered, with big shady trees. He was a man of peace.
In his blood was the urge to settle, to make something, as
his ancestors had made things. He wanted to make wide
fields, to see things grow. He looked enviously at the herds
of royal cattle that they passed. Cows — cows with calves
at foot. All he had were oxen. He loved his oxen, but it
was by cows and ewes and mares that a man lived. It was
by planting, by growing; and a man gained as much by
sowing as by reaping. A man gained by what he put down
in sweat and thought.

There was more ivory waiting at Coenraad's, and gold.
He would send two wagons back to his father, together with
such of his people as wished to go. With Aletta and the
rest he would start again, on the other side of the river; or,

if she would not, he would find the Portuguese and make his home among them.

Fourie was very silent. He kept looking round as if he expected something.

'What are you looking for?' Kaspar said.

'I am looking for nothing,' he answered. 'Why should I look for anything?'

'I do not know,' Kaspar said, 'but it seemed to me as if you sought something.'

'I seek nothing.' He sounded angry.

Kaspar spoke no more, but thought of cows; the kind of cows he would buy, long, deep-bodied, all red, and none more than five years old. He would buy heifers, too. He thought of the teeth of cows; of how he would open their mouths, pulling their tongues sideways, and look at their teeth. A heifer of a year and a half had two teeth set in the middle of her milk teeth. When she was two years old, she had four large teeth, two pairs; when she was three, she had six; when she was four, a grown cow, she had a full mouth of eight. And those teeth stayed until she died, wearing down slowly till they became mere stumps. Then she starved because she could eat no more. On hard, sour veld teeth wore down more swiftly. He laughed at the thought of how his father had once won a bull by telling his age. That had been long ago, and he had been with his father, who had been buying the bull. The bull was young and bad-tempered. They had chased him from a long way to get him into the kraal.

'How old is he?' his father had asked.

'I do not know,' the bull's owner had said, 'but he is a fine little bullikie.'

'I should like to know his age,' his father had gone on.

'He is too wild to be handled,' the man had said.

'Yet I think I could look into his mouth,' his father said.

'What, alone, without catching him?'

'Ja, alone, without catching him.'

'Magtig, if you can do that, you can have him for a present.'

Then his father had thrown a riem over the horns of a young cow and had led her into the kraal. He had not been afraid, for what bull would look at a man when he could see a cow? And the bull, setting himself behind the cow, had stretched himself out to his full length, raising his shoulders and arching his loins. Then he had laid his horns back on his shoulders and wrinkling up his lips, had bared his teeth.

'Your bull is thirty-six months old,' his father had said. 'See, he has three pairs of teeth.'

'Magtig, that is a good trick. He is your bull now.'

His father had taken him. Later he had sent the man a fine riding-horse.

Kaspar's thoughts of his father were dispelled by Links who rode up to him. He had been behind with the spare oxen.

'One of the oxen looks sick, meneer,' he said. 'Come back and see him.'

Kaspar turned his horse. 'Which ox is sick?' he asked. 'They all looked well enough.'

'No ox, but I wish to speak to you,' Links said. 'What do we know of this man Fourie?'

'We know nothing,' Kaspar said, 'save that he came to trade.'

'Is it not strange that his servants are all new? That they are not used to his ways? That he has had to train his beasts himself? What has happened to his servants? And what has happened to the white man who was with him?' Links paused. 'Adam has been into his wagon. I sent him there.'

'And what did he find?' Kaspar walked his horse beside Links.

The Bastard leant over his saddle and took him by the arm. 'He found blood on the wagon-sides above the bed. It is in my heart that Fourie killed his partner in bed, as he slept, and then shot his servants. Therefore, I say, beware!

You are rich; you have gold dust and ivory. You have much more than he, a good wagon, oxen, and two of the finest horses in the world.'

'Even without my servants we are three,' Kaspar said.

'Yes, we are three; but at night we sleep. From now only two of us will sleep. And Adam will watch, too. But be ready, my friend. I may call you my friend?' Links asked anxiously. 'You are not angry? You do not think it presumptuous?'

'You are my friend,' Kaspar said. 'Ja, you and the Silent One. It is in my heart that between men there is no colour. A man's skin can be white and his heart black. A man's skin can be black and his heart white. I have learnt much in these last days, Links, and this is not the smallest of the things that has come to me.'

'Then we will watch this man,' Links said. 'To watch is to be armed; but I like to ride among friends and to keep my enemies apart and in front of me. I will stay with the oxen. Ride forward and talk to him, but show nothing.'

The thought of a man killing for gain was new to Kaspar. He patted his horse's neck and cantered on.

Finding a suitable place, they outspanned and camped. Fourie was silent. He sat smoking. Once he asked Kaspar why he permitted such familiarity from the Bastards.

'I forget that they are Bastards,' Kaspar said. 'They are my friends.'

'Yet you come of great people at the Cape. I know your name.'

'You come from the Cape?' Kaspar asked.

'I have been there. I am from the Bokkeveld.' With that Fourie set to cleaning his gun.

When Kaspar went to bed, he found Adam squatting inside his wagon, with his small bow across his knees. There was an arrow fitted to the string. His eyes were bright with excitement. Now and then a quiver ran over his skin. It twitched like the shoulders of a horse when his body was still. The dogs were not sleeping, but alert. He pointed to the dogs. 'I have told them,' he said. 'They also watch.'

During the night nothing happened. But in the morning Links had news.

'In the night a woman came, Kaspar: one of the King's women; she who is called N'tembi. Before the dawn she went. She came to Fourie's wagon. No good will come of this.'

'What can we do?' Kaspar asked.

'We can do nothing. But something will come of it. We can but wait.'

The day was eventless, save that the wagons had to be double-spanned to cross a drift.

The following night nothing happened. Adam watched again, and in the morning Links said, 'She was here again.'

Again Kaspar rode in front of the wagons with Fourie. Links rode behind with the loose cattle.

Suddenly he put spurs to his horse and galloped up to Kaspar. 'Men are coming,' he said. 'I have seen dust and the flash of spears.'

'We will face them,' Kaspar said to Fourie.

For an instant Fourie's face showed fear; then he swung his horse beside Kaspar's. 'Yes, let us face them,' he said.

The Silent One rode up. A moment later a regiment swung into view. They were in full war-dress: plumed and armed. At their head ran an old induna. They halted.

'Greetings,' Kaspar said.

'Greetings,' the induna said.

'What do you seek?' Kaspar said. 'You are dressed for war.'

'We are dressed for war. We are on the King's business. We seek one of his women. Can we seek her in peace, or must we seek her in war?'

'Seek where you will,' Kaspar said.

The men, spreading out, ran through the veld about the wagon like hunting-dogs while the induna and some others went through the wagons. They found nothing.

'There is nothing here,' the induna said. 'She may have gone elsewhere. But we must find her.'

'And if you do not find her?' Kaspar asked.

The old man looked at him. 'There is only one answer to failure. Either we find the King's heifer or we go to the place of death.' He turned his men and they trotted off as they had come.

An hour after they had left, Kaspar came to the parting of the ways that Ringhals had spoken of.

'We part here,' Kaspar said to Fourie.

'Part? I thought you were going south.'

'I was, but I have changed my mind. I am going first into the west. I hear that there are unicorns there. I would like to shoot a unicorn.'

'You are mad.'

'If I am mad, it is my madness,' Kaspar said, and turned his wagons. 'Tot siens!' he said.

'Tot siens!' Fourie said.

They fired their guns in salutation and farewell.

That night Kaspar was wakened by Links shouting, 'Inspan ... Inspan! We must trek.' The sky all round them was pink with the glow of flames. He sprang up and helped to put in the oxen.

'Where can we go, Links?' he shouted.

'I know this country. There is a place a mile ahead, an outcrop of rock where there is no grass.'

The oxen, frightened by the shouting and the glare, fought against the yokes, but at last they were put in. The trektous slipped over their backs and strained tight as they came into line. The whip cracked and the wagon began to roll. Links led them. Kaspar and the Silent One drove up the loose beasts. The fire was roaring down-wind towards them; it was crawling up-wind. It was burning diagonally across their flanks.

'Use your sjamboks!' Links cried. 'Beat them, kerels, beat them!'

There was nothing accidental about this. Perhaps Links' suspicions had been right. Perhaps it was Fourie's work. Gold dust would not burn.

He heard Links shout, 'This way,' and fire his gun.

They were on a flat of rotten stone. The wagon-wheels turned more easily as they struck the hard ground.

'Tie the beasts!' Links said. 'Lash the wheels and tie everything!'

The spare stock and pole oxen were all tied. Kaspar held Tigernek to calm him. Adam stood by the brown. It grew lighter as the fire came nearer. Everything was painted red by the firelight. They were safe if they did not suffocate on their island of rock, but they were not alone. Out of the veld, from all round them, came every kind of beast. Two wildebeeste, a zebra with a foal, meerkats, rooikats, and snakes. It seemed to Kaspar that all the snakes in the world were with them, under their feet and crawling up the wagon-wheels. Then came a rhinoceros at a gallop. Kaspar thought it was going to strike the wagon, but it swerved away and came to a halt almost beside his horse. There it stood, quite still, his horn black against the red border of the world. By the terror of fire had man and beast, both wild and domestic, become one and at peace. Today there was no war between the beasts. All were still: the buck, and the mice, and the meerkats, and the snakes.

It grew lighter and hotter as the flames approached. They devoured everything, licking at the grass and the trees with long tongues, smothering everything with plumes of rolling smoke. It writhed in curling clouds about them. The horses screamed with fear. The brown lifted Adam off his feet as he reared, but the Bushman clung to him and, as he came down, whispered into his ear. A big python advanced majestically, its little tongue going back and forth out of its closed mouth, towards the wagon. It was like a great, slowly dragged rope, as thick as the thigh of a man and longer than the wagon. Slowly, it reared its bulk against

the back of the wagon, leaned against it, and climbed.
Kaspar watched the canvas tent sagging beneath its weight.
In the red light of the flames its patterned skin made it
the personification of snakes, and of evil. A mamba, swift
as a whip, shot out of the bush, ran over a scrubby tree, and,
curling along a limb, waited. So had the beasts been in the
Ark. So only by terror, by fire or water, could the lion and
the lamb lie down together.

Kaspar pointed this out to Links. 'Behold,' he said, 'the
lion and the lamb at peace. The snake and the mouse are
friends.'

But almost as he spoke, the mamba struck at a rooikat
that climbed near it. The rooikat fell from the tree, twitched
spasmodically for a few minutes, and died. Not even such
danger was enough to reconcile one beast of God's creation
to another.

Links laughed. 'Ja,' he said, 'the lion and the lamb, perhaps, and the mouse and the snake, but not the mamba and
the rooikat. The cat is dead.'

The flames died down. The fire was past them. Kaspar
watched it eating into the distance; watched the columns of
smoke getting fainter. It was moving now, and soon he could
see only smoke; only see it as a haze, no longer watch it
whirling in clouds. The air was thick with birds, little hawks,
shrikes, and bee-eaters, reaping their harvest. The veld was
black, the sky opalescent with smoke; behind them only
was it clear. The wind was from the back.

'Now we must wait,' Links said, 'till the ground is cool.
There is water near here.'

'Everything is full of snakes,' Kaspar said. And it was
so; the ground was covered with them, the wagon filled
with them.

'We will leave the wagon and take the beasts to water,'
Links said. 'By tomorrow the snakes will be gone.' He
laughed. 'The snakes do not like us any more than we like
them,' he said, 'but unless you tread on one they will do

nothing; before God, they are too frightened. Look at that!'

A sable bull had stepped onto the freshly burnt ground
He walked daintily, putting his hoofs down carefully, feeling each piece of ground before he trusted his weight upon
it. His coat was a magnificent shining black, his belly a
brilliant white, his face lined with white. Utterly uncon-
cerned, he passed within twenty yards of them, lowering
his head, with its great curved horns, to smell the ground
at every step. Suddenly, as though satisfied with its condition, he sprang forward into a bounding gallop. The grey-
white ash of the burnt grass sprang up under his feet. Once
he jumped sideways. 'He has burnt himself,' Links said.
And then he disappeared into the haze. The rhinoceros now
lumbered forward. The wildebeeste and zebra followed him,
all walking with daintiness and precision, raising their feet
high.

'We will wait till noon,' Links said, 'and then go down
to the water. Who did it, Kaspar?' he asked suddenly.
'That was no ordinary fire. It came from all round.'

'Ja, who did it?' Kaspar echoed. 'Fourie, do you think?'

'I do not know; but such a fire is the work of man. It
was made to a plan. It hemmed us in.'

They all sat down to wait and drank water from their
bottles and the cask on the wagon. Then they took the
beasts to water. By this time the animals were calm, but
smelt at the ground, blowing up little plumes of white ash
as they sniffed it. Here and there trees still smouldered and
smoke arose in little columns from the game-dung that
burnt more slowly than the grass. It had been a big fire:
they were lucky to be alive.

When they got back to the wagon, they found a party of
warriors waiting for them. They were squatting on their
haunches with their assegais in their hands and their shields
beside them.

'You are to come back with us,' they said.

'Why am I to come back?' Kaspar asked.

'We do not know,' they answered, 'but you are to come back.'

'And if I won't?'

'You will come with us,' they said. 'You will come with us alive, or we will bear you with us dead.'

There were a hundred warriors. To resist was foolish.

'We will come. But where is your captain? Where is the induna?' Kaspar asked.

'He went to take the other wagon. We will meet with him tonight.' They looked exhausted, pale with dust, and their plumes were bedraggled.

'You have come fast,' Kaspar said.

'We have come fast and far,' they answered.

Kaspar pointed to the wagon. 'I cannot inspan until the snakes are gone.'

'We will wait,' the leader said.

In the morning the wagon was turned round, and at dusk they came up with Fourie's wagon. Fourie was a prisoner. They had caught N'tembi with him.

The old induna came to meet Kaspar. He was smiling. He pointed to the captives. 'We have caught them,' he said.

'What will happen to her?' Kaspar asked.

'She will be killed.'

'Killed?' Kaspar said. 'She is young to be killed.'

'It is better that she should be killed than that we should be killed,' the induna said. He looked at his men proudly. 'We are the King's dogs and we have hunted well.' Seeing Kaspar's face, he went on: 'And do not try to do anything. You are safe enough, but if you try to help them, I will have you killed, and that would be a pity.'

'Help them?' Kaspar said. 'I would not help them. He tried to burn us up. And if it had not been for the fire you would not have caught her.'

The induna laughed. 'Look at me,' he said.

Kaspar looked at him.

'Do you see my wounds?' He pointed to his scars, to

his white wounds recently healed and to old black cicatrices. 'Do you think I got them for nothing?' he asked. 'Do you think I command the white shields without knowledge? Has my name of "Leopard" not been earned by my cunning in war? No, white man: had there been no woman, there would have been no fire. It was I who kindled the fire. I made two fires — one about you and one about him, ringing you both in. With you only the snakes and the wild beasts were driven in. But she came in with the buck to him, fleeing in front of the flames. Ai ... like a buck she came, running in, leaping out of the veld.'

'And if the wind had changed?' Kaspar said.

'Then we should have been burnt,' the induna said. 'Men have been burnt before.'

'Why did you not take her at night, in the wagon without making a fire, since you knew she came in?' Kaspar asked.

'The danger was too great. In the night except for the fire she might have slipped away. Ours was the best course. We waited till you were both in places where the fire would not touch you. He was in a sandy place; and then we burnt the world about you. Ai ...' he said, stroking the haft of his assegai, 'when we go out we return triumphant. There is nothing we do not dare.'

'What will happen?' Kaspar asked again.

'She will be killed. If the wife of a man is killed for adultery, how much more will a woman of the King be killed?'

'Perhaps she wished to return to her people,' Kaspar said.

'For the King's women there is no return.'

'And the man?'

'For the man I do not know. The King will be unwilling to kill a white man openly.' He looked at Kaspar. 'We know of your race. We do not fear you, but we seek no trouble. Matched bulls rarely fight. They go their own ways. But he' — the induna nodded at Fourie — 'is bad. We have had word. News has come in that he slew his companion and his servants. Their bones have been found. This is a big land' — he extended his hand to the horizon — 'but little in it is hidden. Always there are watching eyes, always there are feet that follow upon the spoor of those who move in it: men seeking meat or loot. Where a wagon rests something is often forgotten, so wagons are followed; and those who followed him found skulls and clean bones. Ai ... he is a bad man, one who kills sleeping men at night, like a wolf. But fear not, it is in my heart that the King will not blame you. After all, what have you done but bear an ill man company for a space of days?'

Nevertheless Kaspar was uneasy. It might well have been he who had been taken with N'tembi. She might speak. Or someone else might, and then he would be counted equally to blame and suffer the same penalties. He wished that it were over one way or the other. He felt no sympathy for Fourie. He never spoke to him, but could not keep his eyes from N'tembi. So that had been her plan. Her seduction of him had been due to a desire for escape. To escape she had used the only means at her disposal, her body, the price of her freedom. She had played her body and lost it. She even seemed resigned. She bore herself with dignity, a half-smile on her lips. She walked as she had always walked: very erect, with a contemptuous swing. She was a king's daughter. She would remain silent, betraying no one.

5

The judgment was swift.

They were brought before the King. Kaspar was free and unbound, but the girl and Fourie were tied, their hands lashed with riems behind their backs.

Mziligazi sat very still, his eyes moving from one to the other. N'tembi faced him; looking neither to the right nor left, she stared into his eyes.

'Why did you run away?' the King asked.

'I was taken in war,' she said. 'It is my right to run away.

I am a woman and would mate with my own people. Does the deer breed with the river horse?' she asked. She never lowered her eyes.

'River horse!' the King shouted. He raised his hand. 'Kill!' he said.

Three warriors sprang forward. One felled her with a blow on the shoulder; the others, raising their kerries, smashed her joints, breaking her knees and elbows with their great rhinoceros clubs. She was alive; her body moved, but she uttered no sound.

'Take her away,' the King said.

The broken limbs followed the movements of her body, dragging after it as they pulled her. She would die slowly on the veld, tormented by ants and flies, watched by the vultures, fainting and coming to again, and then fainting again. In the night the wolves would kill her, tearing her to pieces while she still lived. The wolves round the great kraal were fat, sleek, and larger than ordinary.

'And you,' the King said to Fourie, 'you have eaten my beef and betrayed it. No doubt you were seduced.'

'I was seduced,' Fourie said. 'She danced before me and I was seduced.' He was leaning for support against the men who held him.

'Among our people,' the King said, 'men are not seduced. When they want women they take them.' He smiled. 'Perhaps that is a lie. Perhaps among our people also it is the woman who chooses whether she will be taken or not; but our men are men, they do not acknowledge it. They do not hide behind a woman's lack of virtue. More, I have had news of you. You killed your companion on the road while he slept. But that is white man's business. You can kill as many as you please. But I will kill no white men.'

Fourie began to thank him.

'Hold your thanks,' the King said. He became thoughtful. Near the kraal there was a young tree. 'Split that tree.'

A warrior split it with an axe.

'Now wedge it open.'

A wedge was inserted into the split tree.

'Take him.' The King pointed to Fourie. 'Set him against the tree so that his left ear is in the cleft.'

They took Fourie and set his ear in the cleft.

'Withdraw the wedge,' the King said.

It was withdrawn and Fourie began to cry out. The splintered wood of the closed tree held him fast.

'Now begin your thanks, white man,' the King said. 'I will not kill you. I will feed you and give you water, but you will stand there till your ear rots off or you gain courage to pluck yourself out, leaving it behind you.' He turned to Kaspar. 'White boy, you may go. Go back to your people and tell them of my justice. Tell them that one day a white man will come back among them. A white man with a crumpled ear, or earless, and that his defect will be a sign to all that he is a slayer of men and a seducer of maidens. So will he go forth branded, and his description circulated among my nation will bring him a swift death if he comes this way again. I have no anger against you, white boy, but my heart is sore against your people. Rest your cattle and tomorrow get you gone.'

6

'It was better, lord, this way.'

Kaspar looked at Ringhals in surprise. 'Better?' he said. There was something terrible about the thought of N'tembi's death: at its simplicity, a woman beaten with kerries; at her end, at her supple body being dragged with broken joints over the veld and thrown to the beasts.

'Better,' Ringhals said. 'Better that it should be the other man who stands with his ear fast to a tree, and better that you can return whence you came in peace.'

'It was terrible to see her killed,' Kaspar said.

'She should not have been killed, lord. But, like all women, she was foolish, and because of her foolishness, she died. I gave her strong moutie, a medicine that would have made her invisible. She was to take it each night at sundown. But no doubt at sundown she did not wish to be invisible. Ai ... that is the way of women. I said to her, "O woman, as the sun sinks in the sky, take this powder, sniffing it up like snuff, and you will be as air, as smoke, impalpable, invisible; and no man, neither friend nor foe, will be able to lay his hand upon you." But because at night she went to the arms of the stranger she heeded me not. Ai ... ai, because of her hot blood, her bones are cracked and cleaned.' Ringhals pulled up his kaross and sank his chin on his knees.

'Why did you send her to me at first?' Kaspar asked. 'Why did you carry her message?'

'I wished to help her. My heart was sore for her. Also, her father is a chief, and she promised me great rewards.'

'Then why, when I was away, did you send her to Fourie?'

'How was I to know that you would return? You are young, lord, and elephants are strong. Besides, had I not promised to watch over you? Therefore, because my word was given, it was better that another should take the risk.'

'You are a good friend,' Kaspar said. 'For the reward she offered, you would have let her go with me. If Fourie had not come, she would have done so and I might be dead.'

'The young lord has spoken truly.' Ringhals' black eyes stared up at him out of the kaross that he had pulled over his head. 'The young lord echoes the words of many; as a friend I am without equal. I am the friend of the living and the dead, the friend of the lost ones, of the ghosts and the spooks that walk by night. I dominate their legions, I lead their impis, and I perceive no reason for your anger. Are you not alive? Do you think I did not know what would occur? I saw it all. I went into the future time, which is one with the past time, and saw. And had she taken my moutie, she would have been safe. A chaste woman would have been safe, but even I am not strong enough to change the heart of a woman nor to prevent a she-cat, at certain seasons, from walking in the night. Also . . .'

'Also? What is there also?'

'Also she knew too much. She had seen me with the snake-woman before the death of Toolah. Truly, lord, the ways of Providence are strange.' He looked up again. 'She calls me her Little Flower and holds me to her breast.'

'The snake-woman holds you?' Kaspar said.

'Ai . . . she holds me. I am a joy to her, a perfume in her nostrils. If I had tobacco, I would prophesy, lord; I am in the mood. The mantle of the lost ones is upon me. It has come suddenly. With tobacco in my hands, I would go into the days that are coming, as messenger, and give you news.' He held out his hands, cupped together.

Kaspar gave him tobacco. The clawlike fingers closed over it. His eyes contracted. He appeared to grow smaller, shrinking into himself. His outline was blurred in the smoke of the fire. It seemed to Kaspar that he could see through him, see the hut against which he leant through his body. Ringhals began to mumble. He spoke words in tongues that Kaspar could not understand. He made little cries, the cries of beasts, of birds. He grew still smaller: he became as small as a child, and then spoke in a thin, high voice:

'I see a great black-bearded man . . . I see a small man, dry like a leaf in winter . . . I see other men — many men — with guns in their hands, and they laugh . . . Ai, they mock a man — a young man . . . It is you that they mock with their laughter . . . and the word goes forth that you have been taken with a heifer of the King . . . that you could not be satisfied with Eve, the Bush girl . . . that you are a man with many concubines. . . . Then I see white women — a small one and a large — that quarrel, after the manner of women, using hard words . . . both desire you. And I see danger in this, for one of them is scorned . . . Ai, ai, a scorned woman is a snake that bites the heel of the scorner. A scorned woman is an adder, marked and patterned with stripes. . . .

And there is another man who . . . holds the snake in his hands, charming her by the magic of his ways . . . Ai . . . ai . . . Aiiii . . .' His voice rose shrilly. 'I see death . . . death by the rope, with men struggling . . .'

Ringhals crouched lower, still staring into the fire; his black eyes were red-rimmed slits.

'You are not among those who hang . . . I see oxen yoked and wagons . . . I see wheels turning . . . I see a woman and a child and cattle — many beasts, cattle, sheep, and horses . . . still they come . . . more beasts. . . . I see a new place, and trouble like a cloud over this land. . . . I see white men fighting black, and white men fighting white men . . . I see it as a contest between bulls. . . . I see a golden cow and a white vulture. . . . It fades . . . it fades . . . Young lord, it fades . . . the future time is thin . . . no longer palpable. The lost ones hover about me. . . . They call me Little Flower. They say, "Tarry with us . . . come to us, Ringhals." They hold out their arms to me in welcome.'

He shivered and grew larger again. His eyes opened. 'I have been, and am back,' he said. 'Now I will give you counsel. Fear nothing, but go on. Do not fear mockery or laughter. When you get back, they will confuse you with this other man, for word of it will have gone forth. Ai . . . the word of it will make much talk in the land, for men must talk, even if it be lies. Also they will say that Eve is your concubine.'

'She is not,' Kaspar said.

'Nevertheless, they will say it. Some will laugh. Some will sneer. But the small one whom you love will believe nothing against you. She will ask you and you will tell her part of the truth. You will say nothing of N'tembi or of your madness with her — only that she was caught with the other man and destroyed. Speak much of Eve. Women are like dogs. They must have a bone to chew upon. So give her a bone with no meat. Let her gnaw upon Eve, since Eve is nothing, and she will go no farther than Eve. Truly, a small woman can cast a great shadow upon a man's life. But the size of a woman, like that of a bird, has little to do with the sweetness of her song.'

7

N'tembi was dead. Fourie was tied to a sapling by his own ear. A number of elephants and rhinoceros had died so that Kaspar's wagons should be filled with ivory and horn. He had been ill and nearly died. These were the facts: Kaspar, riding south on Tigernek, reflected upon them. He thought of Ringhals' words, of van Ek's philosophy, and of the strange similarity between them. He thought of his dreams when he was ill, of his efforts to find a solution; of how sometimes he had thought he had it, and of how each time it had eluded him. He wished that he were different: that he had not this curiosity, this desire to know why, this dissatisfaction of the spirit. It was dissatisfaction which had driven him from his home. He had thought things were not well there. 'I will go elsewhere and see if things are better,' he had said. And what had he found? That they were the same, differently clothed but the same; equality, liberty, fraternity, remained words only. There was one law for the strong, another for the weak; one for women and another for men; one law for the lion, another for the buck. He had proved all this. It had been verified and confirmed conclusively by the deaths he had seen: those of old Frederik, of the Bushmen, of Toolah, of N'tembi.

Kaspar was tired of death, tired of corruption; but he began to see it as a transition. Life lived on death. Without death there could be no life. Seen this way, it was simple but inexplicable. All about one, all the time, even now as he rode over the veld, it was going on, this vast, silent war of beast on beast. How little even man had to do with his own destiny! His own life had been changed by a puppy, and yet it was not only the puppy. It was the factor of time. Had he come later or gone earlier, it would not have happened and he would not have killed the soldier. It was when the time, the place, the circumstance, and the man all met; when opportunity and circumstance forced themselves upon the unwilling hour. It was all chance. Coenraad had said he was lucky. The next few weeks or months would prove his luck. He was going back to put his head in the British lion's mouth. Again, by circumstance, by the series of accidents which had made up his life since he had left Leendert's, he was more fitted to play the part. If he was to gamble with his life, at least now he had the ability to do so.

He was on his way to Aletta. Each day brought him nearer. Life became one with time and time one with the miles that separated him from her. Suddenly he knew that there was nothing strange in his feelings. It was no stranger than the flexing of a muscle on his horse's shoulder. He patted Tigernek. When he knew what caused those muscles to contract, pulling up his horse's leg or extending it down again; when he understood the reason that doves sat pink beak to pink beak, or why young chameleons should stand on their mothers' backs with their tails wrapped round hers, then would he understand everything.

Life, like a loom, wove the subtle thread of consequence through the generations, joining effect to cause, endlessly: no act was unreasonable, no thought sprang from a void, but all were caused, all schemed, all fitted, each a part of some vast device. There could be no understanding. There could only be acceptance: the acceptance of everything, even of the slow passage of the sun each day through the heavens over his head, of its rising on his left, of its setting on his right, and of the miles that were destroyed each day.

The veld was beautiful, but he saw no beauty in the veld. He had no adventures. He shot only for meat. It was as if the country itself conspired to help him, to make things easy. Rivers that had been over-full when he came were low when he went back. No oxen died and none were sick.

Till he got news, till he saw Aletta, his hands were tied. He was crippled, utterly at a loss and perpetually surprised at his own competence, at the way his hands did things perfectly while his mind dreamed. To pass the time when the wagon was not moving, he mended his gear. He made a new sling to his gun; he made a new belt, new velskoen; he strengthened his saddle; and all the time his heart was like a dead thing in his breast, knowing neither joy nor sorrow, beyond both, and able only to count the days and the miles, and to check the one against the other.

A month, a week, two more days.

'Tomorrow we shall be back, Kaspar,' Links said, 'and then you can go to her.'

CHAPTER XXIII

BACK TO THE RIVER

I

COENRAAD was glad to see Kaspar. He clapped him on the back. From his great height he looked down at him.

'Our little cock is home, Christiaan,' he said. 'Before God, elephants are good for boys if they do not kill them.'

'It has done him good,' van Ek said. 'He is like a young dog that is now furnished. Ja, Kaspar,' he said, 'you can go against big game now.'

'Big game!' Kaspar said. 'I have shot elephants.' He was angry at his reception.

Coenraad and van Ek laughed.

'An Englishman is bigger than an elephant, and the day draws near. Much has happened since you were here,' van Ek said. 'The Border is up and the Kaffirs whet their spears.'

Kaspar remembered the kraals he had come through recently; the young men gathered there, and the beating of the drums.

'The English have no place here,' Coenraad said. 'It is our land.'

Van Ek sprang up. It was the first time Kaspar had seen him so moved. He was like a small snake, very sharp and bitter. His lips were drawn back.

'Before God, let them go back to their island. They have no place in Africa,' he said.

'It is said that they have had a great victory,' Coenraad went on, 'and are fat with pride. They blow themselves up like turkey-cocks.'

'Where have they had a victory?' Kaspar asked.

'At Waterloo, in the Low Countries,' van Ek said. 'But many thousands of their best troops have been killed.'

'I am going to Rudolf's,' Kaspar said.

'Rudolf has been here.' Coenraad's voice sounded pleased. 'He is with us.'

'Is all well at Rudolf's?'

'His wife is dead.'

'And the girls?'

'He said nothing of the girls. And since he said nothing, they are well.' Coenraad began to laugh. 'It is the little one,' he said. 'Magtig, before the sweat is dry on your horse you must be after her. Then go; I will give you a man to go with you, not Links or the Silent Willem, they will want to stay with their women. Nor could they get away from them if they wished to. Nee, I will send another, one who, having been long at home, will be glad to go. Ja, it is like that. When a man is with his woman, he tires and wants to rest; and when he is away from her, he becomes hot and strong and can get no peace till once again he becomes tired.' Coenraad slapped his thighs and laughed louder.

Van Ek was silent. He was serious. 'Be careful how you venture. There is money on your head. Before God, we are like vermin to be hunted!' he cried. 'The foxes have their holes, the birds of the air their nests, but we have no place to lay our heads. Come what may, it were better to die in our harness than to live thus. Truly, many of our people will die, but they will lie in peace and their names shall live forevermore, a reproach to them that slew them. The day is near. It is upon us.' He recovered himself and drew forth his pipe. 'Go, Kaspar,' he said, 'but do not stay too long, and be careful. On this side of the Great Fish River you are safe. On the other . . .' He shrugged his shoulders.

'He will come back,' Coenraad said. 'He is a lucky man. He has a spot in his eye.'

'He will come back, or he will not come back,' van Ek said. 'That is to be seen. Only one thing is certain, that unless he dies in the night tomorrow he will be gone.' He smiled and said: 'You would not believe it, Coenraad, but I, too, was once like that.'

'You never told me,' Coenraad said.

'There is nothing to tell. She was very beautiful, and then she died. Since then I have seen much. Since then I have done much. But nothing has been the same. There are plants, Coenraad, that bloom but once if the bloom is plucked. After that they live on, but they have no vigour and they do not thrive. One day, perhaps, I will tell you of it, for it comes to me that I am getting old; that I have waited nearly long enough.' He stroked the lock of his gun, his finger-nails following the lines of the engraving upon it.

He looked very old and tired. He was looking beyond Kaspar into the great space of his age, into the years that he had lived, in emptiness, alone.

'I have news for Gaika,' Coenraad said. 'You can pass that way, Kaspar, and then go on from there. Ja, I have a message for him. His mother was my wife. Sometimes it makes me laugh to have been the husband of a queen and to have a price upon my head. Ja, sometimes it makes me laugh. But sometimes I grow angry. Sometimes I get tired of it, and this time we play to make an end. You had best send your wagons straight to Leendert van Ek and meet them there. They can go safely now that the Bushmen are broken.'

'I will do that,' Kaspar said. 'They can leave when we do tomorrow.'

'You did a good trade,' Coenraad said, 'both with us and with Mziligazi. Your father will be pleased.'

'Ja, my father will be pleased.' His father would be pleased at having three wagonloads of ivory and a quantity of gold. But goods could not replace a son. His father would mourn him. Kaspar wondered if he would ever see his father again or any of his relations. When he got settled, perhaps his father would visit him or his Uncle Hendrik. Hendrik van der Berg had no love of the English and always talked of coming north. It was strange to have an uncle almost of his own age.

Kaspar said good-bye to Coenraad and van Ek and went to his wagons to give Frans his orders. Those of his servants who were going back were making merry, rejoicing at their near return. His servants were going back to the home he would never see again.

2

Kaspar took with him Jeffries, a runaway English sailor. Jeffries came from London. He had been impressed to a fifty-gun frigate. A labourer, he had been dragged from his wife and child. He had had no news of them for five years. He was a big simple man, heavily tattooed. From his left hip to his right shoulder a snake in red and green twined round his body. When he washed, stripped to the waist, and bent down, it writhed with the play of his muscles. His arms were decorated with designs of trees, flags, and women. On the back of his left hand he had a heart transfixed with an arrow. Above the arrow was the letter 'I,' on the left the word 'love,' on the right 'you,' and under it 'Mary.'

'I love you, Mary,' he spelt out. 'That's her name, Mary; and the baby is called Mary, too. She was three when they took me. She'd be eight now.... You shot a soldier,' he said. He looked at Kaspar.

'I shot a soldier,' Kaspar said.

'Wish you'd shot some more of 'em. By God, sir, that's a terrible thing to have done to you. For them to take a man and so treat him that he hates his country!' He was silent. Suddenly he spoke again. 'She came from Shropshire. That's against Wales. I expect she thinks I'm dead. You see, I don't know how to write, and when I got away there was no one to write for me. The *Swallow* — that's the ship I got away from. That's where they made men into sailors, or killed 'em. They made me into a sailor, but they didn't kill me. No, by God, you can't kill Jim Jeffries. I've fought against the French; we fought 'em, a running fight, and then we turned and sank 'em.' There was a strange mixture of pride in the action fought by the *Swallow*, and hatred for his country in Jeffries' voice.

More than ever did Kaspar wonder at the men gathered about Coenraad, the flotsam and jetsam of every land and sea; renegades of every race. And more than ever did he feel himself not at one with them. They were broken men, and he was not broken yet. He might sink to that, or he might be killed. That was a matter between God and himself.

He liked Jeffries. His horsemanship made him laugh. Jeffries was no horseman, but he rode after a fashion of his own, very securely, going up and down on the back of his horse as though it was a dinghy tossing on the waves, guiding him with pulls as if he held the lines of the rudder. But he knew the country, was broken to Africa, and could find his way by the stars, or, as he said, by dead reckoning. He was a good shot and a skilled hunter. He chewed tobacco and did not smoke. He had fought the Americans. Fine sailors, he called them, and able to sail closer to the wind than the English. His conversation entertained Kaspar. It was new. He had, at home, only met Englishmen of a different class and had not liked them. They had seemed to him cold and affected. Kaspar never tired of Jeffries' tales of his voyages. If Aletta would come with him, they would go away and make a place somewhere: in some hidden valley. He was a Boer. The world of Africa was open.

'Tomorrow we will get to Gaika's,' Jeffries said.

'We have to see him about some oxen that he owes Coenraad,' Kaspar said.

'Will we have to bring them back?' Jeffries asked. 'I hate them things. You can't steer 'em.'

3

There were white men at Gaika's. Kaspar was welcomed, and he sat down to listen to what they had to say. His message from Coenraad could wait. It was only a matter of cattle.

'You say that the Boers are ready from the Winterberg to the Cape,' the interpreter said.

'They are ready,' Faber said.

If they were ready, why did they need the Kaffirs? Kaspar wondered.

He looked at Gaika's face. Gaika seemed to be wondering the same thing. He spoke to the interpreter.

The interpreter stood up. 'One day a man met a lion,' he said in Dutch, 'and the man said to the lion: "Oh, lion, what is the matter with the tuft on your tail?" "There is nothing the matter with the tuft on my tail," the lion said. Nor was there anything the matter with the tuft on his tail. It was long and black and stiff, but the words of the stranger made him bashful. He felt ashamed. He felt like a maid when the string of her little apron is broken. Turning round, he looked at the tuft on his tail. It seemed to him good, but less good than it had been. Because of the words of the man, he was disappointed in his tail. Then the man said: "Give me your tail and in a week I will bring you back a fine new one." So the lion bit off the tuft of his tail and gave it to the man. Having no tuft to his tail, the lion did not dare go abroad, but waited concealed in a bush for the return of the stranger with the fine new tuft which had been promised. And in the space of time that the lion waited, it came to him that even a poor tail was better than no tail at all. Also he got hungry and saw other lions passing. They laughed at him, mocking him, and he grew angry. His tail had been as good as theirs, and he saw no advantage in having a finer tail than the others. He was a peaceful lion, and he knew that his new tail, if it were too fine, would excite jealousy among the other lions, who would then conspire together to pluck it off. But when the man returned, it was the lion's old tail that he brought back. It was unchanged. But the lion was so pleased to have any tail that he thanked the man for bringing it, saying: "You bring me back my own tail unchanged, but I am not angry about the deception or the discomfort you have caused me. I will gladly take it and bear no malice towards you." But the man said: "I will only give you back your tail if you pay me for it." So the lion had to pay for his own tail. When he had bitten it off, he had bled a great deal, so at the end, his state was not so good as it had been in the beginning.'

'It is a fine story,' Faber said, 'but I do not understand it.'

'Yet it is simple ... Are you not a man, and is Gaika, my master, not a lion?'

'Then you refuse?'

'My master neither accepts nor refuses. He must have time to ponder. It is his tail you ask for. It is his blood, the blood of his warriors, that he will lose.'

'He would gain many cattle.'

'My master has many cattle and can get more any day that he wills. And might you not say at the end, when the lion is weak and tired, "Now pay us for these cattle"? Is it not simple, O white man? You come to us not out of love; for between white and black there is no love, but because you would borrow our spears for your purpose.' He turned to Gaika and spoke to him. 'My master says that it is likely that he will come in with you. Let that content you.'

With that they got their horses and left.

Kaspar gave the Chief Coenraad's message, spent the night in his kraal, and rode on. He was getting tired of moving, of never resting, of having only the sky for his ceiling. He was sad as he rode down the hill to Frederik's place.

'This is where you killed the soldier,' Jeffries said.

'Ja, it is where I killed the soldier,' Kaspar answered.

His eyes sought the place where that scarlet-coated body had fallen. He could not find it. He could only guess where it was, but it might have been a hundred yards one way or the other, so little did it matter where a man died. Perhaps, like Jeffries, he had had a wife and a child, or a mother. He must have been a man very like Jeffries, a simple, foolish man. He saw the kloof where they had fought, the dark shadow of the cleft, the pool where Frederik had fallen, and where, when he came down from the rock, he had found the big bitch dead.

The wreck of Frederik's house, roofless, its walls blackened with smoke, brooded over the little valley. A roofless house, in an empty valley. As they rode near the house a duiker dived out of the orchard, leaping the stone wall that surrounded it. The water-furrow was broken, and the grass near the house was very green where the escaping water had flowed over it, but the trees in the orchard were dying.

Kaspar dismounted by the threshold and stood hat in hand by the big stone under which his old friend lay. Old Frederik, who had hurt no one; who had, in his simple faith, written to the Governor to explain his actions and had been killed for what, to him, was a first principle of life, the freedom of his land.

Over this place there was a quietness, a quality of sadness. It was a widowed country that asked only to be let alone. It had the sad beauty of a widow: a land that had known happiness; that had been fruitful; that had been loved. Not wild, not virgin, this land had known the loving care of man; had known his tender hand upon it; and was strong to preserve its beauty, its unutterable mournfulness, its uninterrupted dream of dead days long past, and of the dead man, new dead, who had made those days. Baviaan's River was become a place of weeping, of memories; a place where men passing pulled in their horses, sat brooding in their saddles, and rode on.

The grass was long and moved softly, sadly, in the little wind that ruffled it. The willows by the pool drooped, hanging their branches into the deep, shadowed water. The small voices of the wilderness were silent, hushed; they spoke no more.

A big blue-breasted lizard ran along the stone wall, cocked its head sideways at the men on horseback, and dived into a crevice. Kaspar remembered having seen the lizard there before. Of all that had been there, of all the life of man and beast and fowl, only a lizard remained, a blue streak tying the present to the past.

Kaspar had seen this place prosperous. Now he saw it a desolation: a cultivated place being reclaimed by the wilderness from which it had been born. Wild plants and seeds were stronger than the ploughs of men. So would every place be taken back were man reft from the world. Grass would spring up in the streets of the towns; young trees force down strong walls. Man spent his life in an endless war against wild greenery; and greenery, because it was so strong, must win. Man could not conquer Nature. He could only borrow from her, and all his effort, unless continually renewed, was vain against the strength of plants and seeds.

4

The smell of occupation at Leendert's was good to Kaspar. Leendert's smelt different from Coenraad's. One was a camp, the other a dwelling. Here were the scents he knew, and here was the peace of a home. Here the cows in the kraals had been bred on the farm where they gave their calves. There was about the place the continuity of a settled life as opposed to the fortuitous. Hunting and fighting, he had forgotten what a house was like; had forgotten the fruit trees of the orchards; the flowers, the poultry, and the sounds and scents of a farm. Coenraad's had been noisy day and night. At Coenraad's there had been no tomorrow. Here there was a tomorrow. A man could not plough up land for today. When the ploughshare turned the ground, that place was a home, a settlement, a place of waiting while the planted seeds swelled and broke forth into small green shoots that grew, fruited, and were harvested and garnered; a place where man did not merely pause upon the land, but dwelt upon it, serving with heart and mind. Such a place as this had old Frederik's once been, and it was old Frederik's sweat, as much as his blood, that cried out from the ground that he had tilled.

Nothing was changed at Leendert's. As they tied their horses his aunt came out of the house.

'Kaspar!' she cried. 'You are back!'

'I am back, Tanta Sybilla, and I see that my wagons are here.' Kaspar looked at the wagons outspanned near the house. Witvoet, Wolf, and the puppy, hearing his voice, had run to him. His servants were following them.

'Your wagons came yesterday,' his aunt said. 'Off-saddle and come in.'

Kaspar smiled. 'We do not off-saddle,' he said. He turned to Adam. 'Make loose the girths, and water the horses.'

'I will watch,' Jeffries said. He sat down on a tree-stump with his gun beside him, and put a plug of tobacco into his mouth.

'He is an Englishman,' Tanta Sybilla said.

'He is English, but he hates them. Where is my uncle?'

'He is inside. He is very sick, but he will be glad to see you.'

Kaspar thought of the place as he had last seen it: of the wagons, of Afrikander and his men who had met him here, and of the strange beauty of the moonlight. It was here that he had decided to go back to see Aletta, and to get a puppy from old Frederik. He went in to his uncle.

'How goes it?' he asked.

Leendert looked from Kaspar to his wife. 'It goes well,' he said, 'but, magtig, I am tired of being sick. I am a strong man and it irks me . . . but having begun, I must go on. It is at least a simple way to keep out of trouble. Ja, if when things become difficult men would only go to bed, much trouble would be avoided. Nevertheless, my farm suffers. I am too ill to ride, and I do not like to walk.'

Kaspar laughed. His aunt brought in coffee.

'I have got much gold and ivory,' Kaspar said, 'and you must get it back to my father. You must also send back some of my people. It is time that they went back.'

'I am glad you are safe,' Leendert said. 'We heard you had gone hunting and trading.'

'What has happened while I was away?' Kaspar asked.

'Much has happened. The world is gone mad. Opperman has run away.'

'Then who is field cornet?' Kaspar asked.

'Old Willem Kruger: a good old man.'

'But why? I do not understand.'

'Magtig, who can understand?' Leendert said. 'And God knows if I get the stories right. They come from here and there, but Opperman is frightened. Piet Prinsloo stopped at his place and threatened him, calling him a traitor and holding him responsible for old Frederik's death. He said that all who had been concerned in it would pay — Stockenstroom, Rousseau, and himself. Van Wyk, the field cornet of Tarka, tried to set matters right. He went to see the Mullers; they told him much. He saw Johannes and offered to set forth his grievances in a letter to the Government. Johannes agreed and then took back his word. He said he did not know van Wyk well enough to trust him. And then Opperman got news that the Kaffirs were being stirred up. This was enough for Philippus Opperman. Magtig, Kaspar, in the middle of the night he sent a list of his Burgers and his official papers to old Willem Kruger, nominating him field cornet in his place, and went off. Next day old Willem took them back. He did not want to be a field cornet; he is too old and hardly rides now. But when he got there, he found Philippus gone and his wife packing to follow him.'

'This is a big thing,' Kaspar said.

'Nee, it is not a big thing. It is a big little thing. It is big for us because we are in it. It is big enough to send me to my bed. But it is not big to the Government.'

'How many are in it?'

'A handful. The others wish for peace. They wish to farm, but they are threatened. Theunis de Klerk is one of the leaders. He has threatened to kill all who are not with him. He said he would shoot even his own father if he was not with him. He said this to Diedrik Muller, and they are raising more men by threats in the Rhenosterberg. I tell you, things are bad, Kaspar. You had better stay and go to bed like me. Tanta Sybilla can take care of us both. It would be company for me.'

'You forget they seek me,' Kaspar said.

Leendert sat up. 'Ja, I forgot,' he said.

'I come from Gaika's,' Kaspar said. 'I saw Faber there; with him were two others, Frans Marais, the Hungarian who ran away at the battle of Blaauberg, and Adriaan Engelbregt. They were trying to persuade Gaika to come in with them. They said all the Boers were ready and that they had six hundred Hollanders with them. They said all the people from the Baviaan's River through Graaf-Reinet to Kaapstad were ready to rise.'

'And what did Gaika say?'

'Gaika said little. He said he must consult with Ndhlambi and the other chiefs. It is in my heart that he will wait to see how things go before he moves. But his men are ready. I saw many young men.'

'Before God, if they succeed in raising the Kaffirs, this land will swim in blood.'

'I do not think they will succeed. Gaika is slim. He seeks

only profit. It is nothing to him. He only desires cattle, horses, and guns.'

'I say that it cannot be done,' Leendert said. 'The English are a great nation — greater than we. The days of van Tromp are over. I say, besides, what does it matter to us Boers which flag flies over the castle at the Cape? Will our flag make the ewes drop twins, or the wheat bear heavier heads? Or the rains come when we need them? It's madness, Kaspar! A madness that has sent me to my bed. This is the work of malcontents, of Kasteel Hendrik and his like, playing upon Johannes Bezuidenhout and others, whose minds are clouded by hate. And what can they do?' he shouted. 'Before God, what can they do? Nor is the country with them. We need peace to farm, to remake what has been undone. We need help from the Government, and to rebel and raise the Kaffirs is no way to get concessions.'

'Coenraad and old Christiaan are with them,' Kaspar said.

'They are robbers. Coenraad is my friend, but I call him a robber. What are you going to do now?' he asked.

'I am going to Rudolf's.'

His aunt looked up. 'It is Letta,' she said.

'It is Letta.'

Tanta Sybilla sighed with satisfaction. 'I am glad,' she said. 'Letta is a good girl. It was to see Letta that you went last time. I knew it. If only you had stayed there and had not ridden on. Rudolf's child is dead, and Maria is dead.' She refilled Kaspar's cup and sat down with her hands folded on her lap.

'It was for an excuse that I went to Rudolf's,' Kaspar said. 'I had seen the pups and it was a good excuse,' he repeated.

'An excuse,' his aunt echoed. 'What does a man going to see a maiden need an excuse for? That he goes is reason enough. Did you think that she did not know why you went back?'

'I did not know how to say it,' Kaspar said.

'It is a pity you cannot be sick, too, Kaspar,' Leendert said. 'I would have liked you to be sick with me. This is a fine big bed.'

'What will you do,' his aunt asked, 'when you have seen Letta?'

'I am not certain,' Kaspar replied. 'If she will marry me, we will look for a safe place somewhere. I will buy cattle and farm and trade. It is in my heart that I should like to make a place. If she will not marry me, I shall go east and come to the Portuguese. But I must send news to my father and mother from here.'

'We will send news, and you can send a letter with the wagons,' Leendert said.

'I wonder if I shall see them again,' Kaspar said. 'They are no longer young.'

'It would be dangerous to return. And when are you going to Rudolf's?'

'Tomorrow.'

'Then you will sleep with us.'

'I will sleep here, but not with you. I am not safe in houses any more, and I have lost the habit. I will sleep on the veld with Jeffries, Adam, and our horses.'

'Your horses are well?'

'They have never been better.'

His aunt put her hands on his shoulders. 'You have changed much, Kaspar. But you are a good boy. There is no harm in you.'

'He is a man now,' Leendert said.

'Ja, I am a man,' Kaspar said seriously, 'but I am home-less, landless, and quite alone. You do not know, Uncle, how wide our country is. You do not know how rich it is. There is fine grass up there, and game in countless herds. There are fine rivers, big trees, mountains, valleys, all beyond numbering, and all unknown. There is room for all our people. And it is in my heart that one day they will go there;

like the Israelites, they will leave the land of Egypt and find
a Canaan. Ja, before God, I have seen the Promised Land,
and it is empty.'

He got up abruptly. 'I will see you in the morning,
before I ride.'

In his mind was a vision of the north. That was where
he would take Aletta if she would come. Tomorrow he
would know if she would come. He said good-night.

When he had gone, Leendert said: 'I am tired of being
sick. I wish it was over.'

'It is not over,' Tanta Sybilla said, 'and you will remain
sick. Magtig, if men but had the sense of women such
things would not be.'

'Ja, if men were women it would not be, and if all men had
wives like you, it would not be either. I do not see why I
stay in bed like a child.'

His wife was silent. She was thinking of Kaspar: of the
time he had come before; of Frederik's death; of Maria's;
of the baby's. 'It was a beautiful little dress,' she said, 'and
Kaspar never gave back the lappie in which it was wrapped.'

It was strange how one thought of things — that with all
this going on she should think of that dress with its tucks
and gathers and the linen cloth with the red border. It
brought back the past so vividly: the trek up here, the death
of Bokveld. Why in God's name should she think of Bokveld
now? Why think of that ox out of the thousands she had
seen? Perhaps because, when he died, she tried for the last
time to turn Leendert back. And this was the outcome of
their journey. She thought of the Great Fish River; it still
flowed as it had always flowed and the Fish River Bush grew,
getting neither larger nor smaller, but holding its own against
flood and fire; against drought and death; new growth replacing the old; dead branches falling unheard into its depths,
unnoticed, save by the ants that ate the decaying wood.

She thought of the Kaffir villages that pushed nearer and
nearer to the river-bank, and of the Kaffir foraging parties

which penetrated the Zuurveld they coveted. Beasts were stolen, horned cattle and horses. Sheep were killed and devoured; and men lived by their lusts, their avarice, their loves and their hates.

Little ripples from the past swept over the Border: from the distant past of the Dutch East India Company, that had brought men to this continent, setting them down at its tip, so that it might have fresh meat and vegetables to nourish its servants while they ravaged the rich East; from the less distant past of the van Jaarsveld rising, and the bitterness that came out of it; from small hatreds like that of Kasteel Hendrik; from great ones like that of Johannes, who, in his dreams, heard his brother's voice call to him.

And on all sides, from both banks of what, to the English at the Cape, was but a river, a boundary dividing their peasantry from Kaffraria, there was unrest.

In the hot sun events trembled like ripe fruits upon a bough. Yet still men and women lived and died; still were children born; still did cows calve, birds make nests, and small, neat, blue-waisted wasps plant insects, stung to insensibility, beside the eggs they laid in the mud walls. Selina was gone from Baviaan's River, Frederik was dead, and the country was hushed into a frightened stillness. But the mountains remained unchanged, and the little hills and the rivers. Whoever died, the country would endure. The veld that knew neither flag nor nation. Truly, there was much to think of now. Much to regret. But whatever happened Leendert was safe. Sybilla had kept him in bed from the beginning.

CHAPTER XXIV

THE BAVIAAN'S RIVER

I

THE house had become intolerable to Aletta. Taking Kattie by the hand, she went out. She felt she must walk. It was hot, but she needed the heat, the rays of the sun upon her. She went down the vlei, walking quickly on the short grass, Kattie almost running, on fat legs, beside her. It was here that Kaspar had ridden his race against Coenraad. Two herons rose: there had been herons then too; there were always herons here, and soon there must be news of Kaspar. She turned up the hillside, taking a cattle track which followed the slope of the down. It was very narrow, in places so narrow that she had to lean inward to save herself from falling. Coming to some trees, she stopped. There was a fine view of the valley from here. She took Kattie on her knee. Above her the sun shone through a young shoot. In its centre the living fluid of the sap was dark; the big thorns on it were translucent salmon pink, and the shoot itself pale summer green. Behind the shoot was the rest of the tree, and the other trees, a tangle of dark, shadowed branches, trunks and twisted roots. She closed her eyes. The sun shone through her eyelids. They were dyed bright orange by her blood. She was only aware of the bright orange of her eyelids, of the warmth of the air and ground, and the feeling of Klein Kattie crawling over her, touching her face with small, sticky hands that smelt of milk. Something must happen soon: but she had felt this so often, and nothing had happened. Often she had gone out and been certain that when she came back there would be news; had even gone out on purpose, against her will, as if by going out she could make news come, as though things went by contraries; had gone out, so that if Kaspar came she would miss him. It would be so much better to miss him than for him not to come.

She sat up and rubbed her eyes; they ached. She took off her shoe and shook a pebble out of it. Still sitting, she kicked a stone down the hill with her heel. It rolled a little way and stopped. A hare, with long black-tipped ears, hopped slowly past, saw her, and disappeared, flashing its white scut. A big hawk, a lambvanger with a white belly, drifted over her and circled round the vlei, its flight effortlessly adjusted by the tilt of its upswept pinions.

There seemed to be no reason for things: for the hare, the hawk, for her being up here waiting for something to happen that would not happen, or that would happen, irrespective of where she was. Each thing was perfect, poignant in its perfection, yet meaningless when considered in relation to other things. Was life just a series of accidents? Was Kaspar merely an accident? Or was there a pattern, vastly planned, into which everything fitted — herself, Kattie, the hare, the hawk, the trees; were they all part of one thing?

Kattie was sleepy; she lay with her head in Aletta's lap. Aletta began to think of the bread she would make tomorrow. So much flour, so many loaves, with potato water to raise it. She was ready to go back. She wondered why she had come.

2

When she got home, Stephanie met her. She was smiling. 'There is news of Kaspar,' she said. 'A man has just passed. He says that Kaspar was taken in the north with one of the King's women. He has lost his ear.' She laughed. 'They put it in the cleft of a tree and held him there by it till it fell off. He is lucky not to be killed. And more' — she spoke with relish — 'he has a little Bushman girl for a concubine. Magtig, it is shameful! So, while you dream, he fornicates with coloured women. A one-eared man!'

'I do not believe it,' Aletta said.

'Nee, and no doubt when you see him with one ear you still will not believe it.'

'The word of a stranger,' Aletta said. 'Before God, do you take the word of a stranger against a friend?'

'A friend! A man is known by his deeds. Ja, and judged by them, too. And why should it not be true? Did he not go north to trade? Is the north so full of traders that there can be a mistake? Nee, I think it true, and I am not surprised. Why has he sent no word? I will tell you why,' she went on. 'It is because he is ashamed.'

Stephanie smoothed out her dress, looked down at her feet, and went out. She had given her news. How lucky it was that she had been in! The stranger had not off-saddled. He had only stopped to water his horse. She wondered how it would feel to be pinned to a tree. And the stranger had said that the woman had been beaten to death before his eyes.

She moved uneasily. Her frock had not been too tight when she put it on, but now it was strained. It hurt her. She thought of Jacobus' smooth white hands. A child first saw, and then touched for confirmation. This was also the way of men. They saw and touched. Through the tips of their fingers they had to learn. Till a man's hands were on a woman, he knew nothing of her, and through his hands he found comfort in her body.

Kaspar and Jacobus van Zyl were confused in her mind. She felt tired. She wanted to get away. Ever since she could remember she had wanted nothing but this. Then

Kaspar had come, rich, from the south. And after Kaspar there had been Jacobus. She did not understand this talk of freedom. Who wanted freedom? What she wanted was clothes and people, music, routs, dances; all the things that Jacobus spoke of. What was there here to fight for? she wondered. Why should there be all this talk, all this coming and going when nothing was at stake? If she could get some new material, she would make another dress. It would have puffed sleeves and be cut like a picture Jacobus had shown her. It would hang from below her breasts straight to the ground. And she would like to do her hair in a new way. She was tired of wearing it dragged back after the Boer fashion. She wanted it piled up, with ringlets falling down in front of her neck. She wanted jewels, and satin shoes with high red heels. She wondered what it would be like to walk in shoes with high red heels.

3

Soon, any day now, Kaspar would come. He was back from the north. Aletta did not believe a word of what Stephanie had said. Some of it, some of the evil of its intention, clung to her mind, but she dismissed it and went about her work with new hope in her breast. Each morning she said to herself, he may come today; each night when she went to bed she tried to sleep quickly so that the next day, the one on which he might come, would be nearer. And sometimes in the night she woke, crying, not unhappily as she used to cry, but with a strange joy in her heart. Between sleeping and waking her thoughts became real. Kaspar was then tangible. He was there, with his arms about her, his breath in her face. She could feel him beside her, feel with her fingers the harsh softness of his hair, feel with her body the warmth of his body wrapping hers about. Each night now he was with her, enveloping her, telling her that he was coming. So the bright days were dark, something to be filled with tasks; and the dark nights bright with Kaspar.

Once when she cried out in her sleep, Stephanie said: 'You were dreaming of Kaspar. Fancy dreaming of a one-eared man who, the minute he leaves you, takes coloured women into his bed.'

'Ja, I was dreaming of Kaspar,' Aletta said, not wishing to lie. But as she spoke she knew she had lied. She had not been dreaming of Kaspar. He had been with her, lying at her side.

The ways of her life remained the same. She made no plans. She was content to float in a world in which she did everything she had to do by rote while her mind wandered. Stephanie's jokes, her implications, her repetitions and allusions, could no longer hurt her. Kaspar would come to her. He would explain. Till he came, she must wait, and she waited, happily expectant, suspended in a world that was neither the present in which she moved and worked, nor the future which was Kaspar's, but in another, a third kind of existence: one which, based on the past, sent down its roots and bloomed, high above her head, in the days that were to come; but the roots and the bloom were unconnected. The one had existed, the other would exist; and the present, the actual fact of her life, with its daily occurrences, was no more than the slender thread that joined them.

She took more walks with Klein Kattie, and told her tales of fairy princes who came riding on white horses.

'Do they always come?' Kattie asked.

'Ja, they always come.'

'And are the horses always white, Tanta Letta?'

'Not always, Kattie; sometimes they are blue; and they could be brown.'

The sun was low in the sky. Another day would soon be done. Each day brought Kaspar nearer.

She took Kattie by the hand and they went towards the house.

'Uncle Kaspar is not a prince, is he?' Kattie asked.

'Of course he's not a prince,' Aletta said.

'Well, I think he is.' Kattie jumped up and down, skipping first on one foot and then on the other. 'Ja, I think he is, and you should have known it, Tanta Letta. He has a blue horse and a brown.'

4

From Frederik's, Kaspar rode to Rudolf's. It was the old road, the one he had ridden, singing, from Aletta so long ago. He had been free then; free to think, to act and hope. Now he rode it watchfully, with a sailor and a Bushman boy to attend him. It was the road along which he had ridden to the little festival, knowing nothing of Aletta, the road that Selina had directed him to take. He had given Selina needles and cotton as a present. He wondered if she had them yet or if they, too, had been abandoned in her flight.

Kaspar crossed the first drift. He came to the second where the rocks were piled up like watermelons, then he turned up the randjie, keeping well hidden in the bush till he came to the sugar-loaf hill and saw the great fig tree that, from here, almost hid the house. Aletta was down there somewhere. Only with an effort did he prevent himself from spurring down the slope. He knew she was there, and that everything was right between them. It had taken weeks of hunting, it had taken illness and disaster, to make him know this, and then, as suddenly as his certainty had come upon him, it left him. She might have changed, and again he was in doubt. 'Go down, Adam,' he said, 'and see that there are no soldiers there.'

Kaspar dismounted and waited with Jeffries. He thought of the last time he had waited here watching the ant lion's hole while Pierre went down. Caution had become part of his nature now; if it went on long enough, he would become as furtive as the others, who moved like animals among the shadows or sometimes, just to prove that they were not afraid, swaggered over boldly.

5

Jeffries was silent. He sat smoking, looking from Kaspar to the farm below them. It looked quiet, safe, and peaceful; but, by God, you never knew. Pirates disguised their ships as merchantmen and then up came the crew from below. He had heard many such stories in his time, and a great number of men could lie concealed in that house, in those kraals, and among the trees. But the little Bushman would find out. Still watching, he thought of the woman he had at Coenraad's, a Bastard girl. She cooked his food when he was there and he had two children by her. He laughed softly to himself. By God, he thought, I'm one of the few who know whether their children are their own. His children had bright red hair like himself. But that cut both ways. If you bred red-haired children, you had to look out what you did. A red-haired child must have given many a man away.

He thought of Mary; of how she had wanted to go back to Shropshire and to take him with her. If he'd gone back, he would not be here now. But that was the way things came out. Little Mary would be seven. He counted on his fingers — nearly eight. Then it was nine years since he had married her mother. Nine years was a big slice in a man's life, or a woman's, for that matter, and Mary had been pretty. It was funny that a man like him should have had a pretty wife. Pretty women did not starve; but there wasn't much comfort in that either when you came to think it over. And there had been a man, a petty officer, that he'd had to knock down once. He scratched his head. Perhaps there was something in that too. To have him pressed would be a fine way to get rid of a man. It had never struck him till today. Seven years, and only now did he see the rights of it, or perhaps he had not wanted to. Anyway, Mary wasn't in it. She couldn't have been: not a girl like Mary. He stared at the farm again and thought of his two other children: a boy

and a girl. The farm was safe enough. They would go down
in a minute, and when the young chap had done his courting, they would go home again. Suddenly he wanted to get
back to Coenraad's.

Adam came back. It was safe. They mounted and rode
down.

6

When Kaspar came, Aletta could not believe it. There
was no warning. She was in the house: she heard horses:
she heard Kattie cry out. She thought to herself that it
might be Kaspar. One day he will come, and it will be like
this. She went out, and it was Kaspar.

He was mounted on Tigernek. Behind him was another
white man on a black horse and a naked Bushman on the
brown. Kaspar had his gun across his knees. He was burnt
black with the sun. He looked much older, much stronger.
He just sat there smiling at her.

'I have come back,' he said.

'You have come back,' she said. 'I knew you would come
back.'

And she had known. She felt no surprise. No pleasure. It
was as it had to be. Pleasure was for small things, not for
great. It was hard to breathe. Her legs were strangely weak
beneath her, and she felt ill. She put out a hand to steady
herself against the frame of the door, her fingers picking at
the grain of the wood.

Kaspar dismounted. 'I cannot stay for long,' he said. He
still held his gun.

She still could not believe that it was true. He stood by his
horse's head, dappled by the shade of the peach trees. He
was back, and he seemed utterly unreal. She seemed utterly
unreal herself.

'You will have coffee?' she asked.

He nodded his head and came in.

When he had eaten, they went into the shed. She never knew how they went in, only that she found herself there with him, and it was as it had been — a place filled with the scent of the hides, of sheepskins, and of tobacco. A thousand times she had imagined it: imagined being held in his arms; and all the time he held her she felt herself thinking: It is happening: this is Kaspar who holds me. In her mind it had happened so often that in actuality there was no astonishment. A great weight was lifted from her. A great ease, a lassitude, spread over her. A soft clearness and certainty enveloped her. Nothing mattered because there was nothing left to matter. The world was bounded by the mud walls of the shed. It was enclosed by the rafters from which the riems hung.

7

Outside, the white man who had come with Kaspar still stood by his horse. Aletta had not thought of giving him coffee. She asked him to come in. He refused. 'I am watching,' he said, 'but if you would bring me some...'

She brought it. The Bushman stood holding the reins while he drank. She gave him coffee too.

'His name is Adam,' Kaspar said, pointing to the Bushman. Then he introduced the white man. 'This is my friend, Jim Jeffries.'

'Good-day, meneer,' Aletta said.

He smiled at her. She knew that he understood what was between her and Kaspar and was glad.

'I must go,' Kaspar said.

'Ja, you must go, but I will walk a little way with you.' Aletta took his hand.

Kaspar threw the rein over his horse's neck and walked beside her.

'We will follow,' Jeffries said.

There had been few words between Kaspar and Aletta.

There had been small need for words. But now he spoke.

'It might have been different,' he said.

'Ja, Kaspar.' Aletta looked down and blushed. Suddenly she felt shy.

'Those things we thought together, Letta,' Kaspar said — 'those things I was going to come back to tell you. And then I did not come back. I could not.'

'Those thoughts and hopes were real, Kaspar.'

'Ja, Letta, they lived in our hearts.' He was silent a moment. 'They were birds that never sang.' There was more that he wished to say, much more, but his words would take no shape. 'I did not write,' he said. 'I was afraid to. I thought... I tried...' How could he tell her that he had tried to forget her? He began again. 'It came to me afterward that I might have got you with child and that I was a wanderer and homeless.'

Aletta put her hand on his arm. 'Sometimes I wished you had got me with child,' she said. 'It would have been yours. I was never afraid. For a month I hoped.'

She had hoped to have a child: to have his child. Kaspar could not speak. All he could think of was to give her something of his that she could keep by her. From the sack on his saddle he drew a little buckskin bag; in it were the pebbles that had been given to him by Ringhals when he left. 'Take them, Letta,' he said. 'They are pretty.'

'Ja, they are pretty.' She emptied them into her hand.

Drawing her against him, he kissed her closely. Then he mounted and rode away without looking back.

Aletta knew that if he had looked at her from the saddle, he would have turned his horse. She knew if she called he would come back. Twice she opened her mouth, but no sound came. She felt as if her heart were being twisted, wrung out dry, like a cloth. She felt the pebbles, which had been cold, grow warm in her hand. Kaspar was gone. Standing quite still, she watched a hawk moth on a flower. Its body was bright green and carmine; its wings she could not see, they moved too fast. All about her were bees and the grass was soft to her feet. The moth had a long tongue that was curled up like a fine spring. It was like the one that Klein Kattie had killed two days before. She had caught it with her hands and killed it, just to see the colour of its wings.

Aletta's eyes filled with tears. She had said nothing about the Kaffir girl: nothing about the Bushman girl. While Kaspar was there, she had not thought of saying anything about them, yet the thought of them had come between her and Kaspar more than the words she had not said. She had, with part of her, wanted to ask, and with part had been afraid of asking; and he, she felt, had wanted to tell and had been afraid of telling. Both had known that one day it would be spoken of, yet each had felt that it must not be now.

Neither of his ears was hurt. She had looked carefully, distressed that she should do so even as she did it. But had it been true, had one of his ears been gone and the story proved, she could have done nothing. A man was what he was. She would only have been sorry, sad that such things could be. She would have known that she could never understand, and then she would have left the matter, putting it out of her mind.

How tired Kaspar looked! How nervous he was, and how watchful! She thought she had never seen so watchful a man. That was what it meant to be pursued, to be hunted, to have a price upon one's head. Only by his vigilance could he hope to stay alive, and he had risked his life coming to her. And he would come again and again. Nothing she could do would stop him. She thought of the rumour again. Either it was all a malicious invention or there had been another white man up there. One day she would know the truth.

Her mind went back to the last hour. That Aletta, who had given herself to Kaspar so gladly, was another Aletta, and yet all that she did, every action of her life, had been for this end. It was like a tree growing, sending out leaves, branches. blossoms, and fruits, so that the fruits should fall and new trees grow. Yet the burdened branches felt only relief from the weight that bowed them when the fruit fell. It was like the ground, parched and dry, with each particle separate and strained until rain fell upon it and it became whole again. Perhaps women were like the ground. Suddenly she felt a near relationship to the earth and to all that sprang from it. It was like the opening of a flower. And afterwards one was at peace. By unrest, so profound that it tore you open, was peace obtained. She saw a woman's life as a series of rhythms. Like the trees and the flowers, like the beasts of the field, did women have their ebb and flow. She felt serene in her new knowledge. Kaspar was hers. To the end of his life he would be hers. He belonged to her now, though he was riding away. By the right of what had happened she held him between her hands. It was a great responsibility to hold the life of a man between one's hands.

8

Kaspar had not ridden far when he came upon Stephanie. She was sitting on an ant-heap in the shade of a big Kaffir wach'm bietchie, staring up the road away from him. She did not move till he was near her. Then she turned suddenly and sprang up. There was a look of welcome in her face. It changed as she recognised him. 'So it is Meneer Kaspar van der Berg who is back,' she said. 'And he rides from the south.' She sat down, rearranged her dress, and leant back against the tree. Her eyes were mocking as she watched him. 'The mighty hunter is back,' she said, 'and what did he bring for Stephanie? Elephants' teeth? Quills of gold? Come, sit down and talk to me. I had a headache and came here to be alone. Now I no longer desire to be alone.'

He did not dismount. He looked tired, and his eyes were

cold. She could see nothing in them, though he looked straightly at her. He is looking behind me, she thought, and turned to look round. His voice had changed, too. He spoke more slowly and with great indifference. She wanted to pierce his indifference. She wanted to touch his bare forearms, covered with fine golden hairs that sparkled in the sunlight. And he sat so still. Only his eyes moved, roving over the veld. Kaspar had changed greatly.

He took off his hat. 'It is nice to see you, Stephanie,' he said. 'You look well and more beautiful than ever.'

'You learned pretty speeches in the north, meneer,' Stephanie said. 'And did you know that we had news of you?' she asked.

'News? What news?'

'Only that you had gone on a Bushman raid and got a girl for yourself from them. Magtig,' she said, 'I do not understand men. A Bushman girl! Ach sis... I would as soon have an animal in my bed.'

'And what else did you hear?' Kaspar asked. He leant over his horse's neck and spoke very low.

'Not much else except that you were taken with one of the King's women and were punished. You were lucky to escape with only the loss of an ear.'

'I have lost no ears,' Kaspar said. 'But it seems to me that you have long ones and a long, false tongue, Stephanie.'

'What do you mean, meneer?' She sprang up.

'Just what I say, Stephanie.' Kaspar swept her a bow. 'And now I must get on. After all, with my reputation you could hardly wish me to stay with you. Magtig, I might make love to you. Nee, Stephanie, a good maid prefers death to dishonour. Come, Jeffries, we must get on,' he said.

Again he swept off his hat. He was laughing. What was the good of speaking to Stephanie? There was nothing to say. Now he must plan. There was a missionary beyond Coenraad's at Klaarwater. He would marry them. He must clear up his business; send off his wagons; get news to his father; turn his share of ivory into gold, gold was easier to carry, and find a place beyond the river in which to settle.

But there would be difficulties, troubles. What would Rudolf say? He would have to see Rudolf. For the moment all that could be done was done. All that could be said was spoken. And what did the future hold but snatched moments as beautiful, as ephemeral, as this? From now on there would be many such, as delicate as flowers, and tears. From now on there would be many tears: till he could find a way.

He rode slowly. They came to the place where the brown had jumped the sluit and he had broken a leather. He pulled up to rest. It was near here that he had picked the yellow creeper and bound the sweet-scented flowers round his hat.

They watered the horses and had hardly sat down to rest when Kaspar saw someone coming towards them. He was coming from the north. As a rule one could ride these paths for days and meet no one. But today it seemed the veld was as full of folk as a dorp at Nagtmaal. He saddled his horse and, followed by Adam and Jeffries, went to meet the stranger. He would have avoided him if he could have, but he had been seen, and there was no reason for fear; the man was alone.

The horses drew closer to each other. The stranger was a man from over the seas: his seat on a horse was that of a foreigner. He rode with shorter stirrups and sat more erect in the saddle. They drew abreast, almost knee to knee, facing each other. The stranger took off his hat.

'I am Jacobus van Zyl of Amsterdam and the University of Leyden,' he said.

Kaspar removed his hat. 'Greeting, meneer. I am Dirk Coetzee of the Winterberg.'

'It gives me great pleasure to meet you, Meneer Coetzee,' van Zyl said. 'Also' — he paused — 'will you permit me to compliment you on your mount and that of your servant? They look like some horses I once saw at Kaapstad, sons of the Blue Spaniard. In fact' — he reined his own horse back — 'I wager that they have the Blue Spaniard's blood in their veins.'

'I do not know how they are bred,' Kaspar said. 'I bought them as yearlings.'

'Will you sell yours for two hundred pounds?' van Zyl asked.

'It is a great price,' Kaspar said. He appeared to be considering it. 'But if I sold him, either my servant or I should have to walk. This is too rough a country for horses to carry a double burden.'

'I will throw mine in,' van Zyl said.

'And your horse is worth fifty pounds,' Kaspar said. 'He is a good horse. That would make two hundred and fifty for mine.'

'He is worth it.'

'No horse is worth two hundred and fifty pounds,' Kaspar said, 'but if one of them is, if my horse is worth two hundred and fifty pounds to you, meneer, then he is worth it to me. Meneer, I do not know how long you have been among us, but a Boer's horse and his gun and his wife are not for sale. You are from the towns, where things are different, but our horses are part of ourselves. At home we sleep with our wives, but on the veld our horses are our only company, and men do not sell their friends.'

'I am sorry,' van Zyl said. 'I should have liked to buy your horse. If ever you change your mind, tell me, and I will buy him. He looks as if he might win races.'

'Ja, he might win races, meneer,' Kaspar said.

'It has been a pleasure to see you, meneer.' Van Zyl took off his hat again.

'A mutual pleasure,' Kaspar said, 'and I like to have my beasts admired.'

9

Stephanie was impatient. She could not sit still. She leant back against the trunk of the tree, sat forward, resting her elbows on her knees, got up and walked a little way, and then came back and sat down once more. Jacobus was late. He was often late. But when he came he would pay her the compliments she loved, tell her more of the great world, and she would forgive him for having kept her waiting. She could not understand him. He is like a cat, she thought; a cat that walks, looking neither to the right nor to the left. Even when he made love, he did it as if it did not matter; he did it without urgency. It was becoming intolerable that he should take her so casually. She raised her arms and locked her fingers behind her head.

10

'So you are there, my rose, my shepherdess.'

'Ja, I am here, and you are late,' Stephanie said.

'How beautiful you are when you pout,' Jacobus said. 'And that I am late is not my fault. I met company on the road. A man on a grey horse that I tried to buy, but he would not sell.' Jacobus sighed. 'A curious, churlish young man with two servants, a white man who looked a ruffian and a Bushman boy.'

Stephanie looked at him coldly. 'Do you know who he is?' she asked.

'Yes, I know. He told me his name. He is called Coetzee and is from the Winterberg.'

'Then he told you a lie.'

'Who is he? Do you know him?'

'He is Kaspar van der Berg. He has a price on his head,' Stephanie said.

Jacobus dismounted, tied his horse to the tree where she had been sitting, peeled off his gloves, and slipped them under his pistol holsters. So far he had not kissed her. When he left her, he would also be slow and deliberate, would put on his gloves as carefully as he had removed them. 'Come,' he said, and she followed him off the path to a little patch of grass. It was here that they always came, just as it was always by the wach'm bietchie with the red ant-heap built up round its trunk that they always met. Mynheer van Zyl was a man of precise habits. When a thing was good, he saw no reason for change. As he said, the stars do not change nor do the planets vary their orbits.

When Stephanie got back to the house, there were soldiers there. Two dragoons stood by their horses under the big fig tree. The third horse was an officer's charger. She recognised it as Lieutenant Rousseau's. If they had come for Kaspar, they were too late. The bird had flown. Stephanie walked more quickly. She liked the military. Soldiers were gay and flattering. Also it would be amusing to be there, to talk and laugh and be ogled by the lieutenant, knowing what she did and saying nothing. The dragoons removed their arms from their horses' necks as she came. She knew they were watching her as she walked past them, but she did not give them a glance. The lieutenant must be in the house.

He was sitting in Rudolf's chair with his helmet on the table in front of him. Aletta had given him coffee. His face was very burnt up to the line of his helmet. His forehead was quite white and his hair brown and wavy. It was the first time Stephanie had seen his head bare.

When she came in, he got up, his big spurs rattling as he rose.

'Good-day,' he said. 'I was just passing this way and came in to rest.'

He finished his coffee and put on his helmet. 'I must go,' he said. 'I have stayed too long already.' He held out his hand to Aletta. 'Thank you, and I am glad to know that no one has been here. We heard that some of Coenraad de Buys' men were over on this side of the river.'

'If they are, meneer, we have not seen them,' Aletta said. Then she busied herself with the coffee, taking the beaker away and setting the pot by the fire again.

So Lieutenant Rousseau was too busy to talk to a Boer girl, Stephanie thought. As he reached the door she looked at him, put her hand on his arm, and said, 'I am going down to the river.' Aletta was still clattering the coffee things.

Lieutenant Rousseau paused, looked her up and down, and nodded his head.

'Good-bye again, and thank you,' he said in a loud voice.

Standing by the door Stephanie watched him mount. His orderly held his horse's head and leant on the stirrup. He swung up, raised his hand, and rode off, followed by his two men.

Aletta came back. She was very white and trembling.

'What is the matter?' Stephanie asked.

'Nothing, I am tired, it must be the heat.'

'Ja, it must be the heat,' Stephanie said, and left her. She went towards the kraals and then, once hidden from the house, turned down to the river. She was smiling. Lieutenant Rousseau was like all men. You had only to raise your finger and they came.

He had dismounted and was waiting for her. The troopers were some distance off. They had off-saddled and were smoking their pipes. The lieutenant was evidently in no great hurry.

When she came up to him, he took her hand. 'This is a great pleasure,' he said. 'I was disappointed to find that you were not in when I came.'

'My foster sister was there,' Stephanie said.

'Aletta is not Stephanie.'

Stephanie smiled. 'Yet some men think her beautiful.'

'Nee, it is you who are beautiful. Aletta is like a child. She is too small.'

Stephanie could see by his manner that he did not think of her as a child.

'So you came to see me and I was not there.'

'I was on patrol near-by and I came in,' Rousseau said. 'I hoped to see you.'

If only he knew what I know, Stephanie thought. 'You found nothing?' she said. 'No trace of Coenraad's men?'

'I found nothing. How can one find anything in these mountains? If they came at all, which I doubt, they have vanished.'

'If they came at all,' Stephanie laughed.

'I do not care now if it was a wild-goose chase.' Rousseau put his arm round her, tilted up her face, and kissed her.

'You are sure they did not come?' Stephanie said when he let her go.

'I am sure,' he said, kissing her again.

'I am not so sure, meneer.'

'You? What do you know? You know nothing except how to be beautiful.' He touched her bare throat with his hand, slipping it down over her breast.

'Ja, that is what you think — that I know nothing.' Stephanie stepped back from him.

'Why should you know anything?' The lieutenant was angry. What had she met him for like this if it was not to make love? He suspected his men were watching him. They would laugh at his rebuff. They were not even his own men, but borrowed dragoons.

'Ja, why should I know anything, meneer?' Stephanie asked. 'I will tell you why. Because I am not quite a fool. Because I have eyes in my head. Because I can recognise Kaspar van der Berg when I see him.'

Rousseau smiled.

'You don't believe me?' Stephanie stamped her foot and raised her hand to strike him. What fools men were!

'Of course I believe you.' Rousseau took her in his arms again and held her fast. Those dragoons should see that he was her master. Why did she tell these tales and try to make herself important? She was important enough without talking, to him or to any other man, a fine hot piece.

Stephanie broke away from him. She was furious. Her hair was down and her face scarlet.

'Would you believe me if I told you how to take him?'

Perhaps, after all, there might be something in what she said. Perhaps she had seen him or heard of him. Rousseau wanted Kaspar van der Berg. He had shot one of his men, and it rankled.

'Do you want him?' Stephanie asked.

'I want him badly. I have hunted him for months.'

'Then if you have your men ready the day after tomorrow where I tell you, you can take Kaspar van der Berg. I can arrange it.'

'Then you can do more than I can.'

'Sometimes a woman can do more than a man, meneer.'

'Where do you want the men?' Rousseau asked.

'Beyond my house, on the road that goes towards Leendert Labuschagne's,' Stephanie said. 'There is a big wach'm bietchie; it stands alone right by the path and has an ant-heap round the stem. Have them hidden near there.'

'I know the tree. Is that all?'

'Is it not enough that I should get him there for you on a specific day?'

'Yes; but why do you do this?'

'Why must I tell you? What does it matter?' Stephanie stood silent for a moment staring at the river, and then said: 'He is armed, and has two men with him.'

'I will send ten men.'

'Ten should be enough, and tot siens, meneer.' She swept him a curtsey — Jacobus had taught her to do this — and left him.

A plan outlined itself in her mind. A man in love was a fool, and fools were easily snared. With Aletta for bait it could be done, but the trap must be carefully set. Kaspar was no longer a boy to go blundering forward. He was a man. His old diffidence had gone and had been replaced by a cold certainty of purpose. But everything was right. She held

Kaspar's world balanced, ready to fall about him. He would
linger at his uncle's, she was certain of that. He had his affairs to see to, and a note would bring him back. The wording
of it was not yet fixed clearly, but it would come. Aletta
must be sick — hurt in some way and asking for him. A
Kaffir could carry it quickly...

Stephanie thought of Jacobus again. With other men
she had been lucky; perhaps such luck could not hold. In a
few days she would know. In her heart she knew now. But
would he marry her? It often happened that Boer girls had
children a month or so after marriage and it was no disgrace.
She thought of the story of the Englishman who had asked a
young Burger if his child was not premature, and of the
answer — 'Not at all, meneer. The child is a full-time child
and is not early. It is merely that the marriage was a little
late.' But that was a Burger and not a man from overseas.
Jacobus could get away so easily, and she would have to
tell him soon. It was a good thing that Maria was dead.
Maria would have noticed already. As for the other women,
she saw few of them, and with the country in an uproar, disturbed as it was by other matters, there were more important
things to occupy them.

Jacobus would marry her. He would take her back to Holland. She would have fine clothes, shoes with high red heels,
and perhaps her portrait would be painted. Jacobus said
that there were painters who delighted in painting pictures of
beautiful women. But why should he marry her? He came
from a different world; and if he did, how would she comport
herself among the great people that he knew? It was one
thing to dream of red-heeled slippers and another to wear
them. And what would she talk about? They spoke of
books, of pictures, of the families they belonged to. There
were so many beautiful women. All the women Jacobus
knew seemed to be beautiful and cultured. She wondered
what a cultured woman was: one raised delicately like a
flower in a glass house, not a veld bloom like herself. And

what would she do if he did not marry her? What would people say? What would become of her and the child? She blamed Kaspar. It was all Kaspar's fault. Her mind went round and round, torturing her. There was nothing she could do. No one she could ask. She felt trapped like an animal. She no longer doubted that she was with child. She knew it. A wild jealousy of Aletta possessed her, a wild hatred of Kaspar. At last she had acted decisively. The other thing would wait: it would have to wait. Certain things could not be hurried.

'Where have you been?' Aletta asked.

'I have been down to the river.'

'What for?'

'To look at the water, Letta. Why else should I go?' She looked into Aletta's eyes: she believed her. She looked again: Kaspar had made love to her. It was easy to see that he had. Well, he would do it no more. Stephanie's last doubts went. It was even good that he had made love to her, for he would be the more certain to come back when she called.

CHAPTER XXV

AN ACT OF GOD

I

KASPAR was pleased to get back to Leendert's. He would stay and rest for a few days, talking with his Aunt Sybilla and sitting at Leendert's bedside. There might be work to do, too. He felt he wanted work: the solid daily work of a farm: the counting of beasts, the tilling of the soil, the pruning of fruit trees. He almost laughed at his old ideas. Old! — before God, his ideas of less than a year ago when he had thought these things dull and had set out to adventure. Now he saw that there was no freedom anywhere, that only the outward shape of things was changed. The only free people he had seen were the Bushmen, who, until harmed and made revengeful, had lived simple lives, hunting, dancing, and sharing all but their most personal possessions in common. That was what it came to, that these people, whom none deemed human, were the most human of all. He had come to love his little Bushmen. They had the virtues of courage and fidelity. They asked no more than to be happy, to sing and eat and play and dance. They had no beliefs that he could see: a folk law, some customs, and a wonderful sense of life. They seemed to feel themselves as much part of it as the wildebeeste, the zebras, and the giraffes they hunted. He thought of the first one that had been killed by Pierre, the artist, who had died with his pigments slung round his waist, each in a little pot of horn.

He must get two of his wagons back to his father. Perhaps Leendert knew of a white man who would be willing to take them. Tanta Sybilla would be glad about Aletta. There was much to talk to her about. He could talk to her as though she were his mother, or better. It would have been hard to talk to his mother of love. Tanta Sybilla, though she had lived in the wilds so long, was gentler than his mother. She would be able to advise him. He felt a great necessity to talk to a woman of Aletta. When he thought of it, he was surprised at how little he knew of women; astonished that all the time he had been away from Aletta he had kept thinking of things to say to her, and then of how, when he was with her again, he could think of nothing; that when they were together, he became silent, as dumb as a dog able only to wag its tail, to watch her eyes, and try to read what they said. He looked at his hands as they held the reins. They were too big and strong for Aletta. He thought of van Zyl's hands when he had peeled off his gloves — delicate, long-fingered, and soft. What was a man like that doing in these parts? That he had wanted Tigernek, to race him, was proof enough that he was not staying. Two hundred and fifty pounds! Before God, it would not have taken him long to get back his price in races. He laughed at the talk there would be at the Cape if Tigernek was seen there again. Much talk, for those who knew him would know that for Kaspar's horse to be ridden by another would mean that he, Kaspar, was dead.

They were now nearly at Leendert's.

Adam had pulled up and was looking back at Kaspar. Jeffries was at his side. In a minute he would kiss his aunt and laugh with Leendert. He would do these things, laughing and talking as though he had not a care in the world. A man's heart was a very secret thing, hidden sometimes even from himself. There was so much to learn about life, about its mysteries, about the play of one thing upon another, and of what men took to be chance, the juxtaposition of time, place, and circumstance. Even old Christiaan, who knew so much, was wise only because he believed that things happened because they must. He had said, 'For a while life can be fooled, Kaspar. For a while a lappie can be tied over the eyes of men. But not forever. In the end men become what they were intended to become, and in the end all men become the same: all dying; and one body no better than the next; each corrupting and rotting so that none may know from the bones they find whether the flesh of that man were good or evil. And as one man dieth, so dieth the other, all having one breath. If a man beget a hundred children, this is still so, and in the place where the tree falleth, there it shall lie.' Old Christiaan, who knew so much, yet said, 'All that I know more would scarcely fill the egg of a sugar bird.' Van Ek, in his ignorance, was a wise man. He saw things as they were and said, 'Behold, I know nothing.'

They were there. Kaspar swung his leg over his horse's neck. The dogs, which had run out barking, fawned on him.

'It is I,' he said. 'Kaspar, who is returned.'

'Come in,' Leendert shouted from his bed. 'Come in. Give us the news.'

'News!' Kaspar said. 'There is no news.'

'Not even news of Aletta?' Tanta Sybilla asked. 'Did you not see her?'

'I saw her.'

'And she is well?' His aunt was laughing at him.

'She is well.'

'And happy?'

'I think she is happy.'

Tanta Sybilla folded her hands on her knees. She had found out enough. She was satisfied. They would make a well-matched pair. She looked at Kaspar through half-closed eyes. His future might be uncertain. There would be difficulties. But was not everyone's future uncertain and were there not always difficulties? As men went, Kaspar was good, and not more of a child than any other. It had come to her that perhaps when a man stopped being a child, he ceased at the same time to be a man. She began to laugh softly. Her Leendert was such a child — so angry at being kept ill and fed on slops; a big bearded child that roared at her like a bull. But surely it was better to be in bed, or sit wrapped up in a kaross on the stoep, then to be dead? Besides, having begun it, he must go on. Having been ill, he must stay ill till it was over. She picked up her sewing again.

Kaspar had been right. There was work to do. The farm had gone down while Leendert lay fuming. There were cattle to be branded, young bulls to be cut, and stock to be counted. He had a long talk with Leendert about his own affairs. Two wagons loaded with ivory were to go south, together with his older servants. One wagon he was retaining, together with the slaves who wished to stay. It could lie here till he was ready.

'What are your plans?' Leendert asked when Kaspar gave him the letter he had written to his father.

'I have none,' Kaspar said. 'How can I have? But I must see Rudolf. I want to take Letta to the north, and perhaps to the east, to the Portuguese settlements, where we can start again. I am a Boer by blood and I want my place. I want to build, to grow crops, to breed cattle. I want children and a home.'

Leendert touched his arm. 'You will get them,' he said. 'It is in my heart that you will find what you seek. You are safe here. Stay, therefore, a day or two. Rest and make your plans. Before a man does anything, it is necessary that he should have a plan.' He paused. 'But all the same, it is a pity you shot that soldier.'

'Ja, it is a pity,' Kaspar said. 'A pity, too, that I had not the courage to go only to see Letta, but had to go on and get that puppy.'

'She will be a fine bitch,' Leendert said. 'Those dogs of Frederik's were the best up here, and her mother was the pick of his dogs.'

Tanta Sybilla came in. 'There is a letter for Kaspar,' she said. 'A Kaffir brought it.' She was excited — a letter meant news. For a young girl, news meant who was betrothed. For a wife, news meant who was having a child. To an old woman accustomed to birth and past it, news meant who is sick? And who is dead? This was the curiosity of women. First they thought of men, and then of children, and finally of corpses. But always they counted the months of a pregnancy or the ages of the dead, on the fingers of their hands. Always they thought of the essential things — of children, of the men by whom they were begotten, and the dead. Greatly, as they grew older, fearing to be left alone, did they count the dead. Sybilla did not do this yet, but she would do it later. Now she thought of Kaspar and of Aletta and of their children. They would have beautiful children and she would have helped to bring them about.

'Is it bad news?' Leendert asked. He was watching Kaspar's face.

Kaspar handed the letter to him. 'I must go,' he said. 'I will ride at once.'

'Read it out,' Tanta Sybilla said.

Leendert spread it out on his knee. '"Since you left, Letta is ill. She has a fever and asks for you. But do not come to the house. Meet me by the big tree where I was on the road and I will see you safely to her." It is signed, "Your loving cousin, Stephanie."' Leendert put the letter down. 'She writes a good hand,' he said.

Kaspar tightened his belt. Jeffries got up.

'Call Adam,' Kaspar said, 'and tell him to saddle up.'

'You are going at once?' Jeffries asked.

'I am going now. Letta is sick.'

'What can be the matter with her?' Leendert said when they were gone.

'Ja, what can be the matter?' Tanta Sybilla repeated. So much could be the matter with women. So much and so little when they wanted to see a man again. 'Why did she not write herself?' she asked.

She looked at the food she had packed up, which Kaspar had forgotten. It was like a man to forget food.

2

Aletta was ill and Stephanie had sent for him. As he rode through the darkness, Kaspar forgave Stephanie everything. She had sent for him to come to her foster sister. She was kind: and her faults due to her nature and the life she had led. Riding slowly, letting Tigernek pick his way, Kaspar rode on. Sometimes a thorn scratched him, snatching at his shirt as he passed. Sometimes he had to bend beneath an overhanging bough. He wondered how long he would have to wait at the tree and why he could not go forward to the house. The dawn came pink as a flamingo's wing in the east, the west shadowed by it, palely reflecting its colour. He rode faster. Birds began to sing tentatively; a pheasant called. It was a strange roseate world — a world of beauty subtly distilled as they rode beneath the dripping trees where the morning drops hung glistening to the leaves and the grass tops, weighted with dew, hung heavy heads. What could be the matter? Aletta had been well when he left her. He tightened his reins and began to canter. As the sun rose, they reached the tree. Kaspar dismounted and lit his pipe. He remembered with regret the food Tanta Sybilla had prepared. Still, they had biltong with them and tobacco and water. What was the matter with Aletta? What could in so short a time have stricken her?

He was sitting with his back to the tree when Aletta came. His first thought was not wonder at how she should be so well, but relief to see her well. She came quickly through the high grass; the dew had wet her legs, and her dress up to her thighs was dark with water. She broke a spangled cobweb spun between two branches with her hand. A black dringo shrike dived at an insect and returned to its perch.

'Kaspar!' she gasped. 'You must get away!'

'You are not sick,' he said. 'You are well. The letter from Stephanie said you were sick . . . that you asked for me.'

'I am well. It was Stephanie. The soldiers . . .'

There was a shot. Kaspar turned round to find Jeffries standing with his gun raised.

'They are all round us,' he said. 'They shot at Adam.'

Kaspar jumped onto his horse.

'Shall we fight?' Jeffries asked.

Tigernek plunged as Adam came up from under a bush at his head. 'I have killed one,' he said: 'the one who shot at me.' Seizing the brown's mane, he climbed onto his back.

Kaspar slipped the rein over his wrist and held his gun ready.

'Don't fight,' Aletta said. 'Get away while there is time.'

'Must I run again? Before God, must I spend my life running?' Kaspar shouted.

'Go! Go!' Aletta screamed. 'And come back.'

'You are well?' Kaspar said.

'It was a lie,' she said. 'You were betrayed.'

Kaspar wheeled his horse.

'No one can catch you,' Aletta said. 'Ride hard!'

She was gasping for breath. Another minute and she would have been too late. She had run from the house, run till her skirt, wet with dew, had clung round her; then she had walked quickly, fighting for breath. Stephanie had done this, and if the sergeant had not been a fool — if he had not come to the house to make certain of the place — she would have known nothing. She leant against the tree. The veld which had been so quiet was noisy with charging horses and shouting men. Kaspar had swung Tigernek round. She saw the flash of his gun-barrel as he galloped through the bush. Jeffries on the black was beside him, and the little Bushman clung to the mane of the brown, crouching high on its withers, his bow with an arrow fitted held in one hand. All round her troopers shouted. She heard one curse as another cannoned into him. Kaspar was clear. The only man in his path had not been ready for him and he had got past him; the grey, taking the bay troop horse on the shoulder, had thrown it back on its haunches.

There were more shots. The sounds faded. What happened now was in the hands of God.

Getting down on her knees, she prayed: 'Dear Lord, save him. Dear Lord, save Kaspar.' She stayed a long time on her knees by the ant-heap. God had sent her to give Kaspar warning. God meant to save him. She got up and went back, walking slowly along the path. She felt very weak and very much alone.

Stephanie was still in bed when she got back. She sat up, leaning on one arm as she went in.

'I heard shots,' she said.

'Ja, you heard shots,' Aletta said. She paused. 'Why did you betray Kaspar?' she asked.

'I betray him! I know nothing of Kaspar,' Stephanie said. 'Is he dead?' she asked. 'Were those the shots?'

'You sent him a letter in my name,' Aletta said. 'You told him I was ill. You trapped him with Lieutenant Rousseau.'

'Did they take him?' Stephanie had jumped up.

'He has escaped,' Aletta said. 'I warned him.'

'Then he is safe?'

'I did not say he was safe. He has escaped, but the soldiers are after him. They are chasing him as hounds chase a buck.'

'How do you know all this?'

Kaspar was safe. At least he had escaped. Relief swept over Stephanie. She could not understand how she had done this: how she had wished to kill him just to show Lieutenant Rousseau that she knew he had crossed the river.

'How do I know?' Aletta said. 'I know because while you lay in bed the soldiers came to ask which tree he was coming to. They thought it was I who had laid the information. They thanked me. Why did you do it, Stephanie?'

'I do not know,' Stephanie said.

'Then you did do it.' Aletta still found it hard to believe. It was only by chance that she had got up early. Suppose I had not got up, she thought.

Her anger overcame her and she sprang at Stephanie. Without a word she struck her face and shoulders, dragged with sharp fingers at her hair. Stephanie made no effort to defend herself, but allowed herself to be struck; uttering low moans, she tried to shield herself with her hands clasped to her face, her elbows against her breast.

'If I had a sjambok I would beat the skin off you,' Aletta said. 'Before God, I would beat you till the blood ran.' She felt herself possessed; much stronger than Stephanie. And then her strength left her. She felt empty, frightened, and sank onto the bed. Hiding her face in her arms, she began to cry.

Stephanie bent over her. 'I was mad, Letta. I was mad. I think I loved him and he never saw me. He does not know I am there. And I wanted to show Lieutenant Rousseau that I was not a fool.' She flung herself down beside Aletta and put her arms round her. 'He is safe. I am sure he is safe,' she sobbed.

3

Aletta was right. No one could catch Kaspar on Tigernek. There were more shots. He heard men shouting behind him. He must have been early. They had not been ready, and Adam had discovered them. Galloping beside him, Adam said, 'I smelt horses, master, and went to see.' The track narrowed and Kaspar pushed Tigernek forward. They crossed an open glade. Again the three of them were riding neck to neck. There was another shot and Adam's horse went down. Kaspar pulled up. The boy was unhurt. He still held his bow and dived into the scrub like a buck.

'I think there are ten of them,' Jeffries said. 'And that's too many.'

Two miles more and they would reach the river, but the going here was good. The dragoons came into view and for a short distance their corn-fed horses drove them hard. But they were bad shots from the saddle. Kaspar turned and fired at the leading horse. He had no desire to kill another soldier. The horse fell, pitching on his nose, and the dragoon went over his head. Kaspar reloaded. Tigernek was going easily. He still had plenty in him. The speed was telling on Jeffries' horse; the black was extended fully and labouring a little. As they neared the river, Kaspar heard a roaring sound.

'The river is coming down!' he shouted. 'Turn right.' They swung their horses along the bank. There must have been rain in the mountains. There was one chance — to get past the flood. If they failed, they would be caught.

'Drive him, Jeffries!' Kaspar shouted.

They were gaining on the water. It was coming in a slowly moving wall; on the top of it he could see trees and rubbish balanced and swirling as it crept down the bed of the river. They came to a steep bank and slithered down it, their horses almost on their quarters. The heavy sand grasped at their legs, the water coming faster now, a wall that nothing would stop. The troopers had pulled up and dismounted. Their shooting was better and the bullets began to splatter round them.

'Push him!' Kaspar shouted. 'Use your sjambok.'

The black was white with sweat and foam. The bank loomed up ahead of them; raising himself in his stirrups and grasping the mane of his horse, Kaspar flung the grey at it, felt him take it, slip, regain his foothold and reach the top. The black had fallen, but Jeffries was struggling up on foot.

He had dropped his gun. As he reached the top, the water came. The black horse struggled a moment, spun like a top in the stream, was overwhelmed, and, tumbling over and over, was swept down by the flood. There was a final fusillade from the other bank. A bullet knocked Kaspar's gun from his hand. Jeffries fell.

'I am hit,' he said.

Dismounting, Kaspar threw him over his saddle and mounted behind him. Galloping with the double burden, he rode upstream for a mile. Here he put him down. He was badly hit.

'We are safe,' Jeffries said. 'I have heard tell of the river coming down like that, but have never seen it.' He paused. 'There must have been rain somewhere.'

'Yes, there must have been rain in the mountains,' Kaspar said. It was strange to talk about rain to a dying man. They were safe. The river, a mad flood of turgid water, was between them and their enemies. It was a miracle. It was like the parting of the Red Sea for the Israelites.

Jeffries moved uneasily.

'I think I'm going, Kaspar,' he said. He lay very still. 'Will you hold my hand?'

Kaspar took it.

'Not that one. Take my starboard hand, sir, then I can feel you holding it.' He had been hit on the left side of the back.

'Does it hurt much?' Kaspar asked. He felt very helpless. Jeffries was dying and he did not know what to say.

'No. It doesn't hurt. But I feel cold. It isn't cold, is it?'

'No. It isn't cold.'

'By God, it's funny to be dying here. I never thought they'd get me. No, sir. I thought nothing could hurt Jim Jeffries. The Yankees couldn't do it. An' the Frenchies couldn't do it. An' the bos'un on the *Swallow* couldn't do it.

But it's done now, all right, and a fine job at that. You've got your girl, so I'm glad it was me. I'd never have got back home. It's a long way back and I expect she's thought I'm dead this long time ... I'm cold,' he said again.

His hand felt cold.

'It must be the blood that keeps you warm, sir. No blood, no heat. And I'd like you to have my knife. It's all I've got, but it's a good one. Yes, that knife an' me's bin a long time together.'

He closed his eyes, opened them suddenly, and said: 'She had golden hair and so did the baby — red-gold the baby had ... there's nothing like golden hair — long golden hair.' A tremor went through him. He tried to sit up. 'Hold tight, sir. For Christ's sake, hold tight. I'm going this time.'

The big hand that Kaspar held slackened its grip, tightened it till he nearly cried out, and then relaxed. Jim Jeffries was dead.

Death seemed to be infectious, one death to lead to another. They had been out of range when Jeffries was hit. It was a chance bullet sent after them for luck. It seemed pointless that he should ever have lived. What had Jeffries had out of life? What had he done to suffer as he had? The little happiness and love that had been his had been but a fraction of his life. Perhaps love and happiness were only a fraction of most lives. Perhaps they were commodities that had to be exorbitantly paid for.

Kaspar looked down at Jeffries. His eyes were open and his face was at peace. He looked much younger. He pulled the lids down over his eyes; now he looked as if he slept. He loosened the dead man's belt and took off his knife. Jeffries had wanted him to have it. Without knowing what he did, he drew it out of its sheath and tested the blade against his thumb. It was sharp. Then he felt ashamed of having tested it and slipped it on his belt beside his own. Soon that would be all that would be left of Jeffries: his sheath-knife with a bone handle and an English blade. Jeffries had used that knife for years at sea and on land, had eaten with it, had used it to finish off wounded buck, had perhaps killed with it. It had been an integral part of his life. Kaspar knew that for some time he would think of Jeffries each time he used it, and then he would think less often, and, finally, not at all unless someone asked him where he got the knife, for it was of an unusual pattern. So did men die. So were they forgotten.

There was no place to bury the body. The ground was like iron, burnt up and cracked with drought. If he could not bury him, he could at least set him up against a tree and let him lie there. Burials and graves were for women, and men who died in beds like women. Jeffries and his kind, men like himself, would lie where they fell, open to the skies. What did it matter? Perhaps it was better to be eaten by aasvoels than by worms.

He laid him in the shade of a tree, raising his head a little and putting his folded coat under it. Then he mounted.

He wondered where he was. The curse of this country was that one place looked so like another, even the trees being reproduced with great exactitude, so that one thought one recognised them and then found oneself to be wrong. He was unarmed: his gun was broken, and Jeffries' gun was lost. By bearing west he should come to the road leading north and there might find help. He was known as one of Coenraad's men now and in no great danger from marauding Kaffirs. Jeffries was dead, another added to the list; and Adam lost. Adam would somehow find his way back, but the sailor had gone for good. He realised suddenly how fond he had become of Jeffries and how he would miss him.

He walked Tigernek, keeping as near the river as he could, following its convolutions. His biltong was done, but he still had water and could get as much more as he needed from the river. He had also a small piece of raw meat in his saddle-bag. It was putrid, and stank, but he knew that before long, as he had nothing else, he would eat it. A buffalo cow crashed out of the bush and stood looking at him. With a gun he could have lived here for weeks. As it was he just stared at the big beast angrily. There was plenty of game about, and everything, seeming to sense his helplessness, came out to graze all round him. More buffalo, koodoo, steenbok, duiker, and bush-buck made no effort to avoid him.

His tendency was to press on fast, but he controlled it. To go fast one must know where one is going. He must continue west steadily till he picked up the road. I must keep calm, he said to himself. But it was hard to stay calm. The river kept changing direction, bending this way and that, running north, south, east, and west in great bights and bends that confused him. At midday he off-saddled, watered his horse, and let him roll and graze for an hour.

As the sun began to get low in the sky, he looked for a place to camp. He found one at the foot of a big tree and got out the rotten meat and a small frying-pan. He scraped off most of the maggots, kindled a fire, and squatting over the flame began to cook, moving the meat about with his knife. Fried in the rancid sheep's fat the meat was not bad, and he ate it, even to the small worms which, cooked hard, floated like grains of rice in the grease. His stomach was too hungry to be turned by maggots now.

When he had done, he took a drink of water and lit his pipe. He was in a bad way, but he might have been lying beside Jeffries, or have been taken, or his horse might have been hit. Perhaps, as Coenraad had said of him, he was lucky as luck went in these parts. There was no question in his mind now about what had happened. Stephanie had set a trap for him. That was clear. But why had she? What had he done that could possibly make her wish his death? She had set the trap and Aletta had come to warn him. He owed his life to Aletta, and Jeffries, his death to Stephanie. His hatred of the English, which had been in abeyance, flared up again. He must get away from them and the power they represented. He must take Aletta with him. He must see Rudolf and explain, and, above all, he must get out of his present pass himself. In the morning he would change his direction, first watering his horse fully and filling his canteen. Then he would leave the river and set his course northwest so as to cut into the road higher up. If he followed the river with all its bends, it would take him days to get out. His mind made up, he felt happier and slept.

At dawn he saddled up and, picking a tree in the general direction he wanted to go, rode towards it. When he reached it, he picked another, and then another. Lost men drifted in circles. He kept persuading himself that he was not lost. He knew where he was; with the river on his left he was bound to find the road. Lost or not, he was hungry. He looked at the small birds that hopped, twittering, on the bushes. If he could have caught them, he would have eaten them as the Kaffirs did, roasting them whole, just singeing the feathers off and putting them into their mouths. If he had had bread, he could have made a trap with a flat stone and a string and caught them. But he had no bread. He tightened his belt and drank more water. Thoughts of food continued in his mind: first, all the good things he had eaten, and later, thoughts of the food he had scorned: the entrails of elephants, steaks cut from a python. There was nothing by nightfall that he would not have eaten, and he could find no water for his horse.

It was no use turning back. He must go on. He must not lose his head or become afraid. He knew himself to be afraid: and with a new kind of fear. Fighting, a man was frightened, but there was the excitement of the fight to counterbalance it. There was an active enemy to contend with. Here there was nothing. He was alone with a thirsty horse, an empty belly, and perhaps only enough water for another day for himself. He saw buck, but now only the kinds that could go waterless for days. He saw butterflies.

He stopped to watch a blue wasp with red eyes settle on a leaf. It was so slim-waisted that it looked as if its body were detached from its middle part.

As he watched, the wasp grew bigger. It grew and grew till it was as large as a small bird. Had he got fever again, or was it only hunger? His fears returned. He had been trying not to think. He remembered all the stories he had heard of men being lost in the Bush. After this he scarcely dared to look at the small things that moved in the veld. Insects, birds, and even trees lost their true values. Big things seemed small: small things large. Mountain ranges quivered and came nearer to him, or, when he felt himself upon them, receded. Exhaustion, fear, hunger, thirst — he was saving his water — fever and rage, all played their parts; still conscious of reality, Kaspar knew that the things he saw were not real; that, with food and rest, if he could get them, he would recover. He tried to think of Aletta, to see her in his mind as she moved about Rudolf's place playing with Kattie, as she walked, ate, and slept. He was surprised that he found it so hard to think of her, to concentrate on her. But a man, lost and hungry, could not think of women, not even of one woman. He was getting to the state where he could not think at all, not even of food and water and rest.

Whatever happened he must go on. His mouth was so parched that he could no longer talk to Tigernek, but only encourage him by pats. Dismounting, he walked beside him. The horse tried to rest his head on his shoulder and nipped at his cheeks with mousy lips. In the shade of a tree Kaspar stopped. They would rest a little and then go on. He took off his saddle; it weighed over thirty pounds with his blankets and gear. When he went on he would leave it. This looked like the end of his adventure. If nothing happened soon, he would be another who had gone off into the veld and not returned. One day some wandering Kaffir might find his bones and take the pieces of metal that were scattered round them, his knife and Jeffries', the buttons from his coat, and his belt-buckle, for ornaments; and that would be the end of Kaspar van der Berg and his possessions. He stared hopelessly at the sky. Suddenly he sat up. The light flashed on some white wings as a flock of tick-birds flew past in the distance. He remounted. Where there were tick-birds there was water.

4

At last, towards evening, he found it, but the pan was dry. Against a lead-grey sky the dead trees that had shaded the pan were white with tick-birds. They sat almost shoulder to shoulder on every branch, their long beaks resting on their necks. Below them fallen branches, once covered by water, were exposed like bones half sunk in mud.

There was no water here. Only mud, hard and grey, cracked into gaping marbled patterns on the edge and softening to a glutinous semi-liquid towards the centre.

As he watched, some cattle came down to drink, their flanks, between rib and hip, hollow for lack of water, their eyes misty and hopeless. Hesitatingly, they waded through the mud, jumping and plunging as it held them, towards the thick water in the centre, while the mud swirled and closed behind them. Raising their sticky muzzles, they stared at him and then sank them again to suck up such water as they could, trying first one place and then another. Kaspar watched them without interest; his heart was hardened to the beasts. He must have water for himself and for his horse.

Near the bank were three dead beasts, their skin dry and hard about their skulls, their eye-sockets empty. Almost toothless, too weak to extricate themselves, they had died slowly, no vulture or jackal having ventured near to end their misery lest they share their fate. Weakening hour by hour they had slowly died, their last effort a struggle to hold up their heads so that they might breathe. This was what happened under such conditions; because they were old, with worn teeth unable to graze the harsh grass, they became so weak that they died, and while they died, while he died for that matter, he realised that this might well happen now, the tick-birds continued on their way, perching on the dead trees in the evening, flying off in the morning. That man or a beast died slowly, in agony, with glazed eyes and swollen tongue, was nothing to them. While cattle lived, the birds would pull ticks from them dexterously, with long spear-like beaks, since they lived on blood-filled vermin, and when the beasts died, the birds would seek other beasts as a man sought new pasture in a drought.

Truly the ways of God were wonderful. The fish which had lived in the water could lie at rest in the mud till the rains came, while for man a few days waterless was more than he could endure.

Kaspar sat down and tried to think. Tigernek would not drink that water. Horses were fastidious. Could he clean some? Filter it in some way? He rinsed out the horse's mouth with the few drops that remained in his bottle. Where there were cattle there would be men. The cattle had come down a small path. There must be a village near-by; there must be other water. Leading his horse, he skirted the pan and found a cattle track. He followed it and came to some neglected lands; beyond them he saw the thatched roofs of a village. Cries of alarm greeted him. Men rushed out with spears, children stared at him and darted like frightened mice into the low holes of their huts, regained courage, and peeped out as he passed. A tall man, apparently the chief, accompanied by six others, all armed, came towards him.

'Give me water,' Kaspar said.

A girl brought it. He drank some and obtained water for the horse. There was a small spring near-by. Too weak for watering the cattle, it supplied the people. The chief had food brought to him, sour milk in a calabash, Kaffir beer, roasted mealies, and some meat. A man was sent back on his spoor for his saddle and blankets. They gave him a hut in which to sleep and, with the horse loose in the little kraal about the hut, Kaspar lay down to rest. He was safe. He would stay here a day or two and then push on.

In the morning Tigernek seemed to have suffered no ill effects from the gallop, or the trek after it. Kaspar watched the tick-birds running after the cattle. If he had not seen them, he might have been dead by this time. A gun was all he needed now. It was no use going back to Leendert's, nor could he get there with the river full. He would go to Johannes Bezuidenhout's. Johannes, the brother of old Frederik, would let him have a gun if he had one to spare, and he could collect its value from Kaspar's stock of ivory and gold at Leendert's.

From the Winterberg he could send a message to Aletta. Now that he was fed and rested, he thought of her continually. The world revolved round her. He cared more for her than he did for himself; indeed, he had ceased to care for himself at all — that his body required food, that it performed its functions, seemed odd and without significance, almost grotesque, for his mind was not there. He thought with part of his mind of such practical things as the best road to Bezuidenhout's, of a new gun, of the soldiers, and of Adam. But reality was the dream, and the dream reality. He was like a tree bent by a strong wind that kept him from Aletta. That he should be away from her seemed fantastic and without reason; that meeting, they should have to part, ridiculous. Yet still they had met and parted. Having left her, he lived only to return to her side, to get nearer and nearer to her, and he knew that this was so with her, too. As he was drawn, so was she drawn, no less urgently than himself. Separate they were inseparable, each dreaming of the other, each waiting for the time when they should meet again. Yesterday he had hardly been able to think of her. Now he could think of nothing else: to get the gun, to be armed, so that he could go back to her.

One thing was certain, he could not remain much longer on the Border. Once he had obtained his gun and found Adam, he must take Aletta with him and get back to Coenraad's and the mission at Klaarwater. He thought of their marriage. Aletta must come with him. Whether Rudolf were willing or not, she must come. After that, once they were married, he would plan again. They would go north together, or east. With a price on his head, the Border full of troops, and with Stephanie against him, the odds were too great. Besides, he did not wish to become embroiled in the war that was brewing. He could not see it being successful, and all he wanted now was to get away from, and not to fight, the English. They were too strong, but their strength was limited by distance. The farther away he got, the safer he would become. Kaspar was done with war. He wanted peace and rest and security. Above all, he wanted these things with Aletta.

Some more Kaffirs, a small band carrying shields and assegais, came into the village. They were going in his direction and would guide him part of the way. One of them he had seen before at Coenraad's, and the others seemed to know him. They did not state their business, but it did not need stating. They were on a raid of some kind, one of the numerous bodies that had been let loose by the troubled times. Cattle, horses, and guns if they could get them, were their aim.

They marched silently in single file. He followed them, sometimes riding, sometimes leading his horse. Unerringly they took little path after little path. They were completely certain in all their movements. Like animals and as silent as animals. Whatever they were going to do was already planned. There was no necessity for speech among them.

At dark they camped. Kaspar arranged his blankets a few yards away. If he had had a gun, he would have been in danger from them. His horse did not trouble him. Tigernek would let no stranger touch him.

Kaspar woke with the cold. A little wind rustled the leaves on the trees. The sky was grey, like the belly of an elephant. The sleeping Kaffirs stirred. One of them, poking his head out of his kaross, sat up. First he stretched his arms, and then, sitting up with the kaross in folds about his loins, leant forward to feel in the fire at his feet for a hot coal among the ashes. He knelt and blew at it till his eyes watered; as it glowed he piled small bits of grass and twigs against it. Then he rose, washed out his mouth, and poured water on his hands from a calabash. The others began to stir. For a while they sat over the fire feeding it with sticks, their hands held over it, then silently they rolled their karosses, draped them over their shoulders, and with their spears, kerries, and long sticks in their hands stood up. The sky was paling. The leader spoke. Like shadows they followed him in single file along the narrow path through the long wet grass. Already the doves were cooing on the trees and the buck were on the move. They had been there and were gone. The fire was all that was left of them. Kaspar went over to it. As it got lighter, he could see their forms outlined in the red dust. The long marks were where they had lain all night.

5

Once among the trees after his first dive as the horse fell, Adam lay still. He lay quite flat, torn by thorns and lying on others. His yellow skin, spotted by light and shade, made him invisible as the troopers crashed round him, following his master and the other white man. He saw one raise his musket and fire; saw another fall as his horse stumbled; saw the white girl his master had come to see crouch low against the ant-heap by the big tree, as the soldiers galloped by. When they were gone, he lay quiet, waiting, and then, thinking it safe, crawled out of the bush to follow them. First he looked at the dead horse. The ground round it was flattened by its threshing hoofs, blood ran out of its nostrils. The brown was dead. He thought of taking the saddle and bridle and then decided against it. They would cumber him, and no doubt someone from the house would fetch them.

With his bow ready, slipping from tree to tree, he listened to the shouts, making his way towards them. He was shivering with excitement. If they had killed his master, he would kill them all, picking them off one by one, his arrows more than a match for their guns and sabres in the heavy bush of the river. It was his master's body he looked for, or for that of the grey horse. The direction of the sound changed as they swept across his front. They were going down-river. There were more shots. Then he heard them coming back and crawled into an ant bear hole. They were empty-handed. They had lost their quarry and seemed to blame each other. The horses were black with sweat and one of the men supported a comrade in front of him on his horse. When they had gone, Adam ran on. Finding his master's spoor, he followed it. The river was a roaring torrent. His master and the other man had galloped along the bank. He saw where they had gone down into the water. His one idea was to cross too. On the far bank he saw vultures. There was something dead there. His master or the other man or a horse. He could do nothing but wait. In a few hours the river would run down. He shot a dove and ate it raw with some roots that he had in his bag. Then, finding a safe place from which he could watch the water, he curled up and slept. When he woke, the river was still high, but the anger had gone out of it. It was just a flood, fast-flowing, but no longer turbulent with ugly swirls and eddies. It had dropped, too, and, picking up a piece of driftwood as long as himself, he launched it. Holding onto it with both hands and kicking with his legs, he allowed himself to be carried down the stream. Landing, he ran back along the bank till he was opposite the place he had gone in. Here he found the spoor and his master's broken gun. It had been hit by a bullet in the lock and was useless. He picked it up, held it for a moment, smelt it as a dog might have, and put it down. He looked at the spoor again: it was that of his master's horse. There were no other marks. The other horse must have been swept down the river.

He saw where his master had dismounted, noted how the other man had been picked up, saw the blood on the ground and grass, and ran on. Soon he came to the clearing where the horse had slowed up. There were vultures on the trees. One let itself fall off the branch it was perched on, and with two strong beats rose into the air. A moment later it perched again. With twitching nostrils Adam ran towards the bones and torn clothes. They were surrounded with feathers, blood, dung, and mucus. Shreds of cloth, buttons and a leather belt still buckled lay round the tree. Pausing only to pick up the brass buttons and the belt, Adam went on. His master was following the river. The spoor in the marshy ground was easy to find. He could follow it running, almost without looking down.

All round the bends of the river he ran on the spoor. He found where Kaspar had camped and where he had watered his horse. From his footmarks he was walking less strongly. When he found where he had filled his flask and changed direction, Adam hurried. There was no water this way. His master, unless he found him, would die of thirst. The horse was getting tired. He found where his master had dismounted to lead him and the place where he had left his blankets and saddle. There were fragments of the blanket sticking to a thornbush. There was also the spoor of natives roundabout. Still trotting, Adam followed the spoor till he came to the dried-up pan and the village. He circled the village carefully and found the spoor again. His master was well. It was written on the ground. He stopped to eat and went on.

6

'Where is the Baas?' Kaspar slowed his horse.

'The Baas?' The old Hottentot looked vague. 'Which Baas?' he asked.

'Baas Johannes,' Kaspar said.

'Ja, Baas Johannes.' He seemed unwilling to answer. Then suddenly he made up his mind. 'The Baas is down there' — he pointed. 'By the Nek. He is not alone. The Baas has men with him. Many men.'

Many men. Well, if he was with many men he would be easier to find. Riding along the foot of the hills, Kaspar went towards the break in the mountains, and, as he came round the heel of the slope, he saw them. There were a lot of men. He put his heels to his horse and galloped towards them.

Johannes, who was in the middle of the group, turned as he came up.

'Welcome, Kaspar!' he shouted. 'Welcome!' Then to the others he said: 'You see, they come in. Before God, they come in from all parts. Kaspar van der Berg comes from Coenraad Buys.'

'How goes it?' Kaspar said, pulling up.

If it went well, it did not look well. Two men who were dismounted fiddled with their girths.

Kaspar pushed past them till he was level with Johannes. 'I want a gun,' he said.

'Before God,' Johannes shouted, 'we want men with guns. Hey!' he cried. 'Give him a spare gun.'

For Johannes, Kaspar's arrival was opportune. He was desperate. By threats, by oratory about their wrongs and his own, he had raised the country. He, with Kasteel Hendrik Prinsloo, Theunis de Klerk, and Cornelis Faber, had stirred up the Kaffirs, drawing them on with promise of loot. The Zuurveld was to be theirs and the cattle of the military and those of the Burgers who did not join — for those that were not with them were against them and would be put to the spear. Coenraad and Christiaan van Ek were ready, but when everything depended on surprise the news had leaked out and Prinsloo had been taken. Somewhere in their midst there was a traitor.

The whole Border had changed in the twinkling of an eye.

It was thick with troops, with commandos raised by the Government, and Kaffirs restless for plunder. The thing which had at its inception seemed so simple was now grown complex. More messengers had been sent to Gaika, but the answer had come back that Gaika's men sat on their shields. They were ready to move, but did not move. Gaika doubted Johannes' powers, and without Gaika he was helpless. The anger which had been good for stirring up the Boers and the threats he had employed were now useless. His head was too hot, he could not think clearly through the mist of rage that swept over him, and it seemed to him that, as his men wavered, God had sent him Kaspar. Kaspar was a sign from Heaven.

'Where is your own gun?' he asked.

'It was shot out of my hand,' Kaspar said. 'I was pursued and my friend is killed.'

'By the soldiers?'

'Ja, as we ran they shot him.'

'They chased Kaspar,' Johannes cried, standing in his stirrups and holding on to the mane of his horse, 'and they have killed his friend.'

The men round him were still half-hearted. Of those sixty-five there were few he could count on absolutely. They were thinking of their wives and homes. In the night, with that Boer facility for getting out of unpleasant situations, many would slip off. But men could be bound by oaths. They must swear an oath.

'Take off your hats!' Johannes shouted. 'Take them off, and swear to stand by me while I drive the English into the sea. Swear! or, by the living God, I will shoot down the traitors who refuse.'

The men took off their hats slowly and moved uneasily in their saddles.

'Raise your hats,' Johannes said, 'and remember this is an oath before God. Raise your hats high towards heaven and say, "I swear."'

The big hats went up reluctantly. First one and then another swore till all were sworn in. But the oath gave them no cohesion. By the oath they were no more one than before. Their faces were the faces of men beset by doubts.

'Come,' Johannes said, 'we will camp and wait for the others.'

Alone among them he was certain. His face as he spoke was transfigured. He had a mission. It was to avenge his brother's murder, to free his people, to drive the foreigners, the English, into the sea. Soon their beloved soil would be free. Soon Africa would be for those who had taken it from wild men and beasts, who had suffered, who had paid. Before God, how much they had paid! Not a homestead was without its graveyard, and many dead on the veld, killed as they worked or hunted. And they had sworn. An oath could not be broken. They would come with him, and any man who turned away from his duty would be shot.

In a low, shuffling cloud of dust they moved north. They were bowed over their saddles and the horses dragged their feet.

Kaspar was beside Johannes. He began to edge his horse away. Johannes put his hand on the bridle.

'Stay beside me,' he said.

Kaspar rode beside him so closely that their knees touched. Perhaps he would be able to get away at night or next morning. At least he had a gun in his hand again. He had become so used to a gun that he felt incomplete without one.

Suddenly Johannes put his hand on his knee. His eyes were full of tears. 'You would not leave me?' he said. 'You were with Frederik when he was killed. It is for Frederik, and for our people. Is it not said that they that wait upon the Lord shall renew their strength; they shall mount up with wings as eagles? I have been given a message. Ja, my message is to free this land.' He held out his hand.

Kaspar hesitated. He thought of old Frederik and Jeffries. After all, what more had he to lose? He took Johannes' hand. Now he was in it, come what might.

CHAPTER XXVI

JACOBUS

I

STEPHANIE knew of the storm of events. But it was like a storm outside a house while one is occupied within it. Everyone was involved. All the Border was in arms on one side or the other. There were continual rumours of victory, of disaster, the same event being interpreted both ways according to the views of the individual who told of them. Nothing was definite; only that so many dragoons were here, a company of infantry there. The Kaffirs were up, going to sweep the Border with fire and spear. The Kaffirs were not up; they were loyal to King George. Talk, talk, and more talk: all of it meaningless. What would they say if they knew I was going to have a baby? she thought. What would they do? What would she do if Jacobus did nothing? And she could not see Jacobus. The messengers she sent came back saying they could not find him. They said he was in the mountains. Suppose he was shot by the Boers or killed by a leopard or a band of Kaffirs. Suppose she never saw him again. One minute it was Jacobus. Then it was the baby. Then it was Jacobus again. Where was he? What would he do when he knew? Kruger had called up his commando; Cuyler was ready with the troops, and the rebels, with Rudolf among them, were camped on the other side of the river. Terrible times, folk said. Ja, terrible; but no one knew how terrible. I must see Jacobus, she thought. I must. I must.

Several times she had been on the verge of telling Aletta: not for sympathy, but just to talk about it. Just to be able to ask Aletta, who hardly knew Jacobus, what she thought he would do. She even took Klein Kattie out and played with her in the shade of the big fig tree, but Kattie did not want to play with her. Kattie wanted to be with her Tanta Letta or to be alone.

It was very hot. The air, like a blast from an open oven, scorched her, pulling at her skin, drawing it tightly over her face. Little eddies of wind spiralled over the veld, drawing up dust in red cones, plucking up rubbish, carrying it spinning into the air and dropping it again. Stephanie thought of herself a year ago, three months ago. She had been happy then. She tried to remember what being happy was like. It was like nothing at all. When you weren't unhappy you were happy, and so you could not remember it. There was nothing to recall in happiness. I used to sing then, she thought. Then she tried to think how long it was since she had sung. It was a long time. Then she wondered if she would ever sing again as she had done, carelessly, just because she was alive. Even her clothes were no longer a pleasure to her. She would soon be too big for them and they were spoilt for her. Each was mixed up with some memory. She had worn one to try to attract Kaspar. Jacobus had complimented her in another. She took great pains with her black hair, smoothing it, brushing it, oiling it with fine oil so that it was sleek to her head. There was a strange comfort in doing her hair. It occupied her hands, and while she brushed she could not think.

Never before had she been conscious of thinking. There had been no reason to think. Now there was every reason, and all thought inconclusive. By the time she had persuaded herself that Jacobus would marry her, she was convinced that he would not. By the time she had decided to confide in Aletta, she lost her resolution to do so. So it ended as it had begun, each day one of vacillating, of waiting, of trying to do a hundred things, starting them and finishing nothing. The stir about her remained something from which, because of her circumstances, she was utterly divorced. She took to reading the Bible, holding the heavy book on her knees and searching it for counsel. But there was no counsel to be found in it. The Bible was brutally direct. Life was brutally direct. She felt very small, very alone, and weak. What work there was to do Aletta did. Stephanie could see no excuse for taking any of it over suddenly like this, and if she had, she doubted if she could have done it, she often felt so ill.

When Aletta spoke to her, it was of small matters. They spoke to each other only because to speak was easier than to remain always silent. When we were children we used to play together, she thought; play as Klein Kattie did under the fig tree, which in ten years had not changed at all. It seemed even to have the same leaves, and the bough that carried Kattie's swing had carried theirs; the cuts in the polished bark were no deeper. Yes, she thought, in those days we played. We were children then, but now we are no longer children: we are women. Therefore we cannot play and talk, and, before God, what should we talk about? What is there to talk about but one thing for each of us? For me, Jacobus. For her, Kaspar. For both of us marriage.

Near the house, hanging on the branches of a big thorn, there were some finks' nests. They hung like pears. As she looked at them, a small grey hawk flung itself at one of them; striking it open and seizing a young bird in its yellow claws, flew to the top of the tree to eat it. Stephanie watched it land on a branch. It landed cleanly, gripping the branch with one foot, while the other held its prey. The young bird was still living when the hawk began to eat it, ripping at it with its beak. Holding it fast, it pulled at it. Soon she knew that the hawk would have the other nests torn down. It would come daily till all were down and hung, bottomless, as hollow as bells. That was what would happen. There was no going against it. She wondered why she had not tried to save the bird, to frighten the hawk. And she knew suddenly why she had not. It was no good. If she frightened it now, it would come back tomorrow. If she shot it, another hawk would come, or something would come. Stephanie sank her head between her hands. The hot tears ran down the inside of her arms. It is stupid to cry because a hawk has taken a young fink, she thought. She bit her lips, but still she cried. Life was like that, a bird's or a woman's; there were hawks that came and took the song out of it. She went on crying. She was crying for a fink.

2

A farm goes on. No matter what happens, it goes on. Cows calve, ears of grain swell and ripen, tares and weeds spring up, and men and women continue in war or pestilence to serve the fields and the beasts of the field, to reap, to mow, to garner, to thresh, to milk, to castrate, to winnow; and all the time to mend, to repair the things that have, in the course of use, or because of long usage, fallen down or become broken.

At Rudolf's place, with Rudolf away, things were still done, fewer things, but still things. The work was slowed down by his absence, but he could not slow the seasons by being away, nor hurry them by his presence; and the seasons dragged work from the men, from Aletta, even a little from Stephanie when she could be persuaded to move. Only Kattie was left out of it. Too small to work, too young to supervise, she watched, round-eyed, all that went on. She missed her father. Each night she asked for him. She missed sitting on his knee and pulling at his beard; she missed watching him as she sat, held on Aletta's knee, while he read from the Book. It was Aletta who read now, and Kattie, because she would not go to Stephanie, stood listening, her eyes level with the table-top. The big, high-sounding words that Aletta read boomed in her ears, and though they were read softly and she understood only one here and there, they filled her with fear. When her father read in his loud voice, she was not frightened. She was not frightened because he was there. No one could be frightened when her father was there.

At night she slept curled against Aletta. By day she got under Aletta's feet or followed her, pulling at her skirt, raising it in her hand as she dragged. Something was the matter: she did not know what, but the feel of things was different. Her mother had gone to a place called Heaven that was very distant. Her father came and went; so did other men she had never seen. Soldiers passed, big men on bay horses that had short tails. She had never seen short-tailed horses before. It is the English fashion to cut the tails of their horses, Aletta told her. With short tails they were defenceless against the flies and lashed out furiously. Kattie was small, but she knew it was foolish to cut a horse's tail. Left alone, she played under the fig tree or fed the poultry with crumbs and watched them run and scrape.

Above all the others she loved a big cock called Paulus. He was a proud cock and stayed by himself. Kattie thought this very proper. He was too beautiful to mix with the hens, for though the hens were interesting enough they were ugly, dowdy, and only beautiful when their combs were red with laying. Each day Kattie expected something to happen, some change to take place — her mother to come back or her father to come and stay as he used to do; but nothing happened except that it got hotter, and even Tanta Letta became irritable with her when she got in her way.

3

Rudolf was pleased to see Kaspar with Johannes. He wanted to talk to him privately. He was not satisfied with the way things were going and he was frightened. Without knowing quite how it happened, because of his unhappiness he had been dragged into this thing. Now he wanted to get out. Besides, once the Kaffirs were loosed, how would they differentiate between friendly and unfriendly farmers? Actually the friendly ones, because there was no man at home, would fall the easiest prey. What they wanted was loot, as many cattle and horses as they could plunder. He kept thinking of the two girls at home and the child. He kept watching for armed parties of Kaffirs. Johannes was expecting them: he said so. He had sent messengers to Gaika again, and was here, on the other side of the river, waiting for them to return.

Added to Rudolf's fears of the rebellion were all the terrors of a Kaffir war — fire, rapine, and murder by assegai. For nights now the thought of it had kept him awake. Try as he would he could not remember how he had become committed to this course, and all he could think of were the ways in which he could have avoided it. But the hours could not be set backward. It was no use wishing he had done this or that. To save the milk, the crock should not be put on the ground, but Kaspar would advise him. Kaspar was well read: a young man of experience and intelligence who had been a guest at his house. But it was not till they were camped that he got the chance.

'Kaspar,' he said, 'I want to speak to you.'

'Oom Rudolf, I also wish to speak to you.' What was Rudolf going to say? Had he guessed what he wanted? Kaspar stood still, waiting.

'It is about this war,' Rudolf said. 'I do not like it. Nee, magtig, I do not like it at all. There are too many soldiers. We shall have to fight. I have never fought white men. Ja, before God, even if they be English, they are white and brothers of a kind. And there are the girls, Kaspar. I must get back. There are wild Kaffirs loose in the land.' Rudolf's voice broke. He could say no more.

'You must go,' Kaspar said. 'Go now.'

'But the oath. I swore to stay.'

'What is an oath where women are concerned?' Kaspar asked. 'What is an oath given to a man who is mad?'

'But you are staying?'

'Ja, I am staying.'

'Why are you staying, Kaspar? Come with me.'

Kaspar smiled slowly. 'What have I to lose, Oom Rudolf? There is a price on my head. The English soldiers killed my friend; they shot my horse; they broke my gun with their bullets. Before, I felt nothing about them — many were my friends at Kaapstad among the officers and officials — but now I hate them. Ja, and, before God, I will strike one blow against them. That we win, I doubt; but it will be a beginning, and then, if I live, I am coming for Letta. You will give her to me?'

'You want Letta?'

Kaspar nodded.

Rudolf took his hand. 'You will have to take her far away if you are going to be safe.'

'We will be married by the missionary at Klaarwater beyond Coenraad's, and then go on. Now go, Oom Rudolf. Go, as if you were watering your horse, then pretend to have seen a buck, stalk it with your gun ready, and then ride. Good-bye and good luck, Oom Rudolf. When this is over you will see me.'

Rudolf mounted and rode off into the dusk.

'Where are you going?' Johannes shouted.

'To water my horse and stand him in the river. One of his legs is sore.'

So Kaspar wanted Aletta. If he lived he would come and take her, and then they would go off into the wilderness to make a place together, just as he and Stephanie's mother had done: just as every Boer did. A man and a woman trekking alone; then later they were not alone. A family grew round them, and then at the end they were alone again.

Stephanie would go, too, and he would have Klein Kattie. He wondered if he could look after Klein Kattie. There was a certain difficulty about a man living alone with a small girl. What was the good of going on like this, working a farm with no sons to carry on the work? It seemed no good, but he knew he would go on. It was his life, and perhaps the man Stephanie married would have the farm, and her children after her.

Magtig, it would be good to be back. Even in the dark he recognised the landmarks, trees, the outline of mountains against the sky. His horse knew that they were going home and walked faster. A few more hours and he would be back. He tried to imagine what the future would be: to think of his life alone when the girls had gone. He could not. Then he thought of Aletta. She was more to him than his own daughter. He thought of the day old Frederik had brought her to him on his horse. He would tell Aletta about Kaspar: that he had seen him. She would care more about his having seen Kaspar than all the other news; and what news it was! He shivered at the thought of the coming trouble; of the Kaffirs, uncontrolled, running through the land, and of Boers fighting Boers. Johannes had not raised the whole country, only part of it, for many held by the English, and thinking their administration good, were fighting for them.

Soon he would be home. There was comfort in that word. Yet, when he got back after his first ride round, he could not settle down. Some sheep and cattle were missing — stolen, no doubt, by Kaffirs; but there was no one to seek them with him, all the men were on commando. He told Aletta about Kaspar, and she said very little, only asking what he was wearing and if he looked well. Stephanie was sullen and silent. Kattie clung to him. Of them all, only the child had missed him. Without Maria it did not seem like a home at all and, for all the people in it, stark and empty. It seemed strange that he had lived here: strange and purposeless. That there was a reason for life, that it was so ordered by the Almighty God, he did not doubt for an instant. It was only that he could not see that purpose — perhaps it was too big for the understanding of man. It might be right, but it was lonely: very lonely with Maria dead.

4

Jacobus was coming. He had sent Stephanie word to be at the tree. Now she would tell him, and then she would know. Stephanie sang because she was going to see him. Then she stopped singing because she was going to see him. She did her hair: she dressed. Then she let down her hair and did it up again. First she walked fast. Then her feet dragged. What would she say to him? How would she tell him? What would he do? What would he say? She looked at a stone in the road. When she came back, she would pass that stone again. She had passed it so many times, but now it became significant. She was glad she had not stumbled over it. That would have been an evil omen.

When she got to the tree, he was there, waiting for her. He had never been early before. He was waiting beside his horse, fondling its ears with gloved hands. He came towards her.

'My shepherdess,' he said.

Stephanie felt herself push him from her. 'We must talk,' she said. She did not want to talk; she wanted to delay speech and be held in his arms. She wanted to be made much of. Perhaps it would be the last time.

'What is it?' he asked.

She stood facing him, looking into his eyes. It seemed an hour. She knew everything about him: the way his eyes were set too close to his long nose, the way his hair grew: everything.

'Look at me,' she said. 'Can you not see?'

'I see nothing but your beauty,' he said.

'I shall not be beautiful long, Jacobus. I shall be fat. Can you see nothing?' she asked. 'It is in my heart that even the Kaffirs and the servants know.'

He looked at her again. 'Are you ...'

'Yes,' she said. 'I am three months gone.'

'Why did you not tell me?' He was not angry. He looked glad.

Stephanie looked down.

'Come,' Jacobus said, 'let us find Rudolf. We will be married. We must go at once.' He looked at his timepiece.

'You are going to marry me?' Stephanie said.

'Of course I am going to marry you. Are you not the mother of my son?' He undid the reins. 'Come, we must get ready to go. Your father does not know?' he asked.

Stephanie shook her head.

'Then we will say that it must be at once because my work is finished.'

Rudolf was surprised. He had been thinking of losing Aletta to Kaspar, and now Stephanie was to go first. It had come quicker than he thought. He lit his pipe.

'You have been courting her?' he asked.

'Ja, meneer, I have courted her.'

'Then how was it I did not know? Have you been court-ing her in the bushes?' he asked angrily. 'Why, if you wanted to court her, could you not opsit like a Burger in the sit-Kamer with a candle between you?' His sense of decency was outraged. 'You with your gloves and fine ways! Ja, magtig, you have everything but manners and respect for our customs.'

It was now Jacobus' turn for surprise. He had expected the old man to be overwhelmed by having a son-in-law of his quality.

'I have courted her,' he said. 'She is willing.'

'Then the girl is a fool. A popinjay with soft hands! A townsman from foreign parts!'

'Of the City of Amsterdam and the University of Leyden,

meneer.' Van Zyl bowed, putting one leg behind the other and covering his stomach with his hat. It was a very fine bow. He would show the old farmer whether he had manners or not.

'A bowing, scraping popinjay!' Rudolf shouted. 'Before God, if you had wings you would trail them in the dust like a cock.' He had worked himself into a fury.

Evidently it was no use bowing. Van Zyl put on his hat again. Rudolf's anger was burning low. He could think of nothing to say. Van Zyl wanted Stephanie. He had, if he knew anything of his daughter, had her. These things happened even when courting was done decently in the house; how much more, therefore, would they happen when it was done behind bushes on the veld. He looked Stephanie over. He was a farmer and knew what to look for. Not only was Stephanie going to leave him, she was even now all but a mother. He spat and relit his pipe. 'You had better take her quickly,' he said. His eyes were still on Stephanie's stomach.

'We will start for the Cape tomorrow,' van Zyl said, 'and with your permission, meneer, I will take my leave.' He swept off his hat again. By the time it had reached his belly, Rudolf had gone into the house. Not wishing to waste his effort, Jacobus pivoted towards Stephanie, bending low and raising her hand to his lips. 'Till tomorrow, then,' he said.

5

Van Zyl was pleased. Never had he been so pleased about anything. And Stephanie had been afraid that he would not marry her! Poor child, how little she understood him! Indeed, how little had he understood himself. He was to have a child. He, Jacobus Hendrik van Zyl, was to have a son. For the first time in his life he had got a woman with child. Now he could go home. Now his father would acknowledge him again: married and a father. Now he could rest in peace and have no more truck with women. A Hollander, he would go back to Holland. He would grow tulips. He would get fat. He would dress carelessly and throw away his corsets, his scents, his frills. A great nostalgia for his country swept over him. He must take her away at once. He began to calculate the length of the voyage in months: the child would be born at home. He thought of tulips, whole fields of them in narrow beds of black soil with the still water of the canals between them. He thought of the cattle of his home, of the great black-and-white cows with swinging udders; of skating in the winter; and of the books and pictures he would buy. He would set up a little observatory: he would cast horoscopes.

Everything the child did should be calculated in advance, and this stout country blood would replenish the stock of his house. The van Zyls were too old; they had married their cousins for too long. He was an only son of an only son of an only son.... The thin chain of their stock would now be strengthened, and it would be he, Jacobus, who had done it. He thought of his other children, the ones that would come. He could do more for these, casting horoscope after horoscope till the time was favourable. This would have to be years ahead and working back he would pick days for their conception. It might be hard to make Stephanie understand this method, but for a long time he had been convinced that only by so doing could children be born under the best auspices. That was why there were so many failures in life: simply because the infant's course was not charted before its birth. Once Stephanie understood, there would be no difficulty and he would explain it to her fully.

How could anyone doubt the truth of science? he wondered. Was it not known that the tides were governed by the moon? That the twenty-eight-day cycle was a definite rhythm? Thus were the lives of men also controlled by the planets in their orbits, by the fixed stars, by their combinations and proximity or their distance the one from the other. His children should prove to the scoffers what could be done. He would devote a great book to the subject. 'Astrological Conception' he would call it, with a sub-title, 'How Great Men Are Made.' What could be more logical? He thought of the great men in history — of Caesar, Hannibal, Darius, Napoleon. They were successful because they had by some chance been born at the right moment. With his children there would be no accidents; at the most there would be a margin of error. It remained only to convince Stephanie. Already she took an interest in the heavenly bodies. He had taught her to find the Southern Cross and Orion's Belt. Three times out of five she was right and picked them out. Once he got home and she could look at the stars from his observatory through a glass, she would become imbued with his own enthusiasm. There was no question in his mind about this.

6

Stephanie sat on the bed. Jacobus was going to marry her. He was glad she was going to have a child. All round her, spread out, were her clothes. At her feet the wagon-box stood open. It was brightly painted: blue with a device of pink flowers; posy after posy joined together by scrolls and leaves. She looked at the clothes with distaste. Her best seemed poor now. She thought of the pictures Jacobus had shown her. She would have dresses like that. Long, flowing ones that he called Greek. She wondered who the Greeks were. A people who had lived long ago, Jacobus said. What had happened to them? Were there any Greeks left? Did they still wear dresses like that? And had they worn shoes with high red heels?

She began to pack, folding her clothes carefully. Each had memories: a woman was so much part of her clothes. There were clothes you had been happy in; others that you had not been happy in. But even if you did not like them any more, it was hard to part with them. There was the cherry sash, and the green dress that was still marked by the cat. The kittens were almost grown up now. She had never been able to get the marks out. None could see them unless they knew where to look; but she knew. She smoothed the dress over her knee. Knowing she would never wear it again, she packed it. Tomorrow she would be gone: she was leaving. She was surprised at how little she felt leaving her father or Klein Kattie or Aletta, or the home where she had been brought up. She was glad to go. Glad, glad, glad! She was going to places where things happened. She was going to wear shoes with high red heels. She had been so jealous of Aletta. She was no longer jealous. One day she would know whether she had really loved Kaspar. She could not think now. Neither of Kaspar nor of Jacobus. She could think only of her marriage and of the fact that she was going away. She knelt down by the wagon-box and began to pack quickly. She wanted to see the box filled and closed: to see it locked: to see it lashed to the cart that Jacobus was bringing.

He came in the morning, in a Cape cart with four horses. The heavy things were going by wagon. He said good-bye to Rudolf. He bowed over Aletta's hand. A pretty little thing, he thought, but too small. He was a Hollander. He liked big women, voluptuous women, the kind of women that Rubens painted. Stephanie would be big when she was older. Up to a certain age women matured like wine, becoming large and mellow. He helped Stephanie into the cart and turned the horses. They ran back a little and sprang forward, the bar struck the pole, the wheels turned, the pole dropped as the traces tightened, one of the leaders reared, and they were off.

The cart went quickly, pulling a little cloud of dust behind it. Aletta took Rudolf's hand. The cloud grew smaller, disappeared behind some trees, reappeared, now no larger than the hand of a child. Stephanie had gone out of their lives. The trees swam in the heat, moving up and down before Aletta's eyes. Old Rudolf and Klein Kattie and Kaspar had only her to count on now. Somehow she must carry these people — an old man, a young one, and a child. They looked to her.

I

KASPAR could see no reason for delay. If something was going to be done, it must be done quickly. Yet they delayed. The men were restless — weakening. The edge of their enthusiasm was off and they saw to what they had been committed. Most had had no idea of rebellion. They had been called up on commando in the ordinary way and then had found themselves on the wrong side. What were they fighting for? What would they get out of it? And each day the English were becoming stronger, better organised. A few more men had been forced in, passers-by: Bothma, who had been out collecting lost cattle when Johannes met him; Lucas van Vuuren, Cornelis van der Nest. And old Willemse Prinsloo, a cousin of Kasteel Hendrik's, who was travelling the country in search of herbs and simples. He was an inoffensive old man who combined the profession of doctor with the office of undertaker. Once you were in Willemse's hands you stayed there till, one way or the other, he had completed his business. Apart from the herbs he had collected, roots, bulbs, barks, and flowers, his wagon was loaded with wood for coffins.

But these men were unwilling, and, though they swelled the numbers, they weakened the spirit of the rebels still further. To pass the time Prinsloo made a coffin for one of his patients, assured that, as his coming was delayed, the man would die: his worry now, that he would not even get there in time to sell the coffin.

'We were assembled to repel the Kaffirs,' they said. 'Kruger did it. He stood in Opperman's place. We were called upon and we came.'

Johannes was playing for time, but time, as Kaspar saw it, was with the English and against them. Not daring to go home, for dispersed they would be taken, not daring to go on because they had no wish to fight, the commando waited. There was no news from Gaika: none from Coenraad. Kaspar knew definitely now that the rebellion would fail; that the only chance it had ever had, that of surprise, was gone; yet still he stayed. As things were, he could not get back to Aletta and he could not tear himself away from the vicinity of the river where she lived. And he still wished, if he could, to strike a blow for Jeffries; also he hoped in some way to help Johannes, to save him from the inevitable end if he could. So much had happened that he was, in a way, curious to see what more could happen. From the beginning he had been all but passive — a straw caught in the stream of the Border. He seemed to have done little of his own volition. Situations had occurred and he had done what he had to do. He was doing what he had to do now. Till things were settled, his hands were tied. It never struck him to ride off. He had given his hand to Johannes upon it. He tried not to think; he was afraid to. He could only wait. But waiting was not easy. He felt himself being used up.

And here Adam found him. He had traced him as a hound follows a buck, sleeping night after night on his spoor. Leaping over the dogs that chased him, Adam reached Kaspar's feet and sat down. He had found his master. From now on, where they went and what they did would be his master's affair. His master, to Adam, was a god.

Kaspar patted his head. 'I knew you would find me,' he said. 'Soon we cross the river again,' he went on. 'We are going to fight.'

Adam nodded. It did not matter where they went. He had reached his master, and his master was well.

At last Johannes made up his mind and they moved, straggling off to the south. When they got near to Slagtersnek, they saw a cloud of dust advancing towards them. It was made by a number of horsemen, dragoons, perhaps. Trotting their horses, the rebels made their way to the hilltop, Johannes leading them, his lips moving in prayer. But the enemy — it was hard to think of them as that — showed no disposition to attack. Seeing this, Kruger sent a Hottentot down to say that they did not wish to fight. The answer came back: Colonel Cuyler did not wish to fight either unless he was obliged to.

The opposing force came nearer to the foot of the hill and halted. One of their number detached himself and rode up unarmed. As he came nearer, they recognised him. It was Lange, riding a bay horse with flopping ears. When he reached them, he dismounted and left his horse to stand with trailing reins.

'Who are the leaders?' he said. 'I want to talk to the leaders.'

Johannes came forward with Kruger, Marais, and Bothma. Kaspar went with them. Moving away from the others, they sat down.

Lange spoke first. 'Landdros Cuyler has not come in anger,' he said. 'He has come to ask for an explanation and to bid you remember your oath.'

'We will remember it if we may go home,' Kruger said. 'Give us a pardon and we will come down and surrender.'

A bugle sounded.

'I will tell the Landdros your words,' Lange said.

An hour later he was back.

'The Landdros wants the leaders,' he said. 'Johannes

Bezuidenhout, Theunis de Klerk, Kruger, and van der Berg.'

'I will be damned if I surrender! If I go, I shall never be free again!' de Klerk shouted.

Johannes said nothing. He watched with blazing eyes. If it was going to be for nothing they should not take him alive.

'Listen, Burgers, brothers!' Lange said. He was mounted now the better to make himself heard. 'Listen, all of you,' he said again. 'Think of the misery you will bring upon your wives and children if you persist in this madness. Look at the men down there' — he pointed to the foot of the hill — 'and those are only a few. There are more, hundreds more, and what can you do against them? How will you prevail?'

'Before God, we will prevail!' Johannes shouted. 'Before God and by the grace of God, because we are in the right, because you are murderers who slew my brother Frederik. What do we care for numbers? Can numbers prevail against the will of God, against the strength of God and faith?' He stopped exhausted. Faith could move mountains; they had faith. His hands clenched and unclenched as he plucked at his trousers.

Old Kruger began to cry. He was tired. He had been tricked into this. It was Opperman's place to be Field Cornet and he had left him to carry on his duty in ignorance of what was passing.

'Magtig, Lange,' he said, 'I am guilty. Do with me what you will. I will persuade the others. We have been mad. Ja, mad with worms in our brains.' He knelt down and began to pray.

The others took no notice, but without an order distributed themselves along the edge of the hill, taking up positions where they could command the ground below them with their fire.

Kaspar stayed near Johannes. This was different from any action he had yet seen: no real leader, no real motive, no plan, no desire for anything. Each man, except for the leaders, wishing himself elsewhere. He turned round to see Faber coming out of the woody kloof behind them.

He touched Johannes. 'Faber,' he said.

Johannes sprang up. 'He is back from Gaika! The Kaffirs will be coming. With them beside us, we will sweep the land clean.'

A look at Faber's face was enough. He had failed. The Kaffirs were not coming.

'What did he say?' Johannes asked.

'They will not come. They have heard that Prinsloo is taken.'

It was Prinsloo who was the real power. Johannes saw this now: he had been able to stir up others by his devotion to his dead brother. But he had no head for leadership. If Prinsloo had not been captured, it might have been different.

'Did you offer them what I told you?' Johannes asked. 'Did you tell them they were to have the Zuurveld? That they were to get cattle and horses and guns and beads?'

'I told them everything.' Faber was tired out. He had hurried back.

'And what did he say? What were Gaika's words?' Johannes went on. There must be something. The work of weeks could not be lost like this.

'He said we could fight if we wished, but that he had no word from the great King over the water. They still sit on their shields, Johannes, all but a few who are unsettled and ready to murder anyone.'

Kaspar looked down the hill again. The men were moving, advancing up the slope, under Colonel Frazer and Commandant Nel. The dragoons were in the centre supported on either flank by parties of Burgers.

'They are coming,' Faber said. He raised his gun.

The man next to Kaspar waved his hat and shouted to the Boers: 'Keep away from the dragoons! How can we shoot?'

The troops halted again and Potgeiter, a Burger, came forward alone.

'For the love of God, brothers,' he said, 'give in. You can do nothing.'

He sat his horse for a moment, waiting. No one answered him, and he turned and rode back.

A bugle blared. The dragoons leant forward in their saddles and drove their spurs into their horses' flanks. With a rattle of accoutrements, riding stirrup to stirrup, they charged. The Boers on the flanks advanced at the same time.

Johannes sat down with his gun ready to fire when they came within range. Kaspar sat beside him. He had no desire to fire now. He saw Nel and Lange ride up to Kruger round whom some of the younger men stood wavering. No one would fire the first shot.

'Surrender!' Nel shouted, 'and you will suffer no harm.'

'But can you assure us of that? Have you the authority?'

He was right among them now. 'I assure you,' Kaspar heard him say. 'I promise as truly as the wine at the Lord's Supper signifies His Blood and the bread His Flesh, as truly I say, will you suffer no harm.'

They lowered their guns. They had given in. They turned down the hill. They had surrendered. The cause was lost.

'Come, Johannes,' Kaspar said. 'Come quickly. We must get away.'

De Klerk was already mounted. Driving Johannes before him, Kaspar pushed him onto his horse and sprang onto Tigernek. As they galloped down the mountain, the others joined them. They rode till dark, stopped to eat, and then rode on.

'We will go straight through to Rudolf's,' Johannes said. 'We will pass through his place tomorrow night.'

'Then where are we going?'

'I do not know. Into Kaffirland to join Coenraad. But where is Coenraad? Why did he not come?' Johannes asked.

Coenraad could have led them. Coenraad could have done easily what he could never do. He had tried and failed. All that was left now was to get away, and with the country

illed with soldiers even that would not be easy. He must get
back to his wife and son. With a wagon and some gear and
cattle they could start again. Frederik was not avenged, but
he had done all that man could do. It was over and not a
shot fired.

2

Rumour ran more quickly than actual fact. Before the
meeting of the rebels and the troops was over, its story had
gone out. There had been a battle. Many on both sides were
killed. The English were running; the Boers were dispersed;
everybody was killed or a prisoner. Aletta was distracted.
Was Kaspar alive or dead? Wounded, a prisoner? Why,
when he could have stayed out of it, had he entered into this
thing? Surely for her sake he should have kept out. What
would she do if anything happened to him? And where
was he? Dear God, where was he? And could one get no
true report? She could not eat or sleep. Rudolf could not
help her with his awkward sympathy and his clumsy efforts
to talk of other things. The necessity to let him think he
was helping her tormented her still further. There was
nothing to do but wait. It seemed to her that all her life she
had done nothing but wait for news.

And then one of the Hottentots ran in.

'They are coming!' he cried. 'A commando is coming!'

3

When she saw him, Aletta knew that nothing else mattered; knew that, to women, if the dead are not their own
dead, there are no dead. As she watched them stringing past,
tired men sagging over the necks of exhausted horses, she
felt nothing but a great thankfulness; the fact that a great
project had failed was lost and completely forgotten in her
joy at the sight of Kaspar. True, his face was drawn, his eyes

glazed with lack of sleep, as he drooped over his blue roan stallion. The fire had gone from them both, but they were not beaten; they were only tired. Before God, she had never seen men or beasts so tired before. They rode in silence, filing past in fours; their horses — bays, browns, duns, greys, chestnuts, blacks, and roans — all coated with red dust.

Kaspar was alive. Unable to restrain herself, Aletta began to laugh hysterically. Someone shouted a command and the column halted. The horses stood with bent knees and drooping heads as the men slid stiffly from their saddles.

Running up to Kaspar, Aletta flung herself into his arms. Through his shirt she felt his ribs against her. The hammer of the gun he still held in his hand hurt her as it pressed into her back. Opening her eyes, she stared at him. She hated war: war, in which boys became men overnight, and men became corpses. She kissed him again and again. His face was covered with a thick golden down, like the hairs on a young pigeon's breast, and each hair was coated with red dust; the corners of his eyes were crusted with muddy sweat, and he had new wrinkles that were filled in with dirt. He smelt of stale sweat. Tigernek forced his head between them. She put out a hand to rub his ears. As she touched him, he pushed against her.

'I must water him,' Kaspar said, 'and then I must sleep.'

Aletta was unreal to Kaspar. All he could think of was water for himself and his horse and the nightmare of this endless ride. Sleep! Before God, he must sleep and eat! It was a man's world; one in which a man's first duty was to himself; where his only necessity was his own body and the need to recover it. In the last months he had learnt about his body, learnt its needs and how to keep it alive. He looked at Aletta, wondering if she would understand. For some hours he could give her nothing; scarcely alive himself, he could not make new life, and catching up the reins he staggered like a drunken man towards the spruit. Already many horses were rolling their galled backs in the sand. Already many men slept heavily with their heads on their saddles. Behind him, trailing unhappily after him, Aletta followed. Blind with tears, her course was as erratic as his own. She did not understand, but she accepted. While he slept, she would wait near him.

Kaspar woke to find Aletta beside him. She was sitting, half kneeling, looking at him. She had brought blankets from the house to cover him and a pillow for his head. Adam crouched beside her. Kaspar sat up. There were fewer men than there had been the night before.

'They have gone into the mountains,' Aletta said.

He took her hand and held it.

'Where are you going?' she asked.

'I will go with Johannes to Coenraad's and wait there. You will come to me?' he asked.

'I come?' she said. 'How can I now with Stephanie gone and Rudolf and Kattie to watch over?'

'He will let you go, Letta.'

'Ja, he will let me go.' She knew Rudolf would let her go, but could she go? Could she leave him? Not yet. She must wait. She had a feeling that something must be completed first. 'I will come, Kaspar,' she said, 'but you must wait. Things are going to happen. I feel it here.' She put her hand to her breast. 'Now you must go with Johannes; he is saddling up. Adam has Tigernek ready. I have packed more food and powder and ball,' she said.

Kaspar felt rested, but his knees were weak. He bent to kiss her. 'I will go,' he said, 'but I will be back, or you must come to me.'

'If I live I will come to you, Kaspar, but go now.'

Always when they met she seemed to have to drive him from her. Always there was some outside circumstance forcing them apart, threatening them. Why had he got into this? Why had he not lain hidden till it was over and the country quiet?

As if he read her thoughts, Kaspar turned and said, 'They killed my friend.'

'The man who was with you?'

'Ja, Jim Jeffries.'

Aletta said nothing. Hearing from Rudolf that he was alive, she had thought no more of how he had escaped. What had happened seemed so little since he was alive.

'The river came down between us and the soldiers. It saved us,' Kaspar said.

He was mounted. Tigernek snapped playfully at Johannes horse. Adam was behind them on a grey of Rudolf's. He sat very high on the withers, glancing from side to side with dark eyes.

'Good-bye, Letta,' Kaspar said. He did not look at her.

'Good-bye,' Aletta whispered. 'Good-bye and good luck.'

How easy it was to say those words! One said them so often, and often they meant nothing. With good luck, in a while, they would be together; with bad... She turned away. She could not watch them go. She picked up the pillow — it was one from her own bed — and the blankets. There was Kattie to attend to, and Rudolf.

4

Kaspar rode with Johannes. Faber and Stephanus Bothma rode behind them, and Adam brought up the rear.

'We will pick up the women and children, collect the beasts, and trek,' Johannes said. 'Once in Kaffirland we shall be safe.'

'Yes, we shall be safe once we are there,' Kaspar said.

But it was not going to be so easy with women, children, wagons cumbered with gear, and herds of stock. Johannes still did not appear to realise the gravity of what had been done. It was rebellion. It was high treason. Bothma and Faber were silent. Each man was thinking of himself and how he could save himself and his family. At midday they

arted company, Kaspar and Johannes going one way, the
ther two another.

'We must stay together,' Faber said. 'Let us collect our
oods and meet at the bend of the river by the flats.'

'Ja, we will meet there,' Johannes said, 'but no one must
ait. Let the first go on and the others follow on his spoor.'

'Can we not all ride?' Kaspar asked. 'The spoor of four
agons will make us easy to follow.'

'The women cannot ride,' Bothma said. 'They are in no
ondition to ride, and there are small children.'

Faber nodded. He also had young children.

'Tot siens,' they said, raising their guns. 'We will be
here tomorrow. In two days we shall be safe. Then we will
rek slowly to Coenraad's place. No one can take us there.'
hey turned their horses.

Kaspar stopped to write a note to Leendert to tell him
vhat had happened: 'Get news to my father and send off the
vagons. The other wagon, my own with Frans and the
ervants who are remaining hold in readiness to join me at
Coenraad's. I will send news from there.'

He gave the letter to Adam and told him to take it quickly,
nd rode on after Johannes.

The move went off better than Kaspar had expected.
Martha Bezuidenhout acted quickly, packing up food and
ssential gear. Cattle, horses, and sheep were collected, and
he oxen inspanned. Within three hours of their arrival they
vere off, the great wheels groaning, the axles rattling and
hivering as they rolled over the road. Faber had been as
quick as they, and met them at the appointed place. There
vas no sign of Bothma and they went on. Bothma could
ollow. He caught them up an hour later. Having gone on
ill dark, they camped. Next day they went on again.
There was only one road north that the wagons could take.
This worried Kaspar. He spoke to Johannes about it.

'Ja, it is true,' Johannes said; 'there is only one way
hrough, so what can we do? We have been quick. There

was no delay, and God, having brought us so far, will lea
us safely. Have faith, Kaspar, have faith. We have failed
Frederik's blood still cries from the ground, but while I liv
it does not cry in vain. They shall pay, Kaspar. His murde
will yet be avenged.'

It was no good talking to Johannes. He was still inspire
by dreams and visions. To him the world was bounded b
a revenge which Kaspar knew would achieve nothing. If h
could, he would save him, as much from himself as from th
English. He rode up to Faber, who was in front. He wa
mounted and Bothma walked beside him.

'Magtig, this is bad, Kaspar,' Faber said. 'We have bee
mad. Before God, why did we not think? Now it is to
late.'

'Ja, it is bad,' Kaspar said. 'But we are still alive. It
in my heart that from Coenraad's we go east towards th
Portuguese. They will be glad to have us. We will star
new farms side by side.' He put his hand on Faber's shoulde
'We will start again,' he said.

'Ja, Kaspar; God willing, we will start again.'

Kaspar turned round. Johannes was outspanning. H
galloped back to stop him. 'Drive on!' he shouted. 'Driv
on! This is no place to stop.'

The road in front of them was narrow, filled with rock
and surrounded by clumps of heavy bush. Johannes con
tinued outspanning. He stood with the riems in his hand
moving from ox to ox as he freed them. The yokes lay o
the ground.

'Have you no faith, Kaspar?' he asked.

'I have faith,' Kaspar said, 'but no liking for this place
It seems to me you place difficulties in the way of God, wh
gave you more sense than a dumb beast.'

Kaspar was angry. Before God, things were difficul
enough without Johannes' stupidity. He rode forward agair
Faber and Bothma had gone on for water. As he reache
them, a soldier stepped out from behind a rock. Others fo

owed him. An officer shouted, 'Surrender!' They had been ambushed.

Kaspar wheeled his horse. There was a volley from the soldiers. Faber dismounted and knelt down to shoot. There was another shot. Turning in the saddle, Kaspar saw that Faber was hit and the soldiers were running towards him. Bothma was halfway up the hill. Kaspar saw him dive into a crevice between the rocks.

At the wagons Faber and Bothma's wives stood beside their cooking-fires and stared with shaded eyes towards the poort. Johannes had mounted and was coming to him, followed by his wife and son on foot.

'What is it?' he shouted. 'Who is firing?'

'The troops,' Kaspar said. 'They have got in front of us.'

Johannes turned back to the wagon. 'We will fight,' he said. 'Ja, magtig, we will stand at bay.' Almost his brother's words: almost his brother's situation. He would die fighting. He would not be taken.

The soldiers closed in from all round. Kaspar recognised Commandant Nel at their head.

'Surrender!' he shouted, cupping his hands round his mouth.

Bothma, who had been taken, stood between two red-coated soldiers. His head was low on his chest. It was as if he did not want to see. His wife and Faber's came forward with their children. They joined the soldiers.

Kaspar stayed with Johannes. There was no chance of getting away. He tied Tigernek to the wagon and waited. If he surrendered, he would be hanged. There were over a hundred soldiers, dragoons and coloured infantry. As they advanced, Johannes fired. Kaspar heard his bullet strike and saw a soldier fall. Martha handed her husband another gun and picked one up herself. They both fired, the two shots sounding like one. Then the boy fired. Kaspar did nothing. This was the end.

The Bezuidenhouts, man, woman, and child, were with

him behind the wagon. A bugle sounded. The firing ceased and a lieutenant came forward with his helmet placed on the muzzle of a raised musket. 'Surrender!' he shouted.

Nel, on his brown horse, its ears flopping, galloped nearer. 'For God's sake, surrender, Johannes!' he cried. 'You cannot fight.'

Johannes fired. He was muttering to himself. The soldiers began to fire again. A bullet knocked Johannes' gun from his hands. His wife gave him another. It all seemed to be taking so long. Kaspar felt as if it had been going on forever, as if he had stood forever watching Johannes fighting. He felt nothing but surprise at the incredible slowness with which time passed.

Johannes knew it was hopeless. He could not even stave off the end; he could only fight and wait till it came to him. Martha, whom all through this trouble he had forgotten, and his son, stood by him. He had forgotten them, their lives and future, and now they were fighting at his side. He took the gun his wife had reloaded. Kaspar had been right when he had told him to hurry and not to take a wagon. What he had thought, what they all had thought — that up here they were beyond the Law — was wrong. They had been beyond it at one time, but that had been long ago. It had stretched out its hand towards them. Those red coats were the Law. There was no more freedom. Men could no longer live out their lives according to their convictions and the Word of God. As he raised his gun, he felt something hit him. It did not hurt, not sharply, but felt as if he had been struck with a wooden maul. A dull, strong blow which numbed him. His blood ran hotly over him, spilling out where he was broken. Then it turned cold and sticky. Martha bent over him. She was trying to staunch the wound, but it was no good.

'I am finished,' he said. 'Ride, Kaspar!' he shouted, pulling himself up by the spoke of the wagon-wheel. 'Break out while there is time!' There was another volley. Martha and the boy went down. Kaspar began to bandage Martha, but she shook him off.

'Do what Johannes told you. Ride! Get away and tell our people how the Bezuidenhouts were slain,' she said.

He undid the reins and, waiting till the soldiers were nearer, sprang onto his horse's back. Miraculously, no bullet had hit him. Bullets had passed all round him; they were embedded in the wood of the wagon, but neither he nor Tigernek had been touched. They had forgotten about him. He had not fired and the horse had stood hidden behind the wagon tent. Kaspar rode for the nearest soldier. For a second the horse hesitated as he came up to him. But his master's heels and hand on the bridle forced him forward. He swung a little to the left. The next soldier held out his musket like a rail to stop him. Tigernek jumped. From all round the mounted troops galloped towards him, masking him from the fire of the others.

The ground was open in front of him. He was free. He had escaped again. But if it went on, one day he would not escape. And what had it all been for? What had happened? Another soldier was dead: some harmless countryman. Johannes was dead, Martha and the boy wounded, and the others taken. Was the project they had conceived after all so great that men should die for it? Was anything so great that men should die for it?

He felt his strength going. It was a long time since he had eaten, and his fever was coming back. Dropping the rein, he clung to the saddle. Tigernek must get him through. The horse was galloping as though he understood. They crossed the river; they went up mountain-sides; they swung through little paths so narrow that the bush caught at him. He could feel the thorns take hold and tear out of his clothes and flesh. Where was the horse taking him? He had lost all sense of direction and of time. All he could do was to hold on. He was racing at the Cape: he was racing at Rudolf's: Coenraad's big chestnut was behind him. He was escaping from the dragoons with Jeffries; they were galloping knee to knee. He heard Jeffries' voice call to him. He could see his horse's neck black with sweat and white with curds of foam. He could hear him breathing heavily, labouring as he topped each rise. It was dusk, the country seemed familiar, but he had seen so much of this country that it was all familiar. The horse slowed down. There were voices that he knew. Where was he? To whom did the voices belong?

'It is Kaspar!' He fell forward on the horse, his fingers clutched its mane. He kicked his feet free and rolled onto the ground. The horse nuzzled him, its breath coming in great gasps. He was at Leendert's. Leendert and Adam were beside him.

'I must not stay here,' he said. 'Get me away, Leendert, I will bring trouble on you.' He tried to get up. Everything swam: he could see nothing but black marks, each mark surrounded by a luminous white circle that moved, merging into the next. He must get on. 'Give me another horse,' he said, 'and I will ride on.'

Kaspar's fever blotted out everything. Vaguely he remembered Tanta Sybilla, Leendert, Frans, and Adam about him, and that it was very dark. He had memories of its being lighter at intervals and then of its being dark again: memories of trying to eat and vomiting: of being incredibly hungry and unable to hold anything down, of a taste like fur in his mouth, and of sweating interminably. He knew time was passing; that while it passed things were happening. He had dreams, hallucinations of trying to get up and of falling back or being pushed back into his bed; of drinking concoctions that Adam brought him. He could not understand his body failing him. It was as though something disgraceful had happened. He had not been like this when he had been ill with the fever in the north. Then he had still kept his consciousness and been able to perform some of his duties.

But all this came afterwards. At first there was nothing in his mind, nothing in his body. He was suspended, alterately sweating and shivering, between life and death. An hour seemed like a day sometimes; at others, two, three, four, and five days passed like an hour. Every bone and muscle ached. After the first long bout, the illness became more intermittent. He thought he was getting better, but soon came to know that these were just intervals. A feeling of uneasiness would be followed by violent shivering, and when that passed, a throbbing fever swelled his head till he wanted to cry out.

Then delirium: terrors like those he had experienced as a child at night. He was being hunted; Aletta was being killed by Kaffirs and he could do nothing. He would begin to fall. There was no bed, nothing between him and the infinite space through which he fell, and he would clutch at the walls, at the bed, straining onto them till his finger-joints cracked. By now he knew that he was hidden in a cave. His fears changed. He thought he saw soldiers at the entrance. Each time anyone came to him, he thought they were soldiers. He had thought himself brave. Now he knew bravery was allied to health: that a sick man could not be brave. He knew nothing but terror and longed to become unconscious again. He kept watching the shadows on the walls. They moved, they took on the shapes of men and beasts threatening him. Unashamedly and often, he wept, and felt relief from his tears.

At last he was better. He asked Tanta Sybilla for a mirror. She brought it, and he was appalled at the change. Some strange trick had been played on him. The face he looked at was that of an old man. His eyes, twice their normal size, were sunk in their sockets. His hair was long and looked lifeless like tow, like the unravelled strands of a dirty rope. His teeth were yellow between mauve lips, and his body was gone: it was just a skeleton covered with loose skin. The muscles that he had been so proud of had disappeared.

'How long have I been ill?' he asked.

'A long time, Kaspar.' Tanta Sybilla's face was sad, drawn by anxiety. They had taken a great risk nursing Kaspar, but what else could they have done?

'Are my people safe?' he asked. This tortured him: the knowledge that his servants might have suffered.

'They have gone to Coenraad's with your horse, and the other wagons have gone home. There is nothing here to show that you are near. Tigernek was well known.'

Kaspar felt his eyes fill with tears at the thought of his horse being gone.

'And Letta?' he asked.

'Letta is well. I have tried to send her news, but it is hard. She is watched. They think to take you with her. Stephanie is married to Jacobus van Zyl,' she went on. 'He looks like a meerkat.'

'I met him,' Kaspar said.

He was the man who had wanted to buy Tigernek, who had said he looked as if he would win races.

'We thought you would die,' his aunt said. 'Adam saved you with medicines from the Bush. He went away to his own land for them, running day and night.'

'And the rebellion?' Kaspar asked. 'What happened?'

'All are taken, Kaspar. All. And they are being tried.'

That, too, seemed very distant. That abortive little rebellion — the effort, the lives, and the time; all wasted.

'I must get strong,' Kaspar said. 'I must get Letta away. Bring me paper and an ink-horn. I will write.'

He was so weak that writing came hard. The letters looked strange, like those formed by a child; the lines uneven.

'I am alive,' he wrote, 'and will come for you as soon as I am strong. Be ready. Kaspar.'

The effort of writing had exhausted him. He sank back. He would fetch her when he was strong. But how long would it take? From now on only one thing mattered — to regain his strength. The others were taken: he was alive. Coenraad was right: he was lucky.

CHAPTER XXVIII

PAULUS

I

ALETTA stood at the door throwing mealies to the chickens that ran with spread wings towards her. There were a great number of chickens: cockerels and pullets of every colour, old hens, some cocks, and one hen with a late brood as yet only partially feathered.

The day was hot and cloudless. The horses stood listless, head to tail under the dusty trees, flicking long tails at the flies that plagued them. The land was parched under the hot sun and cracked open. It was the kind of day that made children cry and refuse their food.

The poultry had been Tanta Maria's pride, and many of them she had named. There was Mary Magdalene, a wicked speckled hen that was suspected of eating eggs, though she had never been caught in the act. There was Abraham, the father of a multitude; and Paulus, a two-year-old cock that was useless, whom no pullet could seduce. Aletta threw more mealies, scattering the grains in wide arcs and calling to the birds. Klein Kattie clung to her skirt. She was worried about Klein Kattie. The child was sick.

Aletta was terrified about the ordeal of tomorrow. They will never hang them, she thought. It is just to make a show.

But she must go. Everyone had to go. Kattie must eat.
She tried to think of something that would tempt her. Broth
made of chicken with rice might tempt her. She refused
to think of tomorrow and concentrated on the poultry at
her feet. Paulus, the useless cock, was eating fast, filling his
crop without regard for the hens. She would have him
killed. Kattie should have the white meat from his breast
and soup from his flesh. With Maria dead she was responsible
for Kattie. Catching the child up in her arms, she went in.

It was not true — they could not hang those men! Why
she knew them! They had all eaten at the house, at this
very table. Their horses had been tied to the bar beneath
the peach trees. The two Bothmas and old Kruger, de Klerk
and Faber. They had done wrong, but they had surrendered
themselves. Wasn't the death of Johannes enough? Could
not the Law be satisfied with that? It was not possible. Ru
dolf did not think it possible. 'They are doing this to frighten
us,' he said.

Rudolf knew that Aletta was thinking of Kaspar. He was
safe; Tanta Sybilla had hidden him in a cavern. But how
long would he be safe? He was ill and she could not go to
him. There were spies all round them. She could neither
go nor write. She had not seen him since the day the com
mando had passed. The only news she had had was that
which Adam had brought her: a letter saying that he would
come when he was strong. But how was he? And now Kattie
was ailing. It was so hard to be everything to everybody —
a mother to Klein Kattie who was not her child, a daughter
to Rudolf who was not her father, a wife to Kaspar who was
not her husband. She felt herself torn in pieces. There were
so many claims on her. There were so many duties, and to
do one thing right she had to do others wrong. In the past
months since Kaspar had been separated from her, she had
cried so much that she could cry no more. And it was no
good crying. She wondered what would happen. By to
morrow night it would be over. How would she bear seeing

t? It might be Kaspar's turn next. If they caught him, it would be Kaspar's turn. He said he was coming to her. He must be stopped. He must go to Coenraad's.

2

To Klein Kattie Paulus the cock was very beautiful. He was tall, with red hackles like a metal shawl on his neck, a green-and-purple chest, and a tail made of a hundred flowing cycles. Disdaining to walk, he strutted, not with the other chickens, but by himself in isolated grandeur. No cock crowed more loudly or clapped his wings with greater pride than Paulus. And he knew his name, coming when it was called in search of bread. Also — and this meant much to Kattie — he could be seen. Even a small child could look down at a great cock, could observe the beauty of his plumage, could look into his hard golden eyes, could see the arrangement of the scales on his strong legs, and take pleasure in his general brilliance as he walked alone in the sunshine. With cattle and horses it was different. With them she must look upward, and then saw little but their legs and bellies. Cows to Kattie were udders above which their bodies mounted, disappearing into the sky. Oxen were cows without udders — an interesting but almost negligible difference. Horses were mostly legs, too, but their legs were longer. And with a tame horse one could stand beneath him as though he were a house. She had done this once with her father's horse. It had been raining and the water had run down his sides while she stood dry under the roof of his body.

Breaking away from Aletta, she went out. She wanted to watch the chickens. They had nearly finished eating and were hunting for scattered, hidden grains that had fallen behind stones, into cracks in the ground or among tufts of grass.

Sucking her finger, her head almost hidden by the big

kappie she wore, she stood looking at Paulus. What a beautiful bird he was! How she loved him! Ja, she loved him even better than her doll. He was her friend. He was a prince in disguise. A wicked fairy had changed him into a cock, which was why he was so different from the others. Why, she even knew the sound of his crow. It, too, was different, more jerky when it began, sweeter and higher when it ended. Nor was he one of those foolish cocks that, finding food, called upon the hens to come and eat it. On the contrary, he was a wise cock, taking what he found silently and alone, as she did herself. This was a firm bond between them.

And now he was going to be killed. Tanta Letta had told April to kill him. But it could not be true. No one could kill a fairy prince in disguise. It had been said to frighten her, to keep her good and quiet. It was like the stories of the Rooineks — the English who ate little girls. She nodded her head seriously. It was said that the English ate many little girls each day, and little boys, when they could not get girls.

She moved off to the shade of the big fig tree. Her doll Netta was there. Netta had behaved very badly and she told her she would leave her lying on her back in the cleft of a branch till the Rooineks came for her. Of course she had not meant it. She had only meant to frighten Netta and to punish her for being so wicked. How pleased Netta will be to see me! she thought.

She loved the big fig tree with its arching branches. It was like a house without walls; it was like a great forest full of wolves and wild beasts, but safe really and near home, so that if one frightened oneself one could reach safety in a moment. And there were so many fine things to be found under and near it. Everyone worked in its shade; there were odd bits of leather, pieces of iron, nails, a broken plough, and abandoned tools of all kinds. Standing on the root of the tree, she reached for Netta, and then it happened. April, the Kaffir, who did so much about the house,

came out with a throwing-kerrie in his hand. Kattie knew
the kerrie; it was cut from the base of a tree; she had
seen him make it, carving the knob and fining down the
haft till it fitted to his hand. She knew what he was going
to do with it. He was going to kill Paulus. He did not know
who Paulus was. She must tell him. She must tell Tanta
Letta. She must do something. Her mouth began to crumple
and quivered.

April looked about him, blinking in the strong sunlight,
and then raising his kerrie he threw it. It went spinning
through the air, turning over and over. Paulus fell. She
was too late now. She wanted to run, to cry out, but she
could not move. April caught him by the legs and came
towards her. Paulus was giving long screeches. His head
was turned up from his neck like a pipe on its stem. One
of his golden eyes had gone. Where it had been there was a
place that dripped blood. April picked up an axe that was
embedded in the block beside her and laid the cock's neck
on the block. Paulus raised his head from the notched wood.
Kattie covered her face with her hands. It was not true.
It was not happening. She stared from between fingers.
With one bare foot she rubbed the calf of her leg. Up and
down went her instep, rubbing, pressing, as if by pressing
she could make it stop. April's lips were parted in a grin.
The axe went up, was lowered as the bird moved, went
up once more. Kattie shut her eyes and clenched her hands.
There was a dull sound, a tremendous clapping of wings,
a cry from April. As she opened her eyes, Paulus, head-
less, flew straight towards her. Straight, as if he had been
flung, his breast dulled with blood, his great wings clapping,
he struck her. She fell beside him. His wings moved, his
legs twitched. The warm blood ran over her feet. She could
feel it hot, coming in spurts as it ran between her toes. The
front of her frock was splashed where he had struck her —
a red-brown stain already darkened round the edges.

Everything became very clear at that moment to Kattie.

Every crevice in the bark of the fig tree was outlined sharply; the wagon, with its disselboom lying at an angle from the tongue, its tip resting on a stone, was precise and clear. The shining pores of April's skin as he bent over her to pick up the still fluttering bird impressed her as a pattern. She put out her hand to touch his shoulder. The skin looked soft, like the inside of something, like the leather lining of a saddle wet with sweat. It was sleek and warm to her fingers, very pleasant to touch. And then, pulling up her frock so that she was naked, she hid everything from sight and began to cry, sobbing blindly into the blood.

Taking a thin strip of riempie from his belt, April put a slip knot round the dead bird's legs, making it fast below the hocks, and tied it to a branch. The blood dripped slowly. Nearly black, it coagulated into blunt points. The hackles on the cock's neck were ruffled and hung cold, awry. Paulus, the fairy prince, was dead.

3

Rudolf tried to smoke, but his hand shook so that he dropped his pipe. The sentence was terrible, and they were going to have to watch it being carried out. Both Bothmas, Theunis de Klerk, Faber, Hendrik Prinsloo, and Kruger were to be hanged. All but Kruger were to be buried under the gallows, but as a concession Kruger's friends were to be allowed to take possession of his body when he was dead. Marais was to be fastened to the gallows while the others hung, and after that, for the lesser offenders, banishment, and fines. Ach, God! what a thing to happen — that these brave men, friends, that he had lived his life among, should suffer thus. Surely the English could have been merciful. Surely at the last moment there would be a reprieve. And everyone was to watch: everyone; even the women and children. It was to be an example to their nation. It seemed to Rudolf that this example might be double-edged: that the memories of this would eat into the souls of the people and be passed on. That men should be killed fighting was inevitable, but that, having been mistaken, having acknowledged their fault and surrendered, they should be executed was beyond all belief, all possibility of understanding. It meant the end of everything. He would trek. He had talked of it to Aletta. She had said he could go with her and Kaspar. Soon, when tomorrow was over, he would collect his cattle and gear. There were some monies owing him that he would call in, and then they would leave this place. Ja, he would leave the graves of his wife and children. Maria would wish it. But somehow he must get through tomorrow and the time between now and tomorrow.

He looked back on his life. He had been happy and had not known it. Happiness was nothing. It was what you were when you were not unhappy. It was not release or achievement — it was something that came after you had made a fine shot, or sat in the veld listening to the murmur of your Kaffirs, or lived peacefully with your wife and children at home. Happiness was peace, and it made no difference who ruled. He had been happy under the English. And would a change of government stop the locusts coming? Or make the sheep bear more wool? Or the wheat have bigger ears? Nee. That was what men said, but it was not so.

Magtig, he had been happy innumerable times. There had been great spaces of happiness in his life — with his wife, with his children. He thought of hunting trips, of the feel of a young horse under him, of the pleasure of seeing one hound outdistance the rest and pull down a wounded buck; and yet at ordinary times these were only remembered dimly, while danger and disaster stood out. One learned through pain, therefore pain was remembered. A young ox learned his name by having it whipped into him, and it was perhaps thus that men learned the power of God. But young folks thought happiness something they could capture and keep like a tame meerkat in a cage. To them it was always beyond:

if they could have that woman or this horse; if they had
better farm with more water or better grazing; if they wen
on. Ja, their answer to everything was to inspan and to trek
but this was no answer. He was going to trek himself, bu
his heart was not in it. His heart was here, where he lived
Go on, yes. Men must go on, and women; but it was as eas
to leave happiness behind as to find it in front. That wa
what he was going to do, and strangely often one's happines
and unhappiness lay in the same place.

Before God, no man had gone farther than he; no ma
had been more ready to live, even if it killed him, and it ha
not killed him. He was like an old riem, worn in places, bu
still strong in his purpose and wise. It made him sad to thin
of his sudden wisdom. The serpent had come, calling himsel
Freedom, and he had eaten the bitter fruit of experience
His eyes were indeed opened now, and he knew good an
evil; knew that men were as beasts, tearing at each othe
while they yet lived, seeking carrion like vultures, destroyin
the weak like lions, pursuing the slow like leopards.

All this was in his head and heavy on his heart, for ma
was without option, as likely to choose the bad as the good
more able to kill than to procreate, and as willing. Of a
beasts surely man was the most dangerous, the most im
placable. How else did he have mastery over the others.
And of all men a young Christian man was the worst; in th
pride of his young manhood as pointed as a sharpened spear
Youth was cruel under the drive of energy, and age crue
through lack of it. The young cared too much, the old to
little; and all men, young or old, were in fear of something
of illness, of age, of impotence, of penury, of death. Yet al
men died, some ill, some well, according to their natures
plan how they would, they died.

What could he think of now but death, with the deaths
of tomorrow upon him? Perhaps he had not thought of it
enough before. With the deaths of his children, his wives
he had prayed much and thought little, comforting himsel

with the thought that he would join them. The Lord had given, the Lord had taken away. But the Lord was not taking those men tomorrow. Man was taking them. He heard the gallows was already up, that an English predikant was there to administer the last rites, and that great numbers of troops were camped, waiting. The doomed men were waiting also. Everybody was waiting. Till it was over, no work would be done on the Border. Everywhere, in each little house, the people must be sitting as he sat, thinking, not daring to go out.

On a corner of the stoep, where the thatch met the ridge, he saw a lizard dart at a spider. It swallowed the spider and remained still, opening and closing its mouth. The spider had lived on flies. At any moment something, a chicken or a cat or some other beast, might kill the spider.

He fetched the Bible. 'Letta!' he called. 'Come, I will read you from the Book.' He read till his eyes were sore and the light failed, and all the time, as though they were written on the pages, he saw the names of the men who were to die. Stephanus Bothma, Carel Bothma, Kruger, Cornelis Faber, Hendrik Prinsloo, Theunis de Klerk. Where the tree falleth there shall it be.... There is a day for all things, a day for rejoicing and a day for mourning.... 'Let us pray for them, Letta.'

They knelt down. Kattie knelt between them. They were weeping. Kattie had never seen a man cry. She cried, too, as if her heart would break. Her cock was dead.

4

The gallows was up — screwed, bolted, and fast. Mr. Foster rubbed his hands on his trousers. It was a good job — no mistake about that. And it had to be to carry five men — a thousand pounds of men, live weight. It would have been six, but Kruger's sentence had been commuted to transportation for life. 'Bloody rebels, that's what they are,' he said to his servant. 'Bloody rebels.' Now he could eat. Everything was ready. It was lucky he had brought enough timber with him from George. He began to think of what he would do with it afterwards. He hated to cut good timber. He wished he had brought more rope. He had brought only enough for one, but there was more here and it looked good enough — not new like his, but in good order and undamaged by ants.

He went past the horse lines, the tents, the cooking-fires, where an ox was being flayed. No soldier looked up or spoke to him. 'Bastards!' he muttered. 'What have they to be so grand about?' He hated the military. His camp was apart from them on the little knoll. Whatever they thought of him, he was a free man, able to come and go. He turned to- wards the tents and spat. And he drew officer's rations while he was with the army. He began to think of his steak. He would have it grilled over the embers, and if it wasn't right that boy would be sorry. To hang five men all at once! He wondered if it had ever been done before. He picked up the piece of board on which he had made his calculations. He had given them two feet each; a mite less with the mortice into the uprights, but near enough; and if their shoulders touched, what of it?

He got up as Mr. Herold came: the Reverend Mr. Herold, the parson. He was walking with his head sunk between his shoulders, his hands clasped behind his back.

'Good-evening, Mr. Foster,' he said. 'I have come to see you. I thought' — he hesitated — 'that we might pray together.' His hands came from behind his back. He held a small black book. 'I have just left the prisoners. Poor men, they are repentant. They are ready to go.'

So he was to pray with the parson! What about? Mr. Foster lowered his eyes. He was amused. He had hanged plenty of men — black, white, brown — and never prayed before. No, by God, and never lost sleep over it either. But if the parson wanted him to pray, then he would pray. They were rebels, were they not? They had rebelled against His Majesty King George the Third. They had thought that they could drive the English into the sea, but they did not know England. Mr. Foster was very proud of being an Englishman. Why, the fools did not even know that Boney was smashed.

'Yes, Mr. Herold,' he said.

'Then let us pray.' Mr. Herold knelt in the dust, holding his hat in front of him against his chest.

Mr. Herold's prayers were as much for himself as for the prisoners and Foster. He was a young man, devout, enthusiastic, and new to such things as hangings. He had come to the Cape for his health, and he wondered how he would stand what he had to see. It was justice; he knew that. The trial had been fair. These men were being hanged on the evidence of forty-seven witnesses. Their death on the gallows would be a warning. But would he have the strength? Only God could give it to him — not only to witness their deaths, but to give them comfort, to console them, to prepare them to meet their Maker. 'God give me strength,' he prayed.

And he was not the only one. Right through the camp the same feeling permeated. Stockenstroom, Cuyler, Nel; Veld Kornets, Heemraded, everyone was overcome by this terror. It hung like a cloud over them all, from colonel to drummer boy; a feeling that justice was being done, but that somehow justice had failed; that the letter of justice was not the spirit; that these men, repentant and calm, who were accepting their fate, had been betrayed by Fate. They had not known what they did. They had been mad, unthinking. And now, Mr. Herold looked at his watch; in a few hours they must pay the price of their ignorance and prejudice. And so must those who witnessed it. This was something that would be graven on the hearts of all, English and Boer alike. It would influence their lives, make them harder and more unforgiving: make them, because of what they had seen, more cruel.

He must see the prisoners again. He must prepare them further. He must assist them at their end, and when it was over he must bury them. Ashes to ashes, dust to dust. Good Christian men, honest and upright, who had been led by a madman into his own madness. God forgive them. God forgive all concerned.

At Colonel Cuyler's tent two soldiers held a small wizened Kaffir. Unable to stay alone, Mr. Herold came up to them.

Colonel Cuyler came out. 'What's this?' he asked. 'Where did you get this man?'

'He was walking about the camp.'

'Has he stolen anything?'

'He has stolen nothing. He was standing, looking.'

'Who are you?' Cuyler asked. 'What is your name?'

'I have many names, lord.' The old man wrapped his kaross more closely about him. 'I am called Little Cloud,' he said, 'and Little Flower, and Mamba, and Ringhals.'

'Where are you from? What do you do and why are you here?'

'I am from the north,' Ringhals said. 'I am a doctor, and I am here because I go where things come to pass. Ai, lord, I am as curious as a boy, and when I have seen the beginning, it is in my heart to see the end.'

'You saw the beginning?' Cuyler was interested.

'I saw the beginning. I saw the old Baas buried, and this is not the end. It is a new beginning whereby a small red thread of blood will be spun through the land, growing thicker and thicker.'

'Let him go,' Cuyler said. 'He is harmless.'

The soldiers dropped their hands. Ringhals did not go.

'Can I stay, lord?' he asked. 'I am small and old, harmless and as curious as a child.' He sat down and opened his kaross. 'See, lord, I am unarmed and beyond action.'

'Let him stay.' Cuyler went back to his tent.

Ringhals turned to Mr. Herold. 'You are a missionary,' he said.

Mr. Herold could not understand his words. 'What does he say?' he asked his servant.

'He says you are a missionary.'

He was not, but it was near enough to the truth. 'Tell him I am,' Mr. Herold said.

Ringhals nodded. 'We are brothers, then. Ai, brothers and searchers after truth.' His eyes began to sparkle. 'Something is about to happen here which will leave a mark upon the land ... and this is true of any place. At each place you outspan, lord, something of you is left in that place: the mark of your fire, black on the ground beneath the tree where you rested; the bones from the meat you ate; the excrement you voided. Ai, when a man has passed by, a place is no longer the same. He has set his mark upon it. For this reason also there are good places and bad, according to the thoughts and the acts of those who used them. Ai ... there are places which cause gladness or fear in the hearts of those who follow. So also is it with every man and woman that you come upon; every beast that you see takes something of you and leaves its mark upon you. Thus also is the life of a man written upon his face in little lines and the history of a land in its valleys and mountains.'

He got up. Mr. Herold had understood nothing.

'He said you were his brother,' his servant said.

'All men are brothers,' Mr. Herold answered.

'Will the master eat?' his servant said. 'All is prepared.' Of the other words Ringhals had spoken, he said nothing. He did not understand them. They were the vapourings of a wizard and beneath contempt. He was the Reverend Mr. Herold's servant — a Christian.

Mr. Herold turned. Everything was prepared: the gallows, the food. He looked for the old man. He would have liked to speak further to him, but he was gone.

5

Hendrik Prinsloo, Stephanus Bothma, Abraham Bothma, Cornelis Faber, and Theunis de Klerk were to be hanged and be buried beneath the gallows on which they hung. Frans Marais, the Austrian, was to be made fast by a rope round his neck to the gallows. Klopper Bronkhorst, van der Nest, Botha, Nel, van Dyk, and the others were to witness the execution from near-by: banishment, imprisonment, and fines were added to their punishment. And all people, without any exception whatsoever, were to be spectators of the execution. Having participated, in one way or another, in the inception of the rebellion against His Majesty's Government, they were to mark and attest to His Majesty's Government's reply: an executioner to destroy the bodies of the prisoners, a minister to save their souls, and hundreds of soldiers to see that both were done. And to this end — the end of British justice — were the farmers of Baviaan's River, Bruintjes Hooghte, and the Winterberg gathered, with their families and their dependants.

At Slagtersnek, where the oath against England had been taken, was it going to be redeemed.

The rolling country was a camp filled with the outspanned wagons of the Boers, with the transport of the military, with tents, with horses — the small rough horses of the Boers and the chargers of the troops. Standing alone, and separate from everything else, was the hangman's wagon, the one on which he had brought the implements of his trade from George. Herds of oxen grazed peacefully on the slopes. An English groom exercised three couple of foxhounds.

An officer's charger that reminded Aletta of Kaspar's horse was being groomed till it shone like brass. A squadron passed her. She had never seen horses so matched, coming four abreast; each was so like the next that they might have been full brothers. White gauntlets, jackboots, helmets, sabretaches, plumes and standards passed her. Files of in-

fantry, moving as though they were men of wood, marched
by. Their officers were slim-waisted boys whose faces were
red and peeling from the sun. It was an organised tumult
that would forever be painted in her mind, forever engraved upon her heart; a fantastic array of the might of the
nation which, having crushed Napoleon, could well have
spared five Boers. These soldiers should not be here. It
was not their country. Alone, any of them, more helpless
than a Boer child of ten, would have died in the veld. But
massed together, organised, with their transport, leaders,
servants, and equipment, they were able to crush the in-
habitants of the Border beneath their spurred heels, to tread
them under the ironshod hooves of their horses.

All the world was here. Drawn together by the command
of the Government, knitted into silence by the horror of the
moment, the people stood awkwardly behind the soldiers,
the three hundred military who had come to enforce order,
to lend by their blue, green, and scarlet-coated presence the
dignity of authority to an ignoble death.

Detachments of the Sixtieth Rifles in scarlet with blue
facings, of the Eighty-Third Foot in scarlet with yellow
facings, of artillery in blue with red facings, of the Cape
Regiment in green, stood at ease — a narrow, brilliant cord
separating the waiting Boers from the condemned. Above
the infantry towered the helmets and blue tunics of the
light dragoons; a panoply of gleaming bayonets, drawn
sabres, and trampling horse about a gallows. The hot
March sun blazed down on armed troops and unarmed
civilians alike, on the prisoners who stood in their shirts
with their necks bared, on Landdros Stockenstroom, on
Colonel Cuyler, on the Veld Kornets, on the black-robed
minister, on the executioner.

For days this had been expected, but no one yet believed
that it would happen. All waited for it to end. The rebellion
had been crushed. Men had been killed; a show of British
strength had been made. In God's name, surely enough was

done. It would go no further. The gallows was no more than a threat, a grim joke, to show what would happen if such events were repeated.

Aletta could see none of the soldiers' faces, only their wide red backs, the powdered ends of their pigtails, and their ears above their stiff collars. But the stolidity of their stiff backs hurt her. Soldiers were not men. Soldiers were beyond emotion, beyond humanity. They might joke and play; they might have mothers, wives, and sweethearts; but once they were buttoned and buckled into their equipment, they became a part of a composite engine of destruction. Just so many men in red, blue, or green who, acting as one, under orders, were immune from charity, secure from fear, and beyond appeal. It was they who had crushed the rebellion. It was they who had killed old Frederik and Johannes: they who would hunt down Kaspar as their foxhounds hunted a jackal.

She grasped Klein Kattie's hand more tightly and looked at the faces of those about her. Many of the women were crying. The men stood with hunched shoulders muttering to themselves, their hands were clenched. They were not used to being without guns. Big Joachim Joubert pulled out his pipe, lit it with trembling fingers, and then, feeling that he should not smoke on such an occasion, bent down to knock it out on a stone at his feet. He tried to smile at Aletta.

'I will stand in front of you,' he said, 'and then you need not see. Magtig, this is no thing for a maid to see.'

'Baie danke, meneer, but I wish to see. Ja, before God, I wish to see everything: to see all so that I never forget. You say this is not a thing for a maid to see, but I say that it is a thing that all should see. Ja, down to very children in arms. For if it comes to pass a seed will be sown, and it is for us, the women, to plant it in the hearts of our children: a little seed of hatred that will grow, watered by our tears, into a great tree.'

'You are foolish,' he said. 'Look at the soldiers. Look at

what has happened. They are too strong. We are but a handful.'

'A handful, meneer, but a free people, and it will be as I say. Nee, it will not happen in one year. It will not happen in two years. But in fifty, in a hundred, who can tell what will happen, meneer?'

'I do not understand women.' Joachim shrugged his shoulders. 'They were all against this rebellion. They did not care who ruled the land, and now that it has broken, they are all like you.'

'Ja, they are like me. And their children will be like me, and their children's children.'

Aletta was breathing hard. Till Joachim had spoken she had not known what was in her mind. The smell of the sweating crowd nauseated her. The blazing sunshine on the bright clothes of the soldiers and the glittering weapons dazzled her. None of this could be real. Surely she was dreaming it: it was a nightmare: Maria was not dead; Frederik was not dead; Stephanie not gone; Kaspar not a fugitive. But it was not a dream. It was all true. I am alone, she thought. Alone with Kattie and Rudolf. But when this was over, she would go to Kaspar. His letter was between her breasts. Each time she breathed she felt it. She pressed forward, leaning against the quarters of the horse in front of her. The footsoldiers were still coming; line upon line of them, like snakes, swinging into position on their markers. Magtig, she hated soldiers.

The Boers who had not joined in the revolt now wished that they had. These soldiers had no right in these parts. Their marching was a desecration of sacred ground: the ground that they had fought for and were ready to fight for again. Some who had been at the burial of Frederik remembered the words of the old witch doctor. He had foreseen this, and now they foresaw more than this. Ja, this day, this Saturday, this ninth day of March, was a day that would never be forgotten in the annals of their people. Already it was written in words of blood upon the veld. The yoke on their necks was too heavy, the strops about it too tight. Like oxen they were being throttled.

The form of the crowd changed. It surged forward, gasped, and moved back. Bugles were blowing, orders rapped out, metal clinked against metal. A horse, rendered unmanageable by the flies, sprang forward and was forced back, his mouth dripping blood over his bit. Red coats, blue, green, all stiffened. The backs of the men in front of Aletta were arched as they filled their chests with air. That was what they were taught to do — to die, to inflict death, to watch it being inflicted, with straight backs and puffed chests.

She could just see the prisoners standing on the scaffold. They had ropes round their necks. The hangman was arranging the knots below their ears. He worked precisely, conscientiously, cocking his head as he worked: a hangman: a man who murdered for the Law.

The predikant was intoning something from a book. Aletta could not hear the words and wondered if there was a special service for those condemned to death. The predikant looked like a small bird about to fly as the light breeze caught his cassock. The condemned men began to sing. That seemed the hardest of all, that standing with ropes round their necks they should sing to the glory of God. The sound of the hymn rose over the multitude of people. The song of five dead men, their voices harsh and cracked. It faltered and went on; when one voice broke, the others took it up, singing louder. All round her people sang, crying and choking back their tears. Colonel Cuyler, on his white horse, wept openly. The hymn ended in an awful silence. She saw Stephanus Bothma try to step forward. He could not because of the rope. He began to speak.

'Friends and brothers,' he said, 'be cautious what you do and meditate no revenge. Take example from our unfortunate fate. Do not let us die for nothing. We meant no wrong. We meant only to be free...'

There was a sign from Colonel Cuyler. The predikant dropped to his knees as the executioner withdrew the fall.

Aletta closed her eyes. In a minute it will be over; she prayed, 'Dear God, let me see nothing. Let it be over.' With her hands she felt for Kattie's face to cover it.

There was a dreadful cry. She opened her eyes as she was dragged forward. Everyone was shouting, crying, pushing past the soldiers, who beat at them with the flat of their swords, or held crossed muskets in their path. She found herself in the open square, Kattie still holding her hand. The ropes had broken. Only one man was hanged. Four were on their knees in front of Cuyler.

'Forgive them! Let them go!' the people shouted. 'It is a sign from God. They have been saved by God.'

'I can do nothing,' Cuyler said.

Officers reorganised their men, getting them into line and turning them about so that they forced the square open once more. Aletta heard Big Joachim say: 'They are sending for riems. The ropes are rotten. They will hang them with ox riems.' The men were nearly mad, and tried to fight the soldiers with their hands. Aletta saw one man knocked down by a blow from a gun-butt. The cavalry turned their horses and backed them into the surging crowd. Women screamed. A party of green-coated Hottentots, under a sergeant, came through the crowd. They were dragging riems. The body that hung from the gallows — Aletta could not see who it was — no longer twitched.

This time it was quick. The executioner no longer fiddled, but made his knots fast. The drop fell. A sigh like a wind swept through the people. There were no curses, no sobs, no audible prayer.

'Disperse . . . Go home.'

The troops began to form up. There were more orders. A burial party started to dig under the gallows. Aletta had seen them waiting in the beginning with spades and mattocks. So that was what they had been for. Rudolf, who had been separated from her when the ropes broke, found her again.

'Come,' he said, 'let us get out from this place. Aye, from this land.'

6

Once again Rudolf's place was full: this time with mourning and angry men. They ate in silence, cramming the bread and meat into their mouths, gulping down their coffee from Maria's tin beakers, furious at their hunger, at their desire to eat plentifully. Sorrow had made them hungry. Some ate with tears coursing down their cheeks — ate while they wept unashamedly, more ashamed of their hunger than their tears.

There were vacant places, not seats, but places in their hearts and in their community. Five men were dead and others were running on the mountains. There were since the morning five new widows in Baviaan's River and forty children fatherless. Even those who had had neither heart nor hand in the rising were filled with hate. Such a thing should not have been, or, having been, they should not have been forced to see it. God in His Heaven had looked down upon it and had caused the ropes to break as a sign. God in His Heaven was witness that their new hatred was not stillborn; that it would live while Boers rode; live as long as Boer women had tongues to talk to their children and the milk of hate in their breasts to suckle them. One day a leader would arise among them, and, if he failed, more leaders; ever more, till the yoke was thrown off. That the five had been tried by Dutchmen, had been condemned by Dutchmen according to the Roman-Dutch law of the land, meant nothing. These men, Stockenstroom, Nel, and Cloete had betrayed their people, had sold their birthright for a mess of pottage. Today at Slagtersnek the Boer people were one people.

Rudolf looked at Aletta as she served. Her face was

blank, smooth as a leaf. Her hair was as neat as ever, a yellow cap, parted in the middle, drawn back into a knot behind her ears. He felt as if he had never seen her before. He wished he could look into her eyes. But when he saw them, he knew no more. There was no life or meaning in them; they were wide open and unfocussed. They did not meet his, but stared through them, past him. A servant, his dark skin grey with fear — he had seen the hanging — came with more meat. In the dim light of the room the whites of his eyes shone like those of a frightened horse as he glanced sharply from side to side.

The meal was over. Coffee, ever more coffee. A little talk rose: little gusts of talk that swept in eddies like a wind and died flatly, as suddenly as they began. Men stopped talking to mutter into their beards. They moved their heavy legs, tightening their belts. The women who were eating now that the men had done, stooped to wipe the mouths of their children with their aprons or handkerchiefs drawn from their breasts. Two dogs began to fight over a bone. A child, upset by them as they sprang at each other, started to scream, refusing to be calmed. Round and round among the legs of the people the dogs fought, standing on their hind legs, their forelegs wrapped round each other like the arms of wrestlers, as they struggled, snarling, for a throat-hold. Other dogs joined. A twisting mass of snarling, black, white, and yellow hide rolled about the room, overturning more children and chairs. Men shouted and struck at the dogs with their sjamboks, each trying to strike some other man's dog; but before the fight could be stopped, Hans Schoeman's dog was dead. He lay twitching with his throat ripped out, while the house dogs stood with bloody fangs and slowly moving tails.

'So it is over.' Coenraad Buys stood in the door, his bulk filling it.

'You are mad to be here!' Rudolf said.

'Ja, I am mad to be here,' Coenraad said. 'Ja, I am mad.

Or am I sane? Do you think they would seek me here today? And where can a man be safer than among his enemies? If they seek, it will not be here... Besides, I am not alone. Coenraad Buys is never alone.'

Kaspar and van Ek followed him.

'You came too late, Coenraad.'

'Ja, I came too late. I could not cross the river. It rose again.' He bent over the dead dog.

'He was a good dog,' Hans Schoeman said.

Coenraad raised the dog's lips, pulling them open. 'He was a good dog,' he said, 'but he was old.' He straightened himself. 'I came to say that any who flee, or are in fear, are welcome, if they wish, to come to me. Those who do not know the road will find Kaffirs on the bank who await them. Let them tie a white lappie round their bridle hands.' He looked at them contemptuously. 'I was late, but you did not fail because I did not come. You failed because you were divided among yourselves, because, with the bodies of men and the arms of men, you had the hearts of women. Magtig,' he shouted, 'even Gaika doubted you. Now it will all have to be done again, but later. Later, when men have been bred, if men can be bred by women out of women.'

Aletta felt Kaspar's hand on her arm. His fingers closed on it.

'You should not have come, Kaspar,' she said.

'Do I look like Kaspar van der Berg?' he asked.

She looked at him. He did not look like Kaspar van der Berg. His beard had grown, it was loose and untidy. His hair was long and unkempt. His clothes were no longer those of a young farmer, but of a back veld Boer. He wore breyed leather small-clothes, an old jacket of blue duffel, and a large hat that came right over his face. He stooped like an old man and was thin. He looked ill. Her one idea was to get him away safely.

'Aren't you afraid?' she asked. 'Where is your horse?' The question was whispered quickly.

'I am always afraid. I had to see you, and where would it
be safer?'

'You may be recognised,' she said.

'By whom?' he asked. 'And there are no traitors here.
I had to see you,' he went on. 'You got my letter?'

Her hand went up to her breast.

'And you will come?'

She remembered his asking that before.

'You will come?' he repeated.

'I will come. I have always come. But you may have to
wait.' She was thinking of Rudolf and Kattie.

'I had to see you and to see this also. This is something
which one day must be paid for. By the living God,' he
said, 'one day or other we will exact the payment.'

She had never seen him like this. He spoke so softly that
she was afraid.

The people left unwillingly. They did not want to be
alone. But at last they were gone. Kaspar kissed Aletta
suddenly and slipped away with Coenraad and van Ek.
When there was no one left Aletta went out.

Things were the same. She felt they should not have
been the same, felt that if there was peace and quiet it
should have been a brooding, tragic peace; that the leaves of
the trees should have hung with their tips pointing directly
down; that the shadows under the great fig tree should have
been black; that the birds of the air should have sat silent
with folded wings; that the sun itself, instead of shining
brightly, should have been hidden behind dark, rolling
clouds.

After such things places should look different, but they
did not. Rudolf's house looked as it had always looked. It
was as it always had been. She wondered what Rudolf had
hoped for as he made this place; what he had prayed for,
worked for, and to what end. That his two wives and their
children should lie buried on the kopje behind the shining
foliage of the fig tree? That his seed should be scattered —

Stephanie married to an alien traitor and Kattie be left to him alone of them all?

In the open space in front of the house poultry picked for insects, the hens following the cock as he called to them. With a stiff wing trailing in the dust he circled the hens. With a swift run he trod them under him: a young cock full of fire, his brilliant plumage a metallic cloak about him. A flock of orange finks flew past her to the open lands. By the house the flowers were bent down, heavy with bees. Everything was as she always remembered it. Nothing was changed. But soon it would be. Rudolf had said they were to go. The place would stand empty, with gaping windows. Wild grass would grow in front of the house; the peach trees would be unpruned, the water-furrow would be empty.

Stripped of furniture, of domestic beasts and fowls, Rudolf's would lie open: a little ruin, all that was left of a great dream: another place of memory, another abandoned home, another house where riding men would pause no more.

7

Rudolf rode over his farm. He was bidding it farewell. Each day he did this, hoping in his heart to find some reason for not going, trying to plan a way to remain, yet knowing that there was no way. He rode slowly towards the river. To his right and left were the lands that he had wrested from the bush; year after year he had done this, clearing a piece at a time, attacking the thorny trees with pick and axe, with fire and with plough. For this he had driven his Hottentots, to this end his long red spans had worked, dragging away the felled trees and turning up the fat, dark soil, that he and his folk might live. It was an achievement. It was the work of a man to make this where there had been nothing; to set himself, with his meagre equipment, against Nature; to combat the encroachments of wild beasts and wild men; to set himself alone against flood, storm, and drought; against the diseases of man and beast; against accident; against insects; against the tares and weeds. Turning in his saddle, he looked back at his home. It stood, thick-set and squat: a strong place, cool in hot weather, warm in cold, well able to withstand attack; and he had made it. He took off his wide felt hat and sat very still on his horse, wheeling it so that he could look squarely back, and, replacing his hat, he rode on.

Before God, he had been no trek Boer who perched lightly on the soil, hunting, and scratching at its surface. No; he was a man who placed his foot heavily on the ground so that it should bear his spoor forever. He had been young when he came; now he was old. All round him the heads of the Kaffir corn, both red and white, were bent with the weight of the grain they carried and the sucreit, the sweet reed millet, that was as sweet as sugar cane to chew, had turned right over as candles do in great heat. Pumpkins, as large as a man could span between his arms, their haulms dead, lay scattered thickly on the dry red soil, and the cobs of the mealies, very long and thick, hung, head downward, in their dry husks, waiting to be reaped.

The summer's work was done. Yearling calves were weaned and many cows had taken the bull again. Crops, planted, had grown, fruited, and died. As he rode, birds rose from the Kaffir corn, and some guinea fowl, clinging to the ground like lice, ran, calling, between the stems. It was all for nothing. He would never reap the crops. In the distance he saw vultures. Something was sick or dead. He rode towards them.

8

Behind a thick clump of karee boom a Kaffir squatted motionless; he did not even trouble to wipe the flies from his eyelids. Naked and greased, he waited, watching a cow that lay dead a few paces from him. She was dead, slaughtered by the man who sat so placidly watching her. Not an hour ago she had been grazing; a quick slash as she ran from him had hamstrung her. Another gash with his spear in her throat, and she had fallen, her life-blood pouring out a thick purple flood into the ground. The flies on the Kaffir's eyelids divided their time between the dead cow and his face. On the trees about him vultures were perched, and more kept coming. Looking at them, he smiled. These were the messengers of death, accompanying equally the warrior and the cow on their last journey. They watched death with their heads sunk, like old men, into their shoulders. Sometimes they waited for death, sometimes they anticipated it, attacking the eyes and softer parts of their prey while it yet lived.

As he watched, a vulture, bolder than the rest, left the branch where it had been sitting and landed with outspread wings beside the cow. A moment later the others followed it. More fell, like stones, out of the sky, arresting their fall suddenly with wide-stretched, quivering pinions. The Kaffir could smell them as they fought with each other; rank as rotten meat, their hooked beaks covered with blood, their naked necks spattered, they pulled at the cow, tearing out her eyes, attacking her udder and entrails, pulling them out like pale blue snakes from her belly. Driving their heads into the emptiness, dragging and pulling, disappearing even into the cavity of her bowels. A nearly born calf that still moved was dragged out and eaten, its soft skin offering no resistance to their beaks.

The Kaffir heard the sound of a cantering horse. The vultures had fulfilled their purpose. The muscles under his skin ran, flowed like water, rippling, bunching, and dissolving. His fingers tightened round the spear he held. His eyes almost disappeared between his eyelids. With a wet, pink tongue he moistened his thick lips, and as the horse pulled up he sprang out. Without pausing, his hand went back, and before Rudolf could raise his gun the assegai was flung.

9

When April brought Aletta the news of Rudolf's death, it came as a sudden shock, like a blow between the eyes, and then it was over, accepted like a blow which had been dealt. Her mind, evading the personal issues, fastened on the practical implications. His body must be got in and buried. She must plan to leave the farm at once. She was even astonished that she felt so little. Rudolf had ridden out after he had eaten the food she had prepared. She would prepare no more food for him; he had been killed.

She got into the cart beside April. 'Where is he?' she asked.

'Beyond the mealie lands by the little spruit.'

Two other Hottentots clung to the back of the cart. They were all armed and the dogs ran beside it. She held Kattie between her knees; she dared not leave her. What more could happen now? Only that Kaspar should be ill again: that he should die or be captured.

She drove quickly, the horses cantering on the rough road between the tall stalks of the mealies.

'There,' April pointed, 'is where he lies.'

The Hottentots jumped down and began to search the bush. April tied the horses and followed her. 'He has moved,' he said.

The vultures by the dead cow turned their heads to look at them and rose slowly, running a few steps clumsily to get the air under their wings.

Rudolf was not dead.

Aletta ran forward. Klein Kattie, clutching at her skirt, fell whimpering on the ground.

Rudolf opened his eyes. 'A Kaffir,' he said. 'He wanted my gun.' His chest was pierced by an assegai.

Aletta looked at his mouth. There was no blood on it. His lungs were not touched.

'Come, April,' she called. Together they pulled out the

spear. The others came up. 'What did you find?' she asked.

'Nothing,' they said. 'There was only one man. He killed the cow and waited by it.'

Rudolf had been caught by a kill like a lion. They carried him to the cart. He must not die. No one else must die. Aletta felt strong enough to arrest. Rudolf must live. She would take him and Kattie with her to Kaspar.

CHAPTER XXIX

ALL AFRICA

I

KLEIN KATTIE'S world was crumbling round her. Her father had been hurt. This she understood; she had often been hurt herself. But other things were happening: surprising things. Objects that she had thought fixed, round which her life revolved, were being moved. Things were being put into boxes, thrown away, sorted out. That it all had something to do with her father's wound and the recent events was clear. A world in which Paulus could be killed and eaten was no longer the same world. But how and why? Paulus, her father, the milling crowd at what they called the execution, and the soldiers were all one in her mind. It was undoubtedly the fault of the English, and no one, not even Tanta Letta, understood what she had felt for Paulus.

And she was hurt by the fact that her aunt devoted so little time to her.

'What is happening, Tanta Letta?' she asked.

'We are going, Kattie.'

Going . . . Kattie did not understand what her aunt meant. Where could they go? Things were being loaded on the wagons: all sorts of things; things that had been in the house

— chairs, tables, beds, crockery. They looked very strange on the wagons, quite different from the way they had looked in the house.

'Where are we going?' she asked again. There was something very disturbing about this matter.

'We are going to find Kaspar, Kattie. We are going to find your Uncle Kaspar . . .'

'And then are we coming back?'

'We are never coming back.'

They were going to find Uncle Kaspar and were never coming back. Kattie had never been anywhere and not come back. She had been to many places — to her Uncle Frederik's, to her Uncle Leendert's, to . . . oh, so many places on visits and picnics. But they had always come back.

She walked into the house, disconsolately going from one room to the other. She went onto the back stoep. She went under the big fig tree, to the anvil, and the work-place. The anvil was gone, but there was the mark in the ground, the hole where it had stood. She went, her doll held by one arm, its legs trailing in the dust, to sit by the peach trees in front of the house. This was her world, a world where the trees and the stones and the plants all had names; her play-world that was so real; and to each thing, to each place, she told good-bye. 'I am going with Tanta Letta to find Uncle Kaspar,' she said. Under the fig tree there were still a few feathers, bright gold hackles, from the neck of Paulus. Kattie picked them up, fitting them together in her hand like a posy, and began to cry.

The wagons loomed very large above her, larger than she had ever seen them, packed high with unaccustomed gear: the tall things on the outsides against the rails, holding smaller things firmly wedged between them. The heavy stuff — cases, wagon-boxes, implements, and tools — were low in the bed of the wagon to keep it from overturning; and the light things — chairs, packed seat to seat, one upside down upon the other, and covered by a feather mattress —

lay on the top. Strangely shaped, like humped and crippled elephants, the wagons, their loads tied with riems, stood waiting, black against the green sky of evening. Stars began to pierce the green sky. First one or two only, then more till the sky was bespattered with stars that grew brighter as it darkened, and the wagon was black in the starlight.

Nobody put her to bed. She felt very small against the great piled wagons. The dogs came and went uneasily, pushing their heads under her arms, licking her tears, and wandered in circles about the wagons and the house.

Rudolf's place had become a camp. The servants sat by their fires. Aletta came out. She picked Kattie up and put her down again; then picked her up again and laid her on the bed in the first wagon. Kattie was better there than in the almost dismantled house while she saw to the poultry. Lying on the bed Kattie looked at the stars between the black folds of the tent. Lanterns moved, chickens screeched as they were caught and put into crates and baskets. They had to be caught, perched on the walls and roofs of the out-houses and in the branches of the trees at night. Kattie heard Aletta giving orders and the voices of the servants. From the kraals came the lowing of the beasts and the bleating of sheep.

Rudolf's place was being broken. The stars shone coldly upon it. The piled wagons resting on their great wheels stood still.

Aletta came out to fetch Kattie. It was the last night they would sleep in the house. Rudolf was now well enough to travel. She felt certain of that. And here he had nothing to do but think and worry. He kept remembering things, asking about this or that piece of furniture that Maria had loved. How was it packed? If he had been well, he would have packed it in such a fashion. Had the sheep been counted? Were the horses all collected?

Aletta went to look at Rudolf. He was asleep and breathing heavily. The candle-light fell softly; illuminating nothing in the room clearly, it showed only the white outline of the wall where the furniture had stood — clean, distorted patches in the gloom. The brass corners of the Bible, the last tinware on the shelves, and the barrel of Rudolf's gun hung on the wall, gleamed, picking up the flickering light and throwing it back in little fiery twinkles. Chairs, sideboard, table, and chest were gone. But she still saw them, shadowy forms, sunk, heavy-bellied, with the seated hours they had known.

Rudolf's house was already sterile, empty even of death; it was a shell picked clean. Of those who had lived there only she and Kattie remained. Stephanie had gone. Rudolf, sunk into lethargy, was only partly there. And the others were dead. Here, in the surroundings they had known, their death assumed a terrible finality. Only when a man's chair was empty did you realise that you had always thought of it as his chair; that in all your life you had never sat in it; that the riempie seat was shaped by his thousand down-sittings; that its arms were polished by the rubbing of his hands; that the hollow in the floor beneath it was worn away by his feet while he had sat there.

Aletta was frightened. She had put Klein Kattie to bed, and each sound, every rattle and creak that with her mind she could explain as rats, or as a mole snake in the room, made her heart beat faster. She lit more candles, but the shadows only danced more quickly. She heard Maria's soft steps, Rudolf's heavy tread, the sound of his voice as he read from the Bible, following each word with a thick finger, and the quick rustle as he turned the pages came to her ears as though they were real, clearer than when they were real, for then she had never noticed them. It was not the ghosts that frightened: those who died had loved her; but the fact that their presence was so vivid, that not being there, they were so much more there than they had been in life. By some trick of the mind, by something inside herself over which she had no control, she saw them and felt them about her. Since childhood her life had been lived here. There were now great blanks in her life; it was a sky without a sun, or a night sky empty of stars or moon. Again she saw Rudolf and Maria, saw the baby, saw old Frederik, saw the five men dancing on the gibbet. Strung taut by disaster to meet it, she now gave way. With her head pillowed on her arms, she wept. The tears, hot on her face, running down her cheeks, were salt in her mouth. It was all too much; too much had happened, and all the people she counted on were dead. She was left alone. The strong were dead; their strength had availed them nothing; and the weak were left.

Outside a jackal barked and the dogs began to bay with long, quivering howls. It was said that dogs howled when a man died. It was said that they knew. Was Rudolf going to die?

Going to the door, she unbolted it, looked out, and called the dogs in. It would be better with the dogs in the house, she thought. But they refused to settle down, and walked about, their nails rattling on the hard mud floor. They were as uneasy as she was herself: lying down and then getting up to thrust wet muzzles into her hand, or leaving her to search the corners with snuffling noses. What did the dogs know? What did they understand?

She fondled the rough ears of Bosboi, the biggest and most savage of them all. He stood up and, putting his paws on her shoulders, licked her face. But he kept raising his head to look towards the door. Suddenly he jumped away, almost upsetting her, and flung himself at the window growling. His hackles were up, his legs braced. The other dogs followed him, barking angrily. She opened the door for them and they poured out, leaping over each other, a tawny pack of hounds, the smallest higher than her knee. There might be thieving Bushmen about. They would have heard that Rudolf was wounded. But with the dogs she was not afraid. Leendert's dogs not long ago had killed a Bushman, tearing him to pieces. Going to the fireplace, she took down the gun and followed them as they streamed into the moonlight.

A moment later they were back, their tails between their legs. She bolted the door again. I ought to go to bed, she thought. But she could not. She went to look at Kattie. She was lying on her stomach, her head almost buried under the clothes. Beside her on the pillow the tortoiseshell cat slept, curled into a tight ball with a half-grown kitten beside her. Cats were not susceptible to death and sickness.

2

When they left Rudolf's, Coenraad, Kaspar, and van Ek rejoined their men. Kaspar was going back with Coenraad and then on to Klaarwater to make the final arrangements for his wedding with Aletta. The missionary had said he would marry them. That Kaspar was a murderer in the eyes of the law was, he said, something between him and God. He had not meant to kill. He was sorry he had killed. His heart was contrite. The missionary had lived too long among the Bastards not to know how accidents happened and the way things could befall. On his part, Kaspar only wanted rest — somewhere to lay his head. He was tired of running and fighting. He wanted solidity. Comfort he could wait for. It would be enough to have Aletta with him.

'I want a farm,' he said to van Ek. 'I want to make something instead of destroying.'

The old man smiled. 'I had a farm once,' he said.

Kaspar had never thought of Oom Christiaan as a farmer. He had thought of him having always been as he was — an old man, a philosopher in everything but his hatred for the English.

'For a while I had a farm against a mountain. It was a fine mountain, but I did not like it. There were leopards on it and it was too steep to graze my beasts. I came from the Platteland and was helpless before that mountain. I could do nothing with it, so I trekked. I understand that Joachim Johann Joubert has it now and that it will go to the man who marries his second daughter. She is a thin, bad-tempered girl with great whites to her eyes, like a horse that is going to bolt. Nee, I think Joachim will keep his daughter and his mountain for a great space unless an Englishman takes her. They know little of farms and like their women thin.'

'Ja, they like them thin,' Coenraad said. 'Whereas we like them fat and rich with plenty of bottom and substance.' He laughed. 'Ja, that is so. We are all like that but Kaspar, yet, before God, though Letta may be small, she has a big heart.'

The events of the past few days did not seem to have affected Coenraad's humour. He had played and lost, but today he was no worse off than he had been. That men had been hanged, banished, and fined meant little to him. If they could catch him they would hang him too.

Van Ek said nothing. He looked very old and shrivelled on his small dun horse. Suddenly he turned to Kaspar and said: 'I tell you, it is not the complexities of life that puzzle me, but its ultimate and terrible simplicity, the fact that life is not to be put off, that it cannot be turned this way or that, and that in the end possessions are nothing. Herds of cattle can do nothing for a sick man, nor her furniture for a woman in travail. Think of how easy it is to kill a man, how hard and slow to make one. Think of what you need in war; think well and without delusion. Search out your heart. First you want food and water that you may live, for this is the ultimate law, that the living should wish to go on living, and for food men would kill their mothers. Ai, for food they would eat their children. Being fed, you would sleep, and, having slept, you would lie with a woman. And all things that live are like this. In this matter your life or mine is the same as that of a Kaffir; the same as that of an elephant or a little meerkat. This is the simplicity — to be caught in the net of life, to have to live, to have to procreate, willing or unwilling; and, finally, having achieved much or little, to die as a dog dies; or a gemsbok or a slave. As to

God, there may be a God, but for myself I have never seen Him. I am old and near my end. Yet still I refuse to believe in what I have not seen, and so old am I that my mind refutes much of what I have seen, for if the eyes can see water in a mirage where there is none, is it not possible that they also see other things which are not there? And if there are sounds we hear, there may be others that we cannot.'

Coenraad clapped him on the shoulder. 'You are a philosopher,' he said.

'Ja, Coenraad, perhaps I am, and much good has it done me. I have thought and thought and in the end come back to where I started from. I have made a great circle, have learnt many things, and know nothing.'

They were silent. Coenraad's men marched behind them. They were thinking how good it would be to get back. But they spoke of what would have happened if they had come in time, and each, though he did not say it, was glad that they had not come in time. They had avoided a pitched battle with the English. The English had enough to do, with the Border Boers disturbed and wandering bands of Kaffirs raiding the frontier. They would leave them alone. They were alive and safe. Their leader's luck had not deserted him. They rode as they were accustomed to ride with Coenraad's broad back and the powerful quarters of his chestnut in front of them. They spoke of the story they had heard. It was said that Kasteel Hendrik, buried beneath the gallows, had raised his dead hand through the earth that covered him and pointed with outstretched fingers up to heaven.

'It is an omen,' Links said.

'Ja, an omen.' Kaptein Alexander nodded his head till the plume on his hat waved.

3

For Aletta the morning came at last. She felt happy. She was going to Kaspar. At last she was doing something definite. Once started there would be no turning back. She smiled at Rudolf on the kartel of the wagon. He looked comfortable, propped up by pillows and rolled in a jackal-skin kaross. Everything was ready. The cattle, the horses, the sheep with their herders, the poultry in slatted crates beneath the wagons.

'Kom... Springbok... Scotland... Witpentz... Boosveld... Donker. Loop... loop!'

The oxen lowered their heads. The trek-tous tightened. The long whips clapped, the heavy wagons rocked and began to roll.

Aletta stared back at the house. In a few minutes Rudolf's place, empty of life, would stand silent against the great wild fig tree. A house was more to a woman than to a man. The outside world was man's; a house was a place that he came back to and went forth from. But a house was a woman's life. Her happiness, her misery, and her work were enclosed between four walls. Men could live easily, if not in comfort, without dwellings, but for women it was something else. The wide world was too big and not personal enough for women. Aletta found herself thinking of a new house, the one Kaspar would build for her; the home where she would lie safely in his arms, where she would bear his sons. She looked at the peach trees where he had tied his horse that day, at the thatched roof and heavy shadows of the shed where he had made love to her, and her eyes filled with tears. It was a terrible thing to leave a house, to pack one's goods and abandon a home. The wagon was turning. She could feel the skamel move as the pole oxen leant against it. Holding on to the tent, she peered out for a last look at her home. A tree almost hid it, but she could still see it. More trees hid it. They were heavy with leaves. She could see the house no more. She had seen Rudolf's place for the last time. The house by the great wild fig tree was something that had been attempted, had succeeded, and then had failed.

Because of the English had this happened. Because of the English it was broken up. Because of them her people had suffered; the very core of her life shattered; her friends dead or spilt, like chaff scattered over the land, broken and exiled. As neatly as the top on an egg did this climax fit the events of the last few months. Her home was broken and she had left it. Her old life was done, and she was setting out to commence another. Only Kaspar remained: Kaspar, and the hopes that rose like birds in her breast. All this is behind me, she thought — a nightmare that I have lived through. Now it is over: I am going to Kaspar. And the world, because of Kaspar, was beautiful: so beautiful that she could not bear it. Africa called to her — the endless veld, the mountains, the kloofs and krantzes, the long yellow grass and flat-topped trees. There was no end to its beauty — no end to Africa. She would see it with Kaspar. The great wheels crashed over stones, grinding them beneath their iron tyres. Above her the sky was blue; in front of her were freedom and Kaspar.

Klein Kattie slept, curled up beside Rudolf on the kaross. She was dreaming of her cock. He was following her about as he always did, and then the English had come. They were English because they wore red coats. Many hundreds had come and had pursued him, driving him from her with shouts and cries till he had fallen exhausted on his side. Paulus was dead. He was dead because of the English. She woke and began to cry.

'I want Paulus, Tanta Letta! I want my Paulus.'

'Paulus is dead,' Aletta said.

'Ja, he is dead. The verdomde Engels killed him,' the child sobbed. 'Verdomde... verdomde... I hate them!'

4

For Rudolf this going was the end of life. He had thought of something different; thought that he would hold his grandchildren on his knee and end his life in peace. Instead, it had ended with a spear. He knew that he would not live long, and instead of being a help to Aletta he was a burden. He had never been a burden to anyone. It was useless her telling him what she owed him: that he had taken her in as a child. He had wished to be a help and had become a burden. That he was growing better did not help. There appeared to be no reason to grow better. He would never use his arm again. He would not even be able to shoot game for them to eat.

He thought of his house. Ruined, it still would endure. The things a man made were greater than the man who made them: mud and thatch and heaped stone were more durable than flesh and blood. Life had caught up with hope and passed it. He had life still, but little hope. The sword had proved mightier than the ploughshare and the mason's trowel. He had begun his final journey towards Maria. He would be glad when it was ended.

5

Kaspar was waiting for them, van Ek with him. They waited for the wagon to pull up out of the drift, to come level with them, and then swung their horses in behind it.

Kaspar smiled at Aletta.

'I have come,' she said, and looked down. From now on they had one life. She felt van Ek's eyes on her. 'I am glad you have come, Oom Christiaan. Are you going far with us?'

He did not answer, but patted his horse's neck.

'It is Uncle Kaspar,' Kattie said. She scrambled to the end of the wagon and tried to touch Tigernek's nose. Aletta had to hold her to keep her from falling.

'Give her to me,' Kaspar said. He leant forward and gathered her onto his saddle.

'Where are we going?' Aletta said.

'We are going north into the elephant country where I

hunted. I have received permission to live there while I hunt and trade. You will see terrible things, Letta, but they are less terrible than they seem, for they are open. We will be the first, but it is in my heart that more will come; that our folk will go north. Our Africa is a wide country, Letta. None know how wide.'

'Can I have a little horse?' Kattie said.

'Ja, you can have a horse.'

'Can it be white?'

'It can be white.' He held her to him.

6

The wagon was jacked up by a big marula tree; there was a stone behind the off-hind wheel and the axle shone smoothly where it had been rubbed by the bush. Aletta went up to it and touched it with her fingers. It was soft and cool, polished, silky. They had come far.

The yokes lay where they had fallen, cutting the bright curve of the trek chains. Kaspar was working, stripped to the waist. His body was very brown except where, wrinkling away from the trousers, it shone white above the heavy belt. He had grown strong on the trek.

The tyre he was shortening lay glowing in the heart of the big fire on the ground. Sometimes he moved it with an iron bar or piled more embers over it. And suddenly, calling April to help him, he picked it up. Each taking a side, with long tongs, they carried it to the wheel. Fitting it over the felloes they hammered at it, hitting alternate blows, sharp on the paling iron; the blows changed in tone as the tyre burnt into the smoking wood. Then they threw water on it. Hissing steam rose as the dry wood, expanding against the contracting metal, took up.

From where she stood, Aletta could see the bulge of the new weld. Till it was over, Kaspar had not looked up. Then, putting down his hammer, he came towards her.

'The wheel is good,' he said. 'Tomorrow we can go on.'

As they went together towards the place where she had laid out the food, Aletta heard the clatter of iron against iron. April was picking up the tools.

'While you worked today I have baked bread, and there is still some butter. Are you tired, Kaspar?' Aletta looked at him anxiously.

'No, Letta, I am never tired now, but I am hungry. Ach, God, how hungry I am!' Only now, when she spoke of it and he smelt the food, did he realise his hunger. Meat baked in the embers, fresh bread, butter, and strong coffee: his mouth watered. 'You are a good wife, Letta,' he said.

'Ja, I am a good wife.' She laughed.

Soon a cow would calve and they would have milk for their coffee. Two of the cows were very heavy. Aletta wondered which would calve first — Meisie, the one with the white legs, she thought. Already she was very swollen under the tail and her bag was hard.

'Often when they are like that it is a bull?' she said.

'Ja, often it is,' Kaspar answered. 'And listen' — he turned towards her — 'I will tell you something.'

'Ja?'

'If it's not a bull, it will be a heifer.' He laughed. 'Ja, it is like our child that is coming. If it is not a boy, then it will be a girl, and both are good. Sit down, and I will cut the meat.'

Van Ek watched them, smiling. 'Life is like the alphabet,' he said. 'The letters are arranged one after the other in their appointed fashion. B must follow A and C must follow B. Ja, so do events follow upon each other as surely as yoked oxen; pair by pair, span by span. Well and truly is a man yoked to the circumstances of his life and without option but to press on to the last outspan, and not till then will his neck be free of chafing. It takes many years, a lifetime, to make a man, and when it is finished, when he is made, he is ready to die.'

He took the meat Kaspar gave him, and went on: 'His birth and his death are lonely things that no man can arrest, and the sickness of his heart is also his burden that none can ease. Though his wife sit staring at him, beating her breast, he sees her not nor can she feel his sorrow. Heartache and pain are to each man his particular thing, secret; the worm in his bowels, the pain in his ear, his bruised heel, his broken heart, are beyond all aid. Only time, the waxing and the waning of the seasons, will help him. Let such a man, therefore, watch for the dawn, and when he has seen ten dawns, as many dawns as there are fingers to his hand, his pain will be less; let him watch the trees along the river: when they have flowered twice, it will be forgotten; or go to the gardens and see the Kaffir women spitting the seed into the ground as they sow, and then, when the crops are reaped, it will be gone; or to the kraals to see a great bull mounting on a cow, and when that cow calves, he will have forgotten; for while she carries her calf within her, much will have occurred.

'This is the wisdom of the aged — the only crop garnered of my years; for when it comes to pass, no sorrow is so great as we imagined it and no joy experienced equal to that which we expected; therefore, fear not and expect not, for the end is appointed and the pride of man without significance; at any time he may be cut down like a tree. To be born, to live with women, and to die: no more than this is the sum of a man's life; a small thing, one of importance only to himself. To everything there is a season, a time for peace and a time for war; and if two lie together, then they have warmth. How can one be warm alone? And if a man prevail against him that is alone, two shall withstand him' — he looked at Aletta — 'and a threefold cord is not quickly broken. It is in my heart that you will be happy, and make Kaspar happy. You are well mated.'

Poor Oom Christiaan! Had he ever been married? Aletta wondered. When he left them, they would miss him — a strange old man, filled with wisdom.

Kaspar thought of Africa: An endless land in which to wander. He saw it as a vision. He was the first, but his people would come after him and make its hills and plains their own. Magtig, this was a vast, slow land, and could not be hurried.

The wheel was mended: they would go on. While Boers had wheels they would go on, halting only to mend their broken wheels, pausing only to rest on the seventh day. From where they sat he saw this land as the heritage of his race, the land and the freedom to move, to trek.

Old Frederik's bitch pushed her nose into his hand. She had been in season. Next time she came on, he would put her to Witvoet. That was what Frederik had said, 'Breed from her in her second season.' He patted her. So much had happened because of her. Everything had happened because of her. And then suddenly it came to him. 'Magtig, Oom Christiaan,' he said. 'You were right. I have a name for her ... One has only to wait and a name comes.'

'What is it?' Aletta asked. 'What are you going to name her?'

'Geluk,' Kaspar said. 'Good luck ... without her I should never have dared to return to court you.'

'Geluk is a good name,' van Ek said.

They went on eating. Kaspar thought of van Ek's words. Perhaps life was like that — inexplicable: something to be worn like a coat till it was time to take it off.

Rudolf was reading his Bible. Kaspar got up. 'Read to us,' he said. He stood behind him, turning the pages for him as he read. But Aletta, though she listened, heard nothing. She only saw Kaspar, thought only of him and the child she would bear him.

The course of their life together was set. The journey was well begun; the bitch pup well named. She had forgotten the English who had sent them here, forgotten the price they had put upon Kaspar's head.

Kattie had a slight pain in her stomach and was tired of

travelling. Day after day it was the same. Kaspar was always with Tanta Letta. Her father and Oom Christiaan sat smoking and would not play. She wanted the big fig tree and her dolls. She wanted her mother and Paulus the cock. Her face puckered and she began to cry.

Aletta picked her up. She felt guilty. In her happiness she had neglected the child.

'I hate the English,' Kattie sobbed.

Van Ek took his pipe from his mouth and pointed to Klein Kattie. 'She hates,' he said. 'She will always hate. She will teach her children to hate because her tame cock is dead and she has a pain in her belly. Thus is a seed sown. Think back to old Frederik, also, and see how much wood has been kindled by how small a fire.'

'But you also hate the English, Oom Christiaan,' Kaspar said.

'Nee, I hated once, but I hate them no longer. They acted according to their lights and I according to mine. It is in my heart now that both were right: that in all matters there are two sides and little to choose between them.'

Aletta and Kaspar moved nearer to him.

'Listen well,' he said. 'Soon I am going to leave you. To the north there is a great waterfall that the Kaffirs call the Smoking Water. It is a marvel that I would see before I die. All new things that I have heard of I have gone to see, which is why I am homeless.'

He looked at the big marula under which they were camped. 'Seventy-four times since I was born has this tree fruited. Three times before have I passed this way and camped beside it. This is the last time, and yet I am not sad, for the tree is my friend. It is so I have lived, knowing men and women, beasts and trees, regarding them according to their merits, communing with them and watching them. Few but the English have hated me, and many will be sad when they hear that Oom Christiaan is gone. Tell them, when they speak of me, that I went free of hate. From the sole of the foot even unto the head there is no soundness in hatred. It wounds and bruises. It is a putrefying sore that cannot be closed, neither bound up nor mollified with ointment. Memory is the mother of disappointment, Kaspar. In memory the fruit is sweeter, the perfume stronger, the wine more heady. No woman is like the remembered woman: no place like our childhood's home. Listen to the talk of the old men to know this. Their loves, their hates, their battles, and their huntings were greater than ours. Their memories have grown like trees till they overshadow all things. So it was with their fathers before them. So it was with me in my hatred. So it will be with you in your dotage: and yet I can see no change. Elephants are still what they always were, though scarcer, perhaps; leopards still have spots and baboons continue to steal the mealies from the cultivated fields.

'Nee, there is no new thing, no new feeling. Fear, cold, anger, love, remain the same. A full belly still gives satisfaction; young men and maidens still lust after each other. It was thus that they were made and is fact beyond argument, no matter what the predikants may say. What folk seek is peace; and when they find it not, they pass on, not as whoremongers, but as children seeking comfort. You will find this in no book, Kaspar. It is contrary to the precepts of the Reformed Church, but nevertheless it is so. I am old, and this has come to me as I rode the veld, hunting and living my life alone. It is the sum of all that I know. It is the truth, Kaspar, and it has cost me much to obtain it. It is all that I have to give you, for I am without possessions.'

THE END

GLOSSARY OF SOUTH AFRICAN WORDS

Aasvoel = vulture
Agterryers = mounted servant
Alles sal reg kom = everything will come right
Assegai = native spear

Baie danke = thank you very much
Biltong = sun-dried meat
Brey = tan

Daar agter = over there
Disselboom = pole of wagon
Duiwel = devil

Ek weet nee = I do not know

Goed, baie goed = good, very good
Goed genoeg = good enough

Hammel = wether
Hoe gaan dit? = How goes it?

Jong = young man
Jukskeis = yoke skey

Kappie = sunbonnet
Kaptein = captain
Kaross = rug of skins sewn together
Kerels = fellows
Kerrie = a wooden club
Kleinkie = little one
Klompie = small group
Kloof = valley or crack in the hills
Krantz = a cliff
Kyk daar = look there

Laagte = a flat plain

Mak = tame
Mealies = maize, corn

Meisie = girl
Mooi = pretty

Natuurlik = naturally

Opsit = local courting custom

Padjie = small path

Randjie = low ridge
Riem = rawhide thong
Ringhals = African cobra
Rooinek = Englishman; from the way his neck burns red in the sun

Skeis = pegs through ox yoke
Skelm = rascal
Spantou = riem used to tie legs of a cow for milking
Spreeu = starling
Spruit = a small stream

Tier *or* tiger = leopard (Tiger is in common use)
Tollies = young oxen
Tot siens = good-bye
Trek-tous = ropes of twisted hide, to which yokes are fastened

Vang = catch
Velskoen = home-made shoes
Verneuk = cheat, swindle
Versie = heifer
Vlei = marsh
Voertsek = get out
Voorloper = one who leads oxen
Voorslag = whiplash
Vragtag = truly
Vrot = rotten

Wie gaan? = Who goes?